Termination Dust

Tori Minard

Termination Dust
A Northern Lights, Northern Hearts Novel

Tori Minard

Enchanted Lyre Books

Chapter 1

Violation

Anchorage, Alaska. October, 1972

Cass:

I opened the front door of West High and walked into a curtain of snow. Flakes whirled happily out of the sky in a bewildering rush of movement, filling the air with the smell of fresh winter. It was only October, but this was Alaska and snow in October isn't unusual.

Cold air nipped at my legs beneath my long, plaid skirt, somehow finding its way over the tops of my high winter boots. Thank goodness I'd thought to put on the boots this morning, because I'd had no idea it would snow. I was prepared for the weather in spite of myself.

Hat. I needed my hat. I dug around in my book bag and found it, jamming it on my head over the thin layer of snow that had already accumulated there.

To my right, a girl I didn't know tipped her dark head back and stuck out her tongue, capturing flakes that melted as soon as they touched her flesh. She glanced at me and grinned in a surprisingly friendly way. I gave her an answering smile.

Most kids who didn't already know me didn't smile at me. It was an odd sensation.

School buses hunkered down in the snow, a long double line of giant, bright yellow vehicles made hazy by the falling snow. Mine was right in the front. Easy to find, hard to ignore. I trudged toward it, wishing for the umpteenth time that I'd learned to drive over the summer. Now it was snowing and my overprotective parents would never agree to let me learn when there was ice on the roads. I'd have to wait for May.

The metal walls of the school bus bounced the sound of the student riders' voices around in a bewildering roar. The sound made my head hurt. I fought down the urge to turn around and walk back down the bus steps. It was snowing too hard to walk home, considering I lived several miles from school.

The interior smelled like diesel fumes and new snow and, as I moved farther inside, the cheap aftershave of some guy who didn't know when to stop. Apparently, he thought that if a little was good then bathing in it was even better. My nose wanted to wrinkle from the overwhelming stench of it.

It was crowded this afternoon. We must have extra riders, because usually there were more empty seats. Most kids old enough to drive were too cool to ride the bus the way dorky social outcasts like me did.

I hitched my book bag high on my shoulder and made my way carefully down the aisle, avoiding the gazes of the other kids on board. Everyone seemed to be shouting and laughing at the same time, making the vehicle so loud that I couldn't follow any one conversation.

Not that I wanted to.

Riding the bus was something I had to do, not something I enjoyed. I was here because I lacked a car. Only one of my tiny handful of friends rode my route, and she was home sick, so I had to go it alone today. It was something to endure.

I found an empty seat and slid onto the old, brown, fake leather, tucking my ankle-length skirt around me and settling my book bag at my feet. Outside the windows, kids played tag through the gray and white falling snow and tossed snow balls at each other with wild whoops of laughter. I saw a girl get hit in the face. Snow burst all over her features and she lunged at the boy who'd thrown the ball, shrieking. I couldn't tell if her anger was real or just a show.

My parents probably could have afforded a car for me, and I was old enough to drive, but I rode the bus every day anyway. The truth was that I didn't know how to drive and I had no desire to learn. I was content to walk, ride my bike, ride the bus. If I needed to go somewhere far, I hitched a ride with my mom.

That was just one of the oddities that set me apart from all the other kids at school, made me a weirdo and an outcast. I really didn't even know what all the factors were so I couldn't have listed them even if I'd wanted to. But I felt them hanging over my head like a lit-up neon sign as I waited for the driver to start the bus.

Leon Schmidt was sitting directly across the aisle from me, his Three Dog Night concert T-shirt peeking out from under his open navy ski jacket. He was staring at me. I fidgeted nervously.

What was his problem? He was looking at me like he wanted to start something, which was bizarre. I didn't even know the guy. The only reason I was aware of him or knew his name was that my little sister was in his class.

I turned my head to look out the window again. The snowball fights had petered out and most of the kids seemed to either be on buses or in their cars. There wasn't much to look at except the grayish-brown slush of dirty snow covering the parking lot, a thin white frosting of new snow partially hiding the mess, and the impersonal beige bulk of the school building.

In the failing gray light of an Anchorage afternoon, it was a depressing sight.

"Hey," Leon said.

I didn't know who he was talking to and I didn't care. That creepy stare of his was all I needed to know about him.

"Hey," he said again. "Hey, you."

I'd gone to school with this guy for years and never known anything about him except his name. I'd never suspected he was a rude jerk, but he sure was making a bad impression on me today. The person whose attention he was so obnoxiously trying to get clearly didn't want to talk to him.

"Hey, you," he said with more belligerence. "Bag girl. What's your name?"

Oh, God, he was talking to me.

Slowly, reluctantly, I turned my head to look at him. "What?"

He smirked. "You're not very nice, you know that?"

He didn't even know me. Maybe he saw me as an easy target for bullying. Well, I wasn't going to be as easy as he'd hoped.

I just blinked at him, refusing to give him the reaction he wanted. "Oh, yeah?"

"Yeah. I'm trying to say hi and all you do is ignore me."

"I didn't know you were talking to me," I said, hoping he'd drop it.

"Well, I was." His smirk deepened.

He was one of those boy-next-door types, at least in looks, with a roundish face, dark hair, and freckles across his nose. I'd always thought he was kind of cute—not sexy or anything, just nice looking. Until now.

People were starting to notice our conversation, if you could call it that. The girl sitting behind me was listening with eager ears; in my peripheral vision, I could see her intent posture and the way she was staring openly. The guy in front of Leon was listening, too, and that made me want to curl up in a ball and hide.

Dex Morgan, the baddest of the bad boys at West Anchorage High. He had a dark reputation for drug dealing, hard drinking, and God only knew what else. I didn't follow the details, but I definitely knew his rep. According to rumor, he'd even been held back a year at some point and supposedly there was some kind of terrible violence in his past.

What was he even doing on the school bus? Guys like him didn't ride the bus. They drove themselves, or maybe hitched a ride with a friend in an emergency, but they certainly didn't hang out with the lower class-men and the dorks like me who didn't have enough cool to drive ourselves.

His shaggy, dark-blond hair hung over his eyes, but I could tell he was watching me. I hoped he was enjoying the show. Maybe I should stand up on the bench and do a little dance.

Leon was still staring at me, apparently expecting a response.

"Um, okay," I said, feeling my skin start to heat in embarrassment.

"Yeah, whatever," he said. "I heard you were stuck up and it seems like it's true."

I rolled my eyes. "Go bother someone else."

"Your name is Cass, right?" he continued, as if I hadn't spoken. "Weird name. Did they call you after Mama Cass? Hey, I heard you're a virgin. Is that true?"

This information brought a rush of burning heat to my face. "That's none of your business."

He grinned. "I can tell it is. You're a virgin."

At West, it seemed the only virgins were the ones nobody else wanted. At least, the only ones who'd admit to their sexual status. It was the ultimate mark of the outsider, the one no-one desired, the one too weird or ugly to get laid when everyone else seemed to brag about a new sexual conquest or adventure every week.

He was right, of course. I was a virgin. What I couldn't understand was why he'd care or why he'd choose to use that information against me.

I fought the urge to shrink back into the seat and try to disappear. Was Dex listening to this? Of course he was. I didn't look at him because I didn't want him to know how aware I was of his presence, but I could tell he was paying attention.

Unfortunately, I had no witty comeback for Leon. Maybe it was Dex making me so awkward and stupid, or maybe it was just one of those days. Either way, I had nothing. I just stared back at him, my mind blank of everything except the rank embarrassment of being harassed in front of everyone.

"I was told," Leon said, continuing to stare at me, "that you're a virgin island."

Virgin island? Seriously?

"Leave me alone," I said, using my most bored tone, a voice I'd perfected over the years for defense against bullies just like Leon. Pretend you don't care at all what they think and maybe they'll leave you alone. Sometimes it worked well; other times it just seemed to spur them on.

Leon chuckled. "Yeah, you're a virgin. Aren't you?"

"Like I said, none of your business."

Apparently, Leon was the type who couldn't be discouraged with a chilly look. I was starting to feel a tremble in my hands, something I

4

hoped no-one else could see. How far was Leon going to take this? What could I do to shut him up?

"Must be lonely, being so virginal and all," he said.

I'd turned my gaze to the front of the bus, avoiding his, but I could hear the grin in his voice. What an asshole.

"A virgin island. No wonder you're so bitchy. You need to get laid."

"Leave me alone," I said.

"You need to do something about that," he said.

I could feel tears prickling at the backs of my eyelids. Damn it. I wasn't going to cry. I refused to let him make me cry.

"Come on, Cass," he crooned in a sing-song. "Come on, virgin island."

"Leon, back off," Dex said.

"What?" Leon said. "I'm not hurting anything."

"She asked you to leave her alone." Dex's voice was calm, deep, and absolutely authoritative.

I glanced over at him in amazement that he would stand up for someone like me. Or anyone, really. He gazed back at me out of unusual, emerald-green eyes. Beautiful eyes, large and lined with thick, dark lashes. I'd never really noticed Dex Morgan's eyes before, or how good looking he was.

Not like some kind of teen idol, like Peter Frampton or something. Not pretty. Just an angular jaw, full lips that made me feel funny and tingly when I looked at them, stark cheekbones, rough dark-blond hair. And those eyes.

Okay, maybe he did bear a slight resemblance to Frampton. Except his face wasn't as long and it was harsher. Stronger, even though he couldn't be much older than me.

As we stared at each other, a hot bolt of some kind of energy shot through me and settled low in my body. I suppressed a shiver. I'd never felt anything like that before, no matter how good-looking a guy happened to be.

He gave me no real acknowledgment and no sign of his reason for defending me. No smile, no nod, nothing. Just that flat, green-eyed stare.

I dropped my gaze and looked at my lap. The bus pulled out of its spot in the line-up. Leon was talking to Dex now, in apparent good humor. Neither of them seemed angry with the other.

God, boys were so confusing. I could hardly wait to get off this stupid bus and get away from them. Unfortunately, it was Tuesday, so there was a chance I could run into either or both of them tomorrow at school.

As the bus rumbled its way through the subdivision surrounding West, I dared a peek at Dex. He was looking over the back of his bench at

Leon, smiling at something the jerk was saying. There was faint stubble on his jaw and chin, making him look a lot older than the other kids in our grade.

Dex's gaze slid to me and his smile disappeared.

I flushed. Looked away. Pretended to be fascinated with the zipper of my jacket. Why oh why had I looked at him?

No-one else spoke to me during the ride, and when we reached my friend Jenny's stop I was happy to get off. I shuffled down the cramped aisle without meeting Dex's eyes or even acknowledging his presence.

The snow still fell, even harder now. Stomping feet behind me let me know that other kids were getting off at this stop too. I faced forward and headed for Jenny's house. I wanted to stop by and see if she was okay and drop off the homework I'd collected for her; that's why I'd gotten off at her stop and not mine.

Then I recognized Leon and Dex's voices in the cluster of kids behind me. Great. Just great.

I knew both of them lived in the neighborhood. I even knew where Dex's house was—Jenny had pointed it out to me once—so it wasn't all that shocking that they'd get off at the same stop. Maybe they were going to Leon's house to hang out. Not that it mattered to me. I didn't really care what they were doing as long as they did it without involving me.

I picked up speed, my boots crunching through the fluffy, white snow. Jenny's house was right down the block, just a few houses away. I could make it in about three minutes, even in the snow, if I hurried. I could even see its low, yellow walls through the snow and trees.

"Hey, Cass!" Leon called out.

I ignored him and kept walking.

"Love you, baby!" He followed this with loud smooching noises. Then "Ow! What the fuck was that for?"

"I told you to back off," Dex said.

Almost to Jenny's house. Almost there.

Dex and Leon's voices grew slightly fainter, making me think they were moving in the opposite direction from me. No way was I turning around to check, though. Nuh uh.

I made it to her steeply sloped driveway before I chanced a peek over my shoulder. The guys had taken the first left turn instead of heading on straight like I had. They were gone now, out of sight.

Chapter 2

Cock-block

Dex:

I settled onto the fake leather of the bus seat and set my back against the window wall. Then I stretched my feet out in front of me along the length of the seat. The metal wall felt icy against my back, even though I had a winter jacket on. A crappy jacket, but still.

The falling snow made the light weak and gray. Everything seemed dimmer than usual and a little chillier, the colors cooler. Even my red jacket looked dull in that light.

About eight million fucking people were on the bus today, and more kept getting on, each one of them reminding me why I never rode the bus. Yelling, pushing, laughing kids everywhere, most of them freshmen and sophomores. Cause juniors and seniors had their own rides, like I normally did. Only the nerdiest of nerds rode the bus after turning old enough for a driver's license.

Then she got on. She wore a long skirt that brushed against the sides of the aisle as she shuffled along looking for a seat. A blue knit hat with a huge blue and white pompom sat on her head. Lots of people wore hats like that and normally I ignored the effect. It was a hat. So what? But on her it looked cute.

My heart started thumping like an idiot as she got closer. We'd never spoken. She probably had no idea I was alive.

I could have moved my feet. I could have offered to let her sit with me, but she would have said no. Maybe she wouldn't have even acknowledged my voice, so I left my feet where they were.

She sat down across from me except one row down. Technically she was across from Leon.

The bus reeked of Leon's aftershave. Damn. I'd told him just the other day to tone it down, but he still kept sloshing the stuff all over himself like he bathed in it. Didn't he have a sense of smell?

With the doors shut, the odor of that dime store garbage was overwhelming. It reminded me of my dad and not in a good way. I couldn't understand why Leon doused his entire body in it. The bus driver should have left the doors open so we could get some fresh air. It was cold, but at least it smelled clean, like snow.

We were finally getting a major snowfall. So far this year we'd only had a few little dustings of the stuff. The jocks were probably stoked.

Finally, powder! They could run off to Alyeska, the local ski resort, and ski their little hearts out.

I didn't ski. None of my friends skied.

The gray sky reminded me of the way my parents' faces looked when they were coming off a bender. Old, tired, and sick, with nothing to give you but cold, blank, couldn't-give-a-shit. Typical Anchorage winter weather.

It was gonna be colder than shit at my house, too. Mom had forgotten to pay the gas bill again, so no heat unless I could scratch together enough money to get it turned back on. The pipes would freeze unless I did.

The bus lumbered through the falling snow. I stared out the windows at kids walking home, throwing snowballs at each other, laughing. Having fun. They didn't seem to notice the gray.

Leon started in on the girl in the pompom hat. I might have let it go, but she looked so damn miserable I had to shut him down. Then I turned and stared out the window again, because if I didn't, I'd stare at her.

An older guy wearing an orange down parka shoveled the snow off his driveway. It fell down faster than he could get rid of it. Why didn't he wait until it was done snowing before getting out there with the shovel?

Inside the bus, some people talked in hushed voices. Leon, sitting next to me—behind, actually, if we'd been facing forward according to the rules—was quiet. He kept shooting me glares out of the corners of his eyes. If he kept it up, I was gonna have to clobber him.

Nobody would respect me if I let a younger guy like Leon give me shit, even if he was my friend, and I couldn't afford to lose respect. My business depended on it.

I ignored him. My gaze kept wandering stupidly to the girl across the aisle from me. Okay, across the aisle from Leon. Whatever.

I'd seen her around school plenty of times. In fact, she was in my biology class and we'd had history together freshman year. In biology, she sat near me, but in front with her back to me. I don't think she'd ever looked my way once. I looked at her, though. Every chance I got. She never seemed to notice.

Her name was Cass Maslanka. She was one of those good girls, the kind who never smoke or drank or stayed out late at night. The kind who never spoke to me or even looked straight at me.

Like right now, for example. Her eyes remained locked on the book bag at her feet, or else they fixed on the back of the girl in front of her. They never strayed across the aisle to me, no matter how much I stared at her.

Stared at her? Fuck. I was staring.

8

I tore my gaze away and forced it to my shoes, which stuck out in front of me. I was taking up the whole bench seat, so no-one could sit there but me. If I'd known she was going to get on this bus, I'd have put my feet down so she could sit next to me.

Except she wouldn't have. She would have walked right by me like I was invisible and taken the exact same place she was in now. And wouldn't that suck the big one? We'd both have to acknowledge she was too good for me.

She had dark hair, like the color of chocolate chips. And light blue eyes. I had a thing for girls with light blue eyes and dark hair, especially when they had thick, dark eyelashes like she did. She was a real fox.

The funny thing was, it seemed like she didn't know how pretty she was. She never wore make-up—not that she needed it— and she dressed like she didn't care much how she looked. Maybe her parents wouldn't let her wear make-up or short skirts. Right now she had on a plaid skirt that came down almost to her ankles. Under her parka, she had a sweater with a prim neckline that showed nothing.

She was pretty much the opposite of all the girls I normally hung out with. But for some reason, I kept stealing glances at her.

Leon liked her. I could tell. He was an idiot with girls. If he liked one, he'd harass her until she cried or kicked him or her big brother intervened.

Normally, I let him carry on. I figured he wasn't really hurting anyone but himself. This time, though, he'd gone way over the line with that virginity shit. Way over the line.

We were gonna have a talk when we got to his place.

The only reason I was riding the bus today was my '65 Plymouth Barracuda broke down— the starter was dead— and I didn't have the dough to replace the part. If the gas didn't get turned back on, the pipes would freeze and so would all the people in the house. Maybe I wouldn't care about my folks, but my little brother, Joe, was another matter. He needed heat to stay safe.

My car versus the gas bill. Guess who won?

Plus, I had some weed to sell and Leon was in the market. We planned to go to his house, smoke a doobie together and then make the exchange. This little deal would give me just enough to cover that bill and get the heat turned back on. So everybody won.

The bus stopped. Some of the kids stood up, including Leon and me. His house was a block away, mine two blocks. We'd go to his place, get something to eat, hang out. After a while, he'd give me the money and I'd give him the weed.

I'll say one thing for Leon—he was generous. He always fed me when I showed up at his place, which was cool since there wasn't much food at mine.

I'd known the kid since he was five and I was seven. I was the same age as his big brother, Gary, but it was Leon and me who hit it off.

I watched Cass get off the bus ahead of me. She was right in front of me, the huge blue and white pompom on her hat bobbing gently with her movements. My hand itched with the weird urge to reach out and touch her on her shoulder. But no. Not a good idea—too revealing.

We filed off the bus and into the falling snow. The hems of my wide-leg jeans dragged in the stuff. Pretty soon they were gonna be soaked and flapping icy water around my ankles.

I glanced at her again. My heart raced a little and my stomach did this pathetic little flop when she glanced my way. Jesus, what was wrong with me? Maybe I was coming down with something.

Leon bent and scooped up a handful of snow and lobbed it at me. He laughed when it hit my back.

"Fuck you," I said.

"Aren't you gonna fight back?" He bent to get another one.

"Nope." I just walked on, in the direction of his house. He'd get the hint eventually.

Except he didn't. Maybe he was trying to get me back for the shit on the bus, I don't know. He threw one snowball after another at me as I slogged through the white stuff. I just pretended I didn't see him.

The cold bit right through the crappy old coat I wore. It was a hand-me-down from my dad, and he'd gotten it used, so half the stuffing had fallen out of it. I left it unzipped and made like the cold didn't bother me, like I didn't feel it. Like I couldn't feel the snow drift forming on my bare head.

That's right, baby. I'm that tough.

Fuck. She probably wasn't even looking at me.

I was definitely coming down with something. Chicks never affected me this way. Illness was the only reasonable explanation.

With my back turned to him, Leon started hollering at her again. Making kissy noises and telling her he was in love. I rolled my eyes. The second I turned around, he was back at it, making an ass of himself. He never learned.

I swung around and smacked him in the side of the head. "Knock it off."

"Ow!" He ducked like he thought I was going to whale on him a second time. "What the fuck was that for?"

"I told you to back off."

"What the fuck, man?" Leon said, straightening.

I shot him a sideways glance. "What?"

"You shot me down with Cass. Why'd you do that?"

"You were being a dick," I said, giving her a sneaky glance out of the corner of my eye. She was standing on the front stoop of a neat, pale yellow ranch house, her back to us. Like we didn't exist. See what I mean?

"She liked it," my dumbass friend said.

I laughed. "No, Leon, she didn't. You were embarrassing the shit out of her."

"Whatever. She's a bitch anyway."

I blew a lock of hair out of my eyes and carefully did not look at her again. "Is she?"

"Everybody says so." He shrugged. "I thought you knew."

"I wasn't paying attention. She's not my type," I said.

Liar. Big, fucking liar.

"Well, she's mine."

I raised a single eyebrow, a move I'd perfected one summer when I was bored and too young for a job to take up my time. "You like bitches?"

"What do you care anyway? You never cock-blocked me before."

I stopped and stared at him, snow falling into my open mouth. "Cock-blocked you?"

He shrugged. "Yeah, man. What would you call it?"

How do you answer a question like that? If he thought me standing up for a girl amounted to cock-blocking him, he needed to learn a few things about the female sex.

"You gotta learn how to talk to girls," I said, starting to walk again.

"I know how to talk to girls."

I just grinned and shook my head.

Maybe Cass was a bitch. I didn't know. I'd heard the rumors about her standoffishness and that she was stuck up, plus the odd passing comment about her looks, and once something about her being a brain. But rumors aren't necessarily true, and even if she was a bitch, it wouldn't have made a difference to me.

The truth was that I'd wanted to strangle Leon when he went after her. The look on her face—frozen, shocked, afraid. Like he'd pulled back a curtain on her when she was naked and let the whole world see. I'd wanted to protect her.

So what the fuck was that about? I didn't protect anybody but myself.

"You like her, don't you?" Leon said.

"Nope."

"Yeah, you do. You wouldn't have jumped in like that if you didn't."

"Fuck off, Leon."

"Ha!" he crowed. "I knew it! You like her!"

The idiot started dancing around in the snow, whooping and shouting that I liked Cass. Fucking God. Could she hear that?

The only way to find out was to look around and see if she was listening. But if I did that, I'd let her know I cared what she thought. So I just kept walking, head high, like nothing mattered.

Then Leon hit a patch of ice and his feet slipped out from under him. He slammed down on his ass.

I laughed.

He sat in the snow, in the middle of the road, and groaned. "Oh, man, I think I broke my tailbone."

"Serve you right." I stood there and watched him as he struggled to get to his feet.

"Not cool," he said. "I could end up in the hospital."

"Like I said—"

"Anyway, you should just admit that you like her. I saw the way you were looking at her." He clambered awkwardly to his feet.

"I wasn't looking at her." I started walking again.

"Yeah, you were."

"Are we in first grade now? I said I wasn't looking at her."

"Okay, man, whatever." He shook his head, grinning, and I knew I hadn't changed his mind a bit.

Chapter 3

Earth To Cass

Cass:

With a sigh of relief, I dashed up Jenny's drive to the front door of her little yellow ranch house and rang the bell. Even Leon Schmidt wouldn't have the gall to follow me up someone's driveway, and besides they weren't following me. They'd gone the other way.

Jenny's mom opened the door. She had her brown hair in a ponytail. Flared polyester pants and a polyester blouse in an earth-toned avocado green, rust, and cream print completed her outfit. She always looked perfectly turned out even if she was staying home all day.

"Hi, Mrs. June. I'm here to see Jenny."

"Come in, Cass. She's in the living room watching TV."

She must have been feeling awful, like one step away from death's door, then, because there was nothing but soap operas and game shows on TV at this hour. Jenny and I hated soap operas and game shows.

"You might want to go home, though, honey," Mrs. June continued. "I'd hate to see you catch this thing too. It's miserable."

That gave me the bright idea of catching Jenny's virus and any other disease I could snatch out of the air. If I got really, really sick, I could stay out of school for a while. Maybe I could even stretch it to two whole weeks if I worked it hard enough.

I could get my schoolwork from my teachers, via my brother, so I wouldn't fall behind in my classes. And by the time I came back, Leon would have forgotten all about the "virgin island" he'd been harassing.

"I don't mind," I said with a brave smile. "I've got a pretty good immune system."

"Okay. It's your call." She closed the door and led the way through the arctic entry into the main foyer of the house.

Our house didn't have an arctic entry, maybe because it was a split level—or raised ranch, as my cousins in Chicago called it. The June household's entry was small, like the whole house, just a tiny roomlet or portion of the front hall blocked off from the rest of the house by a second exterior door. It supposedly stopped the really cold air from getting in the house, although you could hardly tell since they kept their heat so low all the time. I swear, when Jenny and I used to have winter sleepovers, I would wonder if I'd need to crack the ice in the toilet when I got up in the morning.

They had a sculpted carpet, like we did, only theirs was dark gold instead of green like ours. Their walls were paneled with old-fashioned knotty pine, probably from when the house was built ten or fifteen years earlier. Metal butterflies in a bronze finish flittered across one wall of the entry.

"Would you like a Tab or a Fresca?" Mrs. June said as she turned into their country pine galley kitchen.

"A Fresca, thanks."

I wandered from their entry into the living room. They had a huge picture window that looked out on their back yard. The dark gold carpet almost matched the paneling, and their furniture was all in a burnt orange color, with sixties style angled legs. Gold pinch-pleat drapes framed the window.

I found Jenny stretched out on the couch, still in her flannel nightgown, a brown and gold afghan pulled up to her armpits. *The Price Is Right* was on the TV. She lay there staring blearily at the screen as audience members screamed hysterically and the announcer called for some chick with bouffant blond hair to "come on down!"

It wasn't even the current episode— not really. In Alaska, we got all our TV shows at least two weeks late, since they had to be shipped up via the AlCan Highway, which apparently took at least two weeks for the trucks, even though everyone else could do it in one.

"You're that desperate, huh?" I said.

She gave a little start, as if she hadn't realized I was in the room. Which I guess she hadn't. Then a big grin broke over her face. "Cass!"

"Hey, there. I was wondering if you were still alive."

She looked horrible, her skin pasty, blond hair stringy and lifeless, blue eyes puffy and red behind her owl-like glasses, nose even redder. I hoped I got whatever she had.

"I tried to read, but I couldn't concentrate. I feel like shit," Jenny croaked.

"Jenny June!" her mom said from behind me.

"Sorry!" Jenny kept grinning at me.

I turned to her mom and accepted the Fresca with thanks. The citrus-flavored soda fizzed under my nose. Turning back to Jenny, I said "You do look pretty bad. Do you think you'll be out tomorrow?"

"Probably." She waved vaguely at the TV, where a model was currently ensconced on an antique gold colored sofa— excuse me, a "sofette"—and fondling it like it was her lover while the contestants tried to figure out how much the thing cost. "I'm going crazy with boredom already, though. I don't know if I can take another day of this."

"What's worse, going to school sick or watching soap operas and game shows all day?" I said.

"I'm not sure. I'll have to get back to you on that." She coughed, her eyes watering. "So what'd I miss?"

I collapsed on the floor in front of the couch. "Nothing. Except Dex Morgan was on the bus today."

Jenny's nose wrinkled. "Dex Morgan?"

"Yeah. Leon Schmidt started harassing me and Dex made him shut up."

"Really?" She sat up a little straighter and pushed her glasses up. "With his reputation, I would've thought he would join right in."

"I know," I said, picking at the gold carpet. "It was weird."

"Are you sure it was Dex?"

I rolled my eyes at her. "Yeah, I'm sure. It's not like I could confuse him with anyone else."

"What did he say?"

"Just to back off."

She poked me in my upper arm. "Not to Leon. To you."

"Nothing. He didn't say anything to me. He just looked at me."

"Weird." She blew her nose noisily. "I didn't know he was even aware we were alive."

I shrugged. "I think he was just irritated with Leon for making such a big deal. Everybody was looking at us."

"What did he say to you?"

I picked at the carpet again. "Oh, you know. Stuff."

"Like what kind of stuff?" She pulled another tissue out of the box on her lap.

"Just—" I shrugged, trying to be nonchalant and probably failing miserably. "He teased me about being a virgin."

"No way."

"Yes way."

Her mouth turned down at the corners and her eyes drooped. "What a jerk. What's wrong with him anyway?"

"I have no idea." I recounted the conversation for her. "He was acting like I'd insulted him or something. Like he knew me and had a reason to be mad at me. But I've never talked to him before."

"Wow. I'm sorry that happened to you." She blew her nose again.

"I'm just glad it's over." I elbowed her. "And I'm hoping I get your disease so I can stay home the rest of the week."

She laughed and shook her head. "No, you don't want this. Besides, you've gotta face them or they'll think they can push you around."

She was right of course. If I stayed home, I'd look like I was afraid of Leon. That is, if they even noticed my absence. Part of me thought the incident was just a random bullying thing. You know the kind—hey, there's a weak-looking dork we can pick on. They don't know you and don't really care, but it seems like a fun opportunity.

Another part of me thought Leon might be targeting me personally. I had no real reason for thinking this. It was just my natural paranoia coming to the fore. What I still couldn't figure out was why Dex had intervened. Why he'd stared at me the way he had.

I got a sick, fluttery, completely baffled sensation in the pit of my stomach whenever I pictured those odd green eyes of his fixed on mine. Had he wanted something from me? Should I have thanked him?

"I should have thanked him," I muttered.

"You didn't say thank you?" Jenny said reprovingly.

"No. I was too shocked. I just stared at him and he stared back at me."

She pursed her lips thoughtfully. "I bet he likes you."

"He does not. He's never even noticed me before."

She snorted, and it was not attractive. "How would you know, Miss Oblivious? Guys look at you all the time and you never notice. You never notice anything unless they come right up to you and even then half the time you don't see it."

I rolled my eyes. "Guys don't look at me."

"What we need is something like Candid Camera. They could follow you around and film you on the sly, then show you the footage later. You'd be shocked." She sat up straighter as if galvanized by the idea. "That's a great plan. I think I'll call them."

"Candid Camera is for practical jokes, young lady, and if you ever did something like that to me I'd have to kill you," I said with my best stern-mom voice.

She stuck out her tongue at me. "Anyway, you're trying to change the subject. Dex Morgan likes you."

"Trust me, I'm not his type."

"How would you know what his type is?"

"I'd say his type wears fake eyelashes and miniskirts and go-go boots," I said. "And smokes and drinks every weekend, and maybe on Wednesdays too."

"God, you're so square," she said, laughing hoarsely. "Besides, nobody wears go-go boots anymore. Do they?"

"They do on TV. And you're just as square as I am."

Fashion was even more behind in Alaska than the TV shows, although we did have access to magazines. But when you have to order all your clothes from the Montgomery Ward and Sears catalogs, it's hard to stay at the forefront of fashion. At least, that's what my mom liked to complain about and the way she justified the expense of a couple of shopping trips down to Seattle every year to my dad.

I wasn't especially concerned with high style. Mainly I wanted to keep my butt from freezing off in our long, dark winters without looking too much like the Abominable Snowman. For someone born and raised in this place, I was a complete wimp about the weather and always had been.

"So what're you gonna do about Dex?" Jenny said.

"Do? Nothing." Obviously. By now, he'd forgotten all about the incident, so there was nothing that needed doing.

"Cass, you can't do nothing. You need to have a strategy."

"Why?" I got up and turned down the sound on the TV before returning to my seat on the floor.

"Because," she said in a *do I really have to explain this* tone. "You need to know how to respond. What do you want out of the situation?"

"There is no situation, Jen," I said.

"He likes you. There's a situation. For example, you need to know whether or not you like him back and what you want to do about that."

I took a swallow of the Fresca. Its carbonation made my throat burn pleasantly. "He doesn't like me. I don't like him. There's nothing to decide."

Inside my head, a tiny voice whispered *liar*. Those compelling green eyes, the shaggy blond hair, the deep voice, the long legs...

Stop.

The authoritative way he spoke to Leon and the way Leon instantly obeyed...

Knock it off, Cass.

"Cass?" Jen said. "Earth to Cass. Come in, Cass."

"Huh?"

She laughed. "You were daydreaming about him, weren't you?"

"No," I said, my face heating.

"Yeah, you were. I don't blame you. He's a fox. But, Cass, he's Dex Morgan. You can't really date him, know what I mean?"

"Could if I wanted to," I said with automatic contrariness.

"Could not."

"Could too."

"Could not!" She stuck out her tongue again.

"Wow, I think we've regressed to the second grade." I grinned. "Anyway, it doesn't matter. Really, I'm sure I'm not his type."

"But is he yours?" she said slyly.

"No." My face heated again.

Her living room had plenty of light coming in through the giant picture window that looked out on her chain-link enclosed back yard. Even on a gray and gloomy afternoon like today, a lot of light bounced off the snow, so I was sure she could see just how red my face was getting.

"You really shouldn't lie to me," she said.

"I'm not lying."

"It's not nice to lie to Mother Nature!" She waved her arms dramatically.

"Ugh. I hate that ad." I opened my book bag, more to change the subject than anything else. "I brought some homework for you."

"Thanks. I was hoping you'd say that." She pushed herself upright on the couch.

"You were not."

"Yeah, you're right. I wasn't. If I make you sick, though, we can both stay home and then neither of us will have anyone to bring homework for us to do."

"Sorry to burst your bubble, but my brother would do it for me," I said, opening my geometry book.

"Then we'll have to make him sick too."

I thought for a minute. "How many people would we have to sicken before we could be absolutely sure no-one would bring us any homework?"

"That sounds like an interesting math problem, Miss Maslanka. Let's get to work."

Chapter 4

Meatlocker

Dex:

Leon's house was dark and warm. It smelled clean. We knocked the snow off our shoes and hung our coats up on the hooks in the entry hall.

"You want something to eat?" Leon said.

"Yeah. What you got?"

"Come on and we'll check out the fridge."

I followed him into the kitchen, marveling at how quiet it was here. Nobody yelling. No TV blaring in the living room. Just the soft tick-tick of the wind-up clock they had on the wall of their dining room.

What kind of place did Cass have? Was it quiet like this? Was it warm?

I dug my nails into the palm of my hand. I needed to quit thinking about her. She wasn't for me, wasn't my type, and as I'd mentioned earlier, she'd never even give me a second glance. No sense wasting my time and energy on her, even in my head.

But the image of her long, dark hair hanging out from under her hat, framing her pale face, kept following me around no matter where we went or what we did. Even getting high couldn't erase her from my mind.

I left Leon's place—his bedroom window wide open to get rid of the smoke smell—before his mom came home from work. She taught third grade at Turnagain Elementary, where I'd gone to school. She'd never been my teacher, though.

I wasn't real clear on how much Mrs. Schmidt knew about the things Leon and I did when we hung out. She sure didn't know he smoked pot, or she'd have had him on lock-down. She was a good mom as far as I could tell.

They always had plenty of food in their house. The heat and lights always worked and everybody had decent clothes to wear. And Leon never came to school black and blue, either.

My jeans were still wet when I trudged out into the still-falling snow. My shoes, too. By now, the snow had accumulated to at least half a foot, so it came right over the tops of my shoes and caked on my socks. Colder than fuck-all.

I stuck my hands in my coat pockets to keep them from freezing and bent my head a little to keep the snow out of my eyes. It seemed unnaturally quiet out here, with the snow still falling and muffling the usual town noises. The only thing I could really hear was the scrush-scrush of my shoes in the snow.

I turned onto Susitna and started my trudging journey past split-levels and little ranch houses, all of them dating from the fifties or later. Some had lights on inside, making them look like glowing havens of safety. Up ahead, I saw a slim figure struggling through the snow like me. Only this one wore a long skirt and a knit hat with a big, blue and white pompom on the top.

Could it be Cass? That looked like her hat. I remembered it because it matched the color of her eyes. My stomach did one of those dumbass flip-flops again.

Either she didn't know I was out here or she was ignoring me. I couldn't tell which. She just kept walking, looking ahead, like I didn't exist. And for her, I probably didn't.

Sometimes I thought it would be better for the world if I didn't exist. But then who would take care of my little brother? Nobody, that's who. It was up to me to pull through for him, so I had to keep pushing ahead no matter how bad it hurt.

My house was one of the tiny ones built when the neighborhood was new. In other words, it was old and tired and pathetic. Just one cramped bathroom and two bedrooms. There wasn't enough room in it for two supposed grown-ups, my older brother Sin, plus Joe and me.

The siding needed paint and the roof leaked. The front yard was full of weeds, although right now they were hidden under a nice, clean blanket of snow. I wondered stupidly what Cass would think of it and cringed inside at the obvious answer.

There was no light on at our place, except for the blue flicker of the TV. I could see it through a gap in the ratty old curtains hanging at the window.

Sure as shit, the place felt like a meatlocker when I got there. It smelled like a pile of ground beef left out in the summer sun too long, too. If it hadn't been so cold, the stench would have been unbearable. My nose must have gotten numbed to it during the night, because I hadn't noticed it when I got up. I fucking noticed it now.

Keeping my coat on was a no-brainer. It was too cold to throw it on the pile on the worn-through entryway linoleum with everyone else's shit.

The TV screamed from the living room, like usual, so I went there to see if anyone knew where my little brother was. The picture window that looked out on the front yard was so filthy you could hardly see through it, like it was tinted or something. Cobwebs clung to the corners of the window frame. The brownish carpet—I wasn't sure what its original color had been—was worn through in spots and you could see the subfloor.

Most of our furniture had come from various thrift stores and garage sales over the years, and it was as worn out as the carpet. There was a brown couch, one of those fifties things with the slanted skinny metal legs, its upholstery stained dark in some places, torn, the stuffing poking through. A blue recliner squatted in the corner, facing the TV. That was my dad's chair, and if he was home and one of us sat in it, we caught hell.

The coffee table was a relic from the fifties, too. Its slanting legs matched the ones on the couch, at least in shape. The rectangular top of it had so many dings, scratches, and gouges it looked like it had been through a war. Come to think of it, I guess it had been through a war— the one waged every day in our house.

A picture of a brown horse hung askew on the wall. The paint looked blotchy and the colors were dull. In fact, it reminded me of a paint-by-numbers picture. I never knew what had motivated my mom to hang that thing on our living room wall, but I was pretty sure she'd picked it up for a few pennies at a garage sale. Where else could you get something so ugly?

Discarded food wrappers littered the carpet and the coffee table. I tried to keep the place picked up, but with my parents and Sin determined to make as much of a mess as possible without ever cleaning anything, it was a losing battle.

My mom sprawled all over the ratty brown couch in her green nylon nightgown, a half-empty bottle of cheap whiskey in her hand. She looked up at me blearily as I came in and glared.

"Where you been?" she slurred.

"Out."

"I can see that. Where?"

"A friend's." She didn't need to know I had money. "Where's Joe?"

"How would I know?"

Nice. Real motherly. Some people just shouldn't breed.

I headed down the short hallway, so narrow my shoulders almost touched the walls, toward our shared bedroom. First priority was to stash my cash until I could make it to the gas company to pay the bill. That would be tomorrow, if I could get a ride from somebody.

Some cities had buses. I'd heard this, seen it on TV, read about it. But Anchorage didn't have a public transit system, which meant losers like me had to beg friends for rides or else hoof it everywhere when our cars were on the fritz. I'd find somebody at school who'd be willing to do it.

The reek of pot smoke met my nose before I opened the door to the bedroom. Even wasted as I was, I could smell it; that's how thick it was. Creedence Clearwater Revival pounded away on the record player. Sin must be in there toking up.

I opened the door to a thick haze of smoke. The one dresser we had between us, which looked like it matched the couch and coffee table, and the bunk bed Joe and I shared were almost obscured by the smog. The banged-up pale blue walls were almost invisible. My older brother's lanky frame lay sprawled right in the middle of the smoky cloud, looking passed out on his narrow bed.

Fuck. No sense in hiding the money in here, because if Sin saw where I put it, he'd snag it the minute I turned my back.

He looked out of it, but you never know with junkies. I'd have to use my hidden compartment in the Barracuda.

Ever since he'd come back from 'Nam, Sin did nothing but smoke weed and listen to music. Except when he was out locating more weed, not to mention the smack he shot up his veins, and doing whatever it was he did so he could buy the shit. He never even played his own guitar anymore.

I didn't sell him my stuff and I didn't ask how he acquired his own stash. I didn't want to know.

He looked up from his mattress on the floor, his almost-black hair all tangled and falling in his eyes, much of his face obscured by a bushy black beard. "Dex."

"Hey, Sin. How's it going?"

"It's going." He lifted his joint to his lips and took a long hit.

I could use some myself. The stuff I'd smoked at Leon's was starting to wear off. But I was gonna get a huge contact high just from being in the room with Sin, so I'd save it for another time.

"Where's Joe?" I said.

He blew out the smoke in a long, slow stream. "Fuck if I know."

Nice way to keep track of your little brother.

Sin was twenty-three. Six years older than me and completely, irredeemably fucked up. Sometimes it hurt me to look at him.

We never asked what had happened in the war. My parents didn't give a shit. Joe and I were afraid to know, afraid to push him. All I knew was it had to be bad.

Really bad. Unspeakably bad.

He had tracks on his arms. I never saw him shoot the smack, but I knew he was doing it. Sometimes I'd come home and he'd just be staring at the ceiling with this dreamy smile on his face and I'd know he was gone.

Heroin dreams. They had to be better than the war shit he dreamed about at night.

He'd been so different when he left. Smiling, laughing, carefree. A normal guy, the brother I looked up to, the one who looked out for Joe and me when my folks were too fucked up to do their jobs. Which was most of the time.

Then the war.

He'd come home silent. Angry. He didn't care about Joe and me anymore. Far as I could tell, he didn't care about anything.

So it was up to me to make sure Joe ate every day and did his homework. It was up to me to make sure the bills got paid, the heat stayed on in the winter, and the trash got taken out.

Speaking of trash...I turned on my heel and went back into the kitchen where that unbelievable stench filled the air. Good thing my dad was still gone. Everything was better when he wasn't here.

The trash can overflowed with crap. Crumpled paper towels and napkins, paper plates, a frozen pizza box, tin soup cans. The garbage spilled out of the can and all over the ancient speckled linoleum floor around it, like someone had been too lazy to even bother trying to get the stuff in the bag when they went to throw it away. How had I failed to see this earlier?

"Jesus." I hauled the bag out of the can to give myself some extra space inside it, then bent over and snagged one piece of garbage after another, breathing through my mouth so I wouldn't have to smell it.

I should have done this last night, instead of watching TV. My dad had been out, so we had a rare chance to watch what we wanted instead of what he did. Normally he watched the news and shouted at the screen, then shouted some more at *The Streets Of San Francisco* or *Hawaii Five-O* until he blacked out to some old cowboy flick on the local late night movie program.

That was when he was in a good mood. When he was pissed off, he didn't bother shouting at the TV. He went after my mom or me instead.

Sin was too big for him and besides he was meaner than shit when he wasn't blissed out on heroin and my dad knew it. Nobody messed with Sin unless they wanted to come away missing a limb. Joe, well, my dad would have killed him if he'd beaten him the way he did me. That was why I always got in between the two of them.

Better me than a ten-year-old kid.

The front door opened. I straightened, hoping it wasn't my old man sent home from work early. He worked long hours normally, as some kind of manager in a bank. Made decent money, I think, but we sure didn't see much of it.

I was never sure where that money went, either. Into alcohol, partly, but that didn't seem to explain it all. I suspected the explanation was a woman, or maybe more than one. If he was trying to support two families, that would go a long way toward explaining why ours always suffered.

Joe stomped into the entryway, snow falling off his shoulders and the soles of his shoes. He had dark hair, like Sin, and the same green eyes as everyone else in our family.

He grinned at me as he dropped his bag by the door. "Hi, Dex."

"Where've you been?" I said.

"Frankie's. What about you?"

"I was at Leon's. How come nobody here knew where you were?" I said, frowning, the bag of trash dangling from my hand.

Joe shrugged. "I dunno." He wrinkled his nose. "God, it stinks in here."

"You didn't tell anyone where you were going." I tied the bag.

"I told Mom."

Ah. Well, that explained that. "Next time, leave a note."

"Okay, Dad," he said with heavy sarcasm.

I ruffled his hair. "Someone's gotta keep you on the straight and narrow."

He ducked his head, trying to avoid me. "It's freezing in here." Then he tilted it in the direction of the narrow hallway that led to the bedrooms and bathroom. "Is Sin home?"

"Yeah. It's real smoky in there."

He looked disappointed. He'd probably hoped to have a few minutes to himself.

Ten-year-olds were supposed to be innocent, but nobody could spend half an hour in this household and come away clean. Joe knew the score. He knew Sin was into some heavy illegal shit. He knew I was a dealer too.

I should have a real job. A legal one. But a stint in juvie when I was thirteen had made the local business owners wary of hiring me. I couldn't find a job, so I turned to the only thing available to me. Selling pot.

The hard stuff wasn't part of my business, though. Even I wasn't prepared to go that far. The people who moved that kind of shit were seriously dangerous bastards who wouldn't think twice about breaking my arms and legs if I crossed them, even accidentally. I couldn't afford to take that risk. Not with my little brother needing someone to look out for him.

"You got homework tonight?" I said, pointing at Joe's bag.

"Nah. Just a coloring thing. I can do it by myself."

"You'd better."

"Hey." He gave me a mock-serious glare. "You'd better do your homework too, mister. I don't want to see anything lower than a C on your next report card."

I laughed at him. "Sure, kid."

Chapter 5

Thank You

Cass:

Snow blotted out the whole world and I liked it that way. I loved the way it fell in a still, silent curtain—perfectly still yet always in motion, each individual flake swirling independently of all the others. Soft, white, and cold as death.

When I left Jenny's house at four o'clock in the afternoon, the sun had already gone down. The sky, if I'd been able to see it, would have been black. But the ever-falling snow concealed that blackness from me, the flakes appearing like magic from out of the void over my head.

I was the only person in sight. Flakes accumulated on the shoulders of my red down parka and the ends of my dark-brown hair. It scrunched softly beneath my feet and silenced all other sounds with a million, tiny hushing voices.

On either side of me rose trees even more silent, bearing accumulated snow along every branch like puffy white outlines. They made beautiful, half-realized shapes in the gloom. As unemotional as trees always are, though, I sometimes imagined them watching me with friendly eyes.

It was blissfully quiet out here. Although a busy street lay just a few blocks away, I couldn't hear any traffic noise. Just the crunching of my own footsteps, the soft puffs of my breath, the low whisper of the snow. Soon, the rush-hour traffic would bring noise and cars sliding on the new snow, but for now I had the peace I craved.

The air smelled clean, sweet, and cold. That smell, the scent of snow, along with the crisp fleeting taste of it melting on my tongue, was buried firmly in my earliest memories. When you're born and raised in Alaska, snow feels like more than part of your life. It's part of you, a frigid and highly inconvenient beauty that is never far away even at the height of summer.

Not that we got a real summer in Anchorage. We were lucky if we got two weeks' worth of over-seventy-degree days in the whole season.

I trudged up Susitna, heading for my house. Golden light glowed from windows half obscured by the curtain of snow. Most of the people in these houses, in this neighborhood where I'd lived for ten years, were strangers to me. They lived mysterious lives behind those glowing windows, a fact that gave me a weird kind of thrill as I walked alone along the street.

Out here, alone, I was safe. I was outside the zone of other people's scorn. Out here, nobody ignored me or taunted me. Nobody called me a virgin island.

I passed the house where Jenny claimed Dex lived. It was even smaller than hers, with faded gray paint and an empty yard. No trees, no bushes, just a flat expanse between the house and the street. It looked sad. Lonely. Even the lights glowing through the living room windows seemed dimmer than those in all the other houses.

Was that really his place? Was he there now? If he was, he gave no sign.

My street was one block over from his, with a mix of older houses like Dex's and newer ones. Our house was newly built earlier that year. We'd moved from a small ranch similar to Jenny's into this much bigger house where each of us kids could have our own room.

When I opened the door, the smell of my mom's pot roast hit me. Mom didn't make pot roast very often, but when she did it was so good I tended to eat too much of it. Our little ground level foyer smelled richly of slow-cooked beef, onions, celery, and carrots, and my mouth instantly began to water.

My stomach growled loudly, almost painfully.

The foyer was lit up with golden light coming off the huge amber pendant lamp hanging above my head like some kind of Moorish fantasy. It gave the white walls a kind of warm glow that always made me feel good to come home, even when I dreaded an encounter with my dad. Voices and the sounds of dishes clattering came from somewhere upstairs, where the kitchen and dining room were.

I stomped the snow off my boots on the front stoop before coming inside, so as not to get the floor wet. Then I shucked off all my outdoor clothes and jammed them haphazardly in the closet so I could get upstairs to the food. Running in stocking feet up the avocado-carpeted stairs, I almost ran into my brother coming down.

He grabbed me by my elbows. "Hey, Sis. Where were you? I was going out to find you."

I snorted. "Yeah, right. You were mounting a search party."

"I was. Mom was about to blow a gasket cause you're so late. Where were you?"

I peered into his guileless blue eyes, but could see no deception there. "Tell you in a sec."

He released me so we could go back up the stairs.

We had an open plan living room that sort of melded into the dining room, which was really just a space between living room and kitchen. The same green sculpted carpet covered all of it, except for the green vinyl in the kitchen. My mom loved green.

We had a big, rust-colored sectional couch and two matching rust-colored easy chairs. The coffee table was some kind of dark stained wood with elaborately turned legs that was supposed to look Colonial or something. I hated it and the fancy pleated lampshades on all the lamps, but at least my mom didn't keep the plastic covers on like some people I knew.

My dad sat in the open plan living room with the news on, his attention fixed on the screen. It looked like it needed to have the color adjusted—everything was skewed toward the green end of the spectrum and the anchors were looking seasick.

He glanced up at Adam and me as we tried to tip-toe past him. "Young lady," he said with a frown. "You're late to dinner."

"I know. Sorry. I stayed a little late at Jenny's," I said.

"You worried your mother. You know better than that," he said over the top of Walter Cronkite.

"Like I said, I'm sorry. I guess I should've called."

"Yes, you should have. Go in the kitchen and apologize."

Sheesh, he was laying it on even thicker than usual. I glanced over at Adam, but he only shrugged and grinned. No help from that quarter, although they wouldn't have listened to him anyway. After all, I was the oldest. I was supposed to set an example for the other two.

Sometimes being a good girl was really tiresome.

My mom, her lips tight and compressed with irritation, looked up from a saucepan full of mashed potatoes as we came into the kitchen. "Cass, you're late."

"Yeah. I know." Maybe I should make a sign. *I know I'm late and I'm deeply sorry.* I could carry it around with me for the rest of the evening.

"I was worried about you. You're usually home by now."

"I am home by now," I said, going to the cabinet for a glass of water.

"You know what I mean. You're setting a bad example for Adam and Beth."

Yes. Yes, I was. "Why didn't you call Jenny's? You know I'm usually over there."

She sighed. "I'm a little busy here."

"Well, I'm sorry I'm late. Jenny was sick today and I wanted to make sure she was okay and bring her the homework and stuff."

"Oh." Her angry-mom expression instantly shifted to concern. "Is she okay? I hope it's not anything serious."

"It's just a bad cold."

"You shouldn't have gone over there. You'll get sick too."

I should only be so lucky. "I'll be fine."

"Wash your hands before you touch anything else. I don't want our family coming down with anything."

Yeah, my mom was maybe a little overly concerned about germs. I washed my hands dutifully at the kitchen sink before pouring myself a glass of water. My siblings and I almost never got to stay home from school despite my mom's worries. She was highly focused on prevention, but she never seemed to really believe us when we said we didn't feel well. So even if I did manage to catch Jenny's cold, I'd have a fight on my hands to win the right to stay home. But it was a fight I planned to win, if I were lucky enough to get sick so I could avoid Dex and Leon.

Why was I so spooked about the encounter with Dex? It hadn't even lasted more than a couple of minutes at the most. By now, he'd probably forgotten all about it. He was deep in some kind of drug deal or a bout of partying with Leon and whoever else he spent his time with. Yet here I was, fretting myself over it like the hopeless dork I was.

Girls with backbone didn't spend their evenings worrying over whether a guy who was all wrong for them might be thinking about them.

I counted out five plates and five saucers and carried them to the dining room table, setting them out for my mom. Usually my little sister did this job. "Where's Beth?"

"She's in her room studying for an important math test tomorrow. Adam, go tell her dinner's ready."

Adam sauntered off, whistling tunelessly. It drove me nuts when he did that, but all the nagging in the world couldn't get him to stop. Maybe he did it on purpose to annoy me. Yeah, he probably did.

Little brothers, I tell you. Born to annoy.

"Did you get all your homework done at Jenny's?" my mom said as she brought the pan of potatoes to the table.

"Yeah."

"Good. Maybe you can help Beth with her math later."

* * *

Apparently, sixteen hours isn't enough time for the common cold to incubate, which makes it a bad option as a stay-home sick excuse. On Wednesday morning, I was perfectly healthy. I should have faked it.

The front lobby of the school wasn't any more or less packed than usual. It was always noisy and full of kids, mostly walking from the doors toward the interior of the school. The brutal noise bounced off the green wall tiles and terrazzo floor with its usual intensity. I found the impersonal quality of the roar strangely comforting. It had nothing to do with me, and that was a good thing.

All those kids, all moving in the same direction, made it kind of like a wide river. You either went with the current or you got trampled. Since I didn't like getting trampled, I followed the current toward Junior Hall.

Nobody looked at me. Nobody seemed to know or care what had happened on Tuesday afternoon. At least, not so far.

Leon hadn't been on the bus this morning and neither had Dex. Not that I'd expected Dex and not that I'd have known what to do if he did show up. Die of embarrassment?

Give me a break. He wouldn't notice you if he were here.

He'd certainly never noticed me before yesterday, and the only reason I'd come to his attention was because of the stupid behavior of his buddy. Nope, I was in the clear.

A peculiar settling sensation weighted my stomach. It felt like disappointment, although that couldn't be right. I hated being harassed. I didn't want all of Leon and Dex's friends targeting me for their own amusement while I cringed and tried to become invisible.

More invisible than I already was.

So why was I feeling sorry for myself because the incident had passed unremarked? I didn't want to examine that too closely, so I tucked the thought away in a dark corner of my mind where I could forget about it.

As a junior, I had a locker all to myself. I slipped off my parka and hung it on the hook inside while the girl next to me locked lips with her boyfriend and I pretended not to notice. They were going at it so hot and fast I half expected the clothes to start coming off.

Someone down the hall wolf-whistled, but they didn't seem to hear.

I pulled out my algebra book and shut my locker. When I turned toward the hall, he was there. Dex.

He looked right at me as he walked by in a throng of other people. His green eyes were just as cool and impersonal, just as distant, as they'd been the day before on the bus. Had he known my locker was in this hall?

Of course he hadn't and even if he had, it wouldn't have mattered to him. His heart wasn't jumping around like a crazed rabbit just at the sight of me. He couldn't have cared less.

Now his back was to me and I could see just how broad his shoulders were, how narrow his waist. He wore a simple blue chamois shirt over a gray T-shirt and wide blue jeans. His shaggy hair hung well over his collar.

I still hadn't thanked him.

A guy like Dex Morgan did things for his own reasons that probably had nothing to do with me. He probably wouldn't care if I thanked him or not. But what if he thought I was ignoring him because I looked down on him? What if he felt insulted because I hadn't said anything?

It seemed unlikely, almost impossible, that someone like him would give a damn about the opinion of someone like me. But if he did, then I didn't want to hurt his feelings. He'd really helped me yesterday when he didn't have to. It had meant something to me, although I wasn't sure what.

I started after him, plunging into the roiling current of kids rushing to class. His tall, blond frame stood out above the heads of pretty much everyone else in the hall, so he was easy to track even though he was at least a hundred feet ahead of me by now.

"Cass!"

I turned reluctantly toward the person calling me. It was Mary Agibinik, waving at me, her long black braid swinging back over her shoulder. With a reluctant sigh, I paused to talk to her.

"What's up, Mary?"

"Did you finish reading *Wuthering Heights* yet?" she said, chewing on her upper lip.

"Yeah. I finished it the same night Mr. Brown assigned it," I said, firmly mastering my urge to look back over my shoulder at Dex.

"Really?" Mary's dark eyes widened. "Wow. Everybody else I talked to can't even get past Chapter Three."

"I loved it. Didn't you?"

She shrugged. "I think it's kind of boring, actually. I can't figure out what's going on."

We fell in together as we made our way toward Trigonometry, another class we shared. Maybe I'd have another chance to thank Dex. I was pretty sure he wasn't torn up about it, so it could wait.

* * *

It wasn't until Thursday afternoon that I saw Dex again. I was in the art studio talking to Miss Thornhill, Jenny's ceramics teacher, about how she could make up her work.

The studio smelled like raw clay. Rows of work tables took up most of the space, one row next to the big metal-frame windows looking out on the back lawn and one against the wall opposite. They all had smears of clay on their surfaces from students doing whatever it is you do to clay. I wasn't much of an artist. The last time I'd made anything from clay had been in third grade.

Dex sauntered in, hands in his jeans pockets. I looked up and froze, blushing horribly as I realized who it was.

His gaze just flicked over me and slid away to one of his friends, who was taking his seat for the class about to start. I guessed that meant Dex was taking ceramics. Why hadn't Jenny told me she had a class with him?

Idiot. Because she hadn't known I cared. Heck, I hadn't known I cared.

"Did you hear me, Cass?" Miss Thornhill said.

"Huh?" I blushed all over again as my inattention became obvious to everyone within hearing distance.

"Tell Jenny she can come in after school for some make-up sessions," Miss Thornhill said.

"Oh. Okay, I'll do that. Thank you. I know she loves this class and hates that she's had to miss it this week."

Miss Thornhill beamed. "I'm glad to hear she's enjoying it."

Behind us, the guys were shoving each other and laughing about some guy joke. I could hear the commotion, even though I couldn't see exactly what they were doing.

Was this my best chance to say thank you to Dex? I didn't relish the idea of doing it in front of his friends. But what if I never got another opportunity?

My stomach fluttered wildly. Oh, God. Was I really going to march myself over there and force a conversation?

Yeah, I was. My mom had raised me to be polite.

I swallowed hard and turned around. He was stretched out in his chair, his long legs extended far into the aisle between work tables, his arm casually slung over the chair back. The other two guys with him were the ones in the shoving match. Dex just looked on, evidently amused at their antics but way too cool to join in.

Holy cow. Was I really going to talk to him?

Yeah, I was. Like I said, my mom raised me to be polite.

I forced my feet to march the several yards between Miss Thornhill's desk and the table where Dex sat. His gaze flicked to me again, the way it had when he'd come in, then slid away. Obviously, he didn't expect me to talk to him.

That green gaze shot up to mine when I stopped right in front of him. His buddies quit shoving and laughing as Dex stared warily into my face.

"Hi," I said, feeling like a fool.

"Hi." His voice, deep and slightly rough, had a faint question at the end.

"I—um—I just wanted to say—um—thank you," I stammered, blushing again. "You know. For Monday, on the bus. I—um—I really appreciated what you did."

His lashes lowered over his eyes. They were as thick and dark as I remembered them. He licked his lower lip and the sight made my heart pound and my belly clench.

"You're welcome." He sounded even huskier than before.

"Yeah, I— um—I just—" My weight shifted from one side to the other as my whole body seemed to catch on fire from embarrassment.

His friends snickered.

"Anyway, thanks," I blurted. "Just thanks. That's all I had to say."

I spun on my heel and made for the door before I could humiliate myself any further. Behind me, more shoving and laughter ensued. I wondered if Dex were taking part in it this time. Did he think my apology was funny?

Just as I reached the classroom door, I risked a glance over my shoulder at him. He wasn't shoving and he wasn't laughing. He was staring after me, his face unreadable under the thick, surrounding shag of his hair.

Holy cow. Dex Morgan was staring at me.

* * *

At Jenny's house, an articulated poster-board witch with green skin and a purple and black hat met me at the door. Well, actually she was pinned or taped *to* the door, but let's not quibble. She looked very festive there. Jenny's family hung that witch somewhere on or in their house every Halloween and I looked forward to seeing her.

"Are you going to the dance on Friday?" Jenny said the minute I walked into her living room. She'd gotten her color back, and her blond hair looked clean and shiny again. She was even dressed in jeans and a sweater instead of pajamas.

"Uh...what?" I set my book bag on the floor of her foyer. "You look a lot better, by the way."

She waved an impatient hand. "The dance. On Friday. You know. The Halloween dance?"

"I wasn't planning on it."

"Well, I am. And if I'm going, that means you have to go."

I unzipped my parka. "You're still too sick to go and I don't have to. So there."

"I'm not too sick." She bounced on her toes. "I'm feeling better."

"Does your mom know you're planning to go?"

"She will. She's been bugging me to go back to school."

"Hmm." I pretended thoughtfulness as I toed off my snowy boots before going any farther into her house. "I'll think about it."

"That means no." She pouted. "It always means no when you say you'll think about it."

"I don't want to go. I always feel weird at those things."

"So do I. What's your point?"

"My point is that I don't want to go." I picked up my bag again and walked past her into her living room.

"But you can wear a costume. You can be anything you want to be."

"Can I be the Jolly Green Giant?"

She paused. "Sure. Why not? Or maybe you'd be more believable as his little sister, since you're kinda short."

"Costumes are your thing, Jenny, not mine," I said over my shoulder. "Plus I never get asked to dance."

"Wear your tightest jeans and lowest cut T-shirt or unbutton your blouse an extra button. I hear that's the secret to getting dances."

I made a face. "Ew."

"I'm just passing along a tip," she said airily. "Hey, you could dress up as something sexy, like a can-can dancer."

"A can-can dancer?" Good grief. I could just imagine Dex's face if he saw me in a get-up like that.

Wait a minute. Was I really making plans based on what Dex might think?

"I'm losing my mind," I muttered as I sank to Jenny's couch.

"What's that?"

I glanced at her. As my best friend, she wasn't supposed to judge me. At least, not too harshly. But I sensed she wouldn't approve of me approaching Dex the way I had, given his reputation, so I didn't want to report it to her. On the other hand, if I didn't tell her and she found out from someone else, her trust in me would be compromised. Best friends were supposed to tell each other everything.

"I saw Dex today," I said, looking at my lap. "I thanked him."

"Wow."

"Yeah," I said to my thighs.

"Wow. So you actually talked to him?"

"Uh huh." I flashed her a grin. "Kind of hard to say thank you without talking, right?"

"I thought you might have passed him a note."

Jeez, I hadn't even thought of that. But it would have been cowardly and kind of cheap, like I wasn't willing to be seen speaking to him.

"Nope. I saw him in Miss Thornhill's class when I went to talk to her for you. He was there, so I just went up and said thanks."

"Holy cow." She gaped at me, her eyes wide. "What did he say?"

"He said you're welcome."

Jenny frowned. "Is that all?"

"What should he have said?"

"I don't know." She flounced onto the couch next to me. "Something more, since he likes you."

"He does not."

"Does too. And don't argue with me."

"He doesn't like me, Jen. He looks at me like I'm not really there." Frankly, I wasn't sure why he bothered putting out the energy to direct his gaze toward me if he was so uninterested in the view.

"Well, maybe he doesn't want his friends to know how he feels."

"Why?" I frowned at her. "Because I'm so un-cool?"

"You know how guys are. Especially tough guys like him."

"No. I have no idea how tough guys are, and I don't think you do, either." Jenny didn't have any siblings.

She made a rude noise. "I've known Adam since I was four. Or was it five? Anyway, he's like my own brother, so don't tell me I don't know anything about guys."

"Well, Adam isn't much like Dex." My brother was sweet. A good kid. He wasn't a drug-dealing lowlife like Dex.

I rubbed my forehead. I was seriously confused where Dex was concerned, not sure if I saw him as a dangerously sexy tough guy or just a messed-up kid with a criminal record and a nasty attitude.

"I dare you," Jenny said.

I lifted my head and gave her a questioning look.

"To wear something sexy to the Halloween dance," she said. "Then see how Dex likes it. I bet you'll be surprised."

"He won't be at a stupid high school dance."

She grinned. "Then there's no problem, right?"

"Jen—"

"Oh, come on. We'll both dress up as can-can dancers. You'll see. It'll be fun." She clung to my arm. "You have to do this for me. I could be dying. It's my last wish."

I groaned. "I know I'm going to regret this."

Chapter 6

Costumes

Cass:

The school always seemed kind of weird to me when I came there after hours. Although there were plenty of other people in the lobby and milling around the doors to the gym, it still felt odd to be here so late in the day, especially with dance music blasting away from the gym.

The overhead lights in the lobby glared down at us, the bright illumination contrasting harshly with the darkness I could see in the gym. Clumps of kids stood around, laughing and talking. Some of them gave us curious looks as we approached in our costumes.

Why, oh why had I let Jenny talk me into going to the dance dressed as can-can dancers? I didn't feel sexy. I felt ridiculous.

She'd chosen a bright blue dress for me, to bring out the color of my eyes. Good grief. It had a tight, short-sleeved bodice with low-cut neckline, a full skirt with ruffle, and a frilly petticoat that made the skirt stand out from my legs, plus fishnet stockings. And not one but two feathers. I kid you not, I had two big old ostrich feathers sticking out of my hair. One was blue to match the dress and the other was white.

I even had my hair curled and pinned back with ringlets hanging down the back of my neck. And I was wearing make-up, the whole nine yards. Not just blush and mascara, but heavy black eyeliner and red lipstick. We'd had to put on our outfits in one of the school bathrooms, because both her parents and mine would have had fits if they'd seen the way we looked.

Good Catholic girls didn't go to school dances dressed like saloon girls, or can-can girls either. Sometimes I thought good Catholic girls didn't go to dances at all. Of course, my parents were pretty permissive compared to my aunts and uncles back in Chicago, who forbid my cousins such pagan delights as rock music and dancing, so I guessed I should feel lucky.

Jenny wore a red dress. I wondered who she was trying to impress. Her glasses didn't exactly go with the outfit, but I wasn't going to tell her that.

Something by The Jackson Five was blaring from the speakers as we got our hands stamped. Inside the gym, colored lights flashed and people in all kinds of costumes swayed to the music. I saw someone dressed like a bottle of beer and another as a pregnant nun. Tasteless, sure, maybe even offensive if you were sensitive to that kind of stuff, but not trampy. I felt like a slut with my low-cut bodice showing more cleavage than I'd ever bared in my life.

The air smelled like popcorn and the perfume of the girl standing in line behind us.

I glanced at Jenny. She was going up on her tip-toes like she was looking for someone.

"What are you doing?" I shouted over the music.

"Huh?"

"What are you doing? Are you looking for someone?"

She widened her eyes, the picture of innocence. "No. Just looking around."

Yeah, right. She was up to something. I wasn't sure I wanted to know what it was.

She grabbed my hand. "Come on."

Yeah, she was up to something. She hauled me into the gym like she was on a mission. Had she planned to meet a guy here? I couldn't think of another reason to be so excited about a dance. Usually we spent them standing on the sidelines, being ignored, which eternally raised the question why we bothered going in the first place.

Tonight, she stuck with me for about ten minutes or so. Just enough for that Jackson Five song to end and another two to follow. The last one was "Venus," by Shocking Blue.

I watched a girl in a mini-skirt and halter top—in October in Alaska?—writhe as the singer belted out that she's got it and wondered why I felt so slutty in my saloon-girl get-up. I was modesty personified compared to that chick.

I turned to Jenny to ask her what she thought, but she wasn't there. She'd disappeared on me. That was not her usual behavior; normally she would have let me know if she were leaving.

I scanned the crowd of dancers. There was a guy in a toga made hilariously of flowered sheets, a green-skinned witch, another pregnant nun, and the beer-bottle guy again. A girl floated past in an enormous hoop skirt that took up enough space for three people. But no Jenny.

"You wanna dance?" said a male voice in my ear.

I turned, my heart jumping around like that crazed rabbit again. But it wasn't Dex. Of course it wasn't Dex. It was some guy I didn't know, although he looked vaguely familiar. He was average height, brown-haired and kind of skinny, wearing a polyester paisley shirt unbuttoned to halfway down his flat, pale chest. I suspected he was one of the guys sitting by Dex the day I'd thanked him.

"Uh...okay," I said.

It wasn't the first time I'd been asked to dance, but the experience was unusual enough that I felt weird about it, like everyone was looking at me. The rational part of me knew they weren't, that they were too busy doing their own thing to take notice of me, but the irrational part suspected everyone was making a note. A lot of notes could hide in some of those costumes.

Look at that! Cass Maslanka is dancing! With a boy! Maybe it would make the school newspaper, hah hah.

The kid didn't seem to know what to do with himself on the dance floor, not that I did. He merely swayed from side to side while stepping back and forth. His arms sort of dangled limply next to him. Of course, most of the people dancing looked pretty much the same, so I guessed it was okay. We fit in.

I glanced around and there was Jenny, dancing with a guy dressed as Zorro. He was tall and dark haired, and looked vaguely familiar, but with the black half-mask and cape, I couldn't tell who he was. She grinned and gave me a thumbs-up. We'd both gotten dances within fifteen minutes of arrival. Hmm. Maybe her can-can costume plan was working after all.

My partner's eyes kept traveling over my body, from my neckline down to my waist and then farther down to my thighs. Then back up, over my waist to linger at my chest. Luckily, I was wearing a bra, unlike some of the other girls. Unluckily, I was pretty curvaceous and all that dancing made me bounce around in a way he apparently found interesting.

The can-can dress was working too well. I didn't like the way he kept ogling my breasts.

Five songs later, I was ready to sit down and take a break, not to mention keen to lose my partner. Mr. Polyester Shirt didn't seem to want to let me go, but a slow song was starting and there was no way I was cuddling up to him.

I didn't know him. I didn't want to know him, as his interest in me seemed to begin and end with my chest. So as Roberta Flack started singing, I turned around and walked off the floor.

"Hey." He caught my wrist. "Where are you going?"

"I'm worn out. I need to sit down," I said, wiping my forehead dramatically.

"Let's get something to drink." He nodded toward the exit.

"Isn't there anything in here?" I looked around for the refreshment tables.

"They're out. We can get some water at the drinking fountain, though." He grinned suggestively. "Or I've got some beer in my car."

"No, thanks. I'll stick with water."

"Okay. That's cool."

He still hadn't let go of my wrist. I wasn't sure if I should try to pull away. Would that be rude? He wasn't holding my hand. His fingers were clamped around me right above my watch.

I let it go in the interest of politeness. He was the first guy to take any notice of me in a long time, like since the tenth grade, and while I wasn't attracted to him, I didn't want to be mean to him either.

The hallways, even the lobby, were eerily quiet with almost everyone in the gym. The lighting, lower than normal in these back hallways because it was after hours, made the blue-green wall tiles and floor seem even more watery and swimming-pool-like than usual. We ghosted past the cafeteria and the lobby. He turned right, toward the office.

I tugged at his grip. "Why not use the one in the lobby?"

He nodded in the direction of the office. "The one down here's better."

"Really? Why?"

"It's cleaner, for one thing. Someone spit some gum in the lobby one, and I don't think anyone's cleaned it up yet."

"Ick." Okay, that was a good reason to choose another.

I could hear low, male voices as we got closer to the office area, but I couldn't tell where they were coming from. Maybe one of the classrooms had been left unlocked, or maybe whoever it was had taken over the bathrooms. I didn't care. All I wanted to do was get my drink of water and return to the gym.

The fountain next to the office wasn't especially clean either. It looked like someone had dumped coffee grounds into it earlier in the day. Black specks covered the basin and clogged the drain.

I held my breath and took a sip anyway. What can I say. I was desperate.

My escort bent down after me and slurped up a big mouthful. Great manners.

"What's your name?" I said as he straightened. "I'm Cass."

"I know who you are." He gave me a sly look that made me uncomfortable, although I couldn't say why. "I'm Kurt."

"Hi, Kurt. Are you friends with Dex?"

"We know each other." He slipped his hand from my wrist to my hand, lacing his fingers with mine.

It was not a welcome gesture, but I couldn't quite see how to free myself. Not without openly defying him, at least.

"How do you know who I am?" I said.

"Everyone knows you." He smirked. "You're Cass Maslanka, the untouchable."

"The what?" I said, dumbfounded. Nobody had called me untouchable before.

"The untouchable. The ice queen."

"I'm not an ice queen." Now I was getting irritated. I yanked my hand against his grip, but he didn't let go.

"I know you're not, but lots of people think you are," he said, eyeing me.

We were standing right next to the darkened office. There was a little cubby or niche formed by the doorway. The door was locked, but it was inset a bit, creating this small space and he drew me into it, out of the dim light of the hallway.

I tried to push past him. "I want to go back to the dance now."

"In a minute." He had me up against the door.

The wood felt cold and hard and unforgiving against my back. He was hot and sweaty in front of me, his shirt clammy against the exposed skin of my arms where he boxed me in. He smelled of sweat and cologne.

"What are you trying to do?" I said.

"I want a kiss before we go back." He bent toward me, his breath heavy with the sour smell of beer.

"No." Yuck. He was one of the last guys I'd want to kiss. I regretted dancing with him at all.

"I know you want it, dressed like that." He chuckled and dragged his fingertip along the edge of my neckline. His touch on such an intimate part of me made me shiver with revulsion.

"Let me go." I shoved at him.

He was a lot stronger than he looked. Maybe he had a skinny, flat chest, but I couldn't budge him half an inch.

"Show me you're not an ice queen, Cass," he said, shoving his mouth against mine.

His lips were hard and unyielding. Bruising. I'd only been kissed once, and that had been gentle and hesitant, on both my part and the guy's. This was completely different, an assault, a painful insult.

I could feel his teeth through his lips. Then his tongue. He was trying to force his tongue into my mouth. Well, if he managed to do it, he was going to get a surprise. I'd bite the hell out of him.

Thrashing in his arms, I kicked him. He gave up on the tongue, but kept mashing his lips against mine. It must have been harder to manage the tongue than I thought. I pounded on his back with my fists until he grabbed my hands and forced them over my head. His body shoved against mine, taking all the space away and making it impossible for me to fight back anymore.

For an instant, I thought he was going to do it. Whatever "it" was. I didn't want to think about that.

Then something yanked him off me. Kurt went staggering across the hall to slam into a bank of lockers. Panting, I shoved the hair from my eyes.

Dex stood between me and him, glaring at his friend. "What the fuck is wrong with you?" he growled.

Kurt shoved off the lockers. "Stay out of it, Morgan."

"She doesn't want whatever it was you were trying to do," Dex said, holding a hand out in a stop gesture. "I suggest you leave. Go back to the dance."

"Maybe I don't want to dance anymore," Kurt said. "Maybe I want to get it on."

"She said no. Now get out of here."

"You're not gonna get any further with her," Kurt said with a sneer. "She's like a glacier."

"Don't make me fight you," Dex said. "You don't want that."

Kurt paled. His cocky attitude fled as he took a step backward. "No, man, I don't wanna fight you."

"Get lost."

"Okay. Yeah. Sorry, Dex." Kurt turned on his heel and dashed back toward the dance.

My whole body shook now that Kurt wasn't pushing himself against me anymore. I didn't know if he would have raped me or if that nasty kiss would have satisfied him. I only knew it was over.

My hands shook as I tried to fix my hair, but the elaborate curled style Jenny had created was ruined. One of the feathers hung on my shoulder, broken, and the other sagged over my ear.

Dex turned to me. "You all right?"

"Y-yeah. I think so." I plucked the remaining feather out of my hair.

"Holy shit. It's you."

I peered up at him. He seemed genuinely astonished, looking down at me with his mouth open, his eyes unusually wide for him. His normal cool was temporarily gone.

"Um. Yeah?" I said.

"Cass, right?"

"Uh huh." I crossed my arms over my chest, wondering if he'd give me the eyeball the way Kurt had. My heart was pounding and jumping around, and it wasn't all fear and adrenaline from the Kurt encounter. Some of it was for Dex.

"I'm Dex Morgan," he said, his gaze remaining on my face. No ogling here.

"Yeah, I know," I said.

He lifted one eyebrow. "You do, huh?"

41

"Everyone knows who you are."

Dex snorted. "Yeah. I'm notorious."

I couldn't argue with that, so I didn't say anything. We just stood there and looked at each other for a long, awkward moment.

He wasn't wearing a costume. In fact, his chamois shirt looked like the same blue one I'd seen on him the other day. He was probably way too cool to get dressed up for Halloween.

"I almost didn't recognize you," he said with a swift glance over my form. "You look really different."

"Yeah." I fidgeted nervously, shifting my weight around and playing with a lock of my hair. "My friend did my hair and make-up for me."

"You look really pretty."

I blushed. "Thanks. Um, what are you doing here?"

He gave me a lop-sided smile. "Saving you, apparently."

"No, I meant what are you doing at the dance? It doesn't seem like your thing."

His smile disappeared. "It isn't. I had some business to take care of."

Business? Like a drug deal or something?

I swallowed. "Oh. Well, I don't want to keep you if you've got stuff to do."

"Nah," he said easily. "I'm already done. Why don't I walk you back to the dance?"

I rubbed my arms. "I'm not sure I want to go back just yet. I feel kind of weird." Like all my nerve endings were exposed. I wasn't sure I could face a crowd of people just yet.

On the other hand, I probably wasn't really any safer with Dex than I'd been with Kurt. My intellect knew that, but my heart—or maybe it was my body—disagreed.

He glanced at me. "Are you afraid of Kurt? He won't bother you again."

"I don't know." I shrugged. "I just feel weird." I shook my head. "It doesn't matter. It's not your problem. Thank you for helping me again, though. I really do appreciate it."

"You shouldn't be alone right now," he said, his voice low and thoughtful. "You look pretty shaken up."

"I do?"

He nodded, his eyes serious. "Are you sure you're okay?"

"Yeah. I mean, I don't know. Nothing like this has ever happened to me before."

"Do you want to go home?"

I shrugged again. "I came with my friend Jenny, so I'll have to see if she wants to go."

Her dad had driven us and was going to pick us up at ten o'clock. I touched my fingertip to my lip. It felt swollen and sore. If Jenny or her dad saw me like this, it would get back to my parents. And then there'd be hell to pay for sure.

"I can take you. If you'd like."

I stared at him, surprised at the offer. It was kind. Unless he planned to take advantage of my vulnerability while I was trapped in a car with him.

"That's a very nice offer," I said politely. "But I don't think I know you well enough."

"Suit yourself. But I think I'll stick around for a while, just to make sure he doesn't come back."

I frowned. "I thought you said he wouldn't bother me."

"He probably won't. But if I'm around, I know he won't."

"Aren't you guys friends?" I said suspiciously. Maybe the whole thing had been a set-up.

"Me and Kurt Wilson? No. I barely know the guy."

"But you were sitting next to him in Miss Thornhill's class. I thought you were acting like buddies."

He shook his head. "They're just acquaintances. Sometimes I do some business with them is all."

Business. Was he talking about drugs?

"Oh," I said faintly, wondering how I could get rid of him. My dad would kill me if he found out I'd hung around with a known drug dealer, even for a few minutes.

The problem was that I didn't want to get rid of him. Shameful, I know, but I wanted to find out more about him. I wanted to stand next to him so I could sense the heat of his body near me.

God, I was such a dork. If he knew what I was thinking about him, he'd probably laugh.

"Tell you what," he said. "I'll stick around for a while and we can hang out in the hallway or one of the rooms until you feel better. When you're ready, we'll go back to the dance, I'll disappear, and you can go home with your friend."

I gazed at him dubiously. "You'd do that for me?"

"Sure."

"Why?"

He shrugged. A look of embarrassment flashed over his face, so quickly I wasn't sure if I'd really seen it. "Just 'cause. I don't want Wilson coming back and thinking he can start something with you again."

So he felt responsible for me? That was strange. I told myself this was not, and could never be, because he liked me. Dex Morgan didn't like girls like me. He liked the trashy, easy kind who skipped class to smoke and drink and get laid.

"You know, um..." I paused, biting my lip. "I don't want to be rude or anything, but I'm not like some of the girls I've seen you with. I'm—"

"I know," he interrupted. "You're a good girl and you're not supposed to be seen with someone like me. That's why I'll disappear. I won't embarrass you."

Now my mouth was the one hanging open. "Huh? No, that's not what I meant at all."

"It isn't?" he said, with another skeptical lift of his brow.

"No. I just meant that I'm not—you know—a party girl. I don't drink or anything like that. I'm—" I looked down at the blue satin skirt of my costume dress. "I'm really boring, actually."

"I don't think you're boring."

That brought my head up again. He was looking at me with a slight smile on his full lips, but there wasn't anything mocking about it. I couldn't put my finger on what sort of expression it was, just that he didn't seem to be making fun of me.

"Oh," I said.

"Come on," he said, tilting his head toward the far end of the hallway. The movement made his hair fall to the side. "Let's find a spot to hang out. I promise I won't hurt you, if that's what you're worried about."

Chapter 7

Slow Dance

Cass:

The dim overhead lights of the school hallway cast odd shadows on Dex's face as he gazed soberly down at me. Behind him, the principal's office and administrative areas were dark, mysterious caves. A cool draft teased the skin exposed by my low neckline. I shivered and crossed my arms over my chest.

I could hear the sound of music and voices coming from the gym, and I caught a whiff of popcorn, yet they seemed far away and unimportant. Even Kurt Wilson didn't seem important anymore.

The only significant thing in my world at that moment was Dex.

He didn't seem to want anything from me. Although he said he wanted to make sure I was safe, I didn't get the feeling that he expected anything from me in return. Was I kidding myself?

Maybe it was stupid to trust him, but I did it anyway. He felt safe, oddly enough. This big, rough drug dealer somehow felt safe to me.

Crazy, I know. I should have turned around and run back to the gym as fast as I could. Instead, I let him lead me deeper into the school, past the offices and the cove, down the hall that connected the high school to Romig Junior High and the library they shared. It was just as closed up and locked as the offices.

The atrium-like common area in front of the library, with its stacked carpet-covered cubes for climbing and sitting, seemed lonely without any students. The noises from the dance had faded. It almost seemed too quiet back here.

"It's locked," I said, pointing at the closed doors and the darkened rooms beyond.

Dex reached into his pocket and pulled out a key.

"You have a key to the library?" I said, puzzled.

He glanced at me with a wry smile. "Yep. It comes in handy sometimes."

"Weird."

"It's a skeleton key to the whole school. I can get in any room I want." He unlocked the door. "After you."

"Why would you have a key to the whole school?" I whispered.

"In case I need to rescue a girl and take her somewhere private to recover." He grinned at me, his eyes twinkling with humor I would never have expected to see on his face.

I smiled. "Right."

"Let's go sit in the back where no-one will see us."

Most of the tables were in the center of the room. It was so dark I could hardly see where to put my feet. There were a few tables tucked behind the stacks, and that was where we went. Dex sat on the top of one of them, looping his arm around his bent knee. In the moonlight shining through the windows, his eyes looked dark and mysterious and as remote as ever.

I perched on the wooden seat of one of the chairs, my hands clasped in my lap. Now that we were really, truly alone, I had no idea what to say. Even though I had a brother, my experience with boys was limited. I'd always been either one of the gang or the big sister. Never the girlfriend. Never the date.

Not that this was a date. God, no. I needed to get that idea out of my head immediately.

"So, Cass, what's your costume supposed to be?" he said, watching me with those inscrutable eyes.

"A can-can dancer." Did he even know what that was? A lot of the kids in our school had less than no interest in history.

"Oh, right," he said. "Do you know how to do the dance?"

"No." I was blushing, but in the darkness he surely couldn't see it. "And even if I did, I wouldn't do it."

"How come? It's pretty tame if you ask me."

"Well, yeah. But you're supposed to do those high kicks. My mom and dad would have a cow if they saw me doing something like that."

"They would, huh?"

"Yeah. Like I told you, I'm really boring."

"You need to quit saying that." He reached out and pushed lightly against my upper arm. "You're not boring, Cass Maslanka."

"You know my whole name?"

"Yep."

Huh. What did that mean?

"A lot of people don't know what a can-can dancer is," I said, in an awkward attempt at normal, light conversation.

"That's true." He glanced sidelong at me. "And you're wondering how a low-life like me knows something like that."

"No." Yes.

He laughed softly. "It's okay, Cass. I know who I am. But it might surprise you to know that I like to read."

I attempted to hide my surprise. "Me too. What do you read about?"

"This and that. History. Science fiction. Mechanical stuff."

"Are you a mechanic?"

"I work on cars, yeah." He tilted his head slightly. "Is that a bad thing?"

Wow. He was unsure about himself. I never would have guessed that, never would have imagined any kind of insecurity lay beneath his cool exterior.

"Of course not."

"You sure?"

I thought I could see a dimple in his cheek, but it was hard to tell in the low light.

"Yeah, I'm sure. My grandpa was a mechanic for a while."

"Just for a while?" he said, turning slightly toward me.

"Yeah. He became a carpenter."

"Somehow, I figured you'd come from a family of professionals. Doctors or something."

I shook my head with a little laugh. "Not at all. My dad is from a family of Polish boot and shoemakers in Chicago. My mom's folks are German-American farmers from Wisconsin. No professionals anywhere in my family tree as far as I know."

"But you're a good girl," he said. "A nice girl, and I don't want to get you in trouble."

"Then don't."

He seemed to be studying me through the gloom of the library. Could he see me any better than I could see him? I wondered what he saw in me. There had to be something, or he wouldn't be sitting here with me, and it must be something I'd never noticed in myself. Because I really couldn't understand what it could be.

"You're not afraid to be seen with me?" he said.

"Not if you don't mind being seen with me."

Where was this conversation going? Was he trying to ask me out? Maybe Jenny was right and he really did like me, as unbelievable as that seemed.

"Why would I mind?" he said. "This is all in my favor."

"I figured your reputation might be ruined if you're seen with someone as uncool as I am."

He snorted. "I don't give a shit about that."

"You don't?"

"No. Besides, what makes you think you're uncool?"

I pulled my chin back. "The fact that all the cool people totally ignore me, for one thing. When they're not picking on me."

Dex leaned forward. "Who picks on you?" he said tensely.

"Just people. It's kind of random, actually. My point is that I know I'm not cool and if you're seen with me then you'll be un-cool too."

I could sense his grin even through the darkness. "Baby, my cool will rub off on you, so don't worry about it."

He'd called me baby. The endearment stunned me so much I couldn't answer.

It didn't mean anything. He probably called all the girls that. I told my heart to stop fluttering and be sensible, but it wouldn't listen.

I cleared my throat. "Um, okay. I'll try to remember that."

We sat there smiling at each other for a moment. No amount of darkness could have hidden it. Then I realized what I was doing—making goo-goo eyes at Dex Morgan—and I blushed and looked away.

"Cass?"

"Yeah?" I looked up again.

"Wilson didn't hurt you, did he?" Dex said in a low voice.

"No. Well, my lip is a little sore, but he didn't really do anything too bad."

"You sure? You're not holding out on me?"

"I'm sure. Why?"

He shook his head. "Just wondering. Making sure you're really okay."

If I'd had the nerve, I would have reached out and taken his hand. But I didn't have the nerve. I was a wimp, so my hand stayed in my lap.

"Dex, why did you stand up for me on the bus?" I blurted.

He shifted his weight. The wide leg of his jeans made a sliding sound against the table top. "Leon was embarrassing you."

"So? I mean, you didn't even know me. Why did you care?"

He looked down. "I don't know. Did it bother you?"

"No. I told you. I was—am—grateful. It was just really unexpected. I mean, isn't he one of your friends? You took my side over his."

"Leon is a friend, but I didn't like what he was doing." He sounded self-conscious and his head remained lowered, so I couldn't see his face.

"So my reputation as an ice queen didn't bother you?"

"What are you trying to say?" There was a faint note of something hostile in his voice. Defiance, maybe, or anger.

"I don't know," I said. "Nobody's ever stuck up for me before, that's all."

"Nobody?"

Now he sounded disbelieving. I wished we could turn on the lights so I could see his expression. But then he'd be able to see mine, and maybe the strange sense of intimacy we had here in the dark would be lost.

"Nobody," I said.

He reached across the table and took my hand. It was such an unexpected gesture that I gave a start of surprise, but I didn't pull away. His hand felt strong and gentle around mine, warm and dry and comforting.

"They should have," he said. "You don't deserve that kind of bullshit."

"Thanks." I couldn't look at him. It was too intense.

Instead, I let him continue holding my hand. My fingers slowly curled around his, so I was holding him back. There in the dark, in the quiet of the library, I felt as if I were dreaming. Nothing seemed quite real. The situation was so improbable that it was easy to tell myself it was outside of ordinary reality, a place and time where Dex Morgan could hold hands with Cass Maslanka, and therefore anything could happen.

Well, not anything. There were certain things I wouldn't do, not with anyone. Not even Dex.

"I like science fiction too." My non-sequitur broke the silence awkwardly.

"You do?" He sounded amused. "Who are your favorites?"

"What? You think a girl can't like science fiction?"

"I never said that. What authors do you like?"

"Andre Norton. Ursula K. LeGuin. Robert Silverberg. Isaac Asimov. And Edgar Rice Burroughs."

"Oh, yeah? Are you into Tarzan the ape man?" He gave my hand a teasing little squeeze. "Should I call you Jane?"

My God, was he flirting with me? I blushed and laughed.

"No, don't call me Jane. I like the Tarzan stuff all right, but I was thinking of the Pellucidar books, actually."

"I read one of those. It was pretty good. Although the idea of a whole world in the center of the earth seems kind of silly nowadays." His thumb made a gentle stroking motion across the back of my hand. The touch made little tingles of awareness travel up my arm and all the way through my body to settle deep in my belly.

"Yeah," I said breathlessly. "I know what you mean."

He was not at all what I'd expected. I never thought he'd be the kind of guy to pick up a book at all, let alone the same kind I liked to read. That fact made me wonder if he really was a drug dealer, and if so why. Asking would be rude, though. I mean, I barely knew him and it was none of my business.

Maybe it wasn't true. Maybe it was one of those vicious rumors people liked to spread just for the meanness of it. I wanted to believe that, because the Dex I was getting to know didn't seem like the kind of guy who would sell drugs.

On the other hand, he did have an illicit key to the school.

"Are you feeling better?" he said, continuing to stroke my hand.

I thought about it for a moment. "Yeah, I am. Thanks. This has really helped."

"Good. I'd better get you back to the dance now before your friend notices you're missing."

Oh, yeah. Jenny. I'd been so wrapped up in Dex that I'd completely forgotten about her.

"Okay," I said, reluctant to give up the little bubble of intimacy we'd established.

He kept my hand in his as we left the library. I'd never held hands so long with a guy before, and the prolonged contact made me tingle all over. It made me ache in a way I'd never felt before, made my stomach—and other, less well-known parts of me—flutter with excitement. Which just goes to show you what a terribly dull and safe life I'd led up to that point.

When we reached the lobby, people were wandering in and out of the gym and hanging around in little clusters, talking. Some of them looked over at us, but no-one seemed to make much of the fact that Dex was holding hands with me. Maybe they didn't recognize me.

"Well," he said. "We're here and you're safe enough. Don't go off alone with any more guys."

I looked up at him and smiled. "I went off with you."

"That's different." He smiled back.

He did have a dimple, and when he smiled, his whole face lit up. Those cool green eyes turned warm and even more mesmerizing than ever, making it impossible for me to look away.

I wanted to dance with him. Just one dance. He'd never ask me, though. He had the idea that it would embarrass or compromise me in some way, even though that was ridiculous.

Or maybe he simply didn't want to dance with me. Maybe all that stuff he'd said in the library was him shining me on. Sweet-talking me.

"Dance with me," Dex said.

"What?" I stared up at him stupidly.

He gave our still-connected hands a little tug. "Just one dance. Will you?"

I caught my breath. "Yeah. Of course."

We walked into the gym still holding hands. Miraculously, no-one seemed to notice us together. I suppose they were all too busy doing their own thing to pay any attention to us. This event was probably only momentous in my head.

Santana's "Black Magic Woman" was playing as he led me onto the dance floor. We started moving to the beat. Dex wasn't much better at dancing than Kurt Wilson, but I didn't care. That wasn't the point. Besides, he kept hold of my hand the whole time, and that gave me the most indescribable feeling.

Why was I so over the moon because Dex Morgan was holding my hand? I'd barely paid any attention to his existence before that afternoon on the bus, and I was pretty sure he hadn't noticed mine either. Until he'd intervened between me and Leon, I'd never imagined myself with a guy like him. His type were so foreign to me they might as well have been from another planet...or so I'd thought.

The song ended. I smiled and turned to leave the floor, but he held me back. The song that started to play was a slow one, the kind where you put your arms around your partner.

Dex bent down and put his lips next to my ear. "One more?"

His breath blew gently through my hair and onto my skin. It tickled. I shivered and nodded.

"Okay."

What was I saying? Holding hands was one thing, but now I'd have to press my body up against his. But it was too late to say no, and the truth was that I didn't want to.

He put his hands at my waist. I did the same to him. Holy cow, I had my hands on a guy's waist. And not just any guy. Dex Morgan.

We started shuffling back and forth, slowly turning in a circle, the same way all the other couples on the floor were doing. My heart was racing now. I didn't know whether to look up, into his face, or keep my eyes on his chest. I kept them down.

Slowly, gradually, he drew me in closer until we were pressed together from chest to hips. He felt hot, and as hard as a wooden statue. Except he was unmistakably alive beneath my hands.

His arms tightened around me. I let my head rest against his chest. This was the closest I'd ever been to a boy, even closer than the couple of times I'd been kissed. His body smelled musky, earthy, without a hint of cologne, although I detected a hint of cigarette smoke. I could hear his heart pounding even over the sound of the music.

I let my arms wrap around him. His hand began stroking my back, slowly, up under my hair and then down, all the way to the small of my back. I liked it. I wanted more, but the song seemed to be ending.

Damn.

Someone tapped me on the shoulder and yelled at me over the fading notes of the music. "Cass!"

I turned within Dex's embrace. Jenny was staring at us, her blue eyes wide. Our coats hung over her arm.

She held up her wrist and pointed at her watch. "My dad is here!"

"Okay." I looked up at Dex. "I have to go."

He released me gradually, as if he didn't want to let go. "Okay. Good night, Jane."

I laughed. "Good night, Dex. And thanks again."

"Don't mention it. I'll see you around, Cass."

"Yeah. See you around."

I held his gaze for another moment before turning and following Jenny off the dance floor. My body still tingled and fluttered, and I imagined I could feel his eyes on me as I left.

If Jenny hadn't been there, I wouldn't have gone. I would have stayed with him as long as he wanted me.

This was so unlike me. What happened to sensible Cass, the girl who set a good example for her two younger siblings? She seemed to be on vacation.

Jenny bumped shoulders with me when we got into the lobby. "What the heck was that back there?" she said in a stage whisper.

"A dance."

She gave me wide eyes. "That was more than a dance."

"Not really."

"Why did he call you Jane? Doesn't he know your name?"

"He knows it. That was just a private joke."

"A private joke? Come on, Cass, you have to tell me. You danced with Dex Morgan and he called you Jane. What happened?"

The front doors of the school were only a few yards away. Her dad was waiting in his car outside and I didn't want to have this discussion within his hearing distance.

"He asked me to dance so I said yes," I said lightly, pretending my stomach didn't flutter wildly at the thought of his hands on me.

"And that's it?"

"Yep." I glanced at her chidingly. "It was only a dance, Jen. Really."

"I told you he likes you." Then her eyes narrowed as she stared at my face. "Oh, my God. He kissed you!"

"Jeez, will you keep your voice down? He didn't kiss me."

"Then what happened to your lipstick? It's gone."

"I'll tell you some other time, okay?"

"No. Not okay." She pushed the doors open, letting in a blast of icy winter air.

"I can't talk about it in front of your dad. Just give it a rest."

She looked like she was going to open her mouth and pester me again.

"Who were you dancing with, anyway?" I said, partly out of real curiosity and partly to forestall any more questions on her part.

"That was Bob Rogers. Didn't you recognize him?"

"Not dressed as Zorro." I gave her a closer inspection, noting the blush on her cheeks. "You like him, don't you?"

"Maybe." She giggled. "Yes."

"Tell me all about it."

Bob Rogers was a football player, one of the popular crowd. I never would have put him and Jenny together, any more than I would have done with me and Dex. He seemed nice enough, though, and I was happy for her.

We picked our way carefully down the icy steps. Jenny's dad had pulled up their Chevrolet station wagon right in front, so we didn't have to go far. The running engine sent a cloud of exhaust fumes into the air.

I tapped Jenny on the wrist. "Don't say anything about Dex, okay?"

"Yeah, okay." She grinned at me. "I'll be too busy talking about Bob."

Chapter 8

Reality

Dex:

The gym felt hotter than hell all of a sudden. The air seemed to press in on me. The strobe lights flashed in my eyes—red, blue, red, blue, like the lights on a cop car.

Although the air felt hot, my body was cold without Cass in my arms. I wanted her sweet little body against me again, just to hold.

The DJ was playing another fast song—"Whole Lotta Love" by Led Zeppelin. Not one of my favorites, and besides I'd lost my partner. But I stood there anyway and stared after her like an idiot while around me couples started dancing to the new tune.

The noise of the music and the crowd of dancers seemed to fade away as I watched Cass leave, her blond friend by her side. I should never have asked her to dance.

Hell, I should never have touched her at all, let alone held her hand. All that had done was made me want her even more, and I couldn't have her. She was so far out of my league I'd get a nosebleed if I tried to date her.

Date her?

I didn't date. I fucked. Sometimes I hung out with a chick if I liked her well enough. Dating was not a part of my life.

Cass wasn't the kind of girl I would merely fuck. It would be more than enjoyable, maybe even addictive, but I wouldn't get involved with her on that level. She was the kind of girl who would expect a whole lot more than I was willing to give.

I stuck my hands in my jeans pockets and made my way off the dance floor. I still had a few baggies of weed to sell, so I made my way around the edges of the room, looking for prospects.

I'd paid the gas bill just in time to prevent them from shutting off our heat, and I'd bought the part I needed and fixed my car, but I still needed money. I always needed money.

By the time I headed home, I was significantly richer. I turned into my neighborhood, remembering Cass walking home alone through the snow. Which house belonged to her family? I didn't even know which street was hers.

She probably had one of the nicer houses. Maybe one with a fence around the yard. Flowers in the front in summer, a sprinkler running on the sunny days. Did she have brothers and sisters? Did they run through the sprinkler when it was hot? I'd seen little kids doing that and wondered what it was like.

I shook myself. Who the fuck cared? She wasn't for me, any more than a cute little house with a cute little fence and a sprinkler in the front yard. End of story.

I could see the light from our TV flashing blue through the living room window when I pulled into our driveway. I opened the car door. Sound blared out at me, almost as loud as the school dance had been, tinny gunshots and one of those cheesy, old-fashioned soundtracks. Probably one of my dad's old Westerns again.

Sonofabitch. I had a lot of money in my pocket, and I sure as fuck didn't want it going to my dad. He'd spend it on booze.

I bent down and lifted the lid on the secret compartment I'd put in the floorboards on the passenger side. Stuffing the cash inside, I muttered a short and probably sacrilegious prayer that my dad and Sin wouldn't guess it was there. No way did I want my money going to buy them dope and booze and whores. Yeah, I was pretty sure my dad was screwing around on my mom.

I got up to the door of the house and I could hear the shouting. My mom's voice screeching that she didn't know and my dad should go fuck himself. My dad's answering bellow.

Great. Just great.

My hand hesitated on the tarnished brass of the doorknob. If I went in, I had to face the shitstorm they'd created together. But if I didn't, I'd be leaving Joe to deal with it alone. He was probably hiding under the bottom bunk at the moment. Or maybe in the closet.

Sin sure wouldn't be any help. If he was home at all, he was probably wasted. As always, I was the only one willing and able to do the job.

Fuck me.

I opened the door and strode into the living room without bothering to knock the snow off my shoes. Nobody around here gave a damn anyway.

Mom and Dad didn't seem to notice I'd come in. They stood in the middle of the living room glaring at each other. He was wearing his work clothes—a cheap brown men's suit minus the jacket, his tie loosened and turned half-way across his chest. His comb-over was flopping over the side of his head, too, in a ridiculous black fringe.

Mom wasn't in any better shape. In fact, she was worse. She hadn't even bothered putting on regular clothes. She wore a red velour robe so old the cuffs were falling apart and the zipper seemed permanently stuck at half-mast. Her blond hair, the same color as mine, looked dark and stringy with dirt and oil.

With another shrill scream, she lobbed a dirty plate covered with the smeared remains of a frozen pizza at him. It sailed over his head and crashed against the wall behind him, breaking with a loud shatter. Sauce and globs of melted cheese splattered across the plaster.

He rushed her and grabbed her by the hair. She screeched again and he slapped her.

"Hey," I said, a sick feeling settling into my stomach. "Hey! Knock it off!"

My dad paused with his hand in the air, poised for another slap. "Mind your own business, Dex."

"Do I need to call the cops?"

He laughed. "You wouldn't dare."

Unfortunately, he was right. The cops might search the place and discover my stash and Sin's, and we'd both end up in jail. And Sin was too old for juvie, so he'd be in with the hard adult cases.

I glared at my old man. "Quit hitting her."

"You want me to go after you next?" he said.

"Dex, it's all right," my mom said. "I don't need your help."

She had a red mark on her face where he'd smacked her the first time. Both of them reeked of alcohol. If I left them alone together, God only knew what they'd do to each other.

Maybe they'll kill each other and we'll finally be free of them.

I shut down that nasty little voice. Even I wasn't so low I'd wish my own parents dead.

"Suit yourself," I said.

"Hey," my dad said in a hard tone. "Where'd you get the money to pay the gas bill?"

I gave him one of my coldest stares. "Where do you think?"

He sneered. "My son the drug dealer."

"At least I pay the bills."

"Where's the rest of it?" he said, advancing on me.

"There isn't any. I spent it all." That was true, as far as it went. He didn't need to know I'd gone out and earned more.

"You're lying," he growled, his whiskey breath gusting over me in disgusting waves. "I know you've got more around here somewhere."

"Sorry. I don't. What do you need it for, anyway? The bill's been paid and we've got groceries for the week." Kind of.

"Don't you talk back to me, you sorry little shit. What I need it for is none of your business."

"Well," I said. "I'd like to help you out, but I can't. I'm broke." I shrugged and left them in the living room and tromped down the threadbare carpet of the hallway. Thank God he didn't follow me.

Sin wasn't in the bedroom. I flicked on the light. His comforter and sheets lay in a greasy tangle on his mattress, but he wasn't anywhere to be seen. I wondered if he'd left our brother before or after our crazy parents had started in on each other.

Joe huddled on the top bunk, his arms wrapped around his middle, a haunted look on his face. The air stank of pot smoke.

"Dex!" he whispered. "I'm glad you're back."

I climbed up into the bunk with him. "You okay?"

"Yeah. I'm all right." He shook his head as if to contradict himself. "I hate it when they fight like that."

"Me, too, buddy." I settled in with my back against the wall next to him.

He leaned against me, just lightly. "Did you go to the dance?"

"Yep. Did you do your homework?"

Joe hung his head, shaking it no. "I couldn't. They've been arguing all night long."

Parents sucked. Couldn't they see they were hurting Joe? He was only ten. He shouldn't have to listen to their crap or be afraid one of them would decide to come in here and pick on someone a lot smaller and less able to fight back.

I nudged his shoulder. "That's all right. We'll get it done over the weekend." Maybe our folks would be comatose with drink by then and we'd have some peace for a while.

"Okay." He gave me a strained smile. "I'm supposed to write a story."

"Oh, yeah? What about?"

"The teacher didn't say except it has to have snow in it."

"I bet you can come up with some great ideas," I said.

"Maybe." He looked doubtful.

I wondered if Cass liked telling stories as much as she seemed to enjoy reading them. The time I'd spent with her in the library took on this completely unreal tone, almost like I'd dreamed it. It was a sweet little bubble outside my ordinary life, a place where we could hold hands and talk about stories and...shit. I should've kissed her when I had the chance. I might not get another one.

This...screaming parents, an absent and drug-addicted older brother, no money...this was reality. At least for me.

Chapter 9

Halloween

Cass:

Miss Martha's Stock Pot was especially busy on Sunday. The chatter of voices and clink of tableware against thick, white china almost drowned out the classical music they always played. The air smelled deliciously of the daily special, savory sausage potato soup, and the freshly baked bread and cakes that filled the tempting pastry case near the register.

Our family of five crowded into our unadorned booth, our plates bumping against each other on the heavy, natural wood table top. I'd gotten the daily special plus a cinnamon roll. The Stock Pot had some of the best soup in town, all handmade, nothing out of a can. They baked their own bread and rolls, too.

Hanging spider plants and macramé wall hangings underscored the groovy, hippie vibe of the place. It was almost always bustling with people, full of good cheer, a place where you could either eat a full lunch or just hang out with a coffee and friends if that was what you wanted to do.

On Sunday, my family always went out to lunch after Mass. Sometimes we went to fancier places, sometimes we had pizza, and sometimes we came to Miss Martha's.

"How is school this year, Cass?" my mom said, just as I stuck a bite of soup in my mouth.

I rolled my eyes and pointed to my lips. She had a strict rule that we weren't to talk with our mouths full.

A couple passed by our table. The guy had long, blond hair—really long, past his shoulders—and the girl was wearing a snug T-shirt with no bra underneath. You could tell by the way her breasts hung, lower than they would have with a bra, and the way they jiggled as she moved, and the way her nipples poked at the fabric of her shirt. Her boyfriend had his arm around her shoulder and they were staring at each other in unabashed adoration. Why couldn't someone look at me that way?

"No shame," my mom said, her lips thinning so much they almost disappeared.

"Who?" Adam said around a mouthful of sandwich.

"Adam, don't talk with your mouth full," she said. "I was talking about that girl with no bra. Doesn't she realize everyone can see what she's got?"

"I don't think she cares," Beth remarked.

"Well, she should care. She ought to have some pride in herself, some respect. That boy she's with won't respect her if she doesn't respect herself."

I wasn't sure the girl's choice to go braless was due to a lack of self-respect. It was probably more of a political statement.

"She's a bra-burner, Lucille," my dad said.

My mom gave an unladylike snort. "I'm sure. My mother would have tanned my hide before she'd have allowed me out of the house looking like that."

"I think she's over eighteen," I said.

"Still. It isn't appropriate."

Privately, I agreed that going braless was unattractive. But it was the girl's choice, and I didn't know why my mom always got so worked up about it. Every time she spied a woman without her bra, she had something to say about it, as if her complaining would change anything.

Adam winked at me. "I like it."

"Adam Maslanka!" My mom gave him her most potent Mom-glower.

He grinned. "I can't help it. I'm a man."

"You don't even shave yet," Beth said.

"So?" Adam put on his own glower. "I could if I wanted to."

"Yeah, all three hairs," Beth said, grinning.

"Kids, don't argue," my dad said.

"But it's fun," Beth told him.

Adam subsided and returned to stuffing his ham sandwich into his face. For a few minutes, we had enough peace to get some eating accomplished. I was hungry because I'd skipped breakfast before church, so that was good with me.

Then Beth nudged me with her elbow. "I heard you danced with Dex on Friday."

I widened my eyes at her and gave my head a subtle shake. "Not really."

She wrinkled her nose. "Are you sure? I heard you did."

"Well, yeah, but it was just one silly dance."

Please, please let her drop the subject. I didn't want my parents inquiring into Dex's background, which was exactly what they'd do if they even suspected I was seeing someone. I was reasonably sure they wouldn't like the results, and neither would I.

Adam swallowed his food. "Dex Morgan?"

"It wasn't a big deal," I said, taking an ever-so-casual sip of my water. "Just a dance."

"Wow," he said. "I heard he only—"

I shook my head at him.

"Dates girls with curly hair," he finished lamely.

"Girls with curly hair?" my dad said, frowning in obvious bafflement. "Why would he do that?"

"Who knows, Dad?" I said. "The male mind is a complete mystery to me."

"Me too," Beth said with feeling.

"You're only thirteen," I told her. "You're not supposed to understand boys yet."

"And you are? You're only sixteen," she said, as if that proved something significant.

"The male mind is very simple," Adam said. "Girls."

"Huh?" Beth gave him a dubious sideways glance.

"Girls. That's it. That's what we think about. Girls, girls, girls. And that's all you need to know."

"I take it you're speaking for yourself," I said dryly.

"And every other male on the planet." He lifted his water glass to me in a mock toast.

"Dad, is that true?" Beth said plaintively.

"No, honey, it isn't."

"He's just trying to protect your delicate female sensibilities," Adam told her. "The only time we're not thinking about girls is when we're thinking about older women."

My mom shook her head as if she were losing all hope for humanity. "I can't take you kids anywhere."

"So who's this Dex person?" my dad said.

Damn. I was hoping he'd forgotten about that.

"Just a guy at school," I said nonchalantly. "I barely even know him."

"Are you dating?"

"No! Jeez, Dad, it was just a dance, honestly."

"Okay. But if it goes any further, you need to let me and your mom know. We'll want to meet him."

"Sure. Of course." On the same day that hell froze over.

* * *

It was one of the coldest Halloweens I could remember. We'd gotten so much snow the afternoon of the Leon and Dex Incident that we now

60

had almost a foot accumulated. Normally at this time of year, there was maybe an inch or two.

I sat dressed in regular jeans and a wool sweater in our foyer, the only part of our house on ground level, and read a novel while I waited for trick-or-treaters to show up. The sweet smell of the treats we'd prepared filled the air. It was a Tuesday night and most of the parties were already over. People had done their celebrating over the weekend. The kids, though, wanted to do Halloween on the actual day, and I didn't blame them.

Every time I opened the door to hand out treats, I got frozen all over again. Thick rimes of ice coated our driveway. Cars drove slowly, occasionally sliding sideways toward one side or the other of our street. Clusters of chubby ghosts and bats and witches flitted along in the frozen dark, clutching their plastic jack-o'-lantern treat bags, their costumes made pudgy by all the winter clothes they wore beneath them.

Mom, Beth, and I had made tray after tray of caramel apples, plus we had parceled out the wrapped candy into plastic baggies. Each trick-or-treater got one apple and one bag of candy. The apples—Golden Delicious—were pretty good this year, which was lucky because sometimes all we got in the stores were these tasteless, mealy fruit-shaped objects that only pretended to be apples.

The bell rang again. I opened it to see a little boy dressed as a pirate, with a patch over one eye and a bandanna tied over his head, blousy black sweatpants tucked into his puffy winter boots. Dex Morgan stood next to him. My mouth went dry and my heart and stomach instantly jumped into a contest to see which could flutter the fastest.

He stared at me for an instant, his cool slightly askew. Then a lazy smile spread across his face. "Hi, there, Jane."

I blushed. "Hi, Dex."

The little boy looked up at him. "You know her?"

"Yeah, I do." Dex patted the kid on the shoulder. "This is Cass. Cass, this is my little brother, Joe."

So Dex had a brother. And he was obviously affectionate and protective toward him, which made me like him way more than I should. That thought wasn't helping my nerves any.

"Hi, Joe," I managed to say.

"How come you called her Jane if her name is Cass?" Joe said.

Dex laughed. "I'll explain later." He met my gaze again. "I didn't know this was your house."

"Yeah. Uh, it is." Brilliant conversation there.

"You're not in costume tonight," he observed.

"No. Neither are you."

"Yeah. I don't do costumes."

Joe elbowed him. "I wanted him to be a pirate, too, but he said fuck no."

"Joe! Jesus, watch your language," Dex said with an uncomfortable glance at me.

I laughed. "It's okay."

"So what kind of treats have you got?" Joe extended the tattered pillowcase he held.

"I've got some good stuff." I turned back to my tray of apples and bags of candy. "You can have one each."

"Wow. Caramel apples." Joe grabbed an apple and a baggie and tossed them in his sack. "Thanks, Jane. I mean Cass."

"You're welcome, Captain."

Dex grinned at me. "Thank you."

"Here." I held out the tray. "You get some too."

"Nah. I don't need any."

"Sure you do. Come on. You'll hurt my feelings if you don't take any."

He gave me a surprisingly bashful smile. "Okay. Thanks."

I watched him select an apple. His fingers were long and narrow. Graceful. I'd never thought of a guy's fingers as graceful before. Dex tucked the apple into the pocket of his coat.

"Thanks, Cass."

"Take some candy, too."

He shook his head and laughed a little, but he consented to take a baggie, which he put in his other pocket. I wondered if he'd eat it or give it to Joe.

Now what did I do? Should I ask them to come in? I'd already exhausted my meager store of nerve just by talking to him and boldly urging candy on him. Normally, I would have stood there tongue-tied and stupid, so I wasn't sure what had gotten into me tonight.

Dex had stuffed his hands in his jeans pockets and was kind of rocking back and forth as if nervous. Maybe he needed an excuse to leave. Or maybe he was hoping I'd invite him inside. I opened my mouth.

Joe yanked on Dex's coat sleeve. "Come on. There are still a lot of houses to visit."

"Okay, buddy." Dex lifted his hand. "See ya, Cass."

"'Bye."

If I watched them walk back down the driveway, it would be the most uncool thing ever. Plus, I'd probably turn into solid ice. Reluctantly, I shut the door, wishing I'd asked them in.

But Adam and Beth were upstairs carving pumpkins, and Adam was well aware of Dex's reputation. If the guys had come in, Adam would know Dex and I were acquainted by more than a simple dance.

Would he tell on me? He might. More likely, he'd give me a lecture at some later time and I didn't want to hear it. I wanted to keep my inappropriate attraction to Dex a secret for a little while longer.

* * *

Dex:

Cass's front door was the flat kind, white, like most of the other doors in the neighborhood. Her house had only a small stoop in a little niche-like arrangement between the south wall of the house and the garage, the green walls rising high and faceless over our heads.

It was a typical entry to a typical split-level house. Nothing special. That ordinariness didn't stop me from feeling like crap when she shut the door on me, though.

Joe danced around as we left Cass's driveway. My feet were starting to go numb from the cold, but I'd promised him we could hit as many houses as he wanted tonight and I wasn't going to break my word. His treat bag, which was really the only clean pillowcase I'd been able to find in our house, flopped around, hitting his legs as he hopped on the ice.

"You're gonna fall and break your neck," I said.

"You sound like Frankie's mom."

Jesus. Was I turning into an old lady? Apparently, I was. That's what being responsible for a ten-year-old can do to you.

"She's nice," Joe said. "And really pretty."

"Who, Frankie's mom?" I said, even though I knew he meant Cass.

"No, dummy. Jane. Cass. Whatever her name is." Joe stopped hopping long enough to peer into my face. "Do you like her?"

More than I should. I shrugged. "She's okay."

"I like her. When I get older, I'm gonna ask her out."

I liked her too, more each time I talked to her. She wasn't the bitchy ice-queen rumor made her out to be. In fact, I wasn't sure how that rumor had gotten started.

"Maybe I'll marry her," Joe said.

I laughed. "Yesterday you thought girls were gross. Now you want to get married?"

"They are gross. But Cass is different." He pointed at the next house on the block, another split-level, this one with gold siding instead of green like Cass's. "Let's go there."

"You can tell she's different after talking to her for less than five minutes?"

"Yeah. Can't you?" He started swinging the bag again.

He was right about one thing. Cass was different.

I'd been stupidly hoping she would ask us inside, even though it would have been awkward and weird if she had. She lived in one of the nice houses, just like I'd thought. Nothing fancy, just clean and well-kept, at least from the outside, and only about six months old.

When the building companies had put up the houses on this block over the spring and summer, I'd come and hang out in the foundations with some buddies of mine, smoking and drinking. Even after the walls had gone up, we'd sneak in to party. They were huge compared to my place, with two whole stories. It was a drag when they put the doors on and we couldn't get inside so easy anymore.

Now Cass lived in one of them.

This part of town was kind of a jumble of older, crappier houses like mine and newer, nicer places like hers. All in all, it was a pretty decent neighborhood, but there were a few dumps like the one I lived in.

Of course, our house hadn't been so crappy when we'd moved into it. We'd made it that way. Or maybe that was just my faulty memory; I'd only been Joe's age when we'd taken the place.

"Are you gonna date her while I grow up?" Joe said. "You can if you want, as long as I get her back when I'm ready."

I glanced at him, trying not to laugh. He was kicking some clods of snow, not looking at me. "No, man, I'm not."

"How come? She's cool."

How did I explain to Joe that girls like Cass didn't go out with guys like me? "I don't think she feels that way about me."

"Yeah, she does." He kicked another clump of snow and ice. "I could tell by the way she was looking at you."

My stomach flip-flopped in nervous excitement, but I ignored it. "Oh?" I said, all cool detachment. "Are you an expert now?"

"Yes, I am." He grinned. "Maybe you should marry her instead of me."

"I'm not gonna marry anyone," I said.

"You're not?"

"Nope."

Marriage was not for me. Look how my mom and dad had turned out. They'd married right out of high school, had my older brother, and immediately descended into the hell that was our family life. I had no reason to believe it would work any better for me, and I sure as hell didn't want to end up tied to someone who made me miserable for the rest of my life.

Didn't want kids, either. I didn't want to do anything the same way my folks had.

Chapter 10

Fireweed

Dex:

The hall where I had my locker smelled like puke. Some kid had tossed his cookies all over the floor just a few yards from my spot. Jesus, it was making me feel like hurling myself.

The kid was at the nurse's office, getting his temperature taken or whatever it was they did there. I had no idea, since I'd never visited the school nurse. If I wanted to get out of school, I left. I didn't ask for permission.

Unfortunately, the janitor hadn't shown up yet to clean up the disgusting mess. People were skirting it, looks of revulsion on their faces. I rummaged through the crap in my locker as fast as I could, trying to get out of there and away from the stink.

There it was. My biology textbook. I grabbed it and my binder. Slammed the locker door.

Most of the guys I hung out with cut class on a regular basis and failed to do their homework. They took the easy classes, too, hoping to slide by with C grades in exchange for little or no work. I was an anomaly—a juvenile delinquent who took his classes seriously.

Mostly, it was because I liked learning. I got bored pretty easily, and I liked a challenge. Studying was something to do, and I figured it wouldn't hurt me any. Studying at home sucked, though, because of all the noise and chaos, so I did as much as possible somewhere else.

"Hey, Dex, what's up?"

It was Jake Barrows, a guy I hung with and who occasionally bought some weed from me. He had his arm around Misty Lockhart, a girl I'd screwed a few times. For a while there, I'd suspected she was hoping to be my girlfriend, but like I said before, I don't do girlfriends.

Jake leaned against the locker two doors down from mine, his arm still clamped around Misty. She was giving me the eye and batting her fake lashes at me, even though Jake had his hands on her. She wore no bra, her dark nipples showing right through her thin, white blouse. I also knew for a fact that her poufy, teased platinum-blond hair did not match the rest of her.

"How's it going, Jake?" I said. "Misty."

"It's all right," Jake said.

"I saw you at the dance." Misty licked her shiny lips. "But you didn't say anything."

"Sorry. I was kind of busy."

She pouted. Jake either didn't notice her behavior or didn't care. I wasn't sure which.

"You wanna smoke with us?" Jake said, leaning his head in the direction of the front doors of the school.

"Nah. I got biology."

He lifted his brows. He'd known me for a few years now, ever since seventh grade, and he was still surprised that I took school seriously.

"You sure?" he said. "Biology's boring."

"Yeah, Dex," Misty said, licking her lips again. "You should come."

"Maybe some other time."

I spun the numbers on my padlock, glancing casually toward the middle of the hallway. Cass was standing there against the far wall, looking right at me. She wore jeans today, not the really wide kind most kids wore but the old-fashioned narrow ones. And a high-necked blue sweater with some kind of white design around the top of it. Her dark hair hung loose around her face in soft, natural-looking waves.

Did I acknowledge her? Would it embarrass her if I did? More importantly, would Jake and Misty jump all over her if I did?

Her gaze wavered and fell away, and I had the distinct impression I'd already hurt her feelings by hesitating.

Normally, I wouldn't care whether I hurt the feelings of some random chick I barely knew. But Cass was different. The hurt look on her face made my insides tighten up and ache.

"I see someone I've gotta talk to," I said, leaving Jake and Misty by the lockers.

As I strode toward her, Cass looked up again. I caught her eyes and nodded.

She broke into a huge smile that lit up her face. Damn, she was beautiful. I'd thought she was pretty before, but when she smiled like that, she took my breath.

"You know that chick?" Jake said in apparent disbelief. "She's super square."

Shit. I hadn't realized he and Misty were following.

"Yeah. She's a friend." I hoped.

"Cass Maslanka is a friend of yours?" Misty said with a distinct sneer in her voice. "She's so square and uptight she doesn't talk to anyone. And she's a prude, and probably a nark too."

By this time, we were close enough for Cass to hear what she said. Her blue eyes narrowed on Misty and her back straightened as she gave her a look of cool contempt. She didn't bother answering Misty's claim, though. I admired her self-control.

"Hi, Cass," I said, letting the other kids flow around us.

"Hi." She smiled at me again, but in a more muted way.

Misty leaned all over me like she was marking territory. "I'm Misty."

"I'm Cass."

"I know who you are." Misty stared at Cass as she spoke, and put her arm around my waist.

Cass flushed. Her smile vanished. Her gaze wavered again, and fell.

Jake stuck his hand out toward her. "Hi, Cass. I'm Jake."

He sounded like he was trying not to laugh, and I wasn't sure if he was making fun of her or being genuinely friendly. I tensed, waiting to see if he'd do something obnoxious.

She shook hands with him, a bemused expression on her face. "Hi. It's nice to meet you."

"You wanna go and have a smoke with us?" he said, the grin still in his voice.

Misty glared at him.

"Oh." Cass gave me a startled glance. "Um, no, thank you. It's nice of you to ask, but I have to get to class."

"Told you she's a square," Misty said. "Don't tell her anything or she'll go to the teachers and report us."

"I wouldn't do that," Cass said.

"C'mon." Jake tugged at Misty's free hand, the one not clinging to me. "Let's go before it's too late."

"Come with us, Dex," she said.

"No, thanks." I peeled her arm off me. "Have fun, you two."

Misty pouted, wobbling on her gigantic platform shoes as Jake led her away down the hall.

"Sorry about that," I said to Cass. "Misty can be a bitch when she's jealous."

Cass's dark brows pinched together. "You think she's jealous of me?"

"I know she is." And for good reason. Cass was twice as pretty and at least twice as smart.

Her little nose wrinkled. "Why does it smell so bad in here?"

"Some guy threw up." I took her by the elbow. Her sweater felt soft and warm under my hand, yet slightly prickly. "Let's go somewhere else."

She let me touch her. That fact amazed me too. She didn't seem at all embarrassed to be seen in the middle of the hall with me, like I'd half expected her to.

"What class do you have?" she said.

I gave her a quizzical smile. "Biology. Same as you."

"How do you know that? Wait a minute. You're in my class?"

"You didn't notice?" I felt stupidly disappointed. The teacher called our names at the beginning of every class period, yet Cass had never noticed me.

"No. I guess I—Jeez, I'm sorry." She looked honestly dismayed. "I keep my head down a lot."

"It's okay. You've got other things to think about in there."

"Still—"

"It's okay. Honest." I smiled at her to show how okay it was.

We couldn't talk during class. Our seat assignments were good for the whole semester, and we already had lab partners. But I watched her, the back of her head as she bent over studiously taking notes.

That was nothing new. I realized I'd been watching her ever since the first day of school that year.

It wasn't a welcome observation. When I watched girls, it was to admire tits and ass. Not that Cass didn't have those qualities. She did, and it was clear she had a great body even though she never showed it off. But T and A wasn't why I looked at her. I didn't know why I did it.

There was something about her that drew my attention, my eyes. Something that made me want to get close to her, and maybe even break my rule about no dating.

* * *

When the class bell rang, half the students leaped out of their seats and bolted for the door. The sound level went from practically non-existent to a deafening roar. People pushed and shoved as they all flocked to the single entry and exit point simultaneously.

Outside, in the hallway, there was an answering roar. I could see a couple of guys out there horsing around, pretending to wrestle each other against the lockers as others sped past them.

It was lunch time and everybody was in a rush to grab whatever good time they could before they had to be back for afternoon classes.

"I'm going to The Fireweed Diner for lunch," I said to Cass as we left the biology classroom. "Want to come with?"

Her eyes widened. I couldn't tell if she was happy I'd asked, or nervous to tell me no. "I brought my lunch today," she said.

"So? That doesn't mean you can't eat out, does it?"

"Well, I didn't bring any money."

"It's on me," I said before I could think better of it.

Damn. This was sounding more and more like a date.

"I can't let you pay for me," she said. "It wouldn't be fair."

"Sure it is. Think of it as a loan."

She bit her lip, looking torn, so I stuck my hands in my pockets and slouched a bit, just to show how unconcerned I was. Honestly, it didn't matter whether she said yes or not. I usually ate alone, and that was fine.

She gave a decisive nod. "Okay."

"Okay?" I grinned like an idiot. "You'll come?"

"Yeah." Then she frowned. "How far is it?"

"I have my car. Don't worry about it."

"Oh." Another lip-biting worried look.

"It's not stolen," I said.

She blinked in obvious surprise. "I never thought it was."

"You looked like you were afraid to get in it with me."

Cass blushed. Her pale skin showed every emotion with a flush of color. "Are you a wild driver?"

"Probably." I grinned again. "But I'll take it easy on you."

"Okay. Just let me get my coat."

The howl of an earthquake siren started up, so loud it easily penetrated the walls of the school. Those things had been going off as long as I could remember, and mostly we ignored them. They were like fire drills without the drill, since we never did anything in response to the noise. I guess they were supposed to warn of an impending earthquake, although what we were supposed to do if the earth did start to shake I had no idea. It's not exactly something you can prepare for.

Cass raised her dark eyebrows at me. "Why do they still do those? They don't really think the Russians are going to attack us, do they?"

I gave her a quizzical look. "Russians? It's an earthquake siren."

"Oh." She frowned up at me. "Are you sure? I always thought it was an air-raid siren."

"Maybe I'm wrong." I shrugged. "Either way, they're annoying."

"Why do they do it? If there was an earthquake, it's not like we could escape it."

"I don't know," I said. "Maybe it's just habit."

She laughed. "Like they turned them on years ago and now no-one can find the off switch?"

"Yeah." I grinned. "Something like that."

Misty never would have joked like that with me. None of the girls I normally hung out with would have even understood what I was trying to say. Why did I spend all my time with people like that?

I wasn't sure I really wanted the answer to that question.

By the time we got outside, it had started to snow again. My Barracuda was at the far end of the huge parking lot, where I put it to make getting out easier. I hated being trapped behind a backlog of cars when I wanted to leave.

Now, though, I worried about Cass slipping on the ice as we made our way across the lot. Jesus. Maybe I really was turning into an old lady. Since when did I worry about a girl falling down?

Cass was fine anyhow. She had good boots on, not crazy platforms like Misty, and she walked confidently.

Don't get me wrong. I like sexy shoes. But it does make things easier when a girl can take care of herself.

When she saw my car, she frowned, her eyes widening at the same time. Her steps slowed as she took in the dented black body and the mismatched side panel in rusted green.

"She looks rough, but she handles beautifully," I said.

"Okay."

"I'm fixing her up."

She glanced at me with a dubious expression. "Are you?"

"Yeah. Get in. You'll see."

I came around to the passenger side and unlocked the door for her, holding it as she climbed in. She sat gingerly in the bucket seat, as if she thought the car might rear up and bite her. I tried not to laugh as I shut the door for her.

"It was nice of you to take Joe trick or treating," she said as I got into the driver's side. "Do you go every year?"

"Usually he goes with Frankie Jones, but this year Frankie was sick. He pestered me until I gave in." I started the ignition. The engine gave the same throaty rumble that filled me with satisfaction every time I drove her.

"Riders On The Storm" by The Doors roared out of the speakers. I turned down the sound so we could hear each other talk.

"Well, I think it was great. You looked cute together." She licked her lips. "This car is really loud, isn't it?"

She thought I was cute? That wasn't a good sign. Cute never got the girl.

I slanted a glance at her and pulled the car out of its spot. "I'm a guy. I'm not cute."

She laughed. "Okay. Sorry."

We were alone in the car together. This was the most privacy we'd had since the dance, and though it wasn't a real date it was feeling an awful lot like one. Not that I'd know. I'd never taken a girl out.

I chanced another look at Cass. Did she think of this as a date? It wasn't in the same league as dinner and a movie, but I was paying for her meal and doing the driving. That made it kind of a date.

My hands felt slippery on the wheel. I was nervous, for chrissake. The last time I'd been nervous with a girl was in the sixth grade. The first time I'd kissed someone.

"So Misty is a friend of yours?" Cass said.

"Sort of."

"Oh? What does that mean?"

I hesitated. No way was I gonna tell her everything Misty and I had done. "We've spent some time together."

She twisted her hands together in her lap. She was wearing red knit gloves with pompoms on the wrists. "She doesn't like me."

"Like I said, she's jealous."

"I don't see why. She's really pretty."

"She's all right." I glanced at her to see her chewing her lower lip. "Don't worry about it. She hates most of the other girls. It's just how she is."

"Oh." She leaned her head against the window glass and stared out at the gray and white day. "Okay."

Now what did we talk about? Usually when I was with a girl, we were partying. Drinking, smoking, screwing. Without those crutches, I wasn't sure what to say.

"Read any good books lately?" she said.

"No." Christ. I sucked at this dating thing.

"Not even a Tarzan?"

I laughed. "Nope. You?"

"Just my math book."

"You like math?" I wasn't fond of it myself.

"It's my favorite subject."

"I thought girls weren't any good at math."

She snorted. "We can be good at math. Girls are just as smart as boys, you know."

"I didn't mean it like that. It's just all the girls I know hate it. Except for you." I pulled into the parking lot of the Fireweed Diner.

"Jenny June likes it," she said.

"Is that the blond you were with at the dance?" I shut off the ignition.

"Yeah."

"So you like math and you hate stereotypes about girls," I said.

She lifted her chin. "That's right."

"Are you in favor of the Equal Rights Amendment?" I tried to picture her carrying a sign in a street protest. It didn't seem like something she'd be comfortable with.

"Yeah, I am." She gave me a sly smile. "Do you have a problem with that?"

"Not as long as women are available for the draft," I said.

She nodded seriously, even though I'd been kidding. "I agree."

"You do?" I stared at her in amazement.

"Yeah. Equal rights should mean equal responsibilities."

Wow. "You are not like the other girls."

She bit her lip, a smile fighting to escape. I could tell by the dimple forming in her cheek. "Is that a good thing or a bad thing?"

"Good. Definitely."

God, that dimple was cute. I had the bizarre urge to touch it.

"Let's get some food," I said instead.

* * *

Cass:

I couldn't tell if the Fireweed Diner was named for the magenta-flowered weed that grows so prolifically every Alaskan summer or the street where the diner was located. Fireweed Lane is a busy street not far from the school, with movie theater, restaurants, pawn shops, and all kinds of other businesses along its dusty length. It isn't very pretty, but then most of Anchorage is rough and raw like that, our streets edged with gravel, the medians landscaped only with the weeds and wild trees that volunteer to grow there.

We have a really short growing season, but it's intense while it lasts because of the long days. In November, of course, it's mostly dark and cold.

On this day, the sky was a thin, hard, pale gray. The snow on the roads was a darker gray, brownish from all the grit the city put down for traction. The branches of the naked birches, aspens, and cottonwoods were an even darker gray. In the natural world, only the deeply green, almost black spruces had real color.

The cars and the brightly painted signs on the businesses looked garish against the dreary gray background. I wanted to get out of this ugly town and into the country. Maybe I could convince my family to drive out to the Matanuska Valley or to Alyeska on the weekend. A little escape from the gloom.

The Fireweed Diner was housed in a small, cinder block building near the Fireweed Theater. When we pulled in, the small parking lot, made smaller by the encroaching berms of plowed up snow, was already crowded with several cars.

Inside, it seemed larger than I'd expected. Bright white walls, red upholstery on the banquettes, large windows, and lots of electric light made the place cheerful. I glanced around and saw a table of kids from school, but otherwise the patrons looked like business men on their lunch breaks.

"Do we have enough time to eat here?" I asked Dex as the hostess seated us.

"Sure. They're really fast. Especially if you already know what you want."

I opened the laminated menu. "I have no idea what I want."

"The burgers are good and so is the fried chicken," he said.

I glanced at the items on the menu. Burgers and fried chicken comprised most of it. I decided to get a cheeseburger. It was relatively inexpensive, so I wouldn't put too much of a burden on Dex and besides it would be quick to eat.

With the menu held in front of me, I sent a surreptitious glance in Dex's direction. Were we on a date? He was paying, and usually when a guy paid for a girl's meal, it was a date. Yet it was only our school lunch hour, and that didn't feel especially romantic.

He looked at me from across the table. "Have you decided?"

"Yeah. A cheeseburger."

"We think alike. That's what I'm getting."

I smiled at him. I'd run out of things to say for the moment, or rather I'd run out of nerve to ask the questions I wanted him to answer.

"How do you like biology?" he said.

"It's okay. Look, I'm sorry I didn't realize you were in the same class."

He waved that off. "It doesn't matter."

"Sure it does." I stared down at the folded paper napkin in front of me. "The truth is I assumed guys like you wouldn't be in a class like that."

"Guys like me?" he said, sounding amused.

I was really messing this up. My face flushed. "I mean—you know—"

"Stoners," he finished for me.

"Yeah. I assumed you were in that crowd."

"I am, basically. And most of us aren't in the harder classes."

My gaze lifted back to his. "But you are."

He shrugged. "It's something to do."

"So...do you...you know. Smoke pot?"

The dimple reappeared in his cheek. "Sometimes. Do you?"

I flushed again, even harder. "No."

Dex laughed. "I guessed you didn't. Don't look so torn up about it, Cass. It doesn't matter."

"You don't think I'm going to nark on you?"

"Nah. You could have already if you'd wanted to." He leaned back in the red leatherette seat, watching me, a faint smile curling his lips. "I trust you."

"Oh. Wow." I fidgeted with the napkin. "Thanks. That's pretty big."

"Yeah, it is. I don't do that with everyone." His smile deepened. "I don't know what it is about you."

"The fact that I forced a caramel apple and a bag of candy on you at Halloween?"

He laughed again. "That must be it."

"Did you eat it or give it to Joe?"

"I ate the apple and gave the rest to him. It was a good apple, by the way."

"I'm glad you liked it." Now I wished I'd given him two. "I wanted to invite you in but Joe seemed so excited to visit more houses."

"He was. I think Halloween is his favorite holiday."

"Mine is Christmas," I said.

He nodded and smiled. "I can see that."

The waitress brought our food just as a group of boisterous teens crowded through the door. Among them were some of the popular crowd, the jocks, student government, and honors class kids I rubbed shoulders with during school hours. None of them ever paid me any more attention than Dex's stoner crowd did, but I saw some of them eyeing me with him.

"Kurt Wilson called me untouchable," I blurted.

Dex raised dark-gold brows. "He did? What an ass."

I smiled at him. "Yeah. But apparently he didn't make up that name. People call me that behind my back according to him."

"Don't pay any attention to those assholes. They don't know you." He popped a French fry in his mouth.

"You don't think I'm untouchable?"

Dex shook his head, his eyes smiling at me as he chewed his fry. "I know you're not."

"I knew people didn't like me, but I didn't realize they think I'm an ice queen." And now I sounded like I was whining about it.

"They don't know what to think of you because you don't fit in. You're not like all the other girls and that probably makes them uncomfortable."

"I don't know how to fit in."

"Don't worry about it. You're great the way you are." He took a bite of his burger as if he hadn't just given me the best compliment of my life.

74

Chapter 11

A Good Girl

Cass:

Junior Hall, where I had my locker, was between the offices and Senior Hall, and it always seemed to be packed with people. Most likely it wasn't any more crowded than any of the other hallways, but it felt that way to me. Especially since my next-door-neighbor was caught in another lip-lock with her boyfriend.

The noises of their kissing irritated the heck out of me. Couldn't they control that? They were in public. They were inches away from me, and I felt like an unwilling participant in their love-fest.

"There should be a warning sign right here," Jenny said at my elbow, joining me for lunch.

I glanced at her with a grin. "I agree. Or maybe flashing lights."

"Like a railroad crossing!" She snickered.

"Exactly like that."

On my other side, the lovers continued groping each other, oblivious to me and Jenny. The guy had his hands all over the girl's butt. I had to look away.

"The benches again?" Jenny said.

"Maybe. But I was thinking somewhere different. Maybe the lobby."

"Okay." She held up her bag. "I brought enough chocolate cake for both of us."

"Ooh, chocolate cake." My mouth watered. Her mom baked the best cakes.

"Yeah. She did butter pecan frosting on this..." Her voice faded away as her blue eyes widened.

"What?" I turned in the direction of her gaze and almost ran up against Dex's chest. We were so close together that I caught a whiff of his scent, a mixture of male sweat, cigarette smoke, and whatever laundry detergent his family used. It was a very good smell.

Where had he come from, though? The lovers must have run off while my back was turned, because they were nowhere in sight.

Dex leaned his shoulder ever so casually against the lockers, his hands in his jeans pockets. He wore heavy brown boots, the kind with the thick heel like bikers wear, and a worn-looking red down jacket.

"Hi, Dex." My voice sounded humiliatingly breathy.

He grinned and a dimple appeared in his cheek. "Hi. Going to lunch?"

"Yeah. Jenny and I were going to sit in the lobby. You want to come with us?"

He glanced over my head. "I don't know."

Was he looking at Jenny? Was she glaring at him? I looked back over my shoulder at her, took in her tight lips and tense arms.

"Jenny won't mind, will you?" I said, lifting my brows at her.

She took a visible breath. "I guess not."

Boy, that was enthusiastic.

"See?" I said brightly to Dex. "You should come."

"Okay." He studied my face, his gaze lingering on my mouth. The look in his eyes made my heart race.

"Did you bring something?" I said, sounding even breathier. "I know you usually go out."

"Yeah." He held up a brown paper grocery bag.

Had he brought that just so he could sit with me over lunch? Nah, probably not. Maybe he'd run out of money for restaurant lunches or something.

"Great," I said. "Let's go."

I widened my eyes at Jenny, who only pursed her lips and shrugged. At least she didn't refuse to let Dex join us. For a second there, I'd been afraid she would say no outright.

People thought he was the toughest guy in school, and maybe he was, but he still had feelings. I didn't want her to hurt them. Besides, I really wanted to spend another lunch break with him.

We found a spot in the lobby, right next to the theater doors. West had a huge theater, which doubled as a community performing arts venue in addition to the school productions it hosted, and there was plenty of space around the doors.

I slid down to the floor and opened my lunch bag. I had a roast beef sandwich and an apple—Golden Delicious. Dex sat down beside me and Jenny chose my other side.

"You're in my ceramics class," he said, leaning across me toward Jenny.

"Yeah," she said, not looking at him. "I guess so."

Wow. That was pretty rude.

"How do you like it?" I said to him.

"A lot more than I thought I would. I took it for the easy A, but it's more interesting than I expected."

Jenny snorted softly as she drew out her food.

He ignored her to talk to me. "I usually draw, so ceramics is pretty different for me. Are you taking any art classes?"

76

"No, I'm not much of an artist."

"You're a lady mathematician," he said with a teasing sparkle in his eyes.

"Just a mathematician," I said, rising knowingly to the bait. "The lady part is irrelevant."

"Not to me." He bumped his shoulder against mine. "It's highly relevant to me."

Was he flirting again? I was so square I wasn't even sure. It flustered me. I blushed and bent my head to take a bite of my sandwich.

Dex smiled. He reached into his enormous bag and pulled out peanut butter on white bread. Two sandwiches, plus a bag of what looked like breakfast cereal.

"Is that Cap'n Crunch?" I said.

"Yep."

"I've never eaten that for lunch before."

"It was all we had. I gave the cookies to Joe."

That was nice of him. And he packed his brother's lunch. Wasn't that his mom's job? I wondered what that was all about, but I didn't want to embarrass him so I said nothing. Maybe his mom had to go to work really early in the morning and didn't have time to pack lunches for Joe.

"Are you ready for the trig test tomorrow?" Jenny said to me.

"I've got to study some more tonight," I said.

"You're taking trigonometry?" Dex said, looking impressed.

"Yeah," Jenny said. "We're lady mathematicians."

He gave her a measured look, as if contemplating a come-back. The cool, couldn't give a damn expression in his green eyes brought back everything I'd ever heard about him. The tough, cold, drug dealing low-life who'd scared me had replaced the kind, soft-spoken Dex I'd met at the Halloween dance.

Then his dimple flashed. "Yes, you are. You're probably smarter than me."

"Probably," Jenny snipped.

Dex laughed and shook his head, making his gold hair fall in his eyes. "You don't like me much, do you?"

"I don't know you," she said. "But I know of you. I know your reputation."

"I see." He settled with his back against the tile wall behind us. "And you think I'll get Cass in trouble?"

"Yes."

"She's very protective of you," he said to me.

"I know, and I appreciate her concern, but it isn't necessary." I frowned at her.

"I agree," he said. "It isn't necessary, because I would never do anything to get Cass in trouble."

Jenny rolled her eyes.

"I saw that," he said. "Believe it or not, I don't go around trying to get my friends in trouble. I try to stay out of it myself."

"You do?" she said in obvious disbelief. "That's not what I heard."

"Just because people say it doesn't make it true," he said. "You shouldn't believe everything you hear."

"Yeah, Jenny," I said, nudging her with my elbow. "Give Dex a chance."

"I am. I'm here, aren't I?"

I half expected him to tell her where she could shove her attitude, half expected him to jump to his feet and leave. But he didn't. He just gave me a sidelong glance and a shrug, and took another bite of his peanut butter.

That was when I noticed the mold on his bread. It was a small, green spot on the bottom corner closest to me. He'd already eaten half the sandwich.

I tapped him on his thigh. "I think there's something wrong with your bread."

"Huh?" He examined it. "Shit. You're right."

I watched him pick off the moldy spot and throw it into the plastic bag with the other sandwich. Then he took another bite.

"You're really going to eat that?" I said. "It's gross."

"It's all I've got," he said.

"Here. Have mine." I extended the remainder of my roast beef toward him.

"No. It's yours. You need it."

"I'm full. Besides, I still have an apple." I shook the sandwich at him. "Go on. Take it."

"I'm fine. I'm not very hungry and I have the cereal." His stomach gave a ferociously loud growl.

"You're not hungry?" I said, pulling back my chin in doubt. "It sounds like you're starving."

"Cass—"

"I want you to have my sandwich. Really. You'll hurt my feelings if you don't take it."

He pursed his lips. "You said the same thing on Halloween."

"Halloween?" Jenny said. "What about Halloween?"

For reasons I didn't fully understand, it had become very important to me that he accept my gift. I wasn't in the habit of feeding other people my lunch, but I hated the thought of him going hungry for the rest of the afternoon because his family had no fresh bread at home. I leaned over and placed my food in his lap. "Take it."

"Jesus," he muttered, picking it up. "Fine."

He took a bite. His eyes went round and he looked at me over the bread.

"You like?" I said.

He nodded enthusiastically. I never would have described Dex as cute until that moment, but that move was cute.

"For crying out loud," Jenny grumbled. "I guess I'll have to give him some cake too."

"Let's split each piece three ways," I said. "That way we'll each have the same amount."

* * *

Dex:

Cigarette smoke filled the air around the back doors of the school. It mixed with the fog from our breath until it was impossible to tell the difference. The gray and white clouds looked hazy in the artificial light from the lamps mounted next to the doors, giving the whole scene a weird, dream-like feel.

Above us, the sky looked as black as ink, the stars invisible through Anchorage's standard cloud layer. At nine-thirty in the morning, the sun hadn't come up yet, so we smoked outside in the dark. We weren't supposed to be smoking on school property at all, but nobody paid any attention to that rule unless a teacher came out and yelled at us. The only precaution we took was to keep the weed well out of sight during school hours.

Behind us, the long low stretch of West glowed, all the classrooms brightly lit. The school had once possessed two stories, but in the '64 quake, the top floor had mostly disintegrated. All that was left of it was some band and choir rooms next to the auditorium. I'd never been up there, since I didn't have band or choir.

The smokers, most of whom were stoners too, gathered outside between every class to get a ciggy in before the next round of passing notes and ignoring the teachers' lectures. The air quickly filled with the smell of cigarette smoke—or I assumed it did, since once I lit up, I couldn't smell anything myself. The damned ciggies caused cancer but everyone in my circle smoked them anyway. I don't think any of us planned to live much after thirty and maybe not even that long.

The cold bit right through my chamois shirt and the T-shirt I wore underneath it, but I ignored that. My breath froze in tiny white crystals along my eyebrows, but I ignored that too. I'd chosen to wear my sneakers instead of the biker boots, so my feet were turning into blocks of ice to match the ice under my shoes. We were all out here freezing our asses off in pursuit of a little nicotine.

Jake Barrows sidled up to me, without Misty this time. "Hey, Morgan, got any Maryjane?" he said in a low voice.

"Not on me. How much you need?"

"I was thinking an ounce." He took a long draw on his cigarette and blew out a stream of smoke.

"I can get it to you tomorrow or this afternoon if you want to meet somewhere," I said.

I never invited these guys to my house. This shit needed to stay far away from Joe, so when I needed to make an exchange I made arrangements to meet somewhere.

"This afternoon," Jake said.

He must be getting desperate.

"Smoked your whole stash, huh?" I said with a grin.

"Someone got into it," he said, glowering.

"Oh, yeah? Who?"

"Misty. Who do you think? That chick is a pain in my ass sometimes."

"Better you than me, man."

He gave me a speculative look. "You were with her for a while, weren't you?"

"Define with," I said. "We spent a little time together, but it wasn't anything serious."

"So you don't have any suggestions for me?"

"Nope. Unless you're willing to turn around and run in the opposite direction."

He laughed, his breath puffing out in a thick, white cloud. "You have that much of a hate for her?"

"I don't hate her. I just don't want to have anything to do with her."

He leered. "That's right. You're busy getting it on with Marcia Brady."

"Excuse me?"

My whole body tensed as I waited for Jake to explain himself. Marcia Brady was a pretty girl, but she was totally girl next door and in our circle that wasn't exactly a compliment.

"Your girl," he said obliviously. "She's the goody-two-shoes type, isn't she? A good girl. I still can't figure out what you're doing with her."

It was none of his business what I did with Cass. "She's not my girl. She's nice."

"That's what I mean. She's a nice girl. The kind who goes to church on Sunday and does all her homework."

"So?"

"So do you see any girls like that out here? No. It's weird, man." He took another puff on his cigarette. "Everybody's talking about it."

"If people have something to say, they can say it to my face." I took a drag on my own cigarette. The smoke calmed me down, brought me back to earth.

"Don't get yourself all worked up," he said. "It's cool. I don't care who you date."

"We're not dating."

He looked at me with a skeptical lift of his brows. "You're with her all the time."

"I don't date, Barrows."

"Okay."

He took a puff of his ciggy and I took a drag on mine. We were going to have to go back inside in a minute or two, although if I knew Jake, he'd linger here as long as possible. Hell, he'd spend the whole day out here if he could get away with it and wouldn't freeze to death. I, on the other hand, had classes.

"So, if you're not dating her do you mind if I ask her out?" he said, smoke drifting from his mouth.

"Yes, I do fucking mind," I growled, getting in his face. "Stay away from her."

Jake Barrows would not be good for Cass. He'd screw her and leave her.

"Why?" he said, grinning. "What do you care? She's not your girlfriend."

"And she's not gonna be yours," I said. "Don't make me come after you."

"That intimidation shit might work on Kurt Wilson, but it don't work on me," Jake said.

"When I beat you to a pulp, you'll learn."

He grinned even more widely. "Okay. She's not your girlfriend and no-one else can have her."

"Exactly," I said.

* * *

Cass:

West High was built around two small courtyards. One of the hallways and several classrooms looked out on them. They weren't much to look at; dull, institutional tan walls, weedy dirt, and not much else.

There wasn't any seating, and as far as I could tell, no way to get into them. Of course, there had to be doors for the maintenance guys to get out there and trim back the weeds once in a while, but I'd never been able to figure out where they were.

At this time of year, the courtyards were knee-deep in unbroken snow. The whiteness of the snow reflected a lot of light into Junior Hall, which had windows overlooking both of the enclosed not-quite gardens. For about half the school day, it was dark outside, but by lunch the sun had come up.

Jenny and I liked to sit on the concrete indoor benches that flanked the window walls and eat. We usually brought our lunches. It was a lot cheaper than going out. Besides, neither of us had cars, so going out was kind of a pain.

Today, she seemed a little annoyed with me. She wasn't talking much and just picked at her cheese sandwich. Normally she had a huge appetite for such a small girl.

"Okay," I said. "What's wrong?"

"Nothing. Why?"

"Don't give me that. I can tell you're mad at me."

She lifted her shoulders and picked another crumb of bread off her sandwich. "I'm not mad."

The crumb landed on her lap, a white speck on the red corduroy of her miniskirt. I wanted to brush it off for her.

"Then what's wrong?" I asked instead.

Jenny gave another shrug and pushed her glasses up her nose. "I hardly ever see you anymore, that's all."

"You see me every day."

"Only for a few minutes. We haven't eaten lunch together in I don't know how long." She glanced sideways at me. "You're always with Dex."

"I—I don't think that's true."

"Oh, come on, Cass." She rolled her eyes with a tilt of her head. "You go everywhere with him."

"I'm not with him now." And I felt it. I wanted to see him, but he'd said he had something to do today.

"Yeah, and why is that? Because he's too busy?"

I flushed and looked down at my jeans-clad legs. "Yeah."

"See what I mean?"

"I'm sorry," I said, meeting her eyes. "I haven't meant to neglect you."

"You know you can't date him, Cass." Her eyes were so sincere that I really didn't think she was speaking out of jealousy.

"We're not officially dating."

"You can't be his girlfriend."

I sighed. "He hasn't asked me that." And I didn't think he would.
"Good."
That really irked me. I frowned at her. "Why is it good? You might like him if you gave him a chance."
"He's not like us," Jenny said, leaning forward. "He doesn't respect the rules or the law. He doesn't have a future. He deals drugs. You know this. I don't understand why you're spending time with him. Is it just because he stuck up for you on the bus?"
"It's because I like him. I enjoy being with him. And he doesn't deal drugs."
Her blond brows climbed. "Did he tell you that?"
"Not in so many words, no. But I know he doesn't."
"You know he doesn't?" She rolled her eyes in a downright insulting manner. "Well, you have to admit he smokes the stuff."
"Lots of people smoke pot. That doesn't make them drug dealers."
"Oh, Cass." She shook her head. "You're fooling yourself."
"God, you sound just like my mom."
Her eyes widened. "Did you tell her about him?"
"No, that's not what I meant. You just sound like a grown-up, that's all. I like him. I don't care if he has a future or not, and besides, who are you to say something like that? You sound like you don't even see him as a person. He's just the school bad boy to you."
Now it was her turn to flush. "That's not true."
"It sounds true to me."
"I'm worried about you. I don't think he's the kind of boy you should be spending time with."
"Well, it's not your place to tell me that."
Her chin trembled a little. "I'm your best friend. At least, I thought I was."
I bit my lip. She looked truly hurt, and I hadn't meant to do that. But it hurt me to hear her say such mean things about a guy I liked so much, especially since she seemed to have no interest in my side of things.
"I didn't mean to hurt your feelings," I said. "And we're still best friends. Aren't we?"
Jenny nodded slowly. "I hope so."
"Dex isn't going to take me away from you."
Would she have been as jealous if the guy I liked had been one of our crowd? One of the nerds? Maybe, but Dex was probably extra threatening because he didn't fit in with our group, such as it was. And I didn't fit in with his.
Maybe Jenny was right. Maybe he would hurt me. But I didn't believe for a second that he wasn't good enough for me. The guy who'd

stuck up for me on the bus and saved me from Kurt Wilson and who gave up a good chunk of his Halloween to take his little brother trick or treating was good enough for anyone.

Chapter 12

Everything About You

Dex:

On the Friday before Thanksgiving, we got another major snowstorm. Our house smelled clean enough, since I'd taken out the trash and scrubbed the toilets. It was dark inside the house, with only a couple of table lamps on in the living room. Nobody talked because I was the only one here who was awake.

Sin had made himself scarce again. My mom was passed out on the couch, Joe had gone to Frankie's for dinner, and my dad was working late.

The place felt like a tomb. We still had our gas, since I'd nagged my mom into paying the bill on time, but we kept the heat really low so we didn't "waste" money. Cold, dark, and silent, like a tomb.

I hated it here.

I put on an extra pair of socks and stuck my feet into the motorcycle boots I'd picked up at the Salvation Army. They were pretty beat up, but they kept my feet drier than sneakers could.

My mom didn't even notice when I left. I shut the door behind myself and waded into the snow drift that had already accumulated around our front step. The air outside smelled almost painfully clean, and was cold enough to make my lungs hurt when I took a too-deep breath.

Cass was a dream I'd continually revisited over the last week or two. I saw her in school, mostly in biology. We even went out to the Fireweed Diner again together once. She paid her own way that time.

And I found all kinds of lame excuses to take walks in the neighborhood after school, something I didn't normally do. Oddly, my route almost always took me past her house.

It was always dark when I took these walks and the houses glowed with lights from inside as moms cooked dinner and kids did their homework. At least, that's what I figured must be going on in those places. It's not like I had any personal experience with them.

They looked safe, like refuges. Places you could go where you wouldn't be hit or kicked, or called names, where people rarely or never got drunk and the heat was always on and there was enough food in the fridge and none of it was rotten. But maybe that was just my stupid pipe dream. Maybe the lives lived in those houses were no better than mine.

I set off toward Cass's. She wouldn't be there. I knew that. But it made me feel strange, both good and bad, to walk past her house and imagine her inside, doing whatever it was she did, and that feeling kept drawing me back.

I'd found out she had a brother and a sister, both younger. Maybe she hung out with them after school, or maybe she was with Jenny June at the moment. Those two sometimes seemed to be joined at the hip.

I was going to have to stop this. Stop walking past her house, stop imagining her with her family and friends, stop thinking about her. She wasn't for me, and I sure as hell wasn't for her. This thing I was doing—I didn't have a name for it, but I knew it was dangerous and I had to stop.

Maybe tomorrow.

I rounded the corner to her street. Someone was shoveling her driveway. My heart gave a little jump and started running, like it could dash out ahead of the rest of me and greet her. But it wasn't her, couldn't be her. That would be too easy.

I stuck my hands in my coat pockets and pretended to saunter casually, like I was just happening by at random. The deep snow made this difficult. I kept slipping and stumbling through drifts that came up to my knees.

Then I got close enough to see her face as she looked up and I realized it was Cass after all. She wore her usual parka, with that light-blue hat on her head. Her hands were encased in thick ski gloves. A red muffler covered the lower part of her face. She looked adorably silly all bundled up like that.

"Hi, Dex," she said as I drew nearer.

"Hi. What are you doing?"

"Shoveling the driveway." She grinned and pulled her muffler down to expose her mouth. "Can't you tell?"

"I can barely tell it's you under all those clothes."

"What are you doing?" she said.

"Taking a walk." I gestured toward her shovel. "You want me to do that for you?"

"You don't have to do that. Besides, I'm almost done."

"You know it's only going to snow again and cover up all your hard work," I said.

"Yeah, but at least it'll be smooth and not so icy. Besides, I like shoveling snow."

"You are a very strange girl."

She laughed. "Thank you."

A dog barked inside a nearby house. It sounded like a big one.

"Would you like to take a walk with me?" I said, still all casual-like. Don't let her know you're nervous or that you even care. Keep it cool; keep it easy.

"Sure. Just let me tell my mom."

I lifted my brows. "You have to tell her you're going on a walk?"

"Just in case she needs me for something. I'll be back in a sec." She dashed up her driveway.

Her parents cared where she went and with whom. My parents didn't give a shit whether we were alive or dead.

Cass came running back, her muffler flying out behind her. "Okay. Let's go."

"Did you tell her you were going with me?"

She shrugged. "I just said I was going."

Well, that sort of answered my unspoken question—her parents wouldn't like it if they knew she was with me. Not that I cared. She was sixteen and I figured she was old enough to choose who she wanted to hang out with.

"Want to go down to the bluff?" I said.

"In the winter?"

"Sure. Why not?"

"I don't know. I've never done it, that's all."

"Then it'll be something new."

The bluff was a part of our neighborhood that had once extended a lot farther out toward the Cook Inlet. In the big earthquake of 1964, the front section of the land there had crumbled and slid into the inlet, carrying all the houses with it. Nobody had done anything with the land since, and you could still find remnants of the houses—chunks of broken concrete, twisted pieces of rebar sticking out of the sand on the narrow beach. It was a little spooky sometimes.

I liked it because it was usually deserted. It was a place where a guy like me could get some privacy, a place where I could think. Also, we sometimes partied there.

I turned to go back the way I'd come. The way I normally took down to the bluff was at a park called Lynn Ary. There was a tennis court, flooded and frozen for ice skating in the winter, and down the hill a baseball diamond. The gravel road sloped down past the baseball field and petered out unfinished, swallowed up by the gray clay hillocks and hollows left after the quake.

Cass grabbed my coat sleeve. "Where are you going?" she said.

"To the bluff."

"There's access at the end of my street."

I stopped and looked at her. "There is?"

"Yeah. Come on. I'll show you."

Huh. There was something about this neighborhood I didn't already know, and Cass Maslanka was showing it to me. I never would have predicted that.

We walked silently past two blocks of houses until we came to a spot where the blacktop fell away, revealing a sharp slope down toward the inlet. Everything was covered in almost two feet of snow, but I could see the abrupt drop. The street must have broken there when the quake hit.

I'd only been a little kid when it happened, and I still remember how the ground rocked underneath us. The earth isn't supposed to move and when it does, it freaks you out, especially when it shakes so bad you can hear everything rattling and creaking around you.

We'd just been sitting down to a dinner of canned ravioli heated up on the stove top. My mom had been pregnant with Joe and she'd panicked, screeching her head off as pans and pictures fell off the kitchen walls.

I think that screaming had scared me as much as the quake itself.

Sin grabbed me and hauled me under the table with him and put his arms around me. I hadn't been so scared then, but I had nightmares for years afterward anyhow. The '64 quake was the biggest recorded quake in North America. If it had happened down in California, lots of people probably would have died, but up here in Alaska there just weren't that many people. Besides, we had a lot fewer buildings to collapse and crush people, and the ones we had were mostly one story, so not many died.

In spite of that, the quake had shaped our town, both physically and mentally.

We waded through the thick snow. Alder and willow twigs poked up from the whiteness and caught at our coats and her muffler. The ground continued to drop, causing the houses to seem as if they were rising around us. Snow caked my jeans and crept up underneath them, but my boots kept my feet relatively warm and dry.

Then we were free of the housing development and into the raw land left after the quake. Alders had quickly taken over down here, covering the land in scrubby tree-bushes. They only got about fifteen feet high, but they grew so thickly that, even leafless in winter, they blocked out everything more than a few feet away.

The light from the street lamps faded away, leaving us in a much darker place. Above, the moon shone down and reflected off the whiteness of the snow, so we could easily see where we were going, but it was still pretty dark. The cold moonlight made everything look bluish and strange.

The snow ahead of us was unbroken except for a few lacy little bird tracks. I reached out and grabbed Cass's hand. She smiled at me.

Again, I felt the danger of what I was doing. I'd already done more hanging out with Cass than with any other girl I could remember, just in the few weeks I'd known her. I liked being with her, even though we hadn't kissed yet and rarely touched. I craved her company.

This could not be good. I was in danger of breaking my no-dating rule, if I hadn't done so already. But I couldn't seem to stop myself. I kept taking those boneheaded walks down her street, for example.

"It's so beautiful down here with all the snow," she said, taking a long look around us.

"Yeah, it is."

"I wish I'd come here sooner."

In the moonlight, her eyes looked silver, her hair black beneath her knit hat. She wore no visible make-up, and she was so beautiful I couldn't think straight. The only thing on my mind was how to get closer to her.

"Are you getting ready for Thanksgiving?" she said, her fingers clasping mine.

I shrugged, suddenly uncomfortable. "Nah."

"You're not?" She looked at me, a troubled frown between her pretty brows. "How come?"

"We don't make a big deal out of holidays."

In fact, we didn't really do holidays at all. The closest I'd get to a Thanksgiving meal was a couple of TV dinners—turkey, of course—heated up in the oven for me and Joe. My parents would drink themselves sick and pass out, and Sin probably wouldn't bother to show up. If he was at home at all, he'd be in our room getting high.

"That's too bad," Cass said. "Thanksgiving is always such a big deal at our house. My sister and my mom and I spend the whole day cooking."

"Sounds like a lot of work."

"It is." She smiled, her eyes sparkling like she was thinking of something really good. "But it's fun work."

I couldn't imagine a day spent with either of my parents being fun. More like torture, actually.

"Hey, maybe we could invite your family over," she said, her eyes sparkling even more intensely.

"No."

Cass seemed to shrink in on herself. "Oh. Okay."

I hadn't meant to snap. It just came out that way because all I could think of was the utter disaster a holiday with both our families would be.

"Listen, it's not that I don't want to be with you," I said. "But my folks aren't really friendly. They don't do social events."

"Okay," she said in a small voice.

God, now I felt like shit. "I'm sorry."

"No, it's okay. Really." She gave me a smile so bright I knew it was fake.

"Besides, I doubt your parents would think much of me," I added.

"That's not true," she said quickly.

"Cass—"

"If they got to know you, they'd like you. I know they would."

"Yeah, but they wouldn't get to know me. They'd see this." I gestured at my ratty coat and beat-up, second-hand motorcycle boots. "And make up their minds in a second that I'm not good enough for you."

Jesus. I was talking like we were dating. Really dating. Like boyfriend and girlfriend. How the hell had that happened? How had I let that slip?

We hadn't even kissed yet.

"If that were true—and I'm not saying it is—then they'd be wrong," she said. "And besides, I like the way you look."

I snorted. "You do not."

"Yes, I do," she said quietly. "I like everything about you."

I paused, my feet halting in a shallow spot in the snow. Our breath puffed out in little white clouds. She wasn't looking at me. I think she'd embarrassed herself a little. Maybe she thought I didn't feel the same way about her. But I did, and I wanted to show her how much.

I was nervous as hell. My hands felt slippery and my throat was tight and my stomach kept doing these nauseating little flip-flops. What was wrong with me? I was being a major pussy. This was the first time I'd ever gotten choked up about a girl.

"Cass," I said, my heart racing even faster.

"Yeah?" She still wouldn't look at me.

"I'd really like to kiss you now."

That brought her head up. She stared at me wide-eyed, her lips parted. "You would?"

My free hand came up, all on its own, to palm the side of her face. Her skin felt chilly. "Yeah."

She licked her lower lip. "Okay."

Okay. This was it. She was going to let me do it.

Jesus Christ, you'd think I'd never kissed anyone before.

I leaned in, bending my head nice and slow in case she changed her mind. Her lips were as pretty as the rest of her, kind of delicate and finely shaped and pink. I pressed mine to them briefly, experimentally, and felt her press back. A pause, and I kissed her again, lingering a bit.

She reached up to hold onto my upper arm. I stroked the side of her face with my thumb as I came in again for another kiss.

This time, I used a little tongue, just to see what she would do. She opened for me, right away. We moved toward each other until our bodies pressed against each other. I let go of her hand and put my arm around her, clasping her to me more tightly.

The movements of her lips and tongue felt endearingly awkward, like she'd never done this before. Maybe she hadn't. Maybe Wilson had been her first kiss. That would be shitty if it were true. What a way to start.

I wanted to show her how good kissing could be, to make her forget about that idiot Wilson. So I used my lips and tongue as skillfully as I could, every trick I knew, stroking and licking, giving her little nips with my teeth.

She sighed. Her other arm grabbed me around my waist and held on. I cupped the back of her head, plunging my tongue in deep, tasting her, and she moaned. God, that sound. It drove me nuts, made my cock hard as steel, made me wish we weren't standing in the snow because I couldn't do anything more than kiss her here.

Her other hand, the one on my arm, crept upward until she got to my neck. She stroked the skin on the back of my neck. I'd never thought of that touch as erotic until now. Her fingers moved into my hair, while her body arched into mine. We had two coats and who knew how many other layers of clothing between us, but I could feel every inch of her.

I found myself moaning too. A first kiss had never affected me this way. Hell, no kiss had. Kissing was usually just a prelude to other, more exciting things, but I wasn't going to be getting under Cass's clothes today. For one thing, it was too cold. For another, she wasn't ready for that.

I pulled back, trembling, before I came in my jeans. What had just happened? Nothing had ever felt that good, that necessary. My breath was all rough and unsteady, and so was hers. We stared at each other, right into each other's eyes like a couple of lovers in some sappy movie.

"Wow," she said, gazing at me as if I'd just showed her the universe.

"Yeah." My voice sounded funny, rough and shook up.

"That was—I didn't know it could feel like that."

Neither did I.

"So you liked it?" I grinned.

"Oh, yeah," she said, laughing.

"Good, because I plan on doing it again."

Chapter 13

Kiss

Cass:

The inside of my house smelled like spaghetti sauce. My mom must be cooking Italian tonight. She loved to cook and spaghetti was a family favorite, so we had it a lot.

The air felt astonishingly warm after the snowy outdoors. My cheeks seemed to glow in the heated interior. The warmth felt almost like a hug.

I could hear Beth and Adam upstairs laughing over something. It sounded like they were in the kitchen or dining room, probably helping my mom set the table. I hung my coat in the entry-way closet and shucked off my boots.

Dex had refused my invitation to eat dinner with us. He really thought my family would dislike him. I could tell by the way his posture changed when we reached my driveway. He kind of slumped and his gait changed, too. The take-charge, cocky Dex from school seemed to fade away whenever I mentioned my family.

It hurt me to think he might be right. My parents were really old-fashioned and fairly strict, and they might not take kindly to a boy with a reputation like his. I was convinced that reputation was undeserved, but they would most likely believe it.

I went up the stairs, my stocking feet silent on the green sculptured carpet, to the top floor, my heart torn between joy over the kiss and despair that the boy I liked so much was likely unacceptable to my family.

That kiss. I'd never felt anything like it. I'd never even imagined anything like that, really, in all my daydreaming about kisses and lovemaking. The warm, wet slide of his tongue over mine, the way he tasted...the fact that he had a taste. That was something that had never occurred to me before today.

My whole body still ached with desire for more. I was trembling, too. I could feel it in the shakiness of my hands and my wobbly knees. One kiss would never be enough for me, at least not with Dex. I needed more. Something told me I'd always need more with him.

The living room had one brass lamp burning next to the rust-colored couch we'd bought especially for the new house, but no-one was in there. My dad wasn't home from work yet. I followed the sound of voices into our tiny kitchen.

It seemed like all the houses built around the same time as ours had these little kitchens, even though the houses themselves were pretty large. Jenny's kitchen, in a much smaller house, was twice as big. With my mom, Adam, and Beth in ours, it was too crowded for one more person, so I stood in the dining area, my back against one of our Windsor dining chairs.

Adam looked up and caught my eye. "Cass!"

"Hi. Did I miss dinner?"

"No," Beth said seriously. She pushed her brown hair back over her shoulder. "We're almost ready."

"Good. It smells incredible."

"That's the garlic bread," she said. "I made it myself."

"Wow. Good job, sis."

"Hey, Cass," Adam said. "Can I talk to you for a sec? I have a question about my English class."

"Uh...sure." He was better at English than I, so I wasn't sure why he needed to ask me. But it was okay—that's what older siblings are for, right?

"Let's go in my room," he said. "That's where I left my stuff."

I looked at him more carefully. He was watching me, gauging my reaction. Suddenly I had the feeling this wasn't about English.

"Okay," I said uneasily. "But make it quick because I'm starving."

We ran down to the bottom floor where both our bedrooms were. Our basement wasn't a true basement—it was only half below ground level, with windows just as big as the ones upstairs to let in the sun. It was completely finished, with orange and brown shag in the huge family room and pale wood paneling on the walls. Adam and I, as the oldest two, got to sleep down here, while Beth had to take the room upstairs next to our parents. She didn't seem to mind.

Adam's room was the typical boy's mess, with car posters on the walls and clothes and books strewn all over the chocolate brown shag carpet. It smelled like stale laundry, too. Didn't he ever open a window?

I stood in the doorway shaking my head. "I can't go in there. It isn't safe to walk."

"That's fine. We can talk here." He braced his arm against the white-painted drywall next to his door, frowning down at me.

"What?" I said, as innocently as I could.

"I saw you."

Oh, Jeez, here it came.

I opened my eyes wide. "So?"

"With Dex Morgan."

"So?" I said again, trying to brazen it out.

"Dex Morgan, Cass."

"I heard you."

He sighed and blew a lock of his dark hair from his eyes. Mom claimed it was too long and was constantly after him to cut it. "You guys were holding hands."

I felt myself blush. "Um...okay."

"You know what kind of guy he is."

I rolled my eyes as I heaved an irritated sigh. "Yeah, I do. But I don't think you do."

"Everyone does. He's a drug dealer, for crying out loud."

"I don't think he is. It's just a rumor."

Adam gave me an incredulous expression. "Are you serious?"

"I've never seen him dealing drugs, or taking them either."

"That doesn't mean it isn't true," Adam said patiently, as if explaining something to a small child.

"He's a nice guy. You should give him a chance," I said. "You should see him with his little brother. He's really sweet."

He gave me a pitying look. "He deals pot."

"Prove it." I crossed my arms over my chest as anger rose inside me. "You can't, can you?"

"I don't have to," he said. "I've seen it."

That short sentence made me feel like my chest was filled with ice. "I don't believe it."

"Well, it's true. I've seen him making exchanges and I've heard from plenty of people that he's the guy to see if you want the good stuff."

I shook my head. It couldn't be true.

"How long have you been seeing him?"

"You're my little brother." I glared at him. "It's not your job to keep tabs on me."

"How long, Cass?"

"I don't know. A few weeks."

"How far have you gone?"

"Excuse me?" I gave him a little shove. "That's none of your business."

"I hope you haven't done anything more than hold hands, because being seen with him is going to shred your reputation."

"Oh, please. This isn't the fifties. People don't care what I do."

He leaned back even further, looking offensively relaxed. "Mom and Dad do. And what about Jenny's parents? They'll care."

Unfortunately, he was probably right.

I didn't want my parents, or Jenny's, to think less of me. But I also didn't want to give up Dex. I liked him way too much. Besides, it wasn't right for them to judge him when they didn't even know him.

"What do you want me to do about it?" I said waspishly. "I'm not going to stop seeing him."

"He's going to get you in trouble."

"No. He won't. He cares about me."

Adam laughed. "Yeah, right."

"You don't have to be such a jerk about it. It is possible for a guy to like me, you know."

"Hey." His laughter disappeared. He came off the wall and tilted his head to the side. "I never meant that. Of course guys like you. I hear about it all the time."

I shook my head. "You do not."

"Yeah, I do. Adam, man, your sister is such a fox. I've had a couple of fights about it."

"What?" I stared at him with an open mouth. "You've fought over me? Why?"

"Never mind," he said, looking suddenly embarrassed. "Let's just say I didn't appreciate the way they expressed their admiration."

Boys admired me? They told my brother how much they admired me? That was...incredible. Unbelievable. In fact, I didn't believe it.

I narrowed my eyes. "Are you making this up just to make me feel better?"

"No. I wouldn't do that. I just want you to know that Dex isn't the only guy who thinks you're cute."

Yeah. Kurt Wilson thought I was cute, or maybe just easy. Either way...ick. I didn't want attention from guys like him.

"You know, Adam, that's sweet of you. And it's nice to know some guys like the way I look, but it doesn't change how I feel about Dex. I really enjoy being with him and not because I'm desperate. I like him. I think you would too if you'd give him a chance."

"Maybe he's being so nice because he wants to get in your pants."

I gaped at him again. "Get in my pants? Did you really just say that?"

Adam blushed. "You know what I mean. He wants to score. Guys will say and do anything to score."

"I'm pretty sure Dex could have all kinds of other girls. Why would he spend time with me just to score? There are lots of easier girls around."

Like Misty, for example. It had seemed apparent to me from the moment I'd seen them together that she and Dex had been more than friends at some point. And judging by the way she threw herself at him at every opportunity, she wanted to be more than friends again. All the bad girls in school seemed to want the same thing.

"Maybe you're more of a challenge and that makes you more interesting," my brother said.

"Adam and Cass, are you going to eat?" my mom called from over the upstairs banister.

"In a second, Mom," I yelled back. "Look, Adam, I appreciate how much you care. I really do. But I like Dex and I'm not going to give him up. I'll be okay."

"I think you're going to be disappointed."

"Please don't tell Mom and Dad."

They'd ground me for life if they thought I was dating a drug dealer. Which I wasn't, but that was beside the point.

"I won't. But you need to figure this out. Look into the drug thing," he said. "See if I'm right."

I pressed my lips together. "Fine. Okay, I'll look into it."

But I had no intention of doing any such thing. I trusted Dex.

* * *

The lights at school were too bright. They glared down from the ceiling and irritated my eyes. My wool sweater felt scratchy against my skin, although I'd worn a thin T-shirt underneath to prevent that. The air smelled weird, too, with strange odors coming out of the cafeteria.

The halls seemed even louder and more hectic than usual. People were rushing everywhere, everyone talking at once and as loud as possible. The noise bounced off the hard tile walls, making the din almost unbearable.

Or maybe it was just my jangled nerves.

Did people care what I did after all? Were they watching me? Judging me?

It seemed so unlikely. Just as silly as the notion that boys were secretly—or not so secretly—lusting after me. If they lusted so much, how come none of them had ever approached me? At least not in a nice way.

Mom and Dad had said nothing at all, so I was pretty sure Adam had kept his word. I hadn't heard from Dex all weekend either, which made me wonder if my brother might not be right about him.

Of course, he didn't have my number. But he could have come by and asked for me. I'd stuck around the house all weekend just in case, a fact that now made me ashamed of myself. Who hung around their house waiting helplessly for a boy to call in this day and age? It was nineteen-seventy-two, for crying out loud.

I got to my locker and took off my hat, gloves, scarf, and coat. Everything got stuck into one sleeve of the coat so I wouldn't lose it. Then I hung the coat on the hook in my locker. That was my routine and it worked for me.

"Hey, Jane," said a deep voice in my ear.

I turned around, heart jumping again. "Hi, Dex."

All weekend I'd hoped to see him and now he was here and I couldn't think of anything to say. I felt all flustered and shy. The last time we'd been together, we'd kissed.

He was leaning against the locker next to mine, all cool guy again. His dark-blond hair fell into his eyes. He still had his coat on, and through the ridiculous, mad fluttering of my heart I noticed it was kind of torn up. Like I could see some of the filling sticking out of a tear in the fabric.

Maybe his family couldn't afford good clothes for him. That made me want to buy him a coat for Christmas.

He leaned down and pressed his lips gently to mine. It wasn't hot and heavy, but it did linger, that kiss. It made my heart go even crazier. My hand flew up to the side of his face. I could feel his stubble under my skin and I liked it.

When he pulled away, I noticed some people openly watching us. Misty wasn't around, but there were plenty of others taking note of what we were doing. And Dex had just publicly claimed me, at least in a manner of speaking.

"I missed you," he said, smiling down at me.

"Me too. I was hoping you'd come by."

"I know." He toyed with a piece of my hair. "I didn't want to intrude on your family."

"You wouldn't be intruding."

Adam wouldn't like it, but then it would be a kind of test to see if Dex really was the nice guy I thought. I mean, if he wouldn't even eat a meal with my family, then maybe my brother was right and I shouldn't be with him. On the other hand, we'd only been seeing each other for a few weeks. We'd just had our first kiss. It was pretty early to bring him home to meet the parents, wasn't it?

My experience with boys was so limited I didn't really know the answer to that question.

The words *are you a drug dealer* hovered on my lips. I had to know, although I dreaded getting an answer I wouldn't like. What would I do if he said yes? I had no idea.

He leaned in for another kiss. His lips were so soft and gentle, yet there was something in their movement against mine that suggested a whole world of sensuality. I couldn't help the little sigh that escaped me.

He pulled back slightly, his eyes smiling down into mine, and I couldn't remember what question I'd been about to ask. He smelled like Dex, that piquant mixture of male skin, soap, and cigarette smoke I associated with him. Although I'd rather he didn't smoke—didn't he know it caused cancer?

"I'd like to see you after school today," he said.

"Okay."

He smiled more broadly. "Okay? Just like that?"

"Yep. Just like that."

"Don't you have to ask your parents for permission?"

That would be their position, of course.

I shook my head. "They're used to me hanging out at Jenny's house after school, so they don't expect me right away."

He laced his fingers through mine. "What will Jenny have to say about that?"

"She'll have to deal with it. I'm a big girl."

"I agree." He gave my hand a little squeeze. "But she seems to think she's your watchdog."

We took off down Junior Hall, our hands still intertwined. In my peripheral vision, I could see that people were taking notice of us. It made me feel really weird, like I'd forgotten a crucial piece of clothing at home and was walking around without any pants or shirtless. Vulnerable, that's what the feeling was.

Normally I was invisible to most of the people in school, and I liked it that way. Nobody really saw me for who I was. Of course, until recently I hadn't realized they saw me as the untouchable ice queen. I'd thought it was more that I was beneath their notice. Either way, I'd slipped through the crowds of students without anyone seeming to notice me.

They noticed me now, and I didn't know how I felt about it.

Was Adam right? Would being seen with Dex ruin my reputation?

I didn't really give a damn. The reputation I had wasn't something I wanted or felt I'd earned, so who cared if I destroyed it. Besides, his hand felt too good in mine to let go of it.

"You know," he said, leaning near me, "being seen with me is going to affect your reputation."

"You mean your cool is rubbing off on me?" I said.

"You remember that?"

"Of course I do. I remember everything from that night." I blushed. Maybe that had been too revealing.

He smiled as if it was the best thing anyone had ever told him. "I'm glad to know I made such a good impression."

"You did."

Another cluster of kids walking the opposite direction openly stared at us as they passed. One of them was Bob Rogers, the guy Jenny had been dancing with. I saw the group exchange a glance between themselves and start chattering.

"People are looking," I said.

"Don't let it get to you."

"I'm not. It's just weird. Normally nobody looks at me."

He laughed. "They do. You just don't notice."

Jenny had said the same thing, so I didn't argue. At least, not out loud.

"Anyway," he continued. "It's not you. It's me."

"What does that mean?"

"I don't date. They're not used to seeing me with a girl like this."

Did that mean we were dating? I wasn't sure.

"Wait," I said. "What do you mean you don't date?"

He glanced at me with a wry smile. "What does it sound like? I don't date. I don't take girls out."

"But you're experienced," I said. Then I glanced around, hoping no-one had overheard me.

Everyone else seemed oblivious, and the level of noise in the hall was so high they would have had to be within a few inches of us to have made out what we were saying. Still...what an embarrassing blunder.

Dex didn't seem fazed by it. "Yeah. I am. But my involvement with girls doesn't include dating. Hanging around is as far as it's ever gone."

I frowned. "You took me out to the Fireweed Diner twice."

He lifted our entwined hands. "And I'm holding your hand. That's why people are staring."

I stared. "Why are you doing all that if it's not your way?"

"That's what I like about you. You just blurt out whatever comes into your head."

I blushed again. "I do not."

"Oh?" He grinned. "What are you hiding, then?"

Are you a drug dealer?

"Nothing," I said. "And don't change the subject."

He looked down, swinging our hands between us. His shaggy hair slid into his face, hiding his eyes from me. Maybe I'd pushed him too far with my rude questions. Maybe this was the moment he said it was too much, that he'd made a mistake and he didn't want to spend time with me after all.

Then he looked up, that wry expression back in his beautiful green eyes. "I don't know. You're different."

"So are you," I said. Different from the other guys I'd hung out with. Different from my brother. Different from all my stupid assumptions about him. I just wished my brother and parents could see how different he was; maybe then they'd give him a real chance.

After school, we went out to our usual haunt, the Fireweed, for coffee and snacks. We talked about classes, the other kids, books we'd read, movies we'd seen or wanted to see. It would have felt more friendly than romantic if we hadn't been holding hands through most of the conversation.

The fluttery ache inside me grew and grew over the afternoon. I wanted to go somewhere alone with him so we could kiss again. Really kiss, the way we had down at the bluff. Could we go to Dex's house? We couldn't go to mine; my mom would almost certainly be there and she'd watch us with the eyes of a prison guard in Sing Sing.

"So..." I rubbed my finger through the condensation on my water glass. "What's your house like?"

"It sucks," he said flatly.

"Oh, come on. It can't be that bad."

"Yes, it can." He gave his head a decisive shake. "We can't go there, Cass. I wish I could show you my room and shit, but there's no privacy anyway. Tiny house, crazy mom. It's not a good scene, trust me."

"Oh." I blinked, temporarily at a loss for words. "I'm sorry."

"Don't be sorry. It's just the way things are."

"So...you and your mom don't get along?"

He gave a short, unamused laugh. "You could say that. Besides, I share a room with Joe and our other brother Sin. No privacy, like I said."

"How is Joe anyway?"

He smiled with real affection. "The ankle biter is fine. He likes you."

Aw. That made me all warm inside. "I like him too. He's really cute."

Dex chuckled. "I'll tell him you said that. He wants to marry you."

"What?" I couldn't help laughing. "Why?"

"Like I said, he likes you. All other girls are gross, though. You're special."

He looked at me with such intent when he said that, I thought maybe he meant it for himself and not only for his little brother. I blushed and smiled, and looked away.

Until now, I'd hardly been out on any dates and I'd only had two kisses before Dex. So I didn't really know how this thing was supposed to progress. Did it usually move so fast? Or were we moving slowly? I had nothing to compare with this experience and no-one to ask. Jenny hadn't dated any more than I had.

"We could go to your place," he said.

"Only if you want to sit in the living room and be painfully proper the whole time," I said. "My parents would never let a boy in my room. I would like you to come for dinner some time, though. You wouldn't be imposing at all, so don't say that."

He shut his mouth. Then he opened it again, a smile hovering at the corners of his lips. "Okay, I won't. What floor is your room on?"

"Downstairs. Why?"

His tongue emerged and whisked along the fullness of his lower lip. "Well, I could come to your window. If you wanted me to, that is."

Holy smokes. I hadn't thought of that. Why hadn't I thought of that? Probably because I was a good little girl and I'd never done anything daring in my entire life.

"I would be in so much trouble if we were found out," I said.

"Then we won't." He squeezed my hand again. "I don't want to get you in trouble."

He was too good to be true.

"My brother's room is right next to mine," I said. "We'd have to be super quiet. He thinks he needs to protect me."

"Is he older?"

"No." I rolled my eyes. "A year younger, but that doesn't stop him. I guess it's a brother thing."

"I wouldn't know. I don't have any sisters." He paused, rubbing the top of my hand thoughtfully. "I meant it when I said I don't want to get you in trouble. You're a nice girl and I don't want to ruin that for you."

Maybe I wanted to be ruined.

Now where had that thought come from? I'd always tried so hard to be good, to be the daughter my parents wanted me to be, the big sister my younger siblings could look up to. But maybe that role was beginning to chafe a little.

"How would I know when to be in my room so I could let you in?" I said.

His eyes seemed to get darker as he gazed at me. "It would have to be after dinner, right?"

"Yeah. We eat pretty early, around six." I glanced at my watch. "Shoot, I have to get going. I'm almost late."

"Okay. We don't want to give your folks a reason to distrust you," he said.

I sent him a teasing glance as we got up from our table. "You've done this sneaking around thing before, haven't you?"

"Maybe once or twice."

Chapter 14

Gone

Cass:

The pink paint on the walls of my bedroom seemed unbearably girly, although it was a pale pink, not some godawful bubblegum color. Still...pink. And I had stuffed toys on my bed and collectible dolls on a shelf on one wall and a comforter with a rose pattern on it. And a ruffled lace dust ruffle. Oh, God. It was a little girl's room.

At least I'd stopped at the floor, which was covered in the same chocolate brown shag as Adam's room. No pink carpet. I did have a chandelier, however, in antique brass with crystals hanging from it.

Dex was going to think I was irredeemably dorky when he saw this place. Speaking of Dex, how would he know which window was mine? I'd forgotten to tell him, and Adam's room was right next door. If he knocked on the wrong glass...

I opened my rose-flowered curtains—they matched the comforter—and peered out into the darkness. At least my things weren't Winnie The Pooh or something equally infantile. They were merely pink. Could I help it if I liked pink?

I could see little beyond the glass. The white, unbroken snow that covered our back yard reflected some of the light from the streetlights. In the very back was a narrow kind of hedgerow made of spruce and birch trees and some shrubby undergrowth. It separated our yard from the yards behind us, yards of houses that fronted Susitna.

Dex lived on Susitna.

Just as I had that thought, I saw him emerge from the trees, no more than a dark silhouette in the shadows. He must have cut through our back neighbor's yard. He paused at the edge of the open, snowy expanse a moment before trudging through the drifts.

Footprints. There would be a lot of footprints. I should have thought of that earlier. I'd have to go out and run around back there in order to obscure them.

This sneaking around stuff was more complicated than I'd thought.

I cranked open the window, letting icy air flood my room, and removed the screen. Because my room was on the downstairs floor of a split level, my window was only a few inches above the ground. That made it easy to climb in and out. Not that I'd ever tried it, of course. The ease had been purely theoretical until this moment.

"Everything okay?" Dex said as he crouched down in front of the open window.

"Yeah. Come in."

He peered into my room. "I'm gonna get snow all over your carpet."

"That's okay. Just shake your boots off a little."

He paused, smiling at me, his green eyes so dark in the low light that they looked almost black. Then he gave his right boot a quick shake and stuck his leg through the window opening. He turned, pulling his left leg through as well. With a shimmy, he lowered himself to my floor. He made it look so easy I regretted never trying to climb out myself. Of course, he was a lot taller, so his legs reached the floor faster than mine would.

He turned around and looked at me. "Hi."

"Hi. Let's close the window."

"Oh, right." He turned and cranked it shut. "It's always so cold in my house that I can't tell when the windows are open and when they aren't."

Now that he was here, I was almost as flustered and nervous as if we'd never kissed and held hands. As if we'd never eaten together or walked the halls together. Something about having him in my bedroom changed the tenor of our friendship, or whatever it was that we had. This felt way more intimate than anything else we'd done so far.

He turned back to me. "It's really warm in here. You have a nice room, too."

"Yeah. Uh...sorry about the pink."

"Sorry?" He scrunched up his eyebrows. "Why?"

"You know." I waved vaguely at my ultra-feminine room. "It's so girly."

"I don't mind." His dimple made an appearance. "It's cute. It fits you."

"Oh. It does?"

"Yeah." He took my hands.

His were icy cold, so I wrapped my fingers around them to warm them up. This was really awkward. I shouldn't have invited him in, because I had no idea how to go about this. What did I say to him? I was back to being a tongue-tied, dorky social outcast with no idea how to talk to boys. Not sexy ones, anyway.

"Are you sure we won't be interrupted?" he said.

"No." I glanced over my shoulder at my door, suddenly in a panic. "My door doesn't lock."

"It's okay. We'll just have to be careful. Here, let's sit by the closet. That way I'll have somewhere to hide if I need to."

"Oh. Okay."

My closet took up most of one wall of my room and had louvered folding doors. It wasn't walk-in, but it was still pretty big and Dex could easily hide in it if he needed to. I hated the thought that he might have to do that. It seemed undignified. But my parents would never understand or condone my need to touch a boy, to kiss and be kissed, so if I was determined to go forward with this, I had to sneak.

We settled in on the floor in front of the closet, our backs up against my narrow twin bed. The doors were half open, ready to accept a fugitive teenage boy.

Dex set his coat aside and slung an arm around my shoulders. "Is this okay?"

"It's fine." Wonderful, actually.

"Your house is very warm."

He'd said that already, and the fact he felt the need to repeat it made me wonder how cold his place was. Didn't his parents turn on the heat at all? They had to use it a little, or their pipes would freeze.

I glanced down at his jeans. They were wet up to the knees, and still caked with melting globs of snow. "You must be freezing. You're all wet. Do you want to take those off?"

Oh, Jeez. I hadn't meant it to sound suggestive.

He grinned. "I'd love to but I don't think you're ready for that."

"I only meant so I could put them in the dryer," I said, blushing.

"I know. I was only teasing." His eyes looked so warm as he smiled down at me, the cool detachment I'd seen in them the first time we interacted completely gone.

His smile faded as he gazed at me. His lips parted and his eyes focused on my mouth. I knew he was thinking about kissing me and I wanted him to do it.

I let my own lips part as I leaned in a little closer and lifted my chin. Just enough to suggest to him that the answer to his unspoken question was yes.

His hand played in my hair. He shifted around to face me, his long fingers cupping my chin. I put my hand on his upper arm, feeling the hardness of his muscles all the way through the puffiness of his jacket.

My heart beat so hard and fast I almost felt dizzy and my stomach fluttered madly. My hands trembled.

Dex leaned in and brushed his lips against mine. It felt just as good as I remembered. Somehow, I'd feared that being alone in my room with him might take all the magic out of kissing him. Apparently, that fear was completely unfounded.

He gave a sigh and moved in for a deeper kiss. That sigh did something to my insides, made them ache more sharply than they ever had. I wrapped my arm around his neck and opened my lips to him and his tongue invaded me.

He tasted so good.

The slick glide of his tongue over mine made my whole body come alive. I nipped him, tugging at his lower lip with my teeth, the same way he'd done to mine several times before. Dex responded with a hand at the back of my neck, holding me to him as his kiss grew even deeper and more insistent.

I wanted to feel his hands on me, on places other than my neck. I moved in closer, pressing myself against him, savoring the long, hard column of his body against mine. His other arm came around me, clasping me tightly to him as he plundered my mouth.

Then he slid that hand downward and cupped my rear end. I couldn't help it. I moaned.

His big hand squeezed my left butt cheek. That touch sent more throbs of arousal through me and caused me to arch my body against his. He grabbed my right butt cheek with his other hand, squeezing and releasing the globes of muscle.

I'd never thought that a guy's hands on my butt could feel so good. Maybe it was the naughtiness.

Our breath came in rough little pants and gasps. One of Dex's hands slid up again, this time under my shirt. A good girl would say no at this point, but I wasn't so sure I wanted to be a good girl anymore.

My hand slipped down his arm to his waist. Maybe if I touched him in more places, he'd touch me.

He reached the middle of my back. His hand continued to glide across my flesh, around my rib cage, to the front of me. He paused with his fingertips brushing the bottom curve of my breast.

I moaned against his lips. The sensation of his fingers on such a private part of my body, a part no-one had ever touched but me, made me crazy.

Gradually, his hand moved until he cupped my breast. A low, growly noise escaped him. My body arched against his hand, pushing the roundness of my flesh into his palm. He squeezed, more gently than when he'd massaged my rear end. Just a faint, gentle pressure. He let out another soft, low groan.

I didn't mean to touch his crotch. I surged against him, trying to get closer, and my hand fell into his lap. Dex groaned even more loudly. His jeans strained against a distinct, firm bulge.

I jerked my hand away. "I'm sorry," I whispered.

He gave a shaky laugh. "Don't be sorry. It felt good."

"Would you—" I glanced at the intimidating shape behind his fly. "Would you like me to do it again?"

"I don't know if you're ready for that, babydoll." His voice sounded raspy.

At that moment, I felt ready for anything. "I'd like to make you feel good."

"You do. Believe me." He smiled and traced the shape of my lower lip with his fingertip.

"Can you—you know—touch me like that again?" I said haltingly, my face heating.

"You're so cute when you blush," he said.

That made me blush even harder. "I liked it."

"Would you let me see you?" He lifted the hem of my sweater an inch or so.

"You mean...without my bra?"

He nodded slowly, watching my face, his hands still on my sweater.

I bit my lip. What if he didn't like what he saw? Normally I covered up, wore high-necked blouses and sweaters, things that didn't show much of my shape. He didn't really know what I looked like under all that.

"I don't want to disappoint you," I said.

"Cass. You could never disappoint me."

"But what if—"

"Never." He lifted the sweater up another inch. "Please?"

I sighed. "Okay."

Holding my arms over my head, I allowed him to lift the sweater off me. When it cleared my body, he heaved a sigh. I grabbed the insides of the sweater and tried to pull it back over me.

"You hate it," I said.

"Don't be silly." He refused to let go of the garment. "I love the way you look."

"But—"

"Let go of the sweater, Cass." He sounded so no-nonsense and take charge, like he had that day on the bus.

"O-okay."

He pulled it completely off me. My arms crossed reflexively over my chest, guarding myself.

Dex took my wrists in his hands and tugged. "Let go."

When I let my arms drop, he sat and stared at me for a long time. I knew it even though I wasn't looking into his face because I was afraid to see the expression there. My chest was nothing special, just a B-cup, average size, and my bra was plain white, the cups big enough to almost swallow my breasts.

His hands went to the hooks at my back. "Can I?"

"Okay," I said, even as my pulse screamed.

He undid the hooks so deftly I knew he'd done it many other times, probably with many other girls. That should have bothered me, but instead it made me feel safe. At least one of us had some idea what we were doing.

My bra sagged away from my body and I let it fall. Dex gave another of those heavy sighs. This one sounded almost shaky, as if he were trembling as badly as I was.

"God, Cass," he said in a low voice. "You're so goddamn beautiful."

"I—I am?"

"Yeah. Oh, yeah." He lifted a hand to cup one naked breast. "These are ... they're spectacular."

My lashes fluttered at the touch of his bare hand on my bare breast. My flesh felt heavy, aching, and the only thing I could think of to relieve that feeling was more of Dex's touch.

I pushed myself against his hand. His thumb stroked across my nipple, sending a shock of outrageous pleasure through me and making me jump and gasp.

"You like that?" he said in a husky voice.

"Yes," I whispered.

He did it again. "Me too."

The sensation was incredible, like a sharp pull between my nipple and the place between my legs. As he teased it, my breast only seemed to become more sensitive, more responsive to him.

Then he bent his head and put his mouth on me. My eyes went wide and my mouth opened on a shocked gasp. I had no idea people did that. It seemed wrong, perverse, but it felt too good to ask him to stop.

My hands came up to cradle his head as he suckled on me. The pleasure this caused almost brought a yell from my throat. But I had to be quiet. I didn't want my family to hear what we were doing, so I clenched my teeth to hold back the sounds my body wanted to make.

Dex leaned me back until I lay on the shag beneath him. He kept one hand on a breast while his mouth pleasured the other. My legs scissored back and forth under his weight, restless with desire.

I needed more. More of something. My mouth opened to beg him to take me, to go all the way with me.

He slipped a hand from my breast to my waistband, his fingertips teasing the skin just beneath. Then his hand emerged from the waistband. He cupped me between my legs.

"Dex," I gasped.

"I'd like to touch you here. Will you let me?"

"Yes." I wasn't sure what he was really asking for, but I knew I wanted it.

He unbuttoned my jeans. His hand delved inside, his fingers brushing against the tender space between my legs. It felt so good that I let a small cry escape my mouth.

"Shhh," he said, kissing me. "You've got to stay quiet."

"Sorry."

"Don't be sorry." His fingers brushed me again, a little deeper this time. "God, you're so wet down here."

I buried my face against his shoulder in shame. "That's so gross. I'm sorry."

"Don't be sorry, Cass. It means you want me."

"Oh," I said in a small voice, feeling unutterably stupid and dorkier than ever.

"I like it." His voice seemed to have gotten deeper.

He stroked me right up my center and I moaned against his shirt. That questing finger, simply stroking in feather-light touches, brought the ache inside me to a nearly intolerable pitch.

He pushed his fingertip into the entrance of my body. I gripped his arms hard. Slowly, he inserted the finger more deeply.

I didn't know what to think. It was the strangest feeling, an invasion of sorts that didn't actually hurt. I'd never put anything there before. I never used tampons or touched myself there except for the minimal contact needed to stay clean.

"You're incredibly tight," he whispered.

I whimpered.

He withdrew the finger almost all the way, then slid it back inside, even more deeply this time. My breath caught. When he repeated the action, I let out a sharp moan, muffled by his shirt.

The pleasure inside me curled tighter and tighter, as I gasped and moaned into his shoulder until it burst over me, through me, like an internal explosion. I clung to him, trembling, wondering what had just happened.

Dex petted my hair and crooned wordlessly to me. I lifted my face to him. His mouth came down on mine, hard and demanding, and I wrapped my arms around his neck and kissed him back just as hard.

"What was that?" I whispered when we came up for air.

He smiled. "You came. Haven't you ever come before?"

"No." I blinked at him. "What is coming?"

Dex gave me a dubious look, as if he thought I was pulling his leg. "You don't know what coming is?"

"No. Should I?" Oh, no. We were back to super-dork city.

"Hey, don't worry," he said. "It just means I made you feel really good. When guys do it, they spew out semen."

"Oh." I blinked again. "Oh! I know what that is."

108

His smile deepened. "Yes, you do."

"You look like the cat that ate the canary."

He laughed. "I wish."

What did that mean? I didn't understand. There was so much about sex I didn't know. My parents had sent notes to school "excusing" me every time we'd had a sexual education unit and we Did Not Discuss That at home, so the whole thing was a mystery to me. Jenny got roughly the same treatment from her own parents, and the only information we'd been able to glean was culled from some steamy romance novels we'd discovered at the library. They hadn't been especially instructive.

"Well, you look smug," I clarified.

"I made you come," he said, apparently utterly at ease with the topic of conversation. "Of course I'm smug."

He'd gotten pleasure from giving me pleasure. Would I feel the same way if I made him come? I wanted to find out.

"So guys like to do that to girls?" I said.

He laughed again and kissed my nose. "Yes, we do."

"How many girls have you done it to?"

Oh, God. I really needed to tape my mouth shut.

His grin disappeared. He cupped the side of my face, caressing my cheekbone with his thumb. "Don't think about them. They're gone. Nothing. I hardly even remember them."

I studied his face, his eyes. "You don't mean that."

"Yes, I do. From the minute I saw you, I wanted to be with you."

"Oh, yeah?" I smiled, not believing him. "When was that?"

"Last year, fall semester," he said without hesitation. "You were in my history class."

"I was?" I said, wrinkling my nose. "I don't remember you. How awful. I'm sorry."

"It's okay. I always sat in the back and never talked to anyone." He smiled at me. "But I noticed you, sitting up at the front. I watched you every day."

"Really?" I smiled and stroked my fingertips across his cheekbone. "That's amazing."

"No, it isn't. Half the guys in the class were doing the same thing."

"They were not." I kissed him on the mouth before he could argue with me. "Now I want to take care of you."

"Nah, you don't have to do that." He reached down and adjusted himself. "I'll be fine."

I covered his hand with my own. "I want to, Dex. Please?"

He stared at me for a long moment. "Okay. I'd like that."

He rolled onto his back. Then he unbuttoned and unzipped his fly. His hands paused on the zipper.

"Are you sure? You don't have to do it."

"I want to. Really." I wanted to see what it looked like; I wanted to find out if it was as fun for me to make him come as it was for him to do it to me.

He stared at me for another few seconds. "Okay."

Dex lifted his narrow hips and slid his jeans down and his boxers along with them. His erect penis sprang out, swollen and sticking up like a fence post. My jaw fell open. I hadn't seen a penis since my brother was about seven years old. That had been tiny. This...this was enormous, even accounting for the differences in their heights.

It looked brownish, with a dark red tinge that was darker, almost purple, at the head. The base nestled into a fluff of dark gold curls that also covered the heavy sac that hung beneath.

"Holy smokes. It's huge," I said, half afraid of it.

He laughed. "Thank you."

My hand hovered over the tip. "Can I touch it?"

"I would like that a lot." His voice sounded strained.

I pressed my fingertip experimentally to the head of him. It felt almost velvety. The skin was soft, so soft, yet I could feel the hardness beneath it.

His breath caught as I stroked the length of him, still only with my fingertip. I stroked all along the length a second time, noting the greater tension in the shaft and dragging my finger along the flange at the bottom of the mushroom-like tip.

"Am I doing it right?" I said.

"If you want me to come, put your hand around my dick," he said.

"Like this?" I wrapped my fingers around his shaft.

"Just like that." He closed his eyes. "God."

I moved my hand back and forth, up and down his length, gently so as not to hurt him.

"Harder," he said.

I paused in my movements. "Are you sure?"

"Yes," he said through gritted teeth.

He looked like he was in pain and I didn't want to injure him, but he knew more about sex than I did. I gripped him more tightly and gave him an experimental stroke.

"Yes," he hissed, his hips twitching.

His reaction pleased me. He seemed so strongly affected by that simple motion of my hand. I had Dex Morgan on the floor of my bedroom, at my mercy, panting and gasping because my hand was on his sex.

He showed me what rhythm to use and I pumped him mercilessly until he thrust his head back and groaned deep in his throat. Jets of thick, whitish liquid erupted from the tip of his cock, landing on his lower belly. He continued to shiver and groan as I stroked him, wanting to prolong his pleasure as much as possible. Finally, the shudders stopped. He drew me down and kissed me voraciously.

"That was incredible," he whispered.

"You liked it?" I said, feeling pretty smug myself.

"Yes, I did." He gazed up at me with a lazy, sleepy smile.

"So did I."

"You have a natural talent," he said.

I smiled, pleased. The good little girl wasn't quite so good anymore.

"I really like you, Cass," he said softly. He lifted my hand to his lips and kissed the backs of my fingers.

The tenderness in that gesture almost broke my heart.

"I like you too," I said, although I really meant love. I was falling in love with him.

Chapter 15

The Gift

Cass:

The chattering of hundreds of voices and the thump and clack of feet on terrazzo floors was as deafening as ever on Tuesday morning, yet it seemed very far away from me. The movement of the kids all around me, laughing and shoving and running on their way to classes, seemed to move past me without touching me, as if there were a barrier between me and them. Even Jenny's familiar face looked slightly unreal as we made our way through the throng to our lockers.

I had changed. Technically I was still a virgin, but there seemed to be a gigantic chasm between the me who'd gone home on Monday and the me I was this morning. I had touched a guy and he'd touched me. I'd come. I'd made him come.

I shot Jenny a sidelong glance as she chatted cheerfully about the new unit in our trig class. As far as I knew, she'd never kissed a guy the way I kissed Dex, and she'd certainly never let a guy put his hand down her pants. Did she even know what a penis looked like? She didn't have any brothers, after all.

I couldn't tell her about what I'd done the night before. She wouldn't understand. Besides, she'd want all the details and I didn't think I wanted to describe them to her. How could I?

"You're not listening," she said as we reached Junior Hall.

"Sorry. What did you say?"

"Never mind. It doesn't matter." She gave me a searching look. "Are you all right?"

"Sure. I'm fine."

I'd given Dex an orgasm. What if that was all he wanted from me? What if he was done with me now that he'd gotten what he wanted? Maybe he'd pretend he didn't know me.

"Cass, you're still not paying attention. What's going on with you?"

"Nothing. Why?" I blinked innocent eyes at her.

"It's not nothing." She peered even more intently at my face. "It's Dex, isn't it?"

I shrugged. "Maybe."

"What happened?"

"Nothing. I was only thinking about him."

She rolled her eyes. "Why don't I believe that?"

"I have no idea." I reached my locker and opened it.

Jenny hovered next to me. "Something happened. I can tell. You must reveal the truth to me."

"It's private."

"Ah hah!" She stuck a triumphant finger in the air. "So something did happen."

"Maybe it did, but it's between me and Dex. I can't talk about it."

Her blue eyes rounded. "I hope it's not something that could get you in trouble."

"It isn't." I concentrated heavily on shuffling my textbooks and hoping she'd give up.

"You didn't do the deed?" she whispered.

"What? No!" My face flushed hotly.

"You look like you did."

"Well, I didn't." I shot her a glare. "Now drop it, will you?"

I hung my coat on the hook and smoothed my A-line black and red plaid skirt, tucking in the hem of my red turtleneck sweater, which had come undone when I'd taken off my coat.

"I hope you didn't let him go too far. He seems like the kind of guy you have to string along or he'll lose interest."

"No, he's not," I said firmly, in spite of the fact I'd been wondering the very same thing just a moment earlier.

"Holy smokes, I see him now," she said, gazing over my shoulder.

I turned around. Dex was coming our way, surrounded as usual by a river of students. He wore his standard chamois shirt, this one a dark green, over a T-shirt and wide-leg jeans. He wasn't looking at me. His gaze was fixed somewhere behind me and to my left—the office, maybe.

My heart dropped right through the pit of my stomach. He was going to ignore me. He'd gotten what he wanted and was moving on.

Then his gaze found me and a huge smile broke over his face. He wove his way deftly through the crowd to my side. I couldn't look at Jenny, although part of me wanted to say told you so.

"Hi," he said, putting his hands on my waist. "You look good."

I set my hands on his shoulders. "Good morning."

Dex bent down and fused his mouth with mine. I couldn't help responding with enthusiasm, even though Jenny was right next to us and there were crowds of people around. I gave a little sigh against his mouth and his arms wrapped around me.

He hadn't ignored me after all. I was so glad to be wrong that I hardly noticed the catcalls coming from people walking down the hall.

"Okay, you two, break it up," Jenny said. "The secretary is out in front of the office."

We parted reluctantly. Dex kept his hands on my waist, gazing down into my eyes with more intensity than he'd ever shown before, at least when we were in public. I slid my hands beneath his coat.

"You're cold," I said. He felt chilly even underneath his jacket.

"I just came inside."

"Yeah, but you've got a coat on."

He shrugged. "It's an old coat. I'm fine."

That settled it. I was going to buy him a new one, and I wasn't going to wait until Christmas. I had some money my Grandma Maslanka had given me for an early Christmas present that I hadn't spent yet. I'd planned to get myself something special, but instead I was going to spend it on Dex.

What kind of coat could I buy for twenty dollars? I might have to look on the sales racks.

"I want to see you after school," he murmured in my ear.

"I have something I have to do this afternoon," I said. "Maybe after dinner?"

He kissed me right beneath my ear. "Okay."

* * *

December is a crummy time to buy a winter coat, especially in Alaska. Nothing is on sale. All the stores know you need warm clothing at that time of year, and there isn't much to choose from because the town just isn't that big. A lot of people get their stuff mail-order, but I didn't have time for that.

I told my mom I needed to do some Christmas shopping and had her drop me off at the Sears Mall, the only real mall Anchorage had besides the brand-new University Center, but that was a lot farther away from our house. Neither of them were all that big, either. The Sears Mall had Sears at one end and Carrs Food Center at the other, with a double row of shops in between. I'd been to big malls Outside, so I knew how dinky ours really was, but you have to make do with what you've got.

I figured if Sears didn't carry anything that would work, then I'd probably have to think up a new plan. Montgomery Ward might do, or I could go downtown and check out J.C. Penney's.

As luck would have it, they did carry a ski jacket in a size that looked big enough to fit Dex, and all I had to do was pitch in five of my own non-grandma dollars to get it. I chose one in black, with white stripes along the collar. It looked warm.

I hoped he liked it. I'd never given a guy a present before, except for my brother Adam. And that was different.

Happy Christmas shoppers filled the mall as easy-listening Christmas music played over the sound system. There was a Christmas tree at one end, and big wreaths with bright red bows hanging all over the place. I loved this season. If I'd thought he would accept, I'd invite Dex to Christmas dinner at our house, but I knew he'd say no. Besides, Adam would pitch a fit if I tried that.

I wished my brother would get over the idea that Dex sold drugs. He wouldn't do that. I simply couldn't believe it of him, especially with the way he looked out for Joe.

My mom gave the large Sears bag in my hand a skeptical look when we met up again. "What did you buy?"

"Something for a friend."

"Jenny?"

I shrugged. "Did you do any shopping?"

She was carrying three bags, so she must have bought something. I figured asking her about them would distract her from asking any more questions about my purchase.

"That's for me to know," she said with a secretive smile.

"Oh, come on. Let me see."

"You'll see on Christmas morning."

"Fine." I rolled my eyes, pretending to be put out. "Can we get some caramel corn from Andy's, then?" I said, shifting my coat where it was slung over my arm. "I'm feeling peckish."

"Okay. Then we've got to go home so I can get dinner in the oven."

"I'll help." It was the least I could do after leading her to believe I'd shopped for Jenny when the gift was really for Dex.

* * *

My room seemed to glow in the light of my bedside lamp. That's what I loved about the pink walls. They made the room feel like a beautiful little haven and when I had low light as I did now, the walls seemed almost gem-like.

The bag with the coat inside sat on my bed. I'd carefully torn off the tag so he wouldn't know how much money I'd spent. I hoped he wouldn't mind that I didn't wrap it.

Dex knocked gently on my glass. I went to open the window and let him in, almost bouncing on my toes in my excitement over the gift. Would he like it? Was it too much?

Dex let himself through the window. There seemed to be a new tear in his jacket and I could see the stuffing falling out. It wasn't down, just some kind of fluffy batting that wasn't so fluffy anymore.

He bent down to kiss me. His lips and nose felt cold against my face.

"Did you have fun this afternoon?" he said.

"Yes. I got you something."

Dex cocked his head with a slight, puzzled frown. "You did?"

"Yes. It's right here." I turned and picked up the bag. "For you."

He took it from my hand, still with that puzzled frown. "Why would you get me a present?"

"Because I wanted to." I smiled hopefully, although I was getting more nervous by the second. "Open it."

He peered into the bag. His lips parted as he reached in and pulled out the coat. "You bought this for me?"

"Uh huh." I squeezed my hands together. "Is it all right?"

"Yeah. I mean—yeah. It's—I don't know what to say. No-one's ever done anything like this for me before."

He stared at the coat in his hand as if he didn't know what to do with it. His gaze flew to me. He looked stunned.

"Try it on," I said. "I wasn't sure what size to get."

Dex stared at the coat for another moment. Then he put it and the bag on my bed and shucked off his tired red jacket. He glanced at me with amazement in his eyes as he picked up the new coat and slipped it on.

"Does it fit?" I said.

"Yeah." He moved his arms around. "It's perfect."

"Do you like it?"

"I love it, Cass. But you shouldn't have done this. It's too expensive."

I waved that off. "It's my money. I can do what I want with it."

"How could you afford this? You must have a huge allowance."

"My grandma sent me some money."

He cocked his head again, his lips set in disapproval. "You shouldn't have spent that money on me. It was for you. I'm sure your grandma wouldn't want you buying me stuff with the money she sent you."

"I don't care." I picked up his hands. "I wanted to do it. Your old one is falling apart and I wanted to do something nice for you." I paused. "You're not mad, are you?"

"No. Why would I be mad? It just seems hard to believe." He put his arms around me and drew me in for a tight hug, bending his head down toward mine. "Thank you. I love it. It's the best present I've ever gotten."

That seemed hard to believe. I hugged him back, relieved that he was willing to accept the coat. "You're very welcome."

"I haven't gotten you anything." Now he sounded guilty.

"No, don't do that. There aren't any strings attached. I only wanted you to have something nice."

"You are so sweet," he said. "I can't believe you did that for me."

"You were cold."

"Yeah, but—"

"I care about you. It hurt me to see you cold, so I did something about it."

He sighed. "You didn't have to."

"I know I didn't. That's not the point." I tilted my head back to study his face. "Hasn't anyone ever done something for you just because they care about you?"

"No," he said simply. "Well, my big brother used to a long time ago, but he's different now."

"I'm sorry. That's awful. People should love you."

His lips curled up and his eyes crinkled at the corners. "They should, huh?"

"Yes."

"I feel the same way about you."

I smiled back at him, warmth flooding my heart. This was as close as we'd ever gotten to saying we loved each other. Maybe it wasn't a full declaration, but it was almost as good.

His hand played in my hair. "Do you think we'll have privacy tonight?"

"I hope so. I told my mom I was doing some tough homework."

"I wish you had a lock on your door."

I wrinkled my brow. "I know. But my parents would lose it if I suggested that. They'd think I was hiding drugs or something."

I wasn't sure what they'd think was worse—hiding drugs or a boy. It would probably be a toss-up. Then I wished I hadn't mentioned drugs because of Dex's reputation. He might think I believed those stupid rumors about him.

"I'm going to take this off now," he said, unzipping the jacket. "But only because it's so warm in here."

I grinned. "I'm glad you like it."

He gave me a look I couldn't quite interpret. "If you gave me a burlap sack, I'd like it because it came from you. But the jacket is great. I'm glad you got black."

"Yeah, I figured it would be a good color for you."

"Did you?" He tossed the jacket on my bed.

"Your car is black. And you're kind of a tough guy, so it seemed appropriate."

He drew me into his arms. "Tough guy, huh?"

"Yeah." I put my arms around his neck. "At least that's your reputation. Are you telling me it wasn't earned?"

"Oh, it was earned all right." He bent his head and kissed me.

Chapter 16

Torn

Cass:
The faint draft coming off the window glass had the edge of ice in it. The handle felt cold beneath my hand, although the window was shut and latched. It was a cold night.

Everything outside my window was dark except for the white shimmer of snow in the middle of the yard, where the streetlights could find it. Other houses and trees shadowed the rest of the back yard, so I couldn't tell if Dex were out there or not. He was going to come by tonight, as he did most nights.

My parents were starting to comment on how much time I spent in my room.

I turned from the window to give the room another once-over. I couldn't change the pink walls without going to a lot of trouble, but I'd changed out my dust ruffle for a much less frilly one and I'd put away a few of the stuffed animals. Dex had said he didn't mind my room, but it made me uncomfortable when he came into such a girly place.

A soft tap at the window alerted me. I dashed to open it and let him crawl through. The black ski jacket I'd given him got hung up on the windowsill as he lowered himself to my floor.

"Damn it," he muttered, freeing the garment before it could tear.

"Is it all right?"

"Yeah." He smoothed the fabric. "It looks fine."

"Good. I'm glad you're wearing it, by the way. It looks nice on you."

He grabbed me and yanked me against his body. "Of course I'm wearing it. It's a great jacket and you gave it to me."

I smiled, wrapping my arms around his waist. "I missed you. Where were you today?"

He shrugged, looking slightly uncomfortable. "I had some business to take care of."

It was probably something to do with his little brother. He spent a lot of time looking out for Joe.

"It feels like it's been forever," he said, bending down to conquer my mouth.

I moaned into his kiss. This pleasure had me thoroughly addicted. I couldn't go more than a few hours without beginning to crave his touch, his smell, his taste. Judging by the way he ground his hips against me and groaned, plunging his tongue into me, he felt the same way.

We tumbled onto the floor, still kissing, reaching for anything we could touch. I tugged at his jacket and he rose above me to yank it off and toss it to the side. I had my hands under his shirt before he got back to the floor. His skin didn't feel cold anymore and that was because of the jacket I'd given him. I rubbed my hands all over his powerful back, his sides, his chest.

"Holy shit." It was Adam's voice.

Dex and I jerked apart, breathing heavily. I peeked around his side as a sick feeling invaded my stomach. Adam stood in my doorway staring at us, his mouth open in apparent disgust.

"Adam, what are you doing?" I said.

"The question is what are *you* doing?" he said, glaring at me.

Dex turned to face him. "Don't be mad at her."

"I'll be mad at whoever I want," Adam said. "She's my sister. And you're Dex Morgan."

"No duh," Dex said.

Adam advanced on him, his nostrils flaring. I'd never seen him look like that. He was usually so easy-going. Now his gaze stabbed into us like gimlet spikes, his hands clenched into fists at his sides.

"Do you have any idea how much trouble she'll be in if our parents find out about this?" he growled at Dex.

"Some."

"Some? She'd never see the light of day again. Maybe the girls you're used to hanging with can sleep around and nobody cares, but Cass isn't like that. Our family isn't like that."

"Sleep around?" I snapped. "I'm not sleeping around, for crying out loud. I'm just—" Letting Dex put his hands down my pants. Was that so wrong? My whole body ached and trembled with thwarted desire for him.

"I know she isn't like that," Dex said, his voice remarkably patient. "I like that about her."

"Oh, you do? Then stay the hell away from her."

"Adam," I said. "This isn't any of your business."

"I'm your brother. Of course it's my business."

"You don't have the right to tell me who I can see." I rounded Dex to confront my brother. "I'm sixteen anyway. Almost seventeen. I should be able to spend time with a guy if I want." I'd almost said "date" but I wasn't sure that was what Dex and I were doing. Despite everything, I wasn't sure what we were doing.

"No, you don't. Not according to Mom and Dad."

"Mom and Dad don't know everything," I said. It was the first time I'd articulated that idea out loud, or even to myself. It sounded shocking.

"That's not the point," Adam said.

"It is to Cass." Dex took my hand, which wasn't the wisest thing to do in this situation, given Adam's open hostility. Still, I couldn't reject him so I let him keep it.

"You stay out of this," Adam said.

"Look," Dex told him, "I know I don't have the best reputation, but I care about Cass. I won't hurt her."

Adam snorted, his face twisted in disgust. "Bullshit."

"It's the truth, man."

"Really?" Adam sneered again. "You're a drug dealer. You're infamous. You want me to believe that a guy who deals drugs has my sister's best interests at heart?"

"He isn't a drug dealer," I said.

"Baby—"

"Tell her, Morgan." Adam spoke simultaneously with Dex.

I looked at Dex. "You're not, are you?"

He dropped his gaze and his shoulders fell, and I knew. I'd been lying to myself. All these weeks, all the times I'd gone out to lunch with him or let him in my room, every time I'd kissed him, every time he'd touched me beneath my clothes, I'd told myself he was better than that. Better than a drug dealer. He was too nice a guy to do something that awful. What an idiot I was.

Everyone else had known the truth. Adam and Jenny had tried to tell me and I wouldn't listen. Because he was so nice to me and his little brother, I hadn't wanted to believe he sold drugs.

No, that wasn't the real reason. It was because I was attracted to him and I wanted an excuse to make it okay to see him, so I'd made up a story about how misunderstood he was.

He was misunderstood all right. By me.

I closed my eyes. "I'm so stupid."

"I only sell pot," Dex said, his voice strained. "Not the hard stuff. I thought you knew."

"I told you." Adam sounded triumphant.

I extricated my hand from Dex's and he let it go without a fight. "I didn't want to believe the stories. I wanted to believe you were a good guy."

"Cass." My name sounded like a plea on his lips. "Nothing has changed. I'm still the same guy."

"No." I stepped away from him, suddenly furious. "You're not who I thought you were."

He might not have lied directly to me, but he'd omitted certain facts. Why hadn't he ever talked to me about his "business?" Because he was ashamed of it, probably, and he was right to be ashamed. He ought to be ashamed. I was ashamed that I'd associated with him.

I made myself look at him. The expression on his face was so awful I could hardly stand to see it. My heart hurt that I was doing this to him, and to myself, but it was the right thing. I couldn't be with someone who would blatantly disregard the law or sell addictive substances. Especially to kids.

What about Joe? Had he thought about what kind of an example he was setting for his little brother? Did he want Joe to smoke pot too, or grow up to sell it?

Oh, no. Maybe Joe already smoked it.

"Does Joe smoke that crap too?" I said.

"What?" He gaped at me in what looked like sincere horror. "No. Of course not."

Adam snorted again.

"I don't know if I can believe you," I said.

He took a step toward me, one hand slightly outstretched. "I haven't lied to you. I never said I wasn't a dealer."

"Yeah, but you didn't come out and tell me either." I stepped back.

He shoved his fingers through his hair. "I didn't think I had to. I thought you knew all about me."

"So did I."

He raked his hair again. "Jesus."

"I'm sorry." My voice cracked. "I really am. But I can't see you anymore."

"You knew I smoked," he said, his eyes pleading with me. "I told you. How is this any different?"

"Because selling isn't just your personal choice, for one thing. You're helping other people make the same choice, and I don't think that's right. Besides, you're doing illegal stuff. You could be arrested and sent to McLaughlin."

"I've already been there," he said dryly.

"Oh, my God," I whispered. The boy I'd imagined myself loving was a true juvenile delinquent, with a record and everything.

Well, you didn't want to be a good girl anymore. Looks like you accomplished your objective.

I told my sarcastic inner voice to shut up. She was turning into a real bitch.

"Go home, Morgan," Adam said. "And don't talk to my sister ever again."

"Cass?"

My throat was starting to close up and my eyes stung. If this was the right thing to do, then why did it hurt so bad?

"I'm sorry," I said again. "I'm so sorry, but I think you should go."

For a long, painful moment, he held my gaze. "If this is what you really want then I'll go."

"It is." No, it wasn't. Not at all.

He nodded slowly, grimly. "All right. Take care, Cass."

"You too."

What an awful, mundane, meaningless thing to say when you were rejecting someone you...cared for. Not loved. I didn't love Dex, did I?

He turned away from me. I wanted to ask him to stay, to forget the things I'd said, but I was too weak to do it in front of Adam. And my brother was right. A drug dealer was not for me, even if it was only pot.

Everyone said pot was a gateway drug, that it led to harder drugs and deeper involvement, so the mere fact he stayed away from the hard stuff now didn't mean he wouldn't turn to selling heroin in the future. I couldn't see myself with someone like that, and my parents would either lock me up or disown me if they found out about it.

How could he do it? How could he be the kind of person who would sell illegal substances? He wasn't the person I'd wanted him to be, and that was killing me.

Dex opened my window. He hoisted himself up over the sill and slithered out into the snow wearing nothing but his T-shirt. Where was his jacket? I glanced around and saw it lying on the floor next to my bed.

Scooping it up, I went to him and held it out. "Here. Take your coat."

"No. You keep it," he said roughly. "It's yours anyway."

He wouldn't even look at me. He turned his back on me and plunged into the snow of our back yard, his arms bare to the December cold. I held his coat to my chest. He clearly didn't want it because I'd given it to him. It felt like a slap in the face, but I guessed I kind of deserved it.

"You did the right thing," Adam said behind me.

I rounded on him, my chin trembling. "Go away. I don't want to talk to you."

"Cass, it had to be done," he said, extending a hand to me. "I was only trying to look out for you."

"You were looking out for the family reputation."

Adam shook his head sadly. "That's not true. I love you. You're my sister. I only wanted to keep you safe. Morgan isn't a safe guy."

Tears threatened to overflow my eyes. "I know. Now go away and don't come in my room again."

"Cass."

"Get! Out!" If I'd had something heavy to throw at him, I would have chucked it at his head, but all I had was Dex's coat and I wasn't about to give that up.

"I won't tell Mom and Dad, okay?" he said, standing in the middle of my room like I hadn't just ordered him to leave.

"Get out of here, Adam, or so help me God I will kill you."

"You really liked him, didn't you?" he said in a tone of wonder.

"No duh. Now go away." I showed him my back.

"Cass, come on. Don't be like this."

Maybe if I didn't answer him, refused to acknowledge his presence, he'd get the message and leave.

* * *

Winter in Anchorage is a gray time of year. This December, it seemed grayer than ever. Grayer than I could possibly have imagined a world could be.

The sky, the trees, even the snow seemed gray, because I was gray and colorless in my heart. When I stared out the window at the icy yard, I didn't see the blue peeking through the clouds or the chickadees fluttering from one branch of our cottonwood trees to another. I only saw gray.

And in the afternoon, when the sun went down, I saw black. At the moment, all the light had gone out of the world. Even our neighbors' Christmas lights couldn't lift my mood; their cheerful multicolored twinkle seemed childish and weak to me now. Inside me, there was only the deep darkness of a winter night.

I craved Dex. We hadn't been together all that long, yet somehow I'd become addicted to him. Maybe that was a bad metaphor, considering his occupation. But the longing I felt, the terrible need, seemed as close to my idea of addiction as anything.

I regretted pushing him away. I'd made an awful mistake. I hadn't even tried to work something out, to talk about it with him, and now it was too late.

My mom came into the living room and laid her hand on my shoulder. "Cass, it's time for dinner. I've been calling you."

I glanced back at her. She still wore her apron, a homemade one of blue and white gingham. There was a smear of flour on the bib. She was the only mom I knew who wore aprons. Not even Jenny's mom did that, and she was highly domestic.

"I'm not hungry," I said.

A frown furrowed her dark brows. "Are you feeling all right? You don't look so good."

"I'm fine. Just tired is all."

She pressed the back of her hand to my forehead. "You don't feel feverish."

"I'm all right, Mom, really."

"Well, come to dinner. Even if you don't eat anything. You need to sit with the family."

I heaved a sigh. "Okay."

She wouldn't leave me alone if I tried to resist, so it was easier to go along with what she wanted. Maybe if I stirred the food around on my plate, I could fool her into thinking I'd eaten a bit.

Adam, Beth, and my dad were already at the table, talking and laughing as if it were an ordinary evening. My mom had made baked salmon from fish caught last summer, and mashed potatoes and a huge tossed salad. It smelled and looked just as delicious as always, yet I had no interest in tasting it. My appetite seemed to have turned itself off somehow.

I took my usual seat between Beth and my dad, across from Adam. My brother glanced at me as I sat down, but I didn't return the look. Every time I saw him I wanted to kill him, so it was better if I didn't look at him.

My mom loaded up one of our brown Spanish-mission style plates with some of everything and set it in front of me. "Eat."

"I helped Mom make the fish," Beth said.

I dutifully poked my fork into the salmon. "It looks great, Beth."

She grinned. "It is. I'm an expert cook."

I took a tiny bite and put it in my mouth so as not to hurt her feelings. "It's really good."

It was hard to swallow. I cut another bite and shoved it across the plate, wishing I could hide the food somewhere. If we had a dog, I'd feed him under the table, but we didn't have any pets since our black Lab had died of old age.

"Cass, I could swear you've lost weight," my mom said.

My dad set down his fork to study me. "She looks the same to me, Lucille."

"No, she's thinner. She's got big circles under her eyes, too. Don't you think so, Adam?"

"Yeah, Mom," he said quietly. "She does."

"I'm fine, Mom. Quit fussing, please."

Was that guilt I saw on Adam's face? It was hard to tell, since he had his head bowed and I couldn't see his expression clearly. I hoped it was. He should feel guilty. It was his fault I had no appetite and couldn't sleep.

Except I could have stood up to him. He was my little brother, for crying out loud. I could have told him to buzz off, to mind his own business. I could have stood by Dex. Instead, I'd kicked him out of my life.

Had I done the right thing? My parents would have said yes. But if it was right then why did it hurt so bad?

I'd asked that question the night I rejected him, and I still didn't have an answer. It didn't hurt any less now than it had then. In fact, the pain seemed to get worse every day and I was beginning to think it wouldn't get better.

It was strange how everything could turn around in an instant, how one or two sentences could change your life so profoundly. One minute I'd thought I was falling in love and the next I was telling him to leave me alone forever.

What if I chose a different path? What if I went to him and asked him to forgive me? Would he take me back?

* * *

Dex:

The fluorescent light in the biology classroom was driving me nuts. It buzzed and flickered. Couldn't anyone else see or hear it? The bluish on-and-off shudder of it grated on every nerve in my body.

People's voices grated too. It sounded as if everyone in the room was talking at once and in their loudest voices. Yak, yak, yak, like a bunch of fucking Canada geese on their way to the insane asylum.

The air stank. I'd never noticed all those smells before, but since Cass broke up with me I'd given up smoking. Don't ask me why. It couldn't have been a worse time to kick the habit. I guess I thought that since I felt like shit anyway, I might as well add one more misery to the pile.

I stuck my hands under my shirt to warm them. They were still cold from the walk I'd taken between classes—my substitute for a smoke break—and they couldn't seem to warm up again. My red jacket was gone. Long gone. I'd thrown it in the trash after Cass gave me the black ski jacket, so now I didn't have a coat at all. I was stuck wearing an extra chamois shirt as a substitute, and it wasn't doing the job.

She still sat ahead of me, in the same place as always. I could see the back of her head, her long dark hair hanging loose down her back. The memory of her smell, the softness of her hair against my cheek, her body in my arms, drove through me like a knife to the gut. I wanted her so bad it was a physical pain.

She didn't want me, though. That was plain to see in the way she talked and laughed with her lab partner and never looked my way. Getting rid of me hadn't cost her a thing.

Two could play that game, so I pretended I didn't give a damn. I tried to act like nothing had changed and I was the same old Dex, only unencumbered by a female hanging on my arm. I wasn't much of an actor, though.

I forced my gaze down to my table top and the motorcycle doodle I'd been making on the edge of my paper. I'd already colored in all the figures on my Pee-Chee folder, so now I was working on notebook paper. Anything to take my mind off the new, ugly reality of my school life.

I liked to draw, doodled all the time. When I made pictures or even just abstract designs, my mind calmed down and I temporarily forgot about my problems. It was better than alcohol because it never gave me a hangover. I didn't usually keep my designs, though. It was like the making of them was the important part; once I finished, I forgot about it.

Today, my drawing strategy wasn't working so well. Even art couldn't get my mind off my problems with Cass. I was beginning to think nothing less than a coma would do it.

This was why I should have stuck with my policy of not dating. No girl was worth feeling this crappy, and people were noticing that I wasn't my usual self.

The lunch bell rang and everyone jumped to their feet. I gathered my shit. Ahead of me, Cass calmly walked out of the room as if I didn't exist.

God, I was pathetic. I'd never felt this way about a girl and I didn't want to feel it now. I didn't want to feel anything.

I could have gone to lunch at the Diner with a bunch of my smoking buddies, but I didn't want to. Didn't want the temptation of the smoke, for one thing. Plus I didn't feel like eating.

Instead, I looked for a hidey-hole where I could curl up with the Ben Bova novel I was reading. Somewhere no-one would notice me. I was turning into a hermit.

I headed toward the auditorium, hoping to find some little nook near the stage or maybe in the balcony. I didn't know my way around this part of the school very well, although I had made an exchange once backstage.

I climbed the stairs to the choir and band rooms. Most of the kids who took classes there had already gone to lunch, so it was pretty empty. Just the way I wanted it.

I found a spot in between two classrooms where I could sit down and read. Just as I started to crouch down toward the floor, two girls came around the corner and I froze. I wasn't alone after all.

127

It was Jenny and Cass. Fuck. If I'd known they came up here, I would have gone somewhere else. They were the last people I wanted to run into.

Cass wore plain, narrow Levi's and a light blue sweater with some kind of geometric blue and white design around the neckline. It was the kind of thing a good girl would wear, modest and kind of sweet. The kind of thing a girl who was not and never could be for me would wear.

My heart thumped painfully and my gut twisted. She was so close, just a few feet away, her blue eyes staring at me in dismay. She couldn't have made it more plain that she didn't want to see me.

I flushed all over. "Cass."

I needed to get out of here, get away from her, but in order to leave I'd have to walk past her. That would take me within a foot or less of her and I didn't know if I could take it. What if I couldn't stop myself from reaching out and touching her?

"Dex," she said faintly.

I stuck my book into the back pocket of my jeans. "I'll go."

"No, wait. I—I have something to say to you." She turned to her friend. "Jenny, can you give us a couple of minutes alone?"

Jenny remained expressionless. "Sure."

"No, Jenny, you can stay," I said. "Cass doesn't have anything to say that can't be said in front of you."

Cass frowned. "Yes, I do."

"No. You don't." I made to shoulder my way past them.

"I'm sorry," she blurted.

I paused, almost afraid to look at her face. My heart gave another of those thumps. It hurt even worse this time. "You already said that."

"But I—I shouldn't have sent you away. I regret it more than I can say."

God, that killed me. The weak part of me wanted to fall at her feet and beg her to take me back. The pathetic part. And maybe she wanted that, too, or at least she thought she did at this moment. But what would happen when more of my hideous life smacked her in the face and she couldn't pretend I was like the rest of her friends anymore? Would she reject me all over again?

"I've got to go," I said.

"Please forgive me." She reached out as if to put a hand on my arm.

I flinched away. "You're already forgiven. But I'm still going."

A glance at her face told me she was trying not to cry. Her chin was all trembly and her eyes looked glossy, like they were full of tears. Damn. I didn't want to make her cry.

I could erase that look on her face just by telling her it was okay, that I wanted to be with her again. But what would happen the next time she decided I wasn't good enough for her? I couldn't take it if she pushed me away again. It would tear me up inside, and Joe was depending on me to be strong.

"Please, Dex," she said, her voice uneven. "I miss you."

"That's too bad." I pushed past her.

Our shoulders brushed against each other in the narrow hallway. A bolt of longing shot through me at the contact. I kept going anyway.

My car would be a safer place to read. Anywhere in the school building was a place where she might go, and I didn't want to see her again. Ever.

Chapter 17

Bad For You

Cass:

It was one of those sharp, clear winter days where the sky is pure, pale blue and the air has a cold knife-edge to it and the insides of your nostrils stick together if you breathe in too hard. The air is dry on a day like that and the snow squeaks when you walk on it instead of scrunching.

Everything is pale blue and white, like glacier ice, except the black and gray of the tree branches. It's the kind of day that, even though it's so cold it hurts to breathe, is beautiful enough to make me think I might change my mind and decide to love winter instead of hating it.

Well, usually that's how I see it. This year, while I recognized the beauty in an intellectual way, it just couldn't touch me emotionally. Nothing could.

In an attempt to cheer me up, Jenny had come over early in the morning and baked Christmas cookies with me, Beth, and Mom, so the house smelled like gingerbread and sugar cookies. Every one of our baking racks, laid out on the harvest gold laminate counters, overflowed with cookie Christmas trees and stars and gingerbread people.

I gazed at the bounty, wishing I could share it with Dex. He wouldn't talk to me or really even look at me, though. I didn't know what to do since he'd rejected my apology.

What if I brought some cookies over as a peace offering? He'd probably kick me off his doorstep and slam the door in my face. But it was the only idea I had. I couldn't stop thinking about him and something had to change.

"Well, I'm going to throw this in the wash," my mom said, untying her apron as she walked from the room.

I found a paper plate and started piling on the goodies.

"Are those for me?" Jenny said, rubbing her hands together.

"Dex," I said softly.

"Oh." She lifted her brows. "Do you think that's a good idea? He seemed like he didn't want to see you anymore."

For an instant, all I could do was hang my head. What she'd said was true, but hearing it put so baldly stung pretty bad.

"I can't let things stand the way they are." I glanced at her. "I hurt him really badly and it was wrong. I have to give it another try."

"What if he still won't listen?"

"Then I'll leave the cookies for Joe and come home." I wished she would stop asking questions about how it was going to work. I didn't know and if I gave it too much thought I'd probably chicken out.

"I don't know." She shook her head. "Your folks probably wouldn't like it."

"So? Don't tell them. I sure won't." I finished loading the plate and wrapped it with tin foil.

"You two weren't even dating officially," she said.

I shot her a quelling look. "That doesn't mean I don't care about him and that I don't want him back."

"Okay." She held up her hands. "It's your call."

"Do you want to come with me?"

Normally I would have chosen to see him alone, but something about going to his house made me even more uncomfortable than begging with him in some other location. He'd never invited me over, and in fact had told me his place wasn't a good spot for us to hang out. I wasn't sure cookies were a good enough excuse to visit him, especially considering the way we'd left things at school, but if I had Jenny there as moral support it would be less intimidating. Plus it would be easier to slide the visit past my parents if she went along.

"I don't know," she said uneasily. "He doesn't like me."

"I think it's more the other way around." I displayed the plate by lifting it up under her nose. "You don't have to go if you don't want to, but I'd really appreciate it if you came with."

Her eyes narrowed. "You want me as camouflage."

"Come on, it'll be fun."

"Sure it will," she grumbled. "I get to watch you groveling."

"Isn't that your favorite activity?" I gave her my best attempt at a winsome smile. "I'll be forever grateful."

Jenny winced. "Stop grimacing at me."

"I will if you agree to come."

"All right. Fine. But if he throws me off his property, I'm blaming you."

I only told my mom we were going for a walk. Since he lived so close, it seemed like a believable excuse and we probably wouldn't be there very long.

Bundled in layers of warm clothing, we trudged down the snowy streets to Dex's house. It seemed even less prepossessing than it had that afternoon I'd walked by in the dark. The clear, uncompromising light of day made the house seem sad and tired.

"Are you sure this is his house?" I said, staring at the shack-like building huddled under its coat of snow.

The living room curtains were drawn, shutting the house off to the outside. Dex's car sat in the driveway right next to a dented blue Ford sedan with prominent tail fins, so he must be home.

"Pretty sure. My mom pointed it out to me." She frowned at me with squinty eyes. "Haven't you been here before?"

"No. Dex doesn't think it's a good place to hang out."

"That seems like a reason to stay away, if you ask me."

Well, I hadn't asked her. "I'm going to ring the bell."

I marched up the driveway, the lug soles of my chunky snow boots gripping the ice with ease. The house looked even sadder up close. I could see all the places where the paint was chipping and peeling off. Weeds poked their dried brown heads up over the top of the snow and the linings on the curtains looked frayed, with coffee-colored stains all over them. A row of icicles hung from the eaves.

The door, a slab-style with faded once-dark stain, scuffs and gouges all over it, squatted behind the screen door with an evil air. The screen had multiple tears in it, too. Nobody cared about this place, apparently.

It wasn't a friendly-looking house at all.

I gathered my courage and pressed the doorbell. Nothing happened. People were home, obviously...unless they had a third car and they'd all piled into it and left. I bit my lip and rang the bell again.

Still nothing. Would it be rude to ring a third time? Maybe they didn't want visitors. I glanced at Jenny as she caught up with me. She looked as unenthusiastic as the house did.

The door flew open. A middle-aged woman with the messiest blond hair I'd ever seen and a bulbous red nose glowered out at me. "Yeah? What do you want?"

"Uh..." I fought down the urge to look at Jenny again. "Is this Dex's house?"

"Yeah." She glared at me with a hostility I couldn't understand.

"Um...is he here?"

"He's in his room." She opened the door wider and stood back. "Go ahead."

Now I did glance at Jenny. Her blue eyes were wide with alarm.

"Thank you," I said to the woman. I entered her house with a polite smile.

The front door let directly onto the living room, which was appallingly messy. A threadbare brown carpet in some close-looped style that looked at least fifteen years out of date covered the floor. The furniture was a mix of old and new—mostly old—and all of it looked stained and broken down. The windows were so dirty they hardly let in any light. And the place smelled bad, like mildew with a hint of rotten eggs. I tried to breathe through my mouth.

132

Giving the woman another polite smile, I held out my free hand. "My name's Cass, by the way, and this is Jenny. We're friends of Dex's from school."

"Hi," Jenny chirped brightly.

"Yeah? His room's down there." Ignoring my offered hand, she pointed to a narrow hallway opening off the right of the front room.

The woman—Dex's mom?—turned her back on us and shuffled to the couch. She hadn't even given me a chance to explain about the cookies. The wooden coffee table in front of her seat was littered with plastic drink glasses and plates covered in food debris. No Christmas tree adorned the room, even though it was already December 20th.

I'd never seen anything like it. My mom always kept our house clean and tidy, and we kids helped her do it. If we didn't, we lost privileges like TV. Jenny's family was the same way. I'd never seen anyone living in filth like this.

No wonder Dex didn't want me to come over.

Well, we were here, and it would look weird if we turned around and left without saying hello. So I straightened my back and walked down the little hallway as if I knew what the heck I was doing.

In addition to a bathroom, there were two doors down there. One was shut and the other stood ajar. I peered into the open doorway to see a single large bed, the covers askew. The curtains were pulled, making the room gloomy. Women's clothes lay all over the bed and the floor, so it probably wasn't Dex's room.

God, this was awkward. The temptation to turn and run away almost overcame me. I knew Jenny was hoping I'd lose my nerve—she'd looked just as appalled by the condition of the house and Dex's mom's behavior as I felt. But I'd come this far, and I wasn't going back until I'd seen him.

I knocked on the closed door. At first I didn't hear anything. Then there was a shuffling noise and a low thump. Heavy footsteps approached and the door swung open. My heart started pounding away with infatuated excitement and terror the instant I saw him.

Dex stared down at me with a baffled look in his green eyes. His hair seemed even shaggier than usual, the blond strands standing up in some places and falling into his eyes in others. He sported the scruffy beginnings of a beard, as if he hadn't bothered shaving since I'd last seen him three days ago.

"Cass?" He frowned. "What are you doing here?"

"You wouldn't talk to me in school."

He sighed heavily. "That's because there's nothing to say."

"Yes, there is," I said. "I miss you. I need you." Where Dex was concerned, I seemed to have no shame. I could say the most revealing things, even though Jenny was standing next to me in the cramped hallway, listening. I held up the plate of cookies. "I brought you some treats as a peace offering."

He leaned his elbow against the doorjamb. "You shouldn't have come here."

He was staring at me with hungry eyes that belied his words. His body leaned slightly toward me, as if he couldn't help himself. He still liked me.

"I wanted to see you," I said with growing hope.

He flicked a glance at Jenny. "You probably noticed the house isn't ready for visitors."

"That doesn't matter to me," I lied. "Is it okay if we come in?"

He paused for a moment, staring down at me so coolly I wondered if he'd throw me out. Finally he let out another heavy sigh and opened the door all the way.

"Yeah. Sure."

We filed into his bedroom. It seemed like a haven of cleanliness and order after the chaos of the other rooms, even with three beds—a bunk bed and a mattress on the floor. While there wasn't much floor space, they were using a beach towel for a curtain, and there were a few items of clothing on the floor, it was relatively tidy. The air smelled weird, though. I couldn't place that odor.

The light-blue walls had chips and dings in the plaster and most of the available space was occupied by Playboy centerfolds and car posters. I glanced up at a heavily-endowed blonde with no bra top on—although she did have a bright white pattern of skin where her bikini top had been when she sunbathed—and blushed. Good grief.

Joe sat on the top level of the bunk bed, grinning at me. "Hi, Cass!" He waved.

"Hi, Joe." I was glad for a distraction from that blonde. "How are you?"

"I'm good." He tossed aside the comic book he was reading. "What did you bring?"

"Christmas cookies. We just baked them. This is my friend, Jenny."

"Hi, Jenny." He looked shy all of a sudden.

"Hi, Joe." She glanced at Dex. "I didn't know you had a little brother."

"Well, I do," he said curtly.

At that, Jenny subsided, crossing her arms over her chest and leaning against the closed door. Joe seemed completely unaware of the tension as he clambered down from the bunk.

He bounced on his toes as he contemplated the cookie plate. "What kind are they?"

"Sugar and gingerbread." I pulled off the tin foil. "With icing."

"Cool! Can I have one?"

"Sure. I brought them to share." I held out the plate while he grabbed three cookies, three being equal to one in kid math, at least where cookies are concerned.

"Dex?" I held the plate out to my not-boyfriend.

"No."

I took a breath for patience, and courage. "Okay. I'll put them here." I set the plate on the top of the dresser.

"Is that all you wanted?" he said, glowering at me.

"No. I want to talk to you."

"Well, as you can see I'm kinda busy." He gestured toward his little brother.

"Joe, would you mind if I talk to Dex for a few minutes?" I said.

"Nope." He talked around a mouthful of cookie. "But he's been really grouchy lately, so be careful."

"Joe," Dex said, shaking his head. "You didn't have to tell her that."

"I'll stay here," Jenny said.

"Jesus." Dex grimaced. "Fine. We'll go into my parents' room."

I followed him across the hall and into the other bedroom. It looked even seedier once I got inside it. But I was willing to put up with the surroundings in order to get a chance to be alone with Dex.

Dex shut the door and flicked on the overhead light. "Look, Cass, there's nothing more to say. You don't want to be with me and I understand why."

"I do want to be with you."

"No." He shook his head, making his golden hair sway across his forehead. "You want to be with some fantasy version of me. The version that doesn't deal drugs and live in a shithole like this."

I took a step closer to him, desperate to make him believe me. "Do you think I care about that?"

"Obviously you do, or you wouldn't have kicked me out of your house."

"I was wrong. I was upset and not thinking." One more step closer. "Please."

He backed up. "No."

"I don't know why you deal drugs, but I do know you're a good guy. The way you look out for Joe is wonderful. A bad guy, I guy I couldn't care about, wouldn't do that." I wanted so much to touch him, but I was afraid he'd back away again.

"Cass." He gave me a pleading look. "I can't be with someone who is going to bail on me the second things get rough."

"I won't bail on you."

He raked his fingers through his hair. "Jesus. I can't believe I'm even talking about this. I don't date. Ever." He raked his hair again and blew out his breath. "What am I doing with you? This isn't me. It isn't my life."

It scared me to hear him talk that way. "Maybe it wasn't you before, but it can be now."

"Maybe I don't want it to be me. Maybe I want to go back to the person I was before I met you."

I bit my lip, my stomach doing nauseous rolls in my belly. "Please don't talk like that."

"You have to know this won't work," he said. "Whatever this is that we have. Had. We're not meant to be together, you and me. We're too different."

If I kept pushing and he kept retreating, I was going to cry. I could feel the tears welling up in my eyes.

"I don't know that," I said stubbornly.

"I'm bad for you."

The tears pooled in my eyes. I bit my lip hard to keep them at bay. "You're not. And even if you are, I don't care. I need you. I made a stupid mistake and I wish I'd never said those things."

"Yeah, Cass, I am," he said with complete sincerity. "I don't want to drag you into the shithole that is my life. You don't belong here and that's a good thing." He waved his hand at the door. "We can't really talk about this now anyway, with Joe and Jenny in the next room."

I swallowed hard, trying to get my emotions under control. Then I took a couple of deep breaths for good measure.

"Okay," I said. "But I don't agree with what you just said. I'm going to wait for you to come to my room again so we can talk. I'll be there tonight and tomorrow night. Think about it."

He just looked at me, his face remote, giving me nothing.

"I hope you come," I said.

"I'll think about it." He reached around me, carefully not touching me, and opened the door.

We returned to the boys' room. Joe and Jenny knelt on the floor while Joe used his Evel Knievel action figure, a row of Matchbox cars and a much larger plastic van to demonstrate the stunt man's latest jump over however many vehicles it had been. I never paid any attention to that stuff, so the details had escaped me. But Joe obviously kept careful track.

"And he didn't even break any bones this time!" he said with a grin at my friend.

"Wow. That's really cool," Jenny said, sounding as if she actually meant it.

Dex gave me a rueful glance as he chose a sugar cookie. "Thanks for the cookies. It was really nice of you to do this."

"You're welcome," I said. "I was glad to do it."

"You too, Jenny," he said with a glance at my friend.

Jenny shrugged. "I'm just along for the ride."

"Well, thank you anyway. I didn't mean to snap at you like I did."

She gave another shrug. "It's okay."

The door opened to admit a tall, black-haired guy with a wild and bushy beard. His green eyes were just like Dex's, and the rest of him looked like some desperado or pirate looking for someone to rob. The hem of his gray T-shirt had a Swiss-cheese pattern of holes in it and his ripped jeans hung on his skinny frame.

"What the fuck, man?" he said, glaring at Jenny and me. "Who're these chicks?"

Jenny stiffened, her chin rising. "We're visiting. Who are you?"

"I live here," the black-haired hooligan said.

Dex's jaw worked back and forth for a second. He took a deep breath. "This is Cass and this is Jenny. Girls, this is my older brother Sin."

"Sin? What kind of name is that?" Jenny said with open scorn.

Sin sneered at her. "It's short for Sinatra."

She edged away from him as he came farther into the room. "It's a weird name."

"Yeah?" His gaze trailed over her from her head to her toes and back again. "So is Jenny."

"Jenny isn't weird." She pushed her glasses up. "It's normal. Lots of girls are named Jenny."

He smirked and threw his frame down on the mattress on the floor. "That doesn't mean it isn't weird."

Jenny huffed and gave her head a little toss. "Whatever."

Dex snickered. "Wow. You two are really hitting it off."

"Sin, you should try one of the cookies," Joe said, as oblivious as any other ten year old. "They're really good."

Sin pulled a cigar box out from under his mattress and opened it. "No thanks, bud. You go ahead and have mine."

"Thanks!" Joe looked as excited as he had when he'd first discovered that I'd brought cookies.

I watched as Sin took a cigarette from the box. It was the oddest-looking cigarette, kind of lumpy and uneven and missing a filter. He lit it with a blue plastic lighter and took a deep pull on it.

The odd smell I'd noticed earlier filled the room, along with a thick cloud of smoke. Sin turned on the clock radio next to his bed and the sound of Jimi Hendrix's "Are You Experienced?" filled the room. I shifted, uneasy with the smoke and the music. It was the kind of stuff my parents wouldn't allow in the house.

"Do you have to do that now?" Dex said, staring pointedly at Sin's cigarette.

"Yes, I do." Sin took another long drag on the cigarette, but instead of blowing out the smoke he held it in.

Puzzled, I glanced at Dex. He looked embarrassed and angry, glowering at his older brother as if Sin had done something wrong. The smell of that cigarette was so strange. I'd never smelled tobacco like that before.

Then it dawned on me. It wasn't tobacco; it was marijuana. At least, I thought it might be. I'd never been in a room where someone was smoking pot before.

Holy cow. I was in a room with someone smoking pot.

I exchanged an alarmed look with Jenny. She flicked her eyes toward the door, giving me the signal that she wanted to leave. I wasn't ready to go. I wanted to stay with Dex, yet at the same time Sin's behavior was making me incredibly uncomfortable and I wanted to get away from him.

Not to mention the fact that he'd lit up in front of his ten-year-old brother. That couldn't be good for Joe, but evidently Sin didn't care.

Sin blew out another long, thin stream of smoke. "This is good shit." He held the cigarette out to Dex. "You want a hit?"

"No, thanks. Not right now." Dex glanced at me. "Um...look, can you put that away for now? Cass and Jenny don't smoke."

"It's my room, man, and I need it. You wouldn't believe the shit I had to deal with today."

I saw Dex's jaw move again, as if he were grinding his teeth. His nostrils flared and his eyes narrowed. He opened his mouth and I knew something angry was going to come out of it.

"That's okay," I said. "We were just going anyway."

"Aww," Joe said. "You just got here."

"I know. I'm really sorry, but Jenny and I have some things we have to do. It was nice seeing you again."

He beamed at me. Jenny jumped to her feet and hot-footed it toward the door, not bothering to hide her eagerness to get away. Her hands worked at the hem of her coat.

"You sure you wanna go, Jenny?" Sin said, giving her another lazy once-over I wasn't sure how to interpret. "I'll be glad to share with you."

She blushed. "No. Thank you. I have to go now."

"I'll see you later, Dex," I said with a meaningful glance at him. "Okay?"

"Okay, sure," he said, but I couldn't tell whether he meant it.

Chapter 18

Shaken

Cass:

My room had the same pink glow it always did. I kept the overhead light—the chandelier—off and just burned my bedside lamp. The low, yellow light made the room seem even warmer and more cozy.

I'd cleared the stuffed toys off my bed. They now resided on top of my dresser and along the shelf created by the pony wall of the foundation. The five-inch-wide drywalled top of the pony wall made a nice place to display things.

My idea was that having a bed with no toys on it made the room look more grown-up. I didn't know if it had really worked, though. I mean, the walls were still pink after all.

The pink of my room couldn't comfort me as much as it usually did. I was too nervous. Dex hadn't shown up the night before and I figured he'd continue to not show up, but the silly and hopeful part of me thought he might. So I was in my room, pacing, waiting for him.

I should get some new curtains. Something less girly and more grown-up. I had no idea what that might be, however. Not pink, I knew that much. Boys weren't comfortable in pink rooms, right?

Dex had said it was okay, though. He didn't mind it.

He wasn't going to show up. He'd never talk to me again, so his opinion of pink didn't matter.

A light tap at my window. I jumped about three feet in the air in startlement.

Was it him? Who else would tap on my glass? My heart raced as I went to the window and opened the curtains.

Dex was crouched outside in the snow, coatless, dressed in just his usual jeans, T-shirt, and chamois shirt. No, make that two chamois shirts, one blue and the other dark green. He must be freezing. I cranked open the window.

"You came!"

"Yeah. Can I come in?"

I removed the screen. "Of course."

He let himself into my room and I shut the window. I felt just as queasy and fluttery as I had the day before when Jenny and I had gone to his house. But this time we were alone.

Dex stood next to my bed and looked at me, just waiting. He stuck his hands in the pockets of his jeans, slouching a little. "What did you want to talk about, Cass?"

"You look cold. Where's your coat?"

He shrugged. "I didn't wear it."

Duh. That was obvious.

"Is that what you wanted to say?" His voice was so distant. I hated that.

"No. I—I wanted to say that I don't care if you deal drugs."

He sighed. The sound communicated so much weariness. It didn't seem like a noise a seventeen-year-old should make.

"You should," he said. "It isn't a good thing to do."

"Then why do you do it?"

"Because I need money."

I sat down on my bed. "Can't you get a regular job? I saw a hiring sign at the Fireweed."

Dex leaned back against my wall, crossing his feet at the ankles. "I don't have the best reputation."

"So? I'm sure you could be a busboy or something."

"I was in McLaughlin," he said. "Nobody wants to hire me."

"Oh." McLaughlin was the juvenile detention center. "I see."

"Do you?" His lips curled wryly. "You wanna know why I was in juvie?"

No. Yes. "Tell me."

"I went joyriding with some buddies of mine, cruising up and down the strip, drinking beer we'd lifted from somebody's older brother, hitting on girls, being little assholes and picking fights. None of us even had our learners permit. We crashed the car and totaled it, but somehow we all made it out without a scratch. But there were these other, older guys. We'd argued with them earlier on the strip and they'd followed us. So they jumped us when the car crashed."

I frowned. "So you were convicted of joyriding?"

"Yes, but also assault." He toed my carpet, his eyes on his feet. "I beat the shit out of one of them."

"Oh," I said faintly.

"They started it," he said. "But that's no excuse."

"But...wasn't he a lot bigger than you if he was older?"

Dex tilted his head. "He was a little bigger. I was a lot meaner. I'd already been in a lot of fights by then."

"Oh."

"I'd been in an argument with my dad earlier that day. A bad one. He'd clocked me on the jaw and I had a big bruise from it. When that guy jumped me, I was so pissed off I just kept hitting him even when he was down. It was like I couldn't stop myself. But I could have and I know it."

"You feel bad about it," I said, hurting inside at the thought of Dex's father beating him.

"Yeah. But that doesn't matter to employers. Nobody wants to hire a violent thief."

I had a hard time seeing Dex as violent, even after that story. "You're not like that anymore, right?"

"Cass, it doesn't matter. That's what I'm trying to tell you. Nobody cares. They only see my record."

"So you started selling pot?"

"Yeah." He turned his head and stared at my wall as if looking at something far beyond it. "I need money, like I said. Sometimes my parents forget stuff, like the gas bill or the groceries."

That was horrible. Parents were supposed to be on top of stuff like that. I couldn't picture my own parents forgetting to buy food or to keep the house warm. What was wrong with his mom and dad?

His mother had looked like she was sick, so maybe that was it. Or maybe she just drank too much and didn't care about her kids.

"Where do you get it? The pot, I mean."

He glanced at me briefly. "I know some guys who bring it up from the Lower Forty-eight."

"Would you let me try some?"

"Fuck no." He shook his head. "Excuse my language, but no. You don't need that kind of crap in your life."

I hadn't meant it anyway. Pot held no appeal for me.

"I don't think you need it either," I said. "And it can't be good for Joe, sitting around in all that smoke. That is what Sin was smoking yesterday, right?"

"Yeah. He's been a mess ever since he got home from 'Nam. Nobody can talk to him. All he does is lay around and get high."

Wow. This was way over my head. Dex's family had problems on a level I'd never really imagined before. I mean I'd read novels where people were alcoholics or drug addicts, but I'd never met anyone like that before. Nobody I knew even talked about it except to make occasional pronouncements about the evils of illegal drugs.

I had no idea how to help Dex or what I should do in this situation. The only thing I knew was that I wanted him in my life. I wanted him back, the way we had been. There was no way I was giving up on us. His awful family life wasn't going to discourage me.

"I'm sorry you're going through this," I said. "I wish there was something I could do to help."

"Well, there isn't. Just stay out of it. I don't want you involved."

I tilted my head to the side, watching him. "I'm already involved."

"No. You're not. You were right to break up with me." He flushed. "You know what I mean."

"I wasn't right. I had no idea you were having such a hard time." I got off the bed and came toward him. He couldn't back up because his back was already against the wall, so I grabbed his hands and held on. "I should have talked to you about this stuff instead of getting all freaked out and telling you to leave."

"You did the right thing." He wouldn't look at me.

"No, I didn't." I kept my grip on his hands even as he attempted to pull them away from me. "Don't you get it? I'm miserable without you. I can't stand being away from you. I can't sleep and I don't even want food."

He swallowed so hard I could hear it. "Yeah."

"You feel the same way?"

Dex nodded slowly.

"Then why can't we be together?" I put his hands against my waist. "If we both want the same thing. What's wrong with it?"

"I'm wrong," he said tightly. "I'm bad for you."

I placed my hands on his shoulders and looked right into his eyes. "You are not and anyway I don't care. You're what I want. Please say you'll be with me."

He pinched his eyes shut. "Cass. Please don't make this so difficult."

"I want it to be difficult because I want you to say yes."

His mouth trembled, and twisted into a distorted shape. I could almost see the fight he was waging with himself. It was written on his face. I could feel it in the tension of his hands at my waist.

He shook his head, eyes still shut. His mouth twisted again and he tilted his head back until his skull hit the wall. His hands simply rested at my waist, still in fists, refusing to really engage with me.

I was losing this battle. Dex was going to say no again. He'd leave my room and never speak to me. I could see it in his face. My throat hurt so bad I didn't think I could force out any words to beg him to stay.

Suddenly, he dragged me against his body, his arms coming around me and holding me so tightly I could hardly breathe. I didn't need air. I just held on as he bent his head to mine.

He was shaking. I was shaking. We clung to each other, our breath ragged and uneven. His heart pounded fast and loud beneath my ear.

"I tried so hard to stay away," he whispered.

"I know."

"I thought you didn't even care."

I rubbed my face against his chest. "That's what I thought about you."

142

He gave a soft huff. "I was putting up a front. Trying to be cool."

"Well, it worked. I was totally fooled." I stroked my palms up and down his back.

His body was chilled from being outside. I wanted to make him warm again, to convince him completely and without doubt that he ought to be here, that he belonged. It pained me that he saw himself as wrong and bad. Maybe he'd made some bad decisions, but in his essence he was a good person. I believed that, and I wanted him to believe it too.

Besides, touching him felt so good. It filled the awful emptiness inside me.

"I was pretending too," I said.

"I know that now," he murmured. "But it did piss me off when I saw you at school and you acted like you didn't give a damn."

I lifted my head. "I hope you didn't want to beat me up."

He frowned, looking offended, his lips turning down. "Don't even joke about that."

"Sorry."

"I would never hit you for any reason," he said firmly. "Never."

"Okay."

"I'm serious." He stared intently into my eyes. "I've never hit a girl and I never will. I hate men who beat up on women."

"Okay. I believe you."

He stared at me for another moment. He must have liked something he saw in my eyes, because his shoulders relaxed a little. "You're such a good person. I don't know why you want to be with a guy like me."

"Because you're a good person too." Before he could deny it, I rose on my tiptoes and pressed my lips to his. They were cool, like the rest of him.

He was so cold from being outside and I wanted to warm him. I moved my hands up and down his back, trying to rub some life back into him as we kissed.

The contact felt more comforting than sexual. It dawned on me that I'd needed him not just for sexual pleasure but for this. Comfort. Affection. I hadn't realized how starved I was for physical contact until now.

There were things I wanted to know about him, though, and I didn't want to wait. The visit to his house still haunted me. The titanic mess, his weird and hostile mom, his drug-using brother...And what about his dad? Was the guy ever home? Didn't he care about his kids?

"Dex?" I said softly.

"Mmm?" He pressed his lips across my face—nose, cheek, eyelid.

"Do you have...I mean, do your parents...um..." I sounded like an idiot. Asking him this question made me feel like a nosy bitch. But I wanted to know, to understand him.

"My parents are fucked up, baby," he said, a note of sadness and resignation in his voice. "Is that what you wanted to know?"

"Well, your mom seemed...I thought she might be..."

"Drunk?" he said.

"Yeah."

"She was. She usually is."

"And your dad—"

He rested his head against mine. "He's drunk a lot too. They fight all the time. He beats on her sometimes."

"That's awful. I'm so sorry."

"Don't be." He stroked my back. "It's not your fault."

"That isn't the point." I wished I could make his family problems disappear. "I hate the thought of you living in that place. Of Joe living there. You deserve better than that."

His hand paused in its stroking. "You really believe that?"

"Yeah. Of course I do. Don't you?"

"Not usually. It's just the way things are." He resumed stroking me. "I figured as soon as you saw my place, you'd never want to talk to me again."

"I don't blame you for your parents." I tightened my hold on his waist. "I wish there was something I could do to make it better for you."

"You already are. Seeing you makes it better."

God, that made me feel even more terrible about rejecting him. He needed me and I'd pushed him away. That wasn't going to happen again.

"You make things better too," I said.

"I don't see how."

"I hate it when you talk that way." I tilted my head back. "You make me feel good. You make me laugh."

He looked so serious as he stared back at me. "I do?"

"Uh huh."

"I'd like to make you feel good right now," he said, lowering his lips to mine.

* * *

There's usually something so depressing about January. Christmas is over and spring is so far away you can hardly imagine it, let alone believe it will really happen. Even inside the school, with all the bright lights and activity, things seem gray and dreary. This year was different, though.

The colors seemed brighter. The sickly green tiles on the walls didn't annoy me the way they usually did. The loudness of hundreds of voices and feet and slamming locker doors didn't irritate. I hardly noticed them.

Everything in my world seemed to have a little glow around it, even Junior Hall. I shut my locker door and turned, book bag slung over my shoulder, ready for my first class, English.

I'd worn a special outfit today—a V-neck sweater in blue and jeans with trendy wide legs that my mom had gotten me for Christmas. I even had platform shoes on my feet, chunky oxfords in dark brown leather. It was the most fashionable outfit I'd ever owned and I felt like a model in Seventeen magazine.

Tracy Carpenter and a gaggle of her bitchy little friends had gathered across the hall from me. Normally I ignored them as much as possible. They were part of the so-called popular crowd and mean as a pack of hungry wolves, except they weren't as honest as wolves. They didn't normally attack in the open.

Bob Rogers stood next to the group, waiting for Tracy. I knew they'd been dating and I was glad Jenny wasn't here to see them together. He'd really hurt her feelings by going out with Tracy after they'd shared whatever it was they'd done together at the Halloween dance. She wouldn't tell me what that was.

Tracy and her buddies leaned in together, whispering. She had her hair in the latest style, loose waves that were stiff with hairspray, obviously made with rollers and not natural. Her dark brows had been carefully penciled in and her lips were pale and glossy. She wore a black A-line miniskirt and black go-go boots with a chunky yet skin-tight pale-blue turtleneck belted low on her hips with a black patent-leather belt. That deflated my own fashion confidence, because I knew she had me beat by a mile.

The girls whispered behind their hands. Then they all glanced at me and giggled. They turned back toward each other for more whispering.

Good grief. What now? I shook my head. It wasn't worth fretting myself over. Tracy had been a bitch as long as I'd known her, at least since the third grade.

Before I could make my escape, she and her posse crossed the hallway and surrounded me. I raised my eyebrows, wishing I could do just one the way Dex did. It made him look ice cold and I could use that just now.

"I heard you're one of the stoners now," Tracy said, staring at me with a chilly little smile.

"You heard wrong," I said.

"Are you sure? Aren't you dating Dex Morgan?"

All her friends giggled in unison.

"What does that have to do with anything?" I said, trying to stay cool.

"Are you kidding?" She put her hands on her hips, right over her belt. "Even you must know he deals."

I was not getting in this discussion with her or anyone else. But especially not with her. "So?"

She pursed her pale-pink lips. "So are you a stoner or not? Do you even know what that means?"

I tilted my head and pulled my chin down. "Even you can't be that dumb."

"Excuse me? Did you just call me dumb?" she said in a disbelieving tone. She glanced around at her friends for back-up. "Did you hear what she said to me?"

"I heard," Sherry Nordgren said, her blue eyes gleaming.

Tracy took a step toward me, getting way into my personal space. "Nobody wants to date *you*. You're the biggest spaz in the school and everyone knows it. So if you're dating anyone, even a loser like Dex, you must be putting out."

I flushed as I remembered the night before, when I had in fact put out. Dex hadn't shown up yet. Would he acknowledge me? Would he keep his word, or had he finally gotten everything he wanted from me?

I pretended nonchalance. "Oh, yeah?"

She looked faintly confused, as if she'd expected a different response from me. "Yeah."

I grinned and shook my head. "Whatever you want to think."

"Whatever I want to think?" she said. "It's what everyone thinks."

That made me uneasy. I didn't want people thinking I was a drug addict or anything, and I certainly didn't want to get in trouble with the school. But they'd know as soon as they talked to me that I wasn't guilty, wouldn't they? At any rate, I wasn't going to let Tracy see me squirm.

"So what?" I said carelessly. "Do you have a point, Tracy? Because I'd like to get to class."

She stuck a manicured finger in my face. "You are a stoner. I can tell. Your eyes are all dilated. You're stoned right now."

"Uh, no, I'm not."

"Yeah, you are and I'm going to tell the principle." She turned around as if to march off and nark on me.

A heavy arm wrapped around my shoulders. "You won't tell anyone," Dex said.

I leaned into him in unabashed relief. He was here, and he was acknowledging me in public. My fears were for nothing.

Tracy whipped around to stare open-mouthed at him. "What did you say?"

"You won't tell anyone. First, it isn't true. Cass doesn't smoke anything, not even cigarettes. Second, if you and your boyfriend want me to keep supplying you, you won't tell on Cass."

Brilliant crimson flushed upward from her neck to her hairline as her dark eyes darted nervously from side to side. "Supply? I don't—I mean, we don't—"

"Save it, Tracy," he said. "And leave Cass alone. I don't want to see you messing with her again."

She flushed even more brightly. Her gaze faltered and fell to the floor as she shifted her weight from one foot to the other.

"Well," Sherry said, "I've gotta get to class." She edged away from Tracy's group.

I couldn't remember the last time I saw one of Tracy's entourage making a decision independently. Sherry's action seemed to break the spell on the rest of the girls, because they all turned and followed her, leaving Tracy by herself in the middle of the hallway.

She leveled a poisonous glare at me. "You."

"Yeah, me," I said. "You'd better get going or you'll be late."

She tossed her head, flipping a precisely curled lock of hair back over her shoulder. "Whatever," she said, flouncing off after her friends.

I pressed my lips together to keep from laughing and turned to Dex. "You're here."

"Of course I am. Where else would I be?"

I shrugged. "I know it's dumb, but I keep expecting you to ditch me."

He frowned down at me. "You need to stop that."

"But they think—"

Dex pressed one long forefinger to my lips, hushing me. "Knock it off. I don't give a shit what they think and neither should you. Besides, you were totally holding your own. You didn't even need me."

"Yeah, I did," I said behind his finger. "I'll always need you."

His eyes softened. He bent down and captured my mouth with his own.

Chapter 19

Contraband

Dex:

The party was at some rich guy's house. Bob Rogers. His parents were out of town on some expensive vacation and he'd taken advantage of the situation to throw a monster bash.

I parked the Barracuda a block away so I wouldn't get hemmed in by other cars. Plus I didn't trust the kind of people who would get invites to a party like this. They might think it was funny to fuck up Morgan's ride. Not when they were sober. Nobody sober would be so stupid, but after they'd gotten some booze in them, who knew what they'd decide to do.

I shouldn't have brought Cass along to this job. She didn't belong in a place like this, especially not when I was making a delivery. If anything went wrong, she could get mixed up in it and that would bring serious trouble down on her head.

What the fuck had I been thinking?

I glanced at her as we trudged up the icy street to Rogers' house. Her grip on my hand tightened as if she was nervous. She had on that cute blue hat with the goofy pompom on top. It made her look so innocent I wanted to turn right around and have her wait in the car. Or maybe just ditch this job altogether.

There was a lot of money in it, though, and I couldn't really afford to boge.

"Are you sure it's okay if we go in?" she said, eyeing the lit-up house.

It was one of those enormous, white things with the skinny columns in front that don't look like they really belong with the house because they're so insubstantial. Little shutters flanked the windows. They looked too small for the glass. I wasn't sure if the place was supposed to be a Colonial or some kind of antebellum, *Gone With The Wind* thing. Either way, I knew I didn't belong here and neither did she.

"It'll be okay," I said, squeezing her hand reassuringly. "They know I'm coming and you're with me."

"Okay," she said, but she still sounded worried.

"You don't have to go in if you don't want to," I said. "I don't mind if you wait in the car."

Cass glanced back over her shoulder at the Barracuda. "Um...no, I think I'd rather go in. It's really cold out here."

"I'd give you the key," I said, smiling at her silliness. "I would never make you wait in the cold."

"You would? I mean you wouldn't?"

"Of course not. Do you want to wait in the car?"

She gazed up at the house. We'd reached the end of the long, curved driveway. Brutally loud music thumped away from inside. It was so loud the distortion made it impossible to tell what they were playing. All I could hear was bass. A lot of bass.

"No," Cass said. "I might never get another opportunity to see the inside of one of *their* houses. One of their parties."

"They?" I said.

"You know. The popular kids." She shot me a sidelong glance. "I'll go in."

"Okay." I bent and planted a quick kiss on her cold cheek. "But I don't know what you're talking about when you say popular. You're just as popular as they are."

She made a scoffing sound. "No I'm not. Bob Rogers is on practically every committee in school and the track team. Everyone knows him. Nobody knows me."

"Just because everyone knows a person doesn't mean they like him," I said. "Anyway, if they don't know you then it's their loss."

She gave me such a sweet look that my heart turned over in my chest. "Thanks, Dex."

"It's just the truth," I said roughly.

This thing between us was so huge, had so much force that it brought words out of me that I never would have spoken to anyone else. I'd never even thought them about another person. Sometimes I felt like I was becoming someone completely new, someone I hardly recognized as myself.

We reached the front door. Just as I went to open it, someone threw it open from inside and a couple of guys came tumbling out, laughing drunkenly. They gave us odd sidelong looks and then burst into more laughter.

Whatever.

I drew Cass into the house. Inside, it was hot from all the bodies packed in the place. People were everywhere—crammed elbow to elbow in the living room, the dining room, the kitchen, even on the staircase. The place reeked of booze and pot smoke, sweat and perfume and aftershave. A few of the couples were already locked together, so hot and heavy they might be about to get it on in front of all their friends.

The music turned out to be "White Room" by Cream. At least the guy had good taste in music. People crammed every last nook and cranny of the place. Clearly not all of them could be close friends of Rogers', but most of them that I saw had at least tenuous connections to the so-called popular crowd. Jocks, honors students, student government officers, cheerleaders as far as the eye could see.

I shut the door behind us. "You want to take off your coat?"

"I'll keep it with me," Cass said, eyeing the crowd.

"Probably a good idea. I've gotta find Rogers and then we can go."

She stood next to me in the entryway and scanned the combined living and dining room. The place looked like it had been decorated yesterday. I mean it had the most up-to-date and trendy everything that I'd ever seen. As a guy, I'm not really into all that decorating crap the girls love, but even I could see this was expensive and fashionable.

Everything was in the latest earth tones—brown, rust, gold, and that yellowy green that seemed to be everywhere lately. A big, brass chandelier with globe-shaped lights hung over the modern style dining room table. The carpet was gold and green shag.

The living room was done in the same style. It was like they'd thrown out everything they already had and bought all new. Who did that? Rich people, that's who.

"I don't see him," Cass said.

"Me neither. We'll have to go looking."

She straightened her shoulders like she expected a fight from the people already here. I couldn't see anyone trying to kick her out, even if she hadn't been invited. First, she wasn't hated as much as she thought. Second, she was a girl. Girls are always welcome at a guy's party. As for me, I would never have gotten through the door if I hadn't been packing contraband.

I was the supplier of the pot, and therefore welcome. Real flattering.

Cass didn't seem to know any of those things.

"Come on," I said. "Stick with me."

We got some funny looks as we wandered through the joint, but nobody tried to throw us out, due to the aforementioned contraband.

Or maybe it was my reputation as a badass. Yeah, that might have been it.

Most of the partiers seemed to have paper cups of beer in their hands. I wondered if Cass would like a drink. Had she ever even tasted beer? Probably not.

I bent close to her ear. "You want something?"

"No, thanks. Let's just get this over with."

"Okay." That I could do.

150

Rogers wasn't in the living room or the dining room. We went into the kitchen, where a couple was up against the counter, their embrace so erotic I half expected them to start undressing each other in front of us. The host wasn't in the room, though.

The other people in the kitchen gave us more funny looks. One of them, a hockey jock if I remembered right, detached himself from the group and swaggered over to us with a scowl on his face. He wore a long-sleeved sweater with a pointed collar and horizontal stripes, something that could almost have been the on-the-street uniform of the jock crowd.

"You couldn't have been invited," he said belligerently. "What are you doing here?"

"Looking for Rogers." I slung an arm around Cass's shoulders.

"Why?"

"I'm not discussing that with you," I said. "I want to talk to Rogers. Where is he?"

The jock glanced over at his friends. "Should I throw him out? She can stay, though."

"Nah," said one of the others, a black-haired guy I didn't know. "He's probably making a delivery for Bob."

"You know where he is?" I said.

The black-haired guy inclined his head upward, indicating the second story. "Upstairs. Probably one of the bedrooms."

"Thanks." I turned to go.

Hockey Jock clapped a hand over my shoulder. "She stays here."

"No."

"Yeah, man. The girl stays down here. I want to talk to her."

I glanced down at Cass. She was staring at the guy all wide-eyed and flushed. I couldn't tell if it was fear or some other emotion driving her expression. I only knew I didn't want to leave her alone with these guys.

"She goes with me or no deal," I said.

"Come on, Paul," said the second jock, the black-haired one. "Let her go."

"Why? She came to our party and I want to get to know her." His breath gusted over us, stinking of beer.

"You know my reputation," I said quietly. "You don't want to mess with me."

He sneered. "You're a little outnumbered at the moment, Morgan. Unless you got a gun, there's not much you can do."

"Jesus, Paul, just drop it," the second jock said.

"Nuh uh." He leered down at Cass. "What about it, babe? You want to talk to me?" He gave me a hard look. "I won't let you upstairs with her, so get that tough-guy stare off your face."

"I'll stay," she said.

"Cass—"

"Nothing will happen. He wouldn't dare. There are too many witnesses."

I wasn't so sure. These people tended to stick together, especially against an outsider like Cass. If something were to go wrong, I had no confidence that anyone would defend her.

"I don't want to hurt her, man," Paul said. "I just want to talk."

I pointed a finger at the middle of his chest. "If anything bad happens to her, I will blame you. Maybe I can't do anything about it now, but there's always later. I'll hunt you down and make you wish you were never born if anything happens to her. You got me?"

"Sure, man." He laughed.

I fixed his friends with a stare. "That goes for the rest of you. If anything happens to Cass, I will blame everyone in this room. You better protect her or I'm coming after you."

They exchanged uneasy glances. The second guy, who seemed to be the spokesman for the group, cleared his throat.

"We won't let anything bad happen to her," he said. "Right, guys?"

Everyone nodded. Even Hockey Jock.

"All right," I said, my jaw tense. "Make sure it doesn't."

Letting go of her was one of the hardest things I've ever done. My arm slipped from her shoulders as my stomach churned with anxiety. She gave me a tight smile and went on her toes to kiss me on the cheek.

"Don't be long," she said.

"I'll be back before you know it." I followed this statement with another warning stare at the guys. "Call if you need me."

"I will."

The sick feeling refused to leave my belly as I pushed through the crowd on the stairs and into the upstairs hallway. It was just as fashionable up here, although the shag had stayed downstairs. They had some kind of all-one-color patterned thing going on in the carpet up here, and the overhead lights were all real lamps, made of brass, not those ugly square glass pieces of junk we had at our house.

The first bedroom I came to was occupied by two girls. Both of them wore halter tops and wide-leg jeans and had perfect, fake-looking curls in their hair. One of them sat on a frilly pink bed crying and the other had her arm around her friend. They didn't seem to notice me as I peered around the door, so I shut it softly and tried the next room.

The walls in this one were painted dark brown, almost as dark as black coffee. Shelves full of music albums and hi-fi stereo equipment took up one whole wall. The wall next to it had some kind of fancy desk set-up, and next to that was the bed and fuck me if it wasn't a king-size waterbed with a black leather headboard.

A light dangled over the bed. It looked like a glowing white globe that had gotten partially squashed.

Bob Rogers stood in the middle of the room, his arm around Tracy Carpenter's shoulders. His other hand clutched a rock album as he leaned in really close in order to point out something important in the art work. What he was really doing was looking down her ruffly white blouse.

I stifled a grin. The guy was smooth. At least he thought he was.

He looked up at me with a testy frown. Then he realized who I was and the frown disappeared.

"Hey, Morgan," he said. "You got my stuff?"

"Yep. You wanna take care of it now, or wait until later?" Of course, later wouldn't work for me. Cass was waiting downstairs.

Rogers glanced at the girl next to him. She was staring at me like I was a snake who might sink my poisonous fangs into her precious ankle. I grinned at her, showing off the fangs.

I remembered the way she'd picked on Cass in school. She was cute, but she couldn't hold a candle to my girl, and it really hacked me off when I thought about the way she'd treated her.

Tracy's face turned red when I grinned at her. She dropped her gaze to the floor.

"Baby, can you give us a few minutes?" Rogers said.

"Sure." She gave me another hurried glance. "Um...I'll see you soon?"

"Yeah. Real soon. I'll come and get you," he said.

Tracy walked toward me. I was standing right in the doorway, so she didn't have a way out of the room without going really close to me. A nasty impulse took hold of me to give her a hard time.

She looked more and more nervous the closer she got to me. I guess she didn't want to come close enough to get around me and out the door, since she'd probably have to touch me to do it. And I wasn't moving.

Right in front of me, she stopped and lifted her chin. "Excuse me," she said in a snippy voice.

"For what?" I said.

"Um...excuse me?" She gestured impatiently at the door behind me.

"Oh! Am I in your way?" I said with exaggerated innocence.

She turned red again. She really was pretty. I might have even been turned on by the exchange if it hadn't been for my girl. Cass was the only one I wanted, and besides, Tracy had been a bitch to her. That was practically unforgivable in my book.

"Yes," Tracy said. "You're in my way, as I'm sure you know. Now can you please move?"

"Since you ask so nicely." I stepped aside, grinning at her again as she flounced past me.

She slammed the door on her way out. I laughed.

"You shouldn't mess with Tracy like that," Rogers said.

"Why not?"

He looked at me like I was stupid. "She has a lot of power at school."

I laughed and shook my head. "Like I care. Plus she was mean to Cass. You want me to be nice to Tracy, tell her to back off Cass. Otherwise it's a no-go."

He looked surprised. "Oh, yeah, that's right. You're with Cass Maslanka now. I thought nobody would ever get in that girl's pants." He leered. "Is she an ice princess in bed? I'll bet she's really hot."

"Shut the fuck up," I growled, striding over to get in his face, trembling in rage. "I don't want to ever hear you talking like that about her again."

"Holy shit, man, take it easy." Rogers threw up his hands. "I was only kidding."

"Well, don't." My hands were in fists I couldn't seem to relax. "There's too many guys around here trying to get with her. She's with me, so don't kid around about that shit."

"Okay," he said. "I won't."

He looked pale. I'd scared him. Good.

I clapped him on the shoulder. "It's okay as long as you don't do it again. I don't like it when people treat my girl badly."

He nodded with a shaky smile. "I understand."

"You wanna take care of that buy now?" I said. All I wanted was to get the business done so I could haul ass out of this place. If I hadn't needed the money, I would have just split and they could deal with the loss of their deal.

"Sure," Rogers said, still visibly shaky. "Sure. Let me get my cash."

I stuck my hands in my pockets while Rogers dug in his back pocket for his wallet. My hands still didn't want to release their tension. I'd never fought over a girl before Cass came along, had never known what it meant to be jealous or protective. It freaked me out a little, but it was all good because it was Cass and I loved her.

Yet here I was, dealing drugs. And not just dealing, but selling to these assholes who thought they were better than her. The thing is, if they thought it would save their asses, none of them would hesitate to turn me in to the cops. And then where would we be?

I'd be stuck in McLaughlin again, unable to stand up for Cass, and she'd have to deal with these people on her own. Not to mention the fact that just the thought of being without her for so long made me feel like I was dying inside. I didn't know if I could make it without her.

The drug selling had to stop. It was too risky. And what if I did get caught and Cass somehow got dragged into it? She might end up in juvenile detention too. The thought of my sweet girl getting shoved in with all the hard cases made me sick to my stomach.

This deal was going to be the last of my current stash, except for a tiny amount I had on hand for personal use. I watched Rogers hand over a wad of cash and knew it was the last exchange I would ever make.

"It's all there," he said with another smile.

"I'm sure it is." I counted it anyway, just to be absolutely certain. Only when I confirmed the amount did I bring out the baggie and pass it to him. "Enjoy."

"Thanks, man. And I apologize for Tracy. She shouldn't treat Cass that way."

"Thank you for saying that. By the way, if you need more Maryjane, you'll have to get it from someone else. I'm out of the business."

His eyebrows practically climbed off his head. "What?"

"This is my last deal. I'm going straight. Feel free to pass the word along."

Chapter 20

Party Hearty

Cass:

The Rogers kitchen had brown wood cabinets with no handles on them, and orange laminate counters. It wasn't quite a Halloween jack-o'-lantern orange, but an almost-rust color. A row of lamps that looked kind of like copper box graters hung over the breakfast bar. The vinyl floor was some kind of Spanish-looking pattern in green, and there were green and orange cafe curtains on the windows.

Two shiny metal containers that looked like beer kegs sat on the counter. Wait, those were beer kegs. I'd never actually seen one before, since I'd only heard the term kegger at school. I'd never attended one.

It was a big kitchen, with a gigantic island right in the middle of it. The island was where they had their stove, and where the kegs sat. Our kitchen at home was too small to have an island. In fact, you could probably have fit the entire room on the top of the island in the Rogers kitchen.

The people in the room all watched me like I was an animal in the zoo. Like they were waiting to see how I'd behave. Maybe they were wondering if I'd throw poop at them. Monkeys throw poop.

That ridiculous thought didn't even make me crack a smile. There was too much tension in the air.

Paul still loomed over me, leering, taking me in with slow sweeps of his gaze, up and down. Then up and down again. And again. He took a step closer to me and picked up a lock of my hair. His dark blond lashes lowered as his face took on a smoky expression. He had almost the exact coloring as Dex, yet he did absolutely nothing for me.

I stepped back. "Don't touch me."

"Aw, come on," he said. "I'm not hurting you."

"I don't want to be touched."

"If she doesn't want to be touched, then don't touch her," said one of the others.

Paul snorted. "You afraid of Morgan?"

"Hell, yes. There's no way I want to get on that cat's shit list."

"I've seen you around," Paul said, making no attempt to touch me again.

"I go to West." I glanced at the other guys in the room.

I recognized all of them. They were in many of my classes, the advanced placement ones. The one who'd sort of stuck up for me was Josh Campbell. Next to him were Steve O'Hara, Ben Gibson, and the twins Rob and Rick Atherton. The only other girl was Debbie Wolston, who'd been wrapped around Ben when we'd come into the room.

Now she stood with her back against the counter, biting her lip. When I tried to catch her gaze, she looked away. She wouldn't be any help if things went bad.

I'd never thought of any of these guys as bad kids. They'd always been relatively polite to me in school, just guarded and distant. Not interested in me, as far as I could tell. Now, though, the way Paul kept trying to look down my shirt...

"You're in my English class," he said.

"She sits by me," Steve told him. "Right, Cass?"

"Yeah," I said. "Right."

"How come you never come to our parties?" Paul said.

"No-one ever invited me." I wiped my hands on my thighs and glanced at Debbie again. She still wouldn't look at me.

"I'm inviting you," Paul said. "You can come to any of our things. Right, guys?"

"Sure," Steve said.

"Of course," Ben and Josh said simultaneously.

The twins, Rob and Rick, exchanged a glance and shrugged in unison.

"Why not," Rick said. "I don't mind."

"Tracy won't like it," Debbie said.

"So?" Rick gave her a scornful look. "She doesn't get to decide who we invite."

"What won't I like?" Tracy said.

I turned unhappily. The queen of West High stood in the kitchen doorway, glancing expectantly from one face to another. She wore a white blouse with a low-cut V neckline surrounded by ruffles. Her jeans were the tightest I'd ever seen. White platform sandals peeked out from under the hems of her pants. Had she walked through the snow in those things?

"The guys want Cass to come to their parties," Debbie explained.

"Is that right?" Tracy put one hand on her hip as she looked me up and down. Her once-over was far more insulting than Paul's. Her mouth stretched slowly in a wicked smile. "Paul seems to like her."

"Yeah," Paul said. He took another step toward me, getting right into my personal space.

"I think she likes you too," Tracy said.

"No," I said.

"She said no." Paul gave Tracy a baffled glance.

"She's just saying that because she wants everyone to think she's a good girl." Her evil smile widened. "She really does like you, Paul. I can tell."

"Paul, Tracy's messing with you," Josh said.

Tracy tossed her head indignantly. "No, I'm not."

"You like me, Cass?" Paul said, bending over me.

I leaned back, my heart starting to pound. "As a friend, sure."

He put his hand in my hair. His whole hand, his fingers delving into the thickness of it as they cupped my skull.

"Paul, buddy, don't do that," Josh said.

"Shut up." He bent lower. His breath smelled like beer.

"Paul," said one of the other guys. "Come on, man. Morgan'll be back any second now."

"Fuck off." Paul wrapped his hand around my upper arm. He mashed his mouth clumsily against mine, reminding me of Kurt Wilson.

I smacked him on the back with my free hand, my coat sliding off my arm to the floor. My blow had no effect. His lips continued to slobber disgustingly over mine.

Someone pulled him away. I blinked up into Ben's scowling face as he and Josh hauled Paul a few feet back. He was struggling against them, his face turning red.

"It was just getting good," he said in a slurred voice.

"What the fuck?" Dex sounded both icy and furious behind me.

"Shit," Ben muttered.

My boyfriend stormed into the room, fists clenched and jaw pulsing. He fixed narrowed eyes on Paul. "What the fuck did you do?"

"I just kissed her, man," Paul said. He looked genuinely confused.

I didn't know whether to hate him or pity him.

His friends let go of him. He swayed slightly. Dex's right fist exploded upward, catching Paul on the jaw. The jock grunted, staggering backward and hitting his butt against the edge of the counter.

He sagged and slid down to the vinyl floor. Tracy and Debbie screamed.

Dex leaped on him, his fist raised for another assault. The other guys just stood there watching. Didn't they care that Dex was going to smash their friend to a pulp?

He pounded another blow to Paul's face. The jock's head slammed sideways, hitting the vinyl, blood spewing from his mouth and splattering into his dirty-blond hair. He'd promised not to hurt me or do anything I didn't like, and he'd begun to break that promise. I shouldn't worry about his safety.

But if Dex really hurt him, Dex would be the one to pay.

I jumped in, grabbing my boyfriend's arm as he raised his fist for another strike. "Dex! Dex, stop it."

He growled like an animal, fighting to lower his arm.

"Come on, baby," I said. "He's not worth it."

He shook me off. He was too strong for me to restrain. That big fist came up again, and slammed down into Paul's face. The kid was going to be nothing but bloody pulp by the time Dex was done with him.

I gave up trying to control his arm. As he prepared to hit Paul again, I threw myself between them, my body landing partly over the jock's head. Dex's fist landed like a sledgehammer on my shoulder. I let out a cry of pain.

He reeled backward, falling off Paul and landing on his butt on the vinyl, his face a mask of horror. "Cass!"

Clutching my injured shoulder, I straightened and came onto my knees. "I'm all right."

"Jesus," Ben said, crouching near me with a look of genuine concern on his handsome face. "What did you do to your girlfriend, Morgan? Cass, are you sure you're all right?"

"Don't touch her," Dex snarled as he righted himself.

Ben drew back as if confronted with a poisonous snake. "Okay. I only wanted to make sure she's okay."

"I'm fine." I gave him a strained smile as I climbed to my feet. "It's Paul you should be worried about. He doesn't look so good."

The jock still lay sprawled out on the floor, his face puffy and bleeding. He was going to have a huge collection of facial bruises. I just hoped Dex hadn't broken anything.

Ben and Josh knelt by their friend. I scooped up my coat and went to Dex as he got to his feet. He favored each and every person in the room with a fierce glare.

"Let's go," I said.

"Call the police!" Tracy said. "Don't let him get away with it!"

"You were egging Paul on," Ben said, shaking his head. "You were half the problem here, so don't tell us what to do."

"But he could have killed him." She cut a glare at Dex, her expression more malicious than fierce.

"It's Paul's decision," Josh said.

"Come on, Tracy." Ben stood up and took her by the arm. "I'll take you home."

"But—"

"Home," he said firmly.

"Yeah." I tucked my arm through Dex's. "Let's go home too."

He was shaking, whether in continued rage or its aftermath I couldn't tell. I tugged on his arm and motioned with my head in the direction of the front door.

Party-goers had gathered curiously around the entrance to the kitchen, some of them spilling over into the room itself. I couldn't read their expressions and had no idea if they sympathized with us or with Paul and Tracy. Honestly, I didn't care. I'd had enough of this crowd to last me the rest of my life.

The crowd parted silently to let us pass. Dex let me urge him through the house.

We reached the front door. I yanked it open and burst out into the cold night, my coat still hanging over my arm. The door banged shut behind us and I breathed a deep lungful of icy air in relief.

"Well," I said. "That was an experience."

"Are you sure you're okay?" He peered down at me as I wriggled into my coat.

"Yeah. I'm fine, really. How did your deal go?"

"It went. I should never have brought you along." He grabbed me without warning and yanked me against his body, his head bending down to mine, his breath hard and fast.

He didn't kiss me. Instead, he held me, his cheek resting on the top of my head, his arms wrapped securely around me. My face pressed into the smooth fabric of his ski jacket.

I put my arms around him. "It's okay, Dex. I'm okay. And I don't think you hurt Paul too badly."

"I put you in danger bringing you here," he muttered against my hair. "What the hell is wrong with me?"

"Nothing is wrong with you."

He rocked me from side to side. My body trembled, too. I'd been more frightened than I realized, and now we were out of danger it was sinking in. We could have gotten in serious trouble in there.

"Never again," he said, still rocking me. "I'll never do that again."

"Do what?"

"I'm quitting the business. No more hardcore parties. No more drugs at all."

"What? Really?" I tipped my head back, peering into his face. He looked utterly serious.

"Really. It's not worth it." He shook his head, shuddering. "Jesus, when I think of what could have happened in there. I shouldn't have left you alone for a second."

"Hey." I reached up and smoothed my bare hand over his cheek. "It's over. Let's not worry about it, okay? Maybe we should go have some coffee and talk for a while before you take me home."

"Yeah. Okay."

"You didn't endanger me," I said as we began the walk down the driveway of Bob's house. "I chose to come."

"That doesn't matter." He shook his head, his hand firmly clasped around mine. "I don't ever want you getting hurt, and especially not because of me."

Chapter 21

Meet The Parents

Dex:

Cass's house had avocado green siding. It wasn't wood siding, like our house had, although there was a fake wood texture. And I do mean fake. Looking at it, I could easily see it wasn't real, but I didn't know what the actual material was. Whatever they were making nice houses out of these days.

It was a split level, one of those things where you walk in on the ground floor and the only thing that's there is a tiny little room that serves as a foyer or entry. From the entry, you either go into the garage, down a flight of steps into the daylight basement, or up a flight to the living room, kitchen, and some of the bedrooms. It seemed like seventy-five percent of the new houses I saw these days had the same design. They all looked pretty much the same, too, just big boxes with big plate glass windows.

Their yard had plants in it, too. I mean other than weedy grass, that is. There was a big birch tree in the middle, which I recognized by its black-speckled white bark, and a smaller spruce on one side, plus some bushes that poked bare branches up through the deep snow. The pattern that they made clearly stated that someone had put them there on purpose, with a plan, in order to make the yard look good. They probably really did run the sprinkler on dry summer days.

I'd been inside Cass's room, obviously, but nowhere else. So I was kinda nervous when she finally wore me down and got me to agree to come to dinner at her place. Meeting a girl's parents. Jesus. That wasn't anything I'd ever even considered before, let alone actually carried through.

She met me at the door with a big smile, the kind that made me stupid and willing to do practically anything for her. She wore her usual narrow-legged jeans and her favorite light blue sweater, which she'd once explained to me was called a Fair-Isle. Her dark hair was drawn back into a simple pony-tail, no make-up or jewelry. Her cheeks were flushed pink and her eyes sparkled.

She was so damned beautiful and she didn't even know it. I mean, she was genuinely without a clue about how pretty and desirable she was.

I think that, and her basic shyness, was the reason some people thought of her as a bitch. She never tried to work her looks and she was wary of everyone. People interpreted that as bitchiness, when in reality Cass was the least bitchy girl I'd ever known.

"You came!" she said, sounding a little breathless.

"Yeah. I said I would."

"Come in, come in." She was almost bouncing on her toes.

I grinned at her cuteness. "Excited?"

"Yes. I've been hoping for this for a while."

I knew that, which is why I didn't let her in on the fact that I wasn't so enthusiastic about the dinner. The last thing I wanted to do was bring Cass down, but I had no real hopes that her parents would think I was anything but a thug. A low-life. I'd seen it before with Leon's mom, who tended to blame me for anything bad that happened with her kid. There was no reason to think the Maslanka family would be any different.

The foyer had an enormous lantern hanging from the two-story ceiling. It was made of amber glass and had kind of a Spanish style to it, with dark metal accents. That one fixture was nicer than anything in my house and probably nicer and more expensive than our whole property.

She took my coat—the one she'd given me—and hung it in the entryway closet. I shucked off my sneakers. I'd left the biker boots at home, thinking they'd only underscore what an inappropriate boyfriend I was for their daughter.

Their carpet was new, green like the outside of the house, and had a flowy pattern carved into the pile. When Cass showed me up the stairs, they didn't give a single creak. And the air was just as warm as it always was in her bedroom.

The place smelled really good, like something savory, with onions in it, maybe. And I thought I detected fresh bread. Had her mom actually baked bread? Real bread? Who did that these days?

The stairwell was drywalled, so I couldn't see into the living room until we got all the way up to the top. It was a big room, probably as big as our living room and dining room combined, with maybe some spare space left over. A fireplace surrounded by a wall of fake rock bounded one side of the room. On the opposite wall was a gallery of real paintings, not posters, the kind on canvases with actual oil paint. I'd never seen anything like that in a person's house before. The closest I'd ever come was this one girl who had a painting of Elvis done on black velvet, hanging in her dining room.

They had two huge picture windows that looked out on the darkness of a late Anchorage afternoon. At least three lamps burned, making the room glow brightly and showing off their new-looking furniture—a huge sectional couch in a dark orange, and several easy chairs plus a coffee table that looked like it was supposed to be some Colonial-era antique.

A man who looked a lot like Cass sat in one of the easy chairs, glaring at me. He wore an Oxford shirt, no tie, and casual pants, and had the same dark brown hair and blue eyes that she did. Plus there was something about the shape of his nose that reminded me of her. I met his gaze as squarely as I could.

"Dad, this is Dex," Cass said, still smiling happily. "Dex, this is my dad, Pete Maslanka."

I extended a hand to the man, pretending I didn't notice his expression. "I'm glad to meet you, sir."

No-one I knew talked that way. I'd lifted the line off some TV show where people were polite and acted like they respected each other even when they didn't.

Mr. Maslanka stood up and took my offered hand, giving it a brief, hard shake. "Dex."

"I invited him to dinner," Cass said.

Her dad gave her a dry look. "Yes. That's the fifth time you've said so this evening."

"Oh." She flushed and looked at her stocking-clad feet.

"Thank you for inviting me," I said, mostly because I didn't know what else to say.

Maslanka turned a withering look on me. "I hear you've been seeing my daughter."

"Yes," I said.

"I hope you've been treating her right."

"Of course he has, Dad! Jeez!"

"I'm doing my best to treat her like a queen," I said truthfully.

She grinned again and caught my hand. I could tell by the way he was giving me the hairy eyeball that her dad didn't like us holding hands one bit. If he knew all the other stuff we'd done together, he'd probably haul out the shotgun and fill me full of holes. I let her keep my hand, though, because pulling away would make the situation even worse.

"Your mother has the food on the table already," Mr. Maslanka said, his tone faintly reproving. "So let's go eat."

"I'm sorry I'm a bit late," I said, hoping to smooth things over. "I had a little trouble getting away from work."

"And where is that?" he said as we walked toward the dining room, which was just a nook off the living room.

"Carrs grocery," I said. "I'm bagging."

"I see. I was under the impression you didn't have a real job."

"What would give you that impression?" Cass said. "I never told you that."

Her dad didn't answer. Instead he gestured toward the dining room table and the woman standing next to it. "Lucille, this is Dex Morgan, Cass's boyfriend."

I didn't like the way he emphasized the word boyfriend. It seemed ominous, almost as if he considered it a dirty word. It seemed impossible that Cass could be oblivious to the tension in the room, so I could only interpret her continuing smiles as her attempt to get her parents on our side.

Her mother looked even more like her, although the eyes were a different color. Lucille's were brown. Yet the arrangement of their facial features was nearly identical. Looking at Lucille was like looking at an older Cass but with brown eyes instead of blue. Cass was going to still be a beauty when she got older, if her mom was anyone to go by.

Lucille Maslanka gave me a wary smile. "It's nice to meet you, Dex."

"Thank you for inviting me."

"Oh, you're very welcome. Let's sit. I put you next to Cass."

Adam and a younger girl who also looked very much like Cass bolted into the room, both of them laughing. They pulled up short, their laughter dying as they saw me. Adam drew himself up and glared at me, while the girl merely looked bewildered.

"What are you doing here, Morgan?" Adam said.

"He's staying for dinner," Cass retorted. "Dex, you've met Adam and this is my little sister, Beth."

Beth gave me a shy smile. "Hi, Dex."

"Hi, Beth. It's nice to meet you." Boy, I was using up all my good manners tonight. I hadn't even realized how polite I could be until this moment.

"Same here," she said in a whispery voice.

She seemed even shyer than Cass, which was saying something.

Her blue eyes, just like Cass's, traveled over me, assessing, as her blush deepened. Then she looked away and bit her lip. She was pretty in a cute, junior-high, way-too-young sense, and I liked her because she seemed the least hostile to me out of all the Maslankas.

Cass pulled out her seat, so I took the one next to her. In the center of the table was a huge platter covered in what looked like pot roast, accompanied by onions, carrots, potatoes, and celery. Next to it was another platter, this one with fresh bread.

"You baked," Cass said, looking at her mom.

"Yes, I did. I used that sourdough starter Jenny's mom gave me for Christmas."

"My mouth has been watering all afternoon," Beth said with a shy glance in my direction.

"Grace before food, kids," Mr. Maslanka said. "Beth, will you do the honors?"

Everyone except me put their hands together and bent their heads. I'd seen this once before, at Leon's house when I'd had a Sunday dinner with them. But that was the only time. I had no idea how to say grace, didn't know any prayers, and my stomach sank. They were going to know I didn't know how to participate, and judge me because of it.

I wanted to do this right, so Cass's parents would like me, or at least not hate me. I hated having to prove myself. It pissed me off, made me feel helpless, like I'd turned back into a kid and was at my own dad's mercy. But if I wanted to be with Cass, I had to do this. And I wanted to be with Cass.

"Bless us, oh Lord, and these thy gifts," Beth murmured. "Which we are about to receive through the bounty of Christ our Lord. Amen."

Everyone else murmured Amen with her, so I did it too. I'm pretty sure that was the only time I ever uttered that word.

I wasn't sure whether or not I believed in God. I mean, look at my life. If there's a God who looks out for us and loves us, how do you explain families like mine? It sure felt more like God, if He did exist, didn't give a shit about us. Maybe He was off somewhere having a good time while we squirmed around down here on Earth and wondered why we'd been abandoned.

"Now. Let's eat," Mr. Maslanka said.

They passed the platters around and everyone took whatever they wanted. That was another thing we never did at home. Come to think of it, we never really ate together at home anymore. The last meal I could remember having as a family had been the one interrupted by the Good Friday earthquake in 1964. That meal hadn't ended well, and since then we'd just gone our own ways.

Sin used to get sandwiches or canned soup together for me and Joe. Now I did the same for the two of us, and let my parents and Sin fend for themselves. Most of the time, they seemed to subsist on potato chips, pre-sliced cheese, and TV dinners. Maybe they didn't need calories, with all the alcohol they drank.

I loaded up my plate when the platters came to me. Adam was telling some story about his PE class and how his friend had tripped over his unlaced shoes and bloodied his own lip. While they were distracted, I took an appreciative bite of pot roast.

Damn. That was some of the best food I'd ever tasted. It could have come from a restaurant.

"So, Dex, what does your father do?" Mr. Maslanka said.

I paused in my chewing. "He works for the Last Frontier Bank down on Sixth."

"I see. What does he do there?"

"He's some kind of manager. I'm not sure." I never talked to my dad unless it was absolutely necessary.

"And your mom?" he said.

"She stays at home."

Mrs. Maslanka smiled. "She must be missing you tonight."

I carefully kept my face straight. "I'm sure."

Cass glanced sideways at me. "How's Joe?"

"He's good. He still wants to marry you."

"He what?" Lucille Maslanka said.

"My little brother Joe has a crush on Cass. He's only ten."

"Oh, how sweet." Her mom smiled indulgently.

She wouldn't think there was anything sweet about my family if she ever came to our house and saw how we lived. This, sitting down with the whole family and having a peaceful meal together, was an alien event for me. I felt like I'd been tossed into a foreign country or something. Sure, I spoke the language, but all the customs seemed completely different from what I was used to.

I didn't belong here. Her parents could see it, especially her dad. Adam could see it, too. He kept shooting me glares when he thought Cass wasn't looking.

I didn't even know how to say grace, for Pete's sake. I swore like a fucking sailor, and I had more sexual experience than a lot of sailors too. I was a former drug dealer.

What the fuck had made me think I could stroll into Cass's life and sit down at her dining room table with her family?

I should leave. I should end this farce, say thanks but no thanks, and get the hell out of here. Go somewhere I did belong, where people made sense to me and I made sense to them.

Cass reached under the table and clasped my hand, holding it against her thigh. The sweetness of her touch tethered me, anchored me against the wild urge to go tearing off to someplace where people didn't say grace or try to protect their kids—or give any kind of damn, for that matter. Her hold, her touch, anchored me to the Earth.

I wasn't sure if that touch would save me or condemn me even more deeply.

"There is something that concerns me," Pete Maslanka said with a significant look at me.

"What's that, sir?"

"I asked around about you."

My stomach sank even lower and my appetite disappeared. "Oh?"

"I heard some unpleasant rumors about you, Dex. That you deal drugs, at school and other places as well. Is any of that true?"

167

He stared at me intently. Mrs. Maslanka stared, too, with an assessing air that let me know she wasn't just waiting to hear what I'd say. She wanted to observe how I said it, try to suss out whether or not I was lying.

I took a deep breath. "I used to, but I straightened out."

"So you admit to selling drugs?" Mr. Maslanka's dark brows descended over hard, cold eyes.

"Yeah. But like I said, I'm done with that. It's over. I have a real job now."

"Why would you do something like that?" Mrs. Maslanka said. "Are you an addict?"

"No, ma'am, I'm not. I needed money and nobody wanted to hire me." Jesus. Now the stint at McLaughlin was going to come out.

"Why is that?" Cass's dad said.

"Because I was in juvenile detention," I said, trying to disguise the weariness in my tone, pretending to a nonchalance I didn't feel.

Pete Maslanka shook his head. "I have to tell you that doesn't sound too good."

"I'm aware of that, believe me," I said. "And I'm doing everything I can to overcome my mistakes."

That included quitting the drug dealing, even if it crippled me money-wise. The problem was I suspected it was too late for me, at least where Cass's family was concerned.

* * *

"So, what did you think?" Cass said brightly when we were finally alone together in her room.

Her bedroom was the girliest room I'd ever seen, pink walls and everything. She was embarrassed by it, seemed to think I ought to hate it, but I liked it because it belonged to her. It was her private place and she allowed me into it, and that was all I needed to know in order to love it. Besides, there weren't any pictures of other guys stuck to the wall, like I'd seen in so many other girls' bedrooms. I was the only guy in her life and that was how I wanted things.

I'd changed so much since meeting her that sometimes I hardly recognized myself.

"You have a great family," I said. Of course, they had no idea we were down here alone together. I'd climbed through her window as usual.

"I think they like you." She flopped onto her bed beside me, which left no part of the bed unoccupied. I slung my arm around her to keep her from falling to the floor.

"Baby, they don't like me." I bent my head and kissed her right between her beautiful eyebrows. "They just put up with me for your sake."

Her mouth turned down. "Is that really how you feel?"

"It's what I know. I could tell by the way they were looking at me, not to mention the way they grilled me over my past."

Her shoulders slumped and her mouth turned down a little more. "I hoped they would be open to me having a boyfriend."

"I don't think it's the boyfriend part that's the problem. It's me."

Her lips pinched together. "Well, I don't care if they like you or not. I love you and that's what matters."

I gave her a half-hearted smile and brushed a lock of hair come loose from her ponytail out of her eyes. "At least your dad didn't meet me at the door with a shotgun."

She laughed. "True. That would have been awkward. He actually has one of those, you know."

"It's probably not safe for me to be here with you right now. They'll be extra suspicious after seeing us together at dinner."

She pouted. "I hate having to sneak around."

"Someday we'll be able to be together openly," I said, even though I had no idea if it was really true.

"I hope so."

"At least we have school." For reasons that escaped me completely, she let me hold her hand and put my arms around her at school. She didn't seem to notice the odd looks we got from her honors class schoolmates, or maybe she simply didn't care.

"Yeah," she said wistfully. "At least we have that."

***

Dex:

Cass's birthday party looked almost like it was intended for a much younger girl. Her mom had blown up pink and red balloons to dangle from the dining room chandelier and hung matching crepe paper streamers all over the place. On the dining room table, they had a giant cake with pink frosting and "Happy Birthday, Cass!" written on in red icing.

Not a can of beer or a cigarette in sight. No kissing, groping, or dirty jokes either.

The music playing on the stereo was some kind of sugary sixties pop. I wasn't sure of the band; it wasn't my or Sin's kind of music. A small group of teens clustered in the living room around a game of Monopoly laid out on the floor. Jenny June was there, and a couple of guys I recognized from biology, plus Beth Maslanka and of course Cass. It couldn't have been a sharper contrast with the party we'd crashed the other night at the Rogers house.

Cass looked up and saw me. A huge grin lit up her face. She jumped to her feet and scampered over to me and I almost forgot where I was and grabbed her. She was so damn cute I wanted to kiss her.

Her mom was standing right next to me, though, so I couldn't.

"Dex!" Cass said. "You came."

"Of course I did."

She grabbed my hands. "Do you play Monopoly?"

"Not really."

Her smile disappeared. "Oh."

"It's okay. I can follow along," I said, although I had no idea what I was getting myself into.

We didn't play board games in my family. In fact, none of my other friends played board games. We drank, smoked, and screwed.

She was wearing a frilly dress that reminded me a little of Tracy What's-her-name from the party. It was pale blue and had ruffles at the neckline, but it wasn't low-cut like Tracy's blouse. It was sweet, just like the party decorations.

My hard-bitten side, the one who'd stopped believing in sweetness or innocent fun when I was twelve years old, wanted to roll my eyes and make a wisecrack about the lame little-kid style of the party. Not that I'd ever been such an asshole that I'd actually say that out loud. It was only because the instant I'd set foot in her living room I'd felt like I was marked as different. Wrong.

Putting me in this room with these people was almost like sending a hit-man into a lady's tea party. I didn't belong here. But I was going to try to fit in anyway.

"Guys, this is Dex," Cass said, dragging me over to the group. "This is Dave and Bill." She gestured at the two boys, who looked up at me with suspicion in their eyes. "And you know Jenny and my sister Beth."

I raised my free hand. "Hi."

"Hi, Dex," Beth said. "Do you play Monopoly?"

"I'm learning," I said.

Beth seemed like a genuinely nice girl. A good person. She wasn't so afraid of me anymore, and I liked that. Jenny even smiled at me as I sat down next to Cass.

The boys, though, looked like they wanted to murder me. Maybe they wanted Cass for themselves.

It would be a lot more natural for her to date someone like them than someone like me. These guys probably lived in houses just like hers, or maybe like Leon's. Nice, normal places where people ate hot food for dinner every night. Where parents cared how late their kids stayed out at night. I'd bet neither of them had a criminal record.

"You're in biology with us, aren't you?" one of the boys said as he moved a small metal piece across the game board.

"Yeah," I said.

"Is that how you met Cass?"

"Not exactly," I said. What was he getting at?

"He stood up for me." Cass grabbed a pair of dice and shook them. "Some kid was picking on me on the bus and Dex stepped in."

"Who was it?" the boy said.

"Leon Schmidt." She smiled at me and tossed her dice. "Ooh, I got a twelve." She picked up the hat and moved it twelve spaces around the board to land on something called Reading Railroad.

"Leon Schmidt?" the boy echoed. "He was making fun of Mary Agibinik the other day."

Cass shook her head. "I think there's something wrong with him."

"He doesn't mean to be like that," I said. "He's just an idiot with girls. If he likes one, he'll be mean to her."

Cass wrinkled her nose. "Why? It doesn't make any sense."

"I agree," I said. "I don't know why he does it. I doubt he does, either."

Her nose wrinkled even more. "So are you saying he likes me?"

Shit. I should have kept my mouth shut. "He thinks you're cute," I said uncomfortably.

She shook her head with a small laugh. "Wow. I never would have guessed that."

"You are cute," I said.

Her gaze slid back to me and her smile broadened. She reached for my hand and we laced our fingers together. The others saw it. My neck began to burn and when I glanced at Cass I saw color in her face too. We kept holding hands, though.

I started rubbing my thumb across the back of her hand. I couldn't help myself. Her skin was so soft and smooth and I loved touching her. I did it every chance I got, even when the only part of her I could caress was her hand.

I glanced up and noticed her mom standing in the doorway between the kitchen and living room. She was watching us. I could tell by the set of her mouth that she didn't like seeing me holding hands with Cass, and I wondered if she'd noticed me stroking her daughter. I flushed, but I didn't let Cass go.

"I think that's enough Monopoly," Cass suddenly announced.

"But we don't have a winner yet," Jenny said.

"So? I want to eat."

I shot her a look. Had she seen her mom watching us together? She seemed happy, though, and she kept her hand in mine, so maybe not.

"I'm hungry," she said. "And it's my birthday, so let's get some food."

"You just want to eat because I was winning," Jenny said jokingly.

"You were not," Cass retorted.

"Yes, I was."

"Were not."

"I was too," Jenny said, and stuck out her tongue.

Beth rolled her eyes. "Good grief. You two act like a couple of second graders."

Jenny laughed. "That's the point."

They didn't care about being cool. That was what struck me. At least here, in Cass's home, it didn't matter to them, even though I was here and two other boys.

I'd never really known anyone my own age who didn't have a constant and abiding interest in being seen as cool. They weren't like that because they didn't know any better. Cass and I had talked about it, so I knew she was well aware of her uncool reputation. She and Jenny simply didn't care enough. They were more interested in having fun.

At one time, I would have viewed that choice with some contempt. But now I saw it as brave. They were smart girls. They knew there were repercussions to disregarding the social rules and they did it anyway. That took some courage.

Just like me getting a job bagging groceries, I thought wryly. In my circle, that took courage, because it wasn't cool. Not nearly as cool as dealing had been. My reputation had taken a major hit when word had gotten around that I was a normal wage earner now.

Chapter 22

All The Way

Cass:

The shadows in my room made Dex's hair dark, almost brown looking in some places, but where the light caught it the color turned to shining gold. I had only my bedside lamp burning. I'd drawn the drapes so no-one could see inside. We were enclosed in my quiet bedroom.

My parents and siblings were upstairs watching TV. They thought I was studying. Instead I had my arms wrapped around my boyfriend, deep in a kiss.

His kisses never got old. If anything, they got more arousing, more exciting every time we touched, and Dex seemed to take as much pleasure in them as I did. Besides, his mouth was full and lush, made for kissing.

Not that I had any real experience kissing other guys, but I'd given it some thought. The ones with thin lips just didn't look as enticing.

Or maybe it was all in his technique. He spent plenty of time teasing, brushing his lips over mine, licking me, nipping. He was never in a hurry to stick his tongue down my throat the way Kurt Wilson had tried to do.

The scent of his body made me ache with desire. I wanted his hands on me pronto. I wanted to taste him and stroke my hands all over his hot, smooth skin.

We'd done a lot of heavy petting since that first time. In the last few days, I'd started to wonder what it would be like to go all the way.

He urged me down to the floor, to the blanket I'd spread out for us. I put my hands under his shirt and caressed him over his hard back and along his narrow waist. My touch seemed to enflame him.

He clasped the back of my head, his kiss turning hungry and demanding. I moaned, trembling in excitement. His hands roamed down my back to my butt and squeezed.

Soon, our clothes lay in crumpled heaps all around us. He had the most beautiful body, long and lean but muscular for a sixteen-year-old. I stroked his chest and leaned in to kiss him right on the space between his collar-bones.

"I've been thinking," I said. "I'd like to go all the way."

His gaze snapped to mine, his eyes wide. "You would?"

"Yeah. I think so." My eyes were wide too. "I mean, I'm a little scared, but I want to know what it's like."

He caressed my cheek. "God, I'd love that, but if you're scared, I don't want to do it."

I bit my lip in disappointment. "The thing is I'm not sure I'll ever not be scared. The first time, I mean."

"I know. I was scared the first time."

My eyes went even rounder. "You were?"

"Uh huh." He smiled wryly. "I was afraid I'd make a fool of myself."

"Oh." I hunched my shoulders. "I'm afraid it'll hurt."

Dex sat up and put an arm around my shoulders. "I've been putting my fingers inside you and kind of stretching you, so it might not be so bad. But if you're too scared, we don't have to do it. I'm happy continuing on the way we have been."

I leaned my head on his shoulder and gazed up at him. "Like I said, I'm not sure I'll ever not be afraid. You're awfully big. But I want to have that with you."

His fingers trailed along the line of my cheekbone. "You know it doesn't matter what Leon thinks, right?"

"Leon?"

"He called you a virgin island and I know it embarrassed you. I don't want you to feel bad about that."

"This isn't about Leon. It's about you and me."

"Okay. I think it's good that you haven't slept around like some of the girls I know."

Did he sleep around? I'd gotten the impression he did.

"What about you?" I said.

"What about me?"

"Do you sleep around?"

He gave me a lopsided grin. "I used to but not anymore."

"Oh." Oh. Was he saying he'd given up the other girls for me? I hadn't even asked him to be faithful to me. We hadn't talked about that.

"So you're not seeing anyone else?" I said.

He frowned at me. "No. Did you think I was?"

"I didn't know. I wasn't even sure if we were dating."

Dex lifted my free hand to his lips and kissed it. "Would you be my girlfriend?"

"Yes." I smiled hugely. "So are we going steady?"

"Yes, we are." He looked so serious, almost as if he'd asked me to marry him. This was a big deal for him, just as much as it was for me.

"I want you to take my virginity."

"Cass, you don't have to do that."

I wrapped an arm around his neck. "I know. I want it."

He gazed at me, his eyes dark and solemn, their green color nearly lost in the dim lighting of my bedroom. His hand came up to cup the side of my face. Was he going to say no? The thought both relieved and disappointed me.

I wanted him more than I'd ever wanted anything in my life. Yet the thought of having sex, real all-the-way sex, terrified me with all the stories I'd heard of blood and pain. I longed to cross this barrier and lose my virginity, but I was scared too. My mouth opened to tell him never mind.

"All right," he said. "If you want it."

"I—" I cleared my throat. "Yes. I do."

"I'll be really gentle." He kissed my lips. "If anything hurts, tell me and I'll stop."

He reached for his jeans and pulled a small, square packet from his back pocket.

"What's that?" I said.

"A condom."

I raised my eyebrows. "You carry one with you?"

"A guy can hope, can't he?" He winked at me.

I laughed nervously. "I guess so."

I vaguely expected him to simply lay me on my back, climb on top of me, and have at it. Instead, he took his time caressing me and driving me wild the way he usually did, until I writhed and moaned frantically beneath him. He worked me into not one but two orgasms with his fingers alone. My juices coated his hand as he withdrew it from my body.

"Are you ready?" he whispered.

"Yes." Not really. "Are you?"

"Oh, yeah." He chuckled. "I'm so hard it hurts."

Did that mean it would hurt me? I understood the basics of sex, but there was so much I didn't really know. Like how it would feel to have him—that huge dick of his—inside my vagina. It would have been a terrifying prospect if he hadn't already turned me inside out with pleasure.

He tore open the condom wrapper, producing a thing that looked a bit like a tiny doughnut made of thin rubber. I watched as he placed it over the tip of his cock and rolled it down to the base, leaving a tiny bit loose at the end.

Then he stretched his long body over mine. "Open your legs, baby."

I took a breath and spread my thighs. Dex positioned himself at the entrance of my body. The tip of his cock, warm and blunt, probed me and I tensed, suddenly afraid again.

"Shh," he murmured, kissing me. "It's okay. I'll go slow."

"I'm all right," I lied. The last thing I wanted was for him to back off.

"Okay." He flexed his hips.

His cock slid a little farther inside me. What a strange sensation. It felt so much larger and more invasive than his fingers, although so far it didn't hurt at all. Still, my thighs went rigid with tension and my hands clenched against the skin of his back.

He flexed his hips again and I whimpered.

"Are you all right?" he whispered.

"Yeah, I think so."

"Do you want me to stop?" He sounded strained and his arms trembled.

I took a deep, reassuring breath. "No. Keep going."

He pushed again and I gave another whimper. Then his mouth descended on mine in a wet, hot kiss that utterly distracted me from what was going on lower down. I couldn't help but respond to that kiss the way I always responded to him—with moaning, panting enthusiasm. I plunged my tongue into his mouth as if I could devour him.

Dex gave a mighty surge and seated himself all the way inside me in one smooth stroke. I gasped. A broken groan escaped him.

"Oh, fuck," he moaned.

I turned my head and kissed the side of his throat.

"Are you still okay?" he said roughly.

"Yeah. It doesn't hurt."

He gave me a lopsided smile. "Good."

His hips withdrew in a long, outward slide before plunging forward again. I gave a low, strangled cry at the pleasure of it. While his fingers always felt incredible inside me, this was a deeper, richer sensation.

Instinctively, I pushed my hips upward against his, bringing him even deeper into me.

His body felt hot and solid over me, yet he didn't crush me at all. I wrapped my legs around his waist, my hands braced on his shoulders.

"Is this good?" he said on another thrust.

"Yeah," I moaned.

He pumped his hips against mine in a steady rhythm, moaning. His gold hair slid over his eyes, but they were closed. He looked utterly lost.

I didn't think I would come again, but he reached between our bodies and stroked me between my legs. The touch of his hand set off a firestorm of pleasure that burned through me so violently I had to turn my head and bury my mouth against his muscular arm to muffle my cries. Then he shuddered and clenched his teeth, groaning, and I knew he'd reached his own climax.

I held him, stroking his sweaty back as aftershocks shook his frame. My body trembled too, as if amazed at what had just happened to it. I certainly was.

I'm not a virgin anymore.

Maybe it was wrong of me, but I wanted to jump up and celebrate.

Dex carefully withdrew from my body. Before I could pout at the loss of his heat and warmth, he rolled to his side and tucked me in against him. His big hands stroked my hair and back. He smelled like male sweat and I loved it. Then I wondered if I smelled like sweat too.

"I love you, Cass," he whispered.

All thoughts of sweat vanished.

If he'd said it before sex, I might have wondered if he only told me that to make it easier to get me to say yes. But he didn't have anything to gain by saying it now, so I believed that he meant it.

My heart flooded with the strangest feeling. It was sweet and it felt pleasurable, but it hurt too, with an odd sort of ache. Dex loved me. I'd never been loved before, not this way.

I kissed his bare chest. "I love you too."

We lay together, dozing in each other's arms on the floor, for a long time. I don't know how long. The sound of the TV drifted down from the living room. It sounded like The Brady Bunch. My mom and Beth loved that show. I couldn't figure out what they saw in it.

I grabbed the comforter from my bed and dragged it down to cover us. Dex's hand played softly in my hair. We'd crossed a major line together tonight, and I had no idea how it would feel in the morning.

"I don't want it to be weird," I mumbled.

"Hmmm?"

"Tomorrow. When I see you again. I don't want it to be weird because we've done it."

He tilted his chin downward, smiling at me. "Done it?"

"You know what I mean."

He kissed the crown of my head. "It won't be weird."

"How do you know?"

"Because I love you. And you love me. Nothing can be weird if we love each other."

I snuggled in a little closer, hoping he was right. I'd never fallen in love before. Sure, I'd had crushes, but that was completely different. Crushes were for kids. They're more like fantasies than they're like love.

This was real.

"Your brother is not going to be happy if he finds out you and I are going further than kissing," he said.

"I don't care. He'll just have to deal with it. Anyway, he won't find out."

"Yeah, but I don't want it to be rough on you."
"I can handle Adam," I said.

Chapter 23

Changes

Cass:

The sky above our heads was the color of stainless steel. It seemed to threaten snow, yet no flakes fell. There was only that uniform gray overhead, with not a single break in the cloud layer.

The air smelled like popcorn. Luckily, the nausea that had plagued me every morning for a couple of weeks had settled down now that it was afternoon. Everywhere I looked, flashy painted signs and brightly colored Fur Rendezvous carnival booths, rides and games crowded the parking lot where they'd set up the carnival. A red-framed Ferris wheel turned slowly against the gray clouds and the backdrop of the Chugach mountain range that formed the eastern boundary of the town, the white slopes speckled with black spruce.

Fur Rondy was an annual festival celebrated in Anchorage every February, right before the Iditarod sled races. We had fur and hide auctions, sled races—shorter than the epic Iditarod—plus a variety of athletic events, a carnival, the Miners and Trappers Ball, and even a parade. It probably sounds crazy to hold outdoor celebrations in February in Alaska, but I think that's part of the appeal. It's a way for people to let off some steam and shake off the cabin fever they've been fighting for weeks.

As defense against the February cold, I wore two layers of wool sweaters under my parka, along with long johns beneath my jeans and two layers of wool socks in my boots. Plus, my hat, muffler, and gloves. I was ready for winter action.

Dex had the coat I'd given him. He'd even consented to wear the hat and gloves I'd bought him for Christmas, although I think it hurt his masculine pride to be seen in them. He did it to please me.

Our noses were red with the cold and my toes were starting to hurt despite all my layers. I didn't ask Dex if he felt the same. He would have lied to me anyway if he was uncomfortable.

I carried a cup of hot chocolate that was rapidly cooling in the winter air. He slung his arm around my shoulders as we meandered through the booths, looking for the next amusement that caught our eyes.

"Hey, look," he said. "A photo-booth."

"What's that?"

He laughed. "It's a booth where you can have your picture taken for a few cents. Come on. We'll get one of us together."

I followed him to the booth, gulping down the chocolate so I could get rid of the cup. The booth looked like a tiny shed or house with a curtain for a doorway. We went inside. There was a stool—just one. Dex sat down and pulled me onto his lap.

"Take your hat off," he said. "So I can recognize you later."

"You take off yours too."

He swiped his hat off, his eyes laughing at me. "Obviously."

"So now what do we do?"

He lifted one hip and dug in his pocket, bringing out a few coins which he dropped into a slot in the panel on one side of the booth. "Now we look at the camera. We're gonna get four shots."

I turned in the direction of the camera just before the flash dazzled my eyes. A few seconds later, a warning light began flashing. Dex drew my head around and kissed me, plunging his tongue inside my waiting mouth just as the flash went off again. The third time, we had our noses pressed together like a couple of kids. The fourth time, we pressed our cheeks up against each other and faced the camera together, Dex's arm around my shoulders.

"Now what?" I said.

"Wait a couple of minutes and we'll have our pictures." He glanced at me, smiling. "Is this another thing you've never done?"

"I never even heard of it until now."

"Really?" He wrinkled his brow. "How could that be?"

"I don't know. I guess we don't go to places like this in my family."

He stroked his thumb across my cheekbone. "I'm showing you all kinds of new things, huh?"

I smiled as he settled my hat back on my head. "Yep."

The pictures turned out black and white, and kind of grainy. They looked almost antique. The black and white made our cheekbones look starker, our eyes deeper.

I drew my fingertip along the outer edge of the little strip. "I love them."

"Here. I'll split them evenly."

He took them from me and cut the strip in half with his pocketknife. Then he handed me two—the one where I'd barely had time to look at the camera and the one where we were kissing.

"Thank you," I said, tucking the photo in my inner coat pocket. "I love it."

He smiled and put his half in the pocket of his jeans. "Me too. Let's go find something else."

"When do you have to be at the store?" I said.

180

"Not until five o'clock."

"How about the Ferris wheel, then?" I said.

"I don't know," he said, his eyes twinkling. "It's kinda cold and windy up there. Can you handle it?"

"I have you to warm me up," I said. "Besides, I've never been."

"You've never ridden the Ferris wheel?" His brows rose. "Really?"

"Really."

"Okay, then." He shepherded me in that direction.

A cluster of people in traditional Native parkas walked past us, their coats beautifully made of caribou hide or seal skin with wolf fur ruffs. The hides of small animals—probably squirrels—hung in decorative rows across the backs.

"Someday I'd like to have one of those," I said.

"Yeah? They probably cost a fortune," Dex said.

"Yeah, but they're gorgeous. I like the mukluks, too. The Athabaskan style." The traditional Native boots that came up to the knee were made of smoked moose hide and often sported beadwork and decorative tassels or pompoms out of brightly colored wool.

"I can see you in an outfit like that," he said. "As much as you like to be warm."

I bumped playfully against him. "You're not going to scare me off the Ferris wheel."

"Would I try to scare you off?"

No. Probably not. That was the tactic of my parents, not Dex.

We paid for our ride and got buckled in to one of the cars. As our car rose into the air, the people and booths on the ground seemed to grow smaller and smaller. The wheel creaked and the car swayed as we climbed higher.

I clutched the side of the chair, belatedly remembering how much I disliked heights. "Yikes. We're already really high."

Dex put his arm back around me. "It'll be okay. I won't let anything happen to you."

I smiled nervously at him. "It's not like you could do anything if the machine broke."

"Sure I could," he said with perfect confidence. He leaned down and planted a kiss on the tip of my nose. "We'll be fine."

I hoped he was right. I snuggled more closely into his embrace.

My period was still missing in action. This made two months I'd missed, and I was coming up on a third. It wasn't looking good at all.

I was pretty sure I was pregnant. The only reason I didn't know for certain was that I lacked the nerve to see a doctor. The procrastination had to stop, though. I'd probably start showing soon, and I hadn't even told Dex yet.

I stared out at the vista of Anchorage spread out below us. It isn't the prettiest town, especially in winter when it hasn't snowed for a while and the roads and parking lots are all a big mess of gray from the grit the city puts down. The buildings are almost all utilitarian boxes, and there's no decorative landscaping like cities in the Lower Forty-eight have. Yet it has a raw kind of beauty, with the inlet to the north and the abrupt slopes of the Chugach range to the east.

What was I going to do if my suspicions were correct? I wasn't ready to be a mother, and Dex wasn't ready to be a dad. He had too much pressure on him already. I wanted to finish school. I wanted that for both of us.

Not to mention the fact that my parents would skin me alive if they found out I'd had premarital sex.

How was I going to tell Dex he was going to be a father? I had no idea how he'd take the news. Would he be happy? Terrified? Angry? Would he leave me?

I didn't know a single unwed mother. Nobody I knew had ever gotten pregnant outside of marriage. I'd heard of girls doing it, some of them keeping and raising the babies, but I'd never met one. I had no model for this kind of thing.

Dex and I could get married, if he wanted to, but I wasn't sure that was a good idea. We were so young.

I loved him, and I knew he loved me. But get married? Have a kid? We weren't even old enough to vote yet.

"What're you thinking about?" he said, nuzzling my ear.

"Just stuff."

He kissed me again. "Stuff? Like what?"

"What do you want to do when you graduate?" I said, looking him straight in the eyes.

His lips thinned, turned down at the corners. "I don't really know. Get a job, I guess. My juvenile record supposedly won't follow me once I'm eighteen, so I should be able to find something better than bagging groceries."

"You don't want to go to college?"

He gave me a chiding look. "You know that won't be possible for me."

"No, I don't. Maybe you could go to Anchorage Community College or even the University of Alaska up in Fairbanks. You could take a class or two at a time while you worked."

He gazed thoughtfully out over the town. "I suppose that's true."

"What would you like to do?"

"I don't know. I never considered it." He smiled ruefully. "I've still gotta take care of Joe, no matter what else I do."

I gave a sympathetic sigh. "It isn't fair. Joe's sweet, but it's your parents' job to take care of him, not yours."

Dex snorted. "Fair's got nothing to do with it, baby. It's just the way things are. I can't let him down, now can I?"

"No. You can't." And he wouldn't. Dex was one of the most responsible guys I'd ever met.

It was so strange. Kind of funny, really. He had this terrible, tough-guy reputation. Most people saw him as a hard-ass, a drug dealer, a criminal. They didn't know what a great big brother he was, or how hard he worked to take care of his family. And he didn't deal drugs anymore.

"It's funny," he said. "Before I met you, I never really thought about any of this. There was no point, so why make myself miserable wishing for stuff I could never have? But you changed things."

Yeah. I'd changed things all right. And not for the better if my pregnancy fears were confirmed.

"You deserve a good life. I want you to have good things." I rested my head on his shoulder. "And I think there's a lot you could do if you had the chance."

He squeezed my shoulders, but said nothing.

Having a kid would take away some of his chances. There was no way it wouldn't mess things up for him, and for me too. It's not that I didn't want the baby. I did. We'd made him, or her, together. Dex and I had created a new life, and I welcomed that life, but I also knew it was going to change things for us.

I'd always expected to go to college. In fact, I'd expected to go somewhere Outside, away from Alaska. Now, that opportunity was out of my reach.

Our car reached the top of the wheel. I stared out at the city I'd known all my life. Everything was changing; I was changing, and I didn't want to. I wanted things to stay the same for a while so Dex and I could be young together.

"What do you want to do?" he said.

"I have no idea." Especially if I really was going to be a mom.

"You don't have any great career plans? I thought you and Jenny would go on to be lady mathematicians."

"I would like to do something where I could use math," I said. "But I don't know what. Maybe some kind of engineer."

"Are you going to go Outside for college?" He looked away from me when he asked the question, almost as if he didn't want to know the answer.

"Maybe. But probably not." Especially not if a kid was in the picture.

"Graduation is a whole year away anyhow," he said. "So it's too early to worry about it."

"Yeah. But I'll have to start thinking about where to apply pretty soon."

Or not. What I really needed to do was get a doctor's appointment.

* * *

I came into the living room to find my mom and dad sitting on the new, rust-colored couch they'd bought especially for this house. Waiting for me. It was obvious to me that they were waiting because of the way they sat there and looked expectantly at me as I came in. Had they been watching out the window to see the exact moment that Dex dropped me off?

"Uh..." I said cautiously. "What's going on?"

"Your dad and I need to have a word with you," my mom said.

"Okay." I glanced over my shoulder. "Where are Beth and Adam?"

"Adam is in his room and Beth is at Tammy's house."

Tammy was Beth's best friend.

I glanced at my dad, dreading his answer. "Did I do something wrong?"

"Not exactly," he said. "But we are concerned about this boy you've been seeing."

There it was. I knew they were working up to it.

"What about him?" I said. I could hear the hint of defiance in my voice, but there was nothing I could do about it.

"He's not the kind of boy we want to see you date," my dad said. "He himself admits to being incarcerated."

Incarcerated? Who talked that way?

"Don't you think it's better that he's honest about it?" I said. "He knows he made some serious mistakes."

My dad nodded gravely. "His honesty is admirable, but we're still worried about the kind of environment he lives in and the other kids he spends his time with."

I had to admit that wasn't a point in Dex's favor. "I'm a good influence on him."

My mom smiled. "I'm sure you are, Cass. But what kind of influence does he have on you?"

He makes me come. Nope, I couldn't say that to my parents.

"It's not like he's taking me to parties," I said. "We talk. We like the same kinds of books."

"That's all you do?" My dad looked skeptical. "You talk about books?"

"No. We talk about life and stuff." I had this sick, despairing feeling that I knew where the conversation was headed.

"You spend a lot of time with him," my mom said.

"That's because I lo—I care about him. And he cares about me. He stuck up for me at school when some jerks were trying to start a fight with me."

My mom leaned forward. "Who was trying to start a fight?"

"Oh, just some girl. Tracy something. She's always hated me."

"Is this one of Dex's friends?" my dad said, sounding as if he thought I'd just vindicated his point of view.

"No," I said. "She's one of the honors students. She's class treasurer."

"The fact that he stood up for you doesn't mean he's a good influence," my mom said. "Did you know his family is somewhat notorious among the parents at school?"

"No." I sounded exactly like the sullen teenager I was and I hated it.

"They are," she said. "His mother showed up at a parent-teacher conference drunk. The only time she bothered to show up."

I cringed inwardly on Dex's behalf. "Isn't that confidential information? Should the teachers be telling the parents this stuff?"

"I have no idea whether or not it's confidential," she said. "I only know I don't want you involved with a boy whose mother is an alcoholic, whose brother is a heroin addict, and who has a history of criminal activity himself."

I didn't like those things either, but that didn't mean I was going to reject Dex because of them. "You don't understand, Mom. He's trying really hard to get better. He got a job at Carrs bagging groceries, something totally normal. And he takes really good care of his little brother, Joe. You should see them together."

My dad gave me a slightly sympathetic look, the kind that meant he felt bad about what he had to do but he was going to do it anyway. "Cass, we don't want you to see him as often. We're not saying you can't see him at all. Just slow down a little."

"But—"

"You're too young to be so serious with a boy anyway," my mom said. "You're only seventeen."

"Lots of girls my age have steady boyfriends."

"You're not lots of girls," she said. "You're our girl, and your father and I think you need a few more years before you get so serious."

In other words, they wanted to keep me in a virginal bubble as long as they possibly could. Maybe until the end of my life. I could see I wasn't going to win this argument, especially not by going head to head with them.

I heaved a heavy, resentful sigh and hung my head. "Fine. We'll slow it down."

"You can see him once a week outside of school," my mom said.

"Once a week?" I exclaimed, although I was already thinking about what steps I'd have to take to see him more often than that without them finding out.

"Once a week," my dad said.

"Jeez, you guys are way too strict. Even Jenny's parents aren't that uptight."

"That's because Jenny isn't dating a boy like Dex," my mom said. "If she were, we'd see their rules change overnight. Besides, Jenny isn't under discussion here."

"I need to see him more than once a week."

"Once a week," my dad said. "That's final. If you can't abide by that rule, we'll have to take harsher measures."

"For crying out loud," I muttered. "All right. Fine. Once a week." But I was thinking *we'll see about that.*

* * *

Dex:

Grocery stores are loud when they're busy. People talking, the music playing over the speakers, cash register keys clacking, the drawers dinging when a total is reached, coins rattling in the drawers. The noise seemed to feed the energy that kept me going throughout my shift.

The bright lighting and constant movement kept me from getting too bored. It didn't require the kind of thinking that dealing did, but then again it wouldn't land me in jail.

It wasn't the most exciting or fun job, but it was legal and that was what counted. Plus, cashiers made decent money and I had a chance to move into one of those positions eventually. If I didn't fuck up this one, that is.

I gazed out over the belt, loaded with bananas, lettuce, bread, and a package of cube steak, to the main aisle beyond. There was a line six carts long at my station, all of the carts full to the brim with groceries. The old lady whose stuff I was bagging wore a blue polyester pantsuit, an obvious wig with way too many fake-looking blond curls, and a prim expression. Behind her came a blond mom with three kids under the age of five. After that was another mom, this one with a beautiful Native Alaskan look to her, with two daughters around Joe's age. Then a guy with a painfully bored expression under his scruffy brown beard, and another old lady in a pantsuit.

I bagged as fast as I could to keep up with the cashier, Pam, who could key like lightning. I could hardly keep track of what her fingers were doing. Weekend evenings were always busy like this.

"Morgan, what the fuck?" said a male voice behind me.

I glanced over my shoulder. Jake Barrows stood there with a dumbfounded expression on his face.

"Hey, Barrows," I said, and turned back to the belt.

"You work here?" he said incredulously.

"No. I just like to stand here and bag groceries for the fun of it." I kept my eyes on my work while I talked.

"I never thought I'd see you doing something like this," he said.

Jesus. He was not helping my reputation around the workplace, talking that way.

"It's a good job," I said.

He came around beside me. "But—what about the other stuff?"

"I'm out of it," I said curtly, hoping he'd get the hint and drop the subject.

"You've gotta be shitting me."

The old lady whose groceries I was bagging pressed her red-painted lips together until they disappeared. Pam gave me a look, half curiosity and half reproach.

"I'd love to talk, but I'm kinda busy," I said.

"Sure. Yeah, okay. But I was gonna ask you if you had anything. You know. I'm in the market again."

"I got nothing."

"Man, that sucks." He shook his head mournfully.

You'd think he'd know better than to even hint at a deal in a public setting like this, especially with so many people around openly listening in. He must have been even more desperate than usual. Either that or he was high.

I gave him a searching glance. Sure enough, his eyes were red-rimmed and dilated.

"Barrows, I can't talk right now. I'll get you later."

"Okay, man. Take it easy, man, all right?"

"I'll do that."

"Yeah. Okay, man. See ya later."

I ignored that one and kept bagging. After a moment's pause, Barrows wandered off and I relaxed a little. It was the first time a school mate of mine had approached me here, but unfortunately it probably wouldn't be the last.

"A friend of yours?" Pam said.

"Sorta," I said, eyes on the work.

"You might want to remind him you can't talk while you're working. Not unless he's a customer."

"I'll tell him."

"Good." She rang in the last of the old lady's items. "You're a good worker, Dex. We like you here."

"Nice to know."

"That guy, I don't think he's good for you."

"Don't I know it." I wondered how long it would take before my old cronies got the message that I wasn't dealing anymore. Before they quit pestering me about it. How long would my past follow me around?

Chapter 24

An Inch High

Cass:

The rose-colored walls in my bedroom seemed particularly glowy this afternoon. There was still a hint of light outside, but it was mostly dark and I had my bedside lamp on but not the overhead.

Dex glanced at the door. "I really wish you had a lock on that thing."

"Yeah, I know. But my mom is out today, so we have some time." I smiled hopefully at him.

"Out?" he said, frowning.

"Yeah. She went to the hairdresser's or something. And she mentioned the dry cleaner, too. I think she'll be a while."

"I hope you're right." He took me by the elbows. "So far we've been lucky and that's starting to worry me."

"It'll be fine." I pulled him against me and dragged his head down for a kiss.

He didn't resist very hard. His arms swept me up and bore me down to the bed. We worked feverishly to undress each other.

He stuck his tongue into my navel and I giggled helplessly. It was the weirdest sensation, and not entirely pleasant. His hand slipped between my thighs at the same time, though, distracting me from the slight discomfort of my bellybutton and making me sigh and squirm with pleasure.

A voice intruded on us. I had the vague awareness that it was a female voice, older, coming closer. Before I could pull away from Dex or get a blanket over us, the door opened and my mom stood inside my bedroom, regarding us with open horror. She'd come home early.

"Cass!" she gasped. "What on Earth—what is going on in here?"

Dex struggled to get off me without exposing me to my mom's gaze. Instead, he slid right off the bed and landed on his ass on my carpet. I snatched up my comforter and held it beneath my chin. I was covered in roses, but I was pretty sure I wasn't coming out of this smelling like one.

"Why didn't you knock?" I yelled.

"What in heaven's name—are you two—oh, my goodness." Even in high dudgeon, my mom couldn't bring herself to use harsh language. "Cass Maslanka, I'm speechless."

If only that were true.

Still on the floor, Dex wriggled into his boxers and then his jeans. I glanced at him. He gave me a pained look.

We were caught. The gig was up. If I were lucky, the only thing my parents would do was lock me in a high tower until I graduated from high school. I might never see Dex outside of West High again.

I blinked fast to keep my eyes from flooding with tears. Shit. It wasn't supposed to happen this way. It wasn't supposed to happen at all.

I was such an idiot. I hadn't wanted to play the good-girl role anymore, but I'd never given any serious thought to what would happen if I got caught being bad.

"Dex," my mom said in clipped tones. "You need to go home this instant. And don't come back here unless you want to get shot."

"Mrs. Maslanka, I love your daughter," Dex said, rising from the other side of my bed. He had his jeans on, but no shirt.

"You love her?" my mom said incredulously. "Is that what you call this?"

He looked uncertain. "Yes. I love her."

"Are the two of you engaging in premarital intercourse?"

Good grief. Only my mom would call it premarital intercourse.

Dex and I exchanged a wary glance. Then we both turned back to my mom, tongue-tied.

"I can see that you are," she said. "Have either of you given any thought to what would happen if Cass got pregnant?"

"I'd take care of her," he said promptly, making me want to kiss him.

"You? You're just a kid. You're not capable of taking care of her and a baby."

He frowned. "Mrs. Maslanka, I know I'm young, but I can take care of my family. If anything happens to Cass, I'll be there for her. I'll always be there for her."

"I'm afraid not," she said. "Now you need to get out of here before her father gets home. When he finds out about this, he's going to be livid and if he sees you he just might shoot. I'm not kidding about this."

I could tell she meant it. She really thought Dad would shoot a boy for sleeping with me. Was she right?

My dad was highly protective of all us kids, especially me and Beth, so maybe my mom knew what she was talking about. But shooting Dex? That was illegal, for one thing, and it wouldn't solve the problem, for another.

"Mom, I need Dex," I said. "I love him. We belong together."

"You're seventeen, for heaven's sake. Barely seventeen. You don't know what you want or where you belong."

"Yes, I do." I looked at Dex. He looked back at me with the same expression I felt on my own face. "We belong to each other."

"Well, you live in our house and you follow our rules. Now, I'm telling Dex to get out of here before I have a dead body on my hands."

"I'm going," he said, stuffing his feet in his shoes. He scooped up his jacket and sent me a longing glance. "I'll see you at school, babe."

"Okay." I pressed my lips together in a vain attempt to stop them from trembling. "I love you."

"I love you too."

My mom's nostrils flared and her lips disappeared, the way they always did when she was really pissed off. It was so insulting. Did she really think we were too young to know what love was? Maybe we were only seventeen; that didn't mean our feelings were fake or imaginary. Dex had given up dealing drugs and gotten a normal, boring job for me. That was love.

A terrible feeling came over me as Dex picked up his coat and walked out of my room. He left by the door this time, instead of the window. The sight of his back turned to me, his dark-gold hair caught in his coat collar, his shoulders stiff with worry and defeat, just made me sick inside. I didn't know what exactly was going to happen next, but I knew it would be bad.

An invisible hand seemed to close around my throat. When would I see him again? It felt as if it might be never, and I didn't think I could live with that. He was the best thing I'd ever had, the best thing to ever happen to me, and he was leaving.

"Come upstairs with me," my mom said in an uncompromising tone.

"I have to get some clothes on."

Her lips got even flatter. "Yes, I suppose you do."

"Can I have some privacy?"

"No. I don't trust you not to go out the window."

Really? She didn't trust me?

Of course I knew my mom and dad were conservative when it came to sex, especially between unmarried partners. But it didn't seem to me that what Dex and I had done was so bad. We'd loved each other and showed that love in physical ways. How could that be wrong? It's not as if we were hurting people.

And my mom thought I would run? She thought I'd crawl through the window and disappear?

Maybe I should. Maybe Dex and I could go somewhere together, or I could move in with him.

But I was weak and afraid, and I let her stand there and watch me as I pulled on my jeans and sweater. I let her chivvy me up the stairs and into the living room where we waited for my dad to get home.

It didn't take him long. Beth and Adam were in their rooms, doing homework or reading, completely blind to what was happening with me. That was good. I didn't want them to know.

When the front door opened and my dad came into the house, my stomach gave a sickening flop. I didn't know what he would do, but I knew I wouldn't like it. I was pretty sure he'd try to stop me from seeing Dex, and I didn't think I could handle that.

But he couldn't stop me from seeing him in school. He couldn't stop me from going out to lunch with him and meeting him between classes and whenever else we got the chance. Didn't my mom realize she couldn't really keep me and Dex apart?

My dad came up the stairs and into the living room. His gaze fell on me and my mom, standing there together like a prison warden and a convict.

"What's going on?" he said.

"I caught Cass with Dex. In her room."

My dad frowned. "Alone?"

"Yes. They were ... Pete, they were having sex." Her voice got lower at the end, as if she could hardly bear to say the words out loud.

My dad's frown grew thunderous. "What?"

"Yes. Naked, both of them."

"I knew it." His jaw worked back and forth. "I knew not to trust that shit."

"Don't call him that," I said. "We love each other."

He barked a laugh. "He doesn't love you, Cass. Boys like that only want one thing, and it sounds as if you were about to give it to him."

There was so much disappointment in his voice and face. And not only disappointment. Contempt. He felt contempt for me, his daughter.

I drew up my chin. "I've already given it to him and he still loves me." I threw the words at him like a challenge, a gauntlet tossed down, daring him to fight me.

He only exchanged a sober glance with my mother. "Your mom and I have been looking into this boyfriend of yours."

"Oh?" I said with narrowed eyes.

"Yes. Oh. Did you know his parents are continually behind on their bills? Their electricity and gas are frequently turned off, even in the winter. Both parents are alcoholics."

"Holy smokes, Dad, what did you do? Hire a private detective?"

He gave me an unreadable look. "It doesn't matter. The point is that this is not a family I want you or your siblings to associate with. For

192

heaven's sake, the oldest boy, Sinatra, is a heroin addict. Did you know that?"

"No," I said. "And I don't believe it."

Although, thinking back to Sin's appearance and behavior, it didn't surprise me much.

"He's already been arrested once for possession of a controlled substance," my dad said.

My parents shared a heavy glance. They almost looked as if they were reading each other's minds. That look worried me. I couldn't decipher it, but it couldn't be good.

My mom stared me right in the eyes. "Could you be pregnant?"

My face flamed in humiliation. "No!"

"Why not?" she said with eerie calm. "It looked to me like you were making a strong effort."

"Jeez, Mom." I stared at my lap. "We used protection, okay? Every time."

"Protection doesn't always work," she said quietly.

"How would you know?" I glared resentfully at her. "Catholics don't believe in birth control."

She flushed. "No, and we don't believe in sex before marriage, either."

"Take her to the doctor and have her tested," my dad said, speaking about me in the third person, as if I wasn't in the room.

"That won't be necessary," I said, although I'd worried about pregnancy myself.

The idea of being escorted to an obstetrician by my mother, made to take a pregnancy test and undergo who knew what kind of procedures, it all gave me the heebie-jeebies. Part of me believed they were talking about it as a way to make me feel small. Like I didn't already feel about an inch high.

"I think that's wise," my mom said. "But I want to get her as far away from that boy as possible first."

"Agreed," my dad said. "Take her to Don and Frances, like we discussed."

"What?" I shrieked, too horrified to control my voice. "You can't send me to Chicago."

I hated it there. It was a big, noisy, dirty city with too many people and not enough trees or birds. Dex wasn't there and neither was Jenny. Only my cousins and my super-strict aunts and uncles and grandparents.

"Of course we can, dear," my mom said. "And you'll love it once you get over being mad about it. You'll be with all your cousins. You'll be living with Annie. You know how much you love Annie. You two will go to the same school. St. Hildy's is an excellent school. You'll be in your element."

"I'll be miserable." I bit out the words with a glower.

I did love my cousin Annie. We were the same age and had similar interests. But she wasn't Jenny. She wasn't my best friend. And no-one could ever replace Dex in my life.

My parents intended to rob me of almost everyone I cared about. I wanted to howl with fear and agony at what they were doing to me.

"I won't go," I said. "You can't just put me on a plane at a minute's notice."

"Calm down, Cass," my mom said, frowning.

"No! I won't calm down. I won't go to Chicago."

"Yes, you will."

"You're going to pack me off to Uncle Don and Aunt Frances? What if they don't want me? They've already got ten kids."

"And they have room for one more now that Mary Katherine is in college," my mom said. "We've already discussed it with them. They're looking forward to having you."

I'd just bet they were. Uncle Don and Aunt Frances were the strictest, most conservative parents I'd ever met. They ran their household as if it were a convent, or maybe a prison. They didn't even allow their daughters to cut their hair, for crying out loud, or wear pants, or even talk to boys other than their immediate relatives. They made my parents look like wild-eyed bohemians.

Beth's door opened and my sister ventured into the living room. "Is everything okay? I heard yelling."

"Honey, go to your sister's room and pack a suitcase for her," my mom said. "Put everything in it you think she'd need for a couple of weeks."

Beth's brown eyes rounded. "Is she going somewhere?"

"She's going to visit Uncle Don and Aunt Frances. Doesn't that sound like fun?" my mom said in her falsest, most chipper voice.

"No," Beth said. "It sounds awful." She looked from me to our mom and then to our dad. Then back to me. "What's really going on?"

"Just do what mom wants you to do," I said wearily, defeated. "I'll explain later."

Beth gave us all another bewildered look. "Okay. It might take a while."

"Take all the time you need," I muttered.

Chapter 25

Beaten

Dex:

It started snowing just as I left Cass's house, white flakes swirling down out of a dark, unknowable sky. On both sides of the street, respectable-looking houses with their cheerfully lit windows mocked me as I plodded down the icy street. I'd only been inside one of them. Hers. There was no place in those houses for someone like me.

I'd never given much thought to the way the nice places around here rubbed shoulders with the shitholes like mine. Maybe not all the nice places were truly nice; maybe those tidy exteriors hid alcoholism and violence. That didn't change the fact that there was no way Cass would ever belong to me.

The air had that sharp bite in it, that smell of dry snow, that let me know I was still in Alaska, even if this was a city. There might be paved roads and centrally-heated houses and streetlights all around, but this was still Alaska and she would just as soon kill me as present me with wild berries and freshly caught salmon. It wasn't because she was mean or anything. She just didn't care.

Being a nice guy was exhausting. I was used to doing, and taking, whatever I wanted. I was used to caring about nothing and no-one but myself, and Joe. It had worked well for me, for years, but as I trudged through piles of ice and snow scraped up by the city plows, I knew that way was closed to me. I'd left it behind and even though I'd lost Cass, I knew I wouldn't find my way back to my old life, and that I had no idea what my new life would be.

I'd lost her.

The rational part of me reasoned that I couldn't know for sure. Yeah, her mom was pissed and her dad would be too. They'd probably ground her for a good long time and forbid her from seeing me. But they couldn't keep her out of school, so I'd see her there. We'd find a way to be together.

It sounded reasonable. Believable. Yet my heart sank lower and lower with every step I took.

The way her mother had looked at me...I don't think even my own parents had ever gazed at me with so much disgust in their faces. It made me feel dirty and small. It made me want to hit something.

The lights were on in my living room when I walked up the driveway, which most likely meant my parents were both at home. Just what I needed. Another confrontation with parents.

My muscles tensed and my nervous system went into high alert as I turned the doorknob. Sure enough, the TV blasted from the living room. Tonight it was *Streets Of San Francisco,* an okay show all around but not when watched with my dad. Nothing was okay when watched with my dad.

Nothing was okay at all.

I hung up my coat because she had given it to me. The old red one would have gone into a heap on the floor, if I'd still had it. A gift from Cass got the royal treatment.

I walked into the living room, knowing the bad shit was just going to get worse. My mom and dad weren't fighting each other for once, maybe in part because my mom was passed out on the couch. Her hand dangled off the edge, right near an overturned bottle of cheap Scotch. Whiskey dripped out of the bottle and into the ancient carpet.

My dad looked up blearily from his beat-down old chair. "Where you been?"

"Out."

"I can see that. Where?"

Jesus Christ. As if he gave a damn. I shrugged. "At a friend's place."

"I need some money."

I stared at him, trying to find words. I wasn't sure which ones I was looking for—the ones that would make a temporary peace or the ones that would shatter everything. My whole world seemed to balance on a knife edge, in a way it never had before, and I didn't know where that knowledge came from or what to make of it. The understanding simply hung there, in my mind, part of the air or something.

"I don't have any money," I said. "And if I did, I wouldn't give it to you."

He glowered at me as he levered his big frame a little straighter in the chair. He might be a broken-down alcoholic, but he was still a big guy and a mean-ass fighter. He was taller than me and heavier. Until now, I'd never tried to go head to head with him.

It was a bad idea and I knew that.

"What's that supposed to mean?" he growled.

"You'd waste it all. We need food. We need to pay the gas bill again," I said.

"I'm the parent here, not you."

"Funny. I never noticed that."

My dad climbed to his feet. He still had on the rest of his work clothes—a cheap, navy-blue polyester suit that had probably come from

Montgomery Ward or maybe Sears. His loud, orange and blue paisley tie had a dark stain on it.

"You need to learn a little respect," he said.

I shook my head. "I've got plenty of respect for people who deserve it."

I was poking him, like shoving a stick in the face of a cranky bear. The sane, sensible part of my mind shouted at me to stop, to just go to my room and shut the door and try to forget everything. I ignored it.

"Just what is it you think you bring to this family?" he said, swaying toward me, hands in meaty fists.

"Seems to me I'm the only one who gives a shit," I said. "I'm the one who feeds Joe and checks his homework and talks to his teachers. I'm the one who buys milk and eggs and cereal. So you tell me. What do I bring to this family?"

"Not a goddamn thing," he said. "You're worthless and you always have been."

He was talking out of his ass. Drunk, mean, taking out his frustrations on me. I knew it, and I let it get to me anyway.

"Fuck you," I said.

He laughed. "No, son. Fuck you."

"Don't call me son. You haven't earned it."

That got him going. I saw his face contort in a weird, crumpled-up way and his hand came up and smacked me on the side of my face. My head rocked to the side in a burst of pain.

I righted myself. I touched my lip. Swollen, probably busted and bleeding. Yep, there was some warm liquid bubbling up on it the same way the ugly rage inside me was bubbling up, pushing its ruthless, reckless way outward.

I laughed. "That all you got?"

He sneered. "There's plenty where that came from."

On the couch, my mom gave a mighty snore. Awake, she wouldn't have done me any good. I couldn't remember a time she'd taken my side over the old man's. She never cooked anymore or took any notice of me and Joe. No, my mom's function in life was purely decorative.

"Do you even have a job?" I said, wielding that stick again. "Cause I can't tell. I have no idea whether you even go anywhere when you leave here, other than a dive bar."

"If it wasn't for me, you wouldn't live in a nice house like this," he said, waving a drunken hand around our dump of a living room.

I laughed again. "Wow. Thanks, man."

"You're an ungrateful little bastard, you know that?"

I curled my swollen lip. "Yeah. I know."

"Give me your money, Dex. I'm your dad and it belongs to me anyhow, so you might as well hand it over."

"Sorry." I spread my hands to the sides. "I spent it all and my next paycheck isn't until next Friday."

He lunged at me. I think he meant to grab me and search my pockets, but he never got the chance. I popped him in the jaw.

It was the strangest thing. Almost like my hand acted on its own. It flew out and rammed itself into his face and I don't have any memory of making the decision to hit him.

He staggered back a few steps. Not very far because honestly I hadn't clocked him very hard. Definitely not my best work.

He recovered. Straightened his spine, panting, his tie halfway to his shoulder. Then he roared and launched himself at me.

I could have fought back. I don't know why I didn't.

His fists landed all over me. Everywhere. Head, face, gut. I backed up and something hit me in the calf, forcing my knee to buckle. He clobbered me again and I went down on the floor, right in the whiskey-soaked part of the carpet.

His bare foot slammed into my ribs. I groaned. Before I could react, he kicked me again and I felt something break. I folded around my midsection, trying to protect myself.

With an animal growl, my dad lunged at me and kicked me in the ribs. He still had his shoes on. The fall against the table had immobilized me. Maybe I'd broken something.

All I knew was that I was in too much pain to move or fight back.

"This what you wanted, you little shit?" he yelled. "You want a beating? You got one."

Blow after blow landed on my ribs and my thighs. I curled into a ball, trying to protect myself. On the couch, my mom continued to snore.

He kicked me in the head. Bright lights exploded in my vision.

A loud noise, a bang. Voices shouting. Someone else was there.

Someone yelled. Not me. I didn't know who it was.

The yelling got louder. I groaned because I couldn't make words. My mouth was too fucked up.

He got one more kick in before whoever it was pulled him off me. Big, male hands gently held the sides of my face. I groaned again.

"Dex?" It was Sin's voice. "Can you hear me?"

"Yehh," I said.

"Can you walk?"

"Dunno." I pried my eyes open and peered blearily up into his dark face. "Think he broke some shit."

"God damn it." Sin's scowl was the fiercest I'd ever seen him look. He threw an angry glance over his shoulder, presumably at my dad. "Look what you did to him, you asshole."

"He sassed me." My dad's voice sounded thick, like something was wrong with his mouth. Maybe Sin had punched him.

"So you tried to kill him?" my brother yelled. "Jesus, what is wrong with you?"

Only Sin could talk to our dad like that and get away with it. Apparently, he wasn't stoned at the moment, or he would have been so out of it he wouldn't have noticed or cared that our dad was beating me to death. Guess I got lucky, huh?

"I'm taking him to the hospital." Sin slid an arm behind my shoulders. "Sit up, man."

I struggled to get upright. Stabbing pain made me yelp, but I managed to do it. Panting and nauseated with pain, I clung to Sin like a baby.

"Just hang in there," he said. "We're gonna get you help."

"Uhnhh," I said.

"Do you have your car keys on you?"

"Pocket," I said.

He dragged me to my feet and we hobbled past our dad. The guy stood there and watched and didn't even offer to help.

Sin got me out of the house. I almost threw up before he got me into the passenger side of the car. Once in the seat, I closed my eyes and sat in a blur of pain as Sin went around to the driver's side.

"Joe," I said as he got in.

"He's at Frankie's."

I rolled my head to the side to look at him. The motion made me dizzy and nauseated again. "How do you know?"

"He came by before I left. Said he was going to eat dinner there."

Thank God Joe wouldn't be at home for a while. If he came in when my dad was in that state, and Sin and I were gone, it wouldn't be good.

"See if...you can get him...to spend the night," I said. Talking made me exhausted.

"Okay. I'll call when we get to the emergency room."

I groaned and then everything turned the same shade of black.

* * *

I came to stretched out on one of those gurney-bed things they have in hospitals. It felt hard under my body. The air was chilly. Unforgiving fluorescent light glared down at me from above the bed.

199

My mouth tasted like old blood. I moved my tongue around, searching for missing teeth. Everything seemed to be in its usual place, although my lips felt puffy and distorted.

Looking down at my body, I discovered I wore only a thin hospital gown. I could see the white cotton fabric, printed with little blue diamonds, covering my chest where it showed over the flimsy blanket that hid the rest of me. Sin must have gotten me to the emergency room, but I didn't remember anything after he'd almost carried me out of the house.

I glanced around myself, trying not to move my head. Dull green curtains with metal rings hung on either side of my narrow bed and the tang of hospital disinfectant filled the air. I had a needle in my hand, an IV stand next to my bed. More equipment filled the alcove, but I had no idea what any of it was supposed to do.

My head felt heavy and dull, yet paradoxically my body seemed lighter than normal. There was pain, somewhere, but it was distant, more like an idea I had than something I actually felt. Everything seemed distant, even the constant ache of losing Cass. They must have put something really good in that IV.

"Dr. Harding to the ICU stat," droned an echoing voice over the PA system. "Dr. Harding to the ICU stat please."

Beyond the curtain, a couple of nurses bustled past, both of them wearing scrubs in the same dingy green. One had a green hat that looked a lot like a shower cap over her hair. They were smiling and talking to each other as if the emergency room were a completely normal place to be.

Somewhere nearby, a kid screamed.

I must have made a sound. Suddenly, my brother loomed over me, his face lined with desperation and fear. I could see it even through the giant beard that covered his upper lip and jawline. Sin was worried about me.

"You're awake," he said.

I groaned.

"The doc says you're gonna be okay." He looked like he didn't quite believe it, his mouth pinched and straight with tension.

"What's broken?" I said. Although I had the hazy, floating sensation of some really strong painkillers, I also had a fuzzy memory of something snapping inside me.

"Some ribs and an arm. They set the arm while you were out."

My brow wrinkled. "How'd I—get here?"

"I drove you. I had to pull Dad off first, though. Jesus, I've never seen him like that before. I really think he would've killed you if I hadn't gotten there in the middle of it."

200

"Thanks, man," I rasped.

He grabbed my hand, his eyes glittering as if he were about to cry. "Hey, no problem. You're my little brother."

He didn't ask what we'd been fighting about, probably because he knew it didn't matter. The subject of the fight was never what the fight was really about; it was only a pretext. The real reason was that my dad was a drunken asshole who liked to hurt people.

"Good thing...you weren't stoned," I said.

He grimaced and looked away. "Yeah. No shit."

"I was only kidding."

"Well, I wasn't." Sin shook his shaggy black head. "I've gotta stop doing that shit."

I couldn't argue with that. Joe and I needed him.

I thought of Cass. The look on her face when her mom had discovered us. The way she'd tried to defend me.

"Cass..." I mumbled. "Her mom...broke us up."

"Shit, man. I'm sorry." Sin grabbed a metal and plastic chair, dragged it close to the bed and sat down, still holding my hand like he thought I might die on him.

"Yeah," I said. "I love her."

Shit. I hadn't meant to say that. It must be the morphine in my system, making me stupid and loose-lipped.

"Yeah?" Sin said. There was no judgment on his face. "She seemed like a cool girl."

"She's the coolest." I was never going to see her again and somehow that was worse than the broken ribs. A hundred times worse.

Chapter 26

Ice

Cass:

The floor in the obstetrician's examining room had at least five different colors of speckles in it and all of them were ugly. Tan, sickly pink, a crappy green, white, and black. Maybe it was meant to hide stains, although with this being a medical office you'd think they'd want the stains to show so they'd know where to clean extra hard.

My mom had insisted on taking me to the doctor the minute we could get an appointment, which turned out to be the morning after we'd arrived in Chicago. He was my Aunt Frances's doctor. She'd gotten me in as a family emergency.

That was me. A family emergency.

I could hear vague sounds of footsteps in the corridor outside, and low voices. Other patients—unlike me, they were all respectable married ladies—plus the doctors and their nurses. They all sounded happy to be here, their voices well-modulated and soft. Nobody cried or yelled. Nobody threw anything.

Couldn't they see what an ugly place this was? Couldn't they feel the cold judgment in its walls?

Maybe, for them, those things didn't exist.

I shifted on the exam table, the paper crackling under my butt. To my right, a wall of cabinetry held mysterious objects in its drawers and on its shelves. My stomach tried to rebel as I imagined what kind of tools the doctor might use and how they would feel.

I rolled a lime-flavored Life Saver around in my mouth, letting the familiar sweetness reassure me. Once I got out of here, I was going to eat the rest of the roll. Forget about the calories.

No-one had thought about making this awful place seem happy or kind. Women came here for a kind of exam that seemed worse to me than a dentist poking at teeth with one of those sharp needle-like tools they used. But it seemed like no attempt had been made at all to create an exam room that wasn't terrifying.

The walls were a hard, unforgiving white and the fluorescent lamps overhead seemed designed to make the patient look as bad as possible. Not that I cared what the doctor thought of my looks. I only wanted to get this idiotic exam over with as soon as possible.

I'd already peed into their cup, so they had what they needed to do the pregnancy test. But my mom and Aunt Frances had insisted I get a full pelvic exam. My first.

I crossed my arms over my chest, shivering as the chilly air passed right through the hideous hospital-style gown they'd given me to wear. It smelled like some kind of vile chemical had been poured over every surface in the room. Maybe they'd pour some over me.

I'd never forget the prim judgment that had lain beneath the nurse's bustling professional exterior. It matched what I'd been getting from Aunt Frances, so I was hardly surprised, but it still hurt. I loved Dex and he loved me. If I was pregnant, it had been created out of that love, yet these people sent me contemptuous glances and pursed their lips as if I'd brought something dirty into their lives.

If Frances thought that way, why had she agreed to take me on? It's not like I wanted to live with her and Uncle Don.

The pictures of Dex and me at Fur Rondy were hidden in my coat pocket. I wanted to get up off the exam table and take them out. Stare at them, the way I'd done on the plane every time I thought my mom wasn't paying attention. But the doctor might come in at any moment and I didn't want him or anyone else to see me looking at them. Those pictures were private, for me and Dex. If someone else looked at them, especially with that superior expression all these adults kept giving me, it would soil the only beautiful thing I still had in my life—my memories of him.

The familiar sting of tears almost ambushed me. I bit down hard on my lower lip to drive them back. No crying. Not here. Not now.

The door opened and a man old enough to be my grandfather strode briskly into the room. He wore thick, black glasses that perched on a beak-like nose, and a somber expression.

"I'm Doctor Wachowsky," he said. "I hear this is your first pelvic exam."

"Yes." My voice came out flattened and colorless, like the walls.

"Don't worry," he said. "It doesn't hurt."

"Um...okay."

"Now if you'll lay back and put your feet in the stirrups, we'll get started."

"Stirrups?" I said.

He pointed at the weird projections on the end of the table. "That's where you put your feet."

"Oh." I swallowed.

He was a doctor. He was only going to look at me, not hurt me. Besides, if I really was pregnant, there would be a lot more examinations and medical stuff to endure, not to mention the birth itself.

Oh, God. I might be pregnant. I wanted to puke.

But the doctor was watching me, none too patiently, so I rested my back gingerly against the exam table and put my feet in the stirrups. The paper-covered vinyl felt cold against my back.

The doctor sat down on one of those rotating stools and shoved it right up between my legs. "Scoot down for me."

God. He was looking right at my—I took a deep breath, closed my eyes, and scooted down.

"A little farther," he said. "I need your pelvis to be right at the edge of the table."

Ick. No wonder they needed stirrups. With another deep breath, I scooted a little nearer to him.

"That's fine."

He stood up again and started to press all over my abdomen with cold fingers. I still couldn't look at him. No-one had seen that part of me since I was a small child, except for Dex. This was as different from Dex as I could imagine, harshly impersonal rather than loving. I wanted to jump off the table and put my clothes back on.

The doctor took a seat on the stool again. He picked up a tool. I could hear the metallic sound of it, but my legs were in the way and I couldn't see what it was. A weird squishy noise followed.

My hands tensed on the paper table cover. Suddenly, something ice-cold and hard probed the entrance to my vagina and shoved its way inside. I gasped, arching my back off the table.

"Hold still, now, Cass," he said. "I'm only inserting the speculum."

"The what?" I said, grasping at any distraction that might take my mind of what was happening to me.

"It's a tool we use to expand the walls of the patient's vagina so we can see what we're doing."

"Oh," I said in a small voice.

"Now I'm going to open it."

The cold pressure on my vagina increased. I gritted my teeth. My fingernails dug into the paper.

"It's less uncomfortable if you relax," he said.

"It's like ice. I can't relax."

Anyway, how would he know if it hurt or not? He didn't even have a vagina.

I endured some mysterious probing and prodding until he removed the instrument of torture. Then he did something worse. He stuck his hand inside me.

Not his whole hand, but it kind of felt that way. His fingers were big and hard and cold, and completely unsympathetic. Why did women have to go through this? I never wanted to experience anything like this again.

And then he stuck a finger in my rear end. I gasped again, grinding the back of my skull against the table as I gritted my teeth. Jesus Christ on a bicycle. What th hell was he doing that for?

Finally, he removed his hand and snapped off the gloves. I waited for whatever indignity would come next, but he only pushed the stool away from the table and stood. I watched him walk to the sink and wash his hands.

"All signs point to a pregnancy," he said. "We'll know for sure when the test comes back, but for now you should consider yourself pregnant, young lady."

Pregnant. Me. My breath caught and the tears fought their way to the surface again. I was going to have a baby. Dex's baby.

He didn't even know. He ought to know he was going to become a father. But my parents and my aunt and uncle had all forbidden me from contacting him. How was I going to get word to him?

Would they force me to give up the child? Knowing my family, they'd at least try.

God, I needed him. I didn't know what good he could do, since he was really just a kid like me, but I needed him anyway. We loved each other. Together, surely we'd figure out a way to survive.

"You can sit up now," the doctor said, going to the door. "The nurse will call your mother and aunt in and we'll all have a talk."

I didn't want to have a talk. I wanted to go home to Dex.

Chapter 27

Shotgun

Dex:

It was one of those black Anchorage mornings when you can't even imagine spring, although the calendars claim it's right around the corner. Cold as fuck, the sun nowhere in sight and not due to rise for hours. Snow everywhere, practically up to the windowsills on the one-story houses.

Spring. What the hell is that, anyway?

I stood in my shared bedroom and put on the coat Cass had given me, awkward and painful because of my broken arm hanging in a cast and sling. When I finally got the coat on, I stuck my feet in my motorcycle boots. Nobody in my house was awake yet, except for me.

No sound emerged from our parents' bedroom. In our room, Sin sprawled all over his bed, apparently at peace for once. His face looked so drawn, though, so haggard. Jesus. If he didn't get off the smack and soon, I was scared he wouldn't wake up one day. On the top bunk, Joe snored loudly, oblivious under his Evel Knievel comforter.

I hated the way I'd left Cass alone with her mother. Anything could have happened after I went home. I hadn't even been able to call because of the fight with my dad and going to the hospital. It had kept me up for hours, worrying about her, whether they'd punished her and how.

My body hurt all over from the beating, from my scalp to my toenails, but that didn't matter. I had to find out how my girl was doing, even if they dragged me physically off their property. That was okay, as long as I knew she was all right.

I didn't know when I'd be back, although I probably wouldn't be gone for long. I couldn't see Cass's parents letting her talk to me for more than about thirty seconds, if that long.

Outside, the neighborhood houses seemed to sleep under their caps of snow. It was too early on a Saturday morning for anyone to be up and about, except for lunatics like me. Even the ravens and chickadees were still in bed.

I clumped my way up the Maslanka driveway. Only a block and a half away from my house, yet it might as well have been on another planet. Their driveway was neatly shoveled and relatively free of ice and the yard looked tidy under its blanket of snow. There weren't any tell-tale weeds or rogue bushes sticking up in awkward places to ruin the serenity of the place.

Lights gleamed in their upstairs windows, so presumably someone was awake in there. My heart picked up speed at the thought of seeing Cass again. I had to see her. Had to make sure she was all right.

My ribs ached like the devil. The doctor in the ER had bound them, but he'd warned me that broken ribs are painful and they take a while to heal. I probably shouldn't be walking over icy streets in my condition. Like I gave a shit.

I looked like I'd been run over, or maybe attacked by a whole bar full of pissed off bikers. My dad had done a serious number on me. I didn't care. There was no way I was lazing around in bed when I could be talking to Cass.

My stomach churned nervously as I rang the bell. Her parents weren't going to like seeing me again, not that I would allow that to change my mind. Her mom had looked so grim when I'd left her that I'd worried, even in the hospital. What if they hurt her? What if they took out their anger with me on Cass? I couldn't stand it if that happened.

Light footsteps thumped down the stairs inside. The chain rattled. The door opened to reveal Beth Maslanka, dressed in a red bathrobe and moccasin-style slippers, her long dark hair in a single braid. Her eyes widened and her mouth fell open on a gasp when she saw me.

"Did my dad do that to you?" she said.

"Hi, Beth." My voice came out sounding remarkably calm and even. "It was my dad, not yours, and I need to talk to Cass."

Her pale skin turned red. "Um...she's not here."

"Not here? Come on, it's seven thirty on a Saturday. Please let me talk to her."

She shook her head. "I can't. Really, Dex. She's not here."

"Then where is she? Jenny's?" It seemed awful early for her to be out visiting, even if Jenny's house was just a couple blocks away.

"No." Beth's gaze dropped to the floor. "She's not at Jenny's."

I frowned, my worry returning. "Then where is she?"

Beth shook her head, looking miserable. "I'm sorry, but I'm not supposed to tell you."

Jesus Christ. I gripped the molding around the door. "Beth, where is she? Is she all right?"

The younger girl gave a non-committal motion of her head. "She's...she's just not here."

"Is she all right? Did they hurt her?"

Beth's head came up, her mouth open in a startled O. "Of course not. They wouldn't do that."

"Then where did she go? I need to see her. I need to know she's okay." My hand tightened on the wood. "Please, Beth. I need to know."

"What happened to you, anyway? Did your dad really beat you up?"

"You could say that. And you didn't answer my question."

"Beth?" said an older man's voice. "What's going on?"

Crap. Her dad.

"Nothing, Dad," she called. "I've got it." She turned back to me. "You've got to go. He's going to hit the roof if he sees you."

"Just tell me where she went." I was begging like a pussy. "I have to know."

She shook her head, looking alarmed. Then she glanced over her right shoulder. Pete Maslanka appeared behind her in the entryway. He, too, wore a bathrobe. His was dark blue. His feet were bare.

He glowered at me like I was some low, filthy insect that had fallen in his soup. "What are you doing here? I thought my wife told you to stay away."

That look was no more than I'd expected. I lifted my chin and squared my shoulders. "I have to see Cass."

"No. You have to get off my property before I call the police. Beth, go upstairs."

"Yes, Dad." She turned and left me there with him, no protest at all.

"Mr. Maslanka, I need to see her. I just need to know she's all right."

His face contorted in what looked like barely controlled rage. "You don't need anything where Cass is concerned. Get out of here or I will call the police."

"Just tell me she's all right."

He barked out a harsh laugh. "Get lost, Dex. You don't belong here."

"I know that. But I care about your daughter. I— I swallowed. "I love her. I need to know she's safe."

"You don't love her. If you did, you wouldn't have endangered her the way you did." He loomed at me, although he really wasn't any taller than I was. I couldn't tell how he did it, but he made himself seem a whole lot bigger. "Get off my property. I won't ask again."

He wasn't asking in the first place, but I decided not to remind him of that.

I stuck out my jaw. "You're not even going to tell me if she's safe? What did you do to her? Huh? How do I know she's okay?"

He barked an incredulous laugh. "You have some nerve, you know that? I'm her dad and I'm telling you she's okay. That's how you know."

"That's not good enough," I growled, my heart pounding desperately, my stomach sick. It was true. They'd done something to

208

her, something horrible. It was the only reason I could think of for his behavior.

"Look, you cocky little shit," Maslanka snapped. "Take your beat-up, white-trash self out of here or I'll shoot you. You got that? I'm gonna go get my shotgun. You'd better be gone by the time I get back."

I stared at him as a sense of unreality settled over me. Cass's dad had just threatened to shoot me. I wondered if he'd do it or if he was only bluffing. And if he did shoot me, would he then call an ambulance or would he leave me to bleed out on his doorstep?

I couldn't leave Cass undefended, but I also couldn't see what I could do to help her.

"Jesus Christ," I muttered.

"Don't you dare blaspheme at my door," he thundered.

I shook my head. Was this guy for real? "You are something else, man."

"Out." He pointed back down the driveway. "I'm going to shut and lock this door. When I come back, I'll have my shotgun loaded and ready for you. Stay if you want me to fill you full of buckshot."

He slammed the door in my face. I stood there staring at the flat white expanse of it for what felt like five whole minutes. If I left, I'd be abandoning Cass. But if I stayed, I had no doubt Maslanka would fire that shotgun right into my belly.

With a sense of doom hanging over me, I turned around and walked away. He'd beaten me, just as much, just as badly, as my father had. The defeat sat so heavily on my shoulders I had trouble walking.

It wasn't the first time I'd felt the powerlessness of being young and poor. When they'd thrown my ass in McLaughlin, I'd wanted to die. This was worse, though. This time, it wasn't just me in trouble and there was nothing I could do to help the girl I loved.

Not one fucking thing.

Chapter 28

Alone

Cass:

The living room and some of the less used areas of Aunt Frances and Uncle Don's house had this funny smell, kind of mildewy, that made my nose wrinkle. Maybe it was the age of the house, which seemed to be at least seventy years old. It was made of brick and had a deep front porch with thick, tapered columns, and inside it was dark, the windows small except for the front one in the living room.

The trim was all dark wood, too, and the walls had ancient-looking wallpaper on them. In the living room it was dull green vines and leaves on a buff-colored background that might have been white or ivory at one time. In the kitchen, it was dull green cabbage roses on brownish-white, and in the dining room it was some kind of dark abstract scrolling pattern, also green on muddy ivory or white. I guess someone living here once upon a time had really loved green.

The fixtures looked as old as the house. The one next to the living room couch had a fancy fabric shade with beaded fringe dangling from it. I couldn't decide if it was the coolest, hippie-groovy thing I'd ever seen or if it was hideously ugly.

The curtains in the living room were probably as old as that lamp. There was a layer of dusty-smelling brownish lace and then a layer of dark green cotton velvet drapes over that. I pushed the lace aside as I stared out at the front yard.

My mom was leaving me. She opened the passenger door of Uncle Don's Chevy station wagon as he threw her luggage in the back. She was going home, and I was stuck here indefinitely.

Somewhere behind me, in the kitchen I guessed, Aunt Frances was talking to one of my girl cousins, Annie. They were making dinner. I could hear the click and clank of kitchen tools against bowls and pans as they worked.

My tiny black and white photos of Dex and me, taken at that photo booth at Fur Rondy, seemed to burn my skin right through the pocket of my jeans. My mom didn't know I had them. She'd never asked and I sure wasn't going to tell. Anyone.

The pictures were all I had of him. Other than the baby, that was, and they weren't going to let me keep the baby. The idea of just giving my baby away, to people I would never meet, made me sick. I would have no guarantee they'd love my child, although I got constant reassurances from Aunt Frances that "it would go to a good family."

Maslanka girls did not have babies out of wedlock. It wasn't done. I'd never live it down and neither would my parents—we'd be ostracized by all our relatives and so would the child. I'd have to give him or her up to an adoption service unless I wanted to leave the family behind and strike out on my own.

The thought had occurred to me more than once. I could take my kid and get a tiny apartment somewhere, and a job. Heck, I could go on welfare if I had to, just until I figured out how to support myself. But the thought terrified me and I wasn't sure I was capable of it.

I'd never had a job before. I know that's ridiculous, for someone as old as seventeen, but it was true. My parents wanted us kids to concentrate on school, and besides they seemed to believe jobs were unnecessary for girls. Adam, of course, planned to get one in the summers, starting next year, but Beth and I were expected to stay home and learn to be wives and mothers.

My parents hadn't gotten the message that it was the seventies now. In their minds, I guess the sixties had never happened and we were still living in a post-war, women stay home world. They hated the women's movement and everything associated with it.

My lack of real-world experience hit me now, harder than it ever had before. Maybe it was because my mom was leaving. She was in the car now, not looking at me or even at the house, as if she wanted to forget I existed. My parents were so offended by what I'd done that they felt the need to pack me out of state, for crying out loud. I knew what would happen if I chose to keep the baby. They would disown me, and I'd truly be alone in the world. Alone, except for a helpless child.

I wished with sudden ferocity that I'd fought them harder when I had the chance. Sure, it would have made our home life more difficult and maybe I wouldn't have been the Good Girl, the Admirable and Responsible Older Sister. But I might have had more resources by now, more experience with getting by on my own, something I truly hadn't understood how much I needed until now.

I gave into temptation and slid the photos from my pocket. We looked so happy in them. Dex was looking at me as if I were the only thing in his world that mattered.

What was happening to him now? Was he okay? Did he miss me? Did he even know where I was?

My throat seized up and my eyes burned. I stuffed the pictures back in my pocket and leaned my forehead against the cold, wavy glass of the window. What if I never saw him again? What would I do?

I'd go on, of course. I would have to, especially if I kept the baby.

Oh, God, was I going to keep the baby?

Uncle Don got into the driver's side and shut the door with a metallic slam. He started the engine. Finally, my mom glanced over at the house. I couldn't tell whether or not she could see me standing at the window. She gave no sign. The car backed out of the driveway and took off down the street.

"Cass, honey, come help us fix dinner," my Aunt Frances called.

I wiped my eyes. "Okay. Coming."

Annie gave me a tentative smile as I came into the old-fashioned kitchen with its free-standing stove and cupboards. There was virtually no counter space because they had no built-in cupboards, only cabinets that stood separately from each other. All work happened on the gigantic kitchen table.

I couldn't smile back at my cousin. At that moment, I didn't think I'd ever smile again. All I could think was that I needed a way out of this mess and no-one was going to help me find it. I had to figure it out for myself.

That evening, as I got ready for bed in the upstairs bathroom, I found blood in my underpants. The bathroom looked more like a converted bedroom than a regular bathroom. The ceiling was high and the room square, not rectangular and narrow like most bathrooms. It featured a claw-foot tub that I had to admit was pretty cool looking, and one of those wall-mount white sinks where you can see the plumbing underneath. The toilet looked as vintage as the rest of the fittings.

I had a nightgown draped over one of the freestanding wooden bookshelf-things to either side of the sink that played the role of a counter and cabinet. I could have undressed in the room I shared with Annie, but I didn't know her all that well, so I changed my clothes in the bathroom. And when I pulled my underpants down, there was the evidence. I was bleeding.

I stared down at the wet, red stain and my heart began to pound. This couldn't be normal.

A few drops might be okay, but this was more than a few drops. It covered the whole crotch of my underwear. I sat down on the toilet with my panties around my knees and stared up at the green plaster of the bathroom ceiling.

Could it be a miscarriage? I thought I'd read somewhere that a little spotting during pregnancy, especially in the early months, was normal. But this seemed much too heavy to be normal.

My mom would probably be happy if I miscarried. Okay, not exactly happy, just less furious and afraid. I could picture the look of relief on her face so clearly, almost as if she stood in front of me. Not that it would make a difference to her and my dad's plans to keep me in

Chicago; I'd already asked and they said even if I turned out to not be pregnant, I still had to finish high school down here.

They really wanted to keep me away from Dex. He didn't even know he'd gotten me pregnant. He might never know how close he'd come to being a father. It hurt my heart to think of him up in Anchorage, without me, facing his parents and all the pressures of his life with no love and no support.

Bringing a baby into that picture would have been difficult. Maybe disastrous. But he should at least know what was happening, shouldn't he?

My belly cramped with sudden violence. It was worse than any menstrual cramp I'd ever had. I doubled over, my palms pressing against my lower abdomen as cold sweat bloomed all over my body.

If I'd had any doubts I was miscarrying, that pain erased them. The child that hadn't seemed real to me until now seemed to be leaving. I closed my eyes as more wetness pooled between my legs.

I hadn't wanted to be a mother. I hadn't known what I was going to do if I decided to keep the baby. Yet I'd never wished that tiny life away, and I didn't want it to leave me now.

"Stay," I whispered. "Please stay."

But the cramps continued on their vicious way. My stomach threatened to empty itself all over the chipped, black and white hex tile floor. I didn't know if the nausea was part of the miscarriage or just due to my overwrought emotional state.

Someone knocked on the bathroom door. I jumped.

"Yes?"

"Cass, are you all right in there?" Aunt Frances said. "You've been a while."

I did not want to talk to her right now, but someone needed to know what was happening to me. So I forced myself to pull up my bloody panties and walk to the door of the bathroom and open it.

Aunt Frances always wore dresses. Today she was in a blue and white striped cotton shirtdress with pearl snaps down the front, sensible oxford shoes on her feet. Her brown hair was in a bouffant style that flipped up on the ends.

She glanced over my half-dressed state with wide eyes. "What's going on?"

"I think I'm miscarrying," I said baldly. "I'm bleeding."

"May I come in?" she said, hand on the door.

"A-all right." I stepped back so she could enter.

Frances closed the bathroom door behind herself. "How much blood is there?" she said in a matter-of-fact tone that reassured me.

"It looks like a lot." I pulled down my panties and showed her. Embarrassing, but what else could I do?

"That is a lot," she said. "It looks like much more than normal spotting."

"Should I go to the doctor?"

She tilted her head, considering. "I don't think so, unless you're feverish or in a lot of pain. Are you?"

"The pain is bad. But I think it's manageable."

She pressed the back of her hand to my forehead. "I'll take your temperature, but I don't think you're running a fever. Why don't I give you some aspirin for the pain and we'll wait and see?"

I bit my lip and nodded, afraid to speak. I hadn't wanted this baby. I might have been forced to give it up, and if I'd managed to keep it then becoming a mother would have changed my life forever and not for the better. Yet I didn't want to lose it.

"Do you think there's some way to save it?" I whispered.

Her face softened. She laid a gentle hand on my shoulder. "Only God can do that, dear. We'll get you to bed and see how you are in an hour. That's probably all the doctor would say to do anyway, but if the bleeding gets any worse you let me know immediately. Okay? Send Annie in to me if you feel like it's too hard to get up."

I nodded again, speechless.

"This is a blessing, Cass," she said softly. "You're too young to be a mother, especially unwed. Believe me, it's no small thing to raise a child and being unwed and young makes it infinitely harder."

"I know," I choked out. "But I want to save it."

"Oh, honey." She took me in her arms. "It'll be okay. You'll see. Uncle Don and I love you. Your mom and dad love you. It'll be okay."

I didn't believe her.

Chapter 29

Brothers

Dex:

"Dex, wake up."

I groaned, sleep still wrapped thickly around me. "Whuh?"

"Wake up." It was Sin's voice. "Come on, buddy, I need you to wake up."

I blinked up at him. The bedroom was unlit except for the nightlight I'd put in for Joe back when he was still afraid of the dark. In its dim glow, I could barely see my older brother hanging over me, his black hair falling in his face. He looked like an animated skeleton.

Sin never woke me up. I mean never. Not since before he'd left for the war. I couldn't figure out what he was doing.

I rubbed my face. "What the fuck, Sin? What time is it?"

"Three o'clock."

"In the morning?" I struggled to sit up. "What's going on?"

"The cops are here."

"Oh, fuck." That got me upright and fully awake, my heart racing. "You put your stash somewhere they can't find it?" I whispered urgently.

"They're not here for me. Or you either. It's about Mom and Dad."

I rubbed my eyes again. "I'm not following you."

Sin's eyes looked bleak, even for him. He wore an old white undershirt and a pair of ragged jeans that hung off his emaciated frame. His shoulders drooped as he gazed down at me. He looked unsure of himself, like he had something to say but wasn't sure how to put it into words. Whatever it was must be bad.

"Just tell me," I said, bracing myself. "Waiting won't help."

"They're dead, Dex."

I frowned, trying to make sense of his words. My brain wasn't fully awake yet after all. It had sounded like he said our parents were dead.

"Mom and Dad," he said. "They died in a car crash."

I continued to stare dully at him. "A car crash?"

"Remember that party they were going to? They were on the way home and ran into a moose."

I narrowed my eyes at him. "You're shitting me."

"It's the truth."

I couldn't help it. I gave a snort of laughter. "A moose? Come on, Sin, give me a break here. Couldn't you at least wait until I woke up on my own to bullshit me?"

He didn't smile. His green eyes remained just as somber, as serious as ever. "I wish I were joking, but I'm not."

I rubbed my face again. "A moose. Mom and Dad are dead because they hit a moose?"

"Yeah. The thing broke their windshield. The car ran off the road and hit a telephone pole and that's what killed them. I guess they weren't wearing seatbelts."

I couldn't take it in. Our parents were dead?

My sorrow over losing Cass still boiled under the surface of me, barely controllable. And now this. I couldn't see the future, couldn't picture it with our parents gone. They'd been terrible parents, but still...they'd been all we had. And now we didn't have them anymore.

What would we do? A seventeen-year-old and a twenty-year-old, only one part-time job between them, with a little brother in elementary school. What were we going to do?

"So...they must have been going pretty fast," I said, still bewildered although the haze of sleep had left.

"Yeah. About sixty, the cops said. They were both hammered." Sin grimaced. "Probably fighting."

"Jesus Christ," I said. I glanced up at the top bunk. "What are we gonna tell Joe?"

"The truth, I guess." He ran bony fingers through his hair. "I don't know what's gonna happen now, man. I don't know if we'll stay together."

"We'd better go out and talk to the cops," I said. "Or else they'll think we're up to something back here."

That was our normal response to anything involving the law. Paranoia born of long and painful experience. Cops were not our friends.

"You're right," he said.

I forced myself out of bed, wearing only my briefs and a ratty old T-shirt. "Let's go."

Sin stood there a moment, staring up at the top bunk where our youngest brother lay. I couldn't quite read the expression on his face. He'd checked out years ago, probably long before he'd come back to us from the war. He'd been present in body only for so long I had no idea what to expect from him. Could we count on him or was he going to drag us down into the heroin depths with him?

Fuck no. No, he wasn't, because I wouldn't allow that to happen. Somehow I was going to keep me and Joe together, keep us alive and well.

Sin caught me looking at him. He straightened and gave me a nod. "It's gonna be all right, Dex. I know this seems bad, but it's gonna be all right."

"Is it?"

"Yeah." His voice cracked a little. He raked his fingers through his hair again. "I know I haven't been the big brother you've needed for a long time now. But I'm gonna pull myself together. I'm gonna make sure you and Joe are okay."

Funny, that's just what I'd been telling myself.

"I don't know if I can believe that," I said. "I want to, but—"

"I know." He hung his head. "I haven't done shit for a long time. But I'm gonna be better now. I have to be. I love you guys, you know?"

I clapped him on the back. "Yeah. Me too."

I really wanted to believe him, and myself. I wanted to believe it would turn out all right, but I just didn't know. I didn't know anything anymore.

Chapter 30

The End

Chicago, 1975
Cass:
The room I shared with my cousin Annie had tiny pink flowers all over the walls. I think it was the only room in the house that wasn't predominantly green. It looked out on a huge maple tree that turned astonishing colors of red, orange, and gold in the fall and which took up most of the small back yard.

There were lace curtains on the windows. I suspected the house had last been decorated over thirty years before, but I hadn't been rude enough to actually ask anyone if I was right. Every room was full of lace and dark colors and fussy wallpaper, and it smelled old.

Our beds had pink comforters. Pink was still my favorite color, but I'd never liked those beds or the bedding. The principle of the thing, I guess.

Annie was a sweet girl, but her home was my prison. I'd never wanted to come here and I didn't want to stay. She knew I could hardly wait to go back to Alaska, and my chance had finally come.

I'd graduated from high school today and I'd been eighteen for a few months. No-one could legally hold me here, or anywhere I didn't want to be. I was officially an adult.

I took off my graduation gown—in royal blue with a white cap, the school colors for Saint Hildegard's Catholic High School For Girls—the minute Uncle Don and Aunt Francis brought me and Annie home from the ceremony, glad to get back into my everyday skirt and T-shirt. High school was over and I was over eighteen. Freedom beckoned.

I glanced at Annie, sitting on her bed across from the one I used. I still thought of it as *her* room, not ours. She'd divested herself of her gown, too, and was busily re-braiding her waist-length brown hair.

"Are you excited?" I said.

"I don't know what I am." She grimaced. "Loyola next year. I think I'll be excited in September. Right now I'm kind of numb."

"Yeah. Me too."

Someone knocked on Annie's door.

"Come in," she yelled.

The door opened and her little brother Michael stuck his head inside. "Cass, there's a phone call for you."

"Okay, thanks." I stood up and brushed some imaginary dust off my denim skirt.

The house had only one phone and it was a wall mounted one in the kitchen, the old-fashioned black kind. I pounded down the stairs after Michael.

In the kitchen, his twin brother Jimmy tried to do pull-ups by laying on the floor under the table and using the top as his bar. He could only pull himself up about half way, grimacing and red-faced.

Aunt Frances held the phone out to me with a huge smile.

"It's your mom and dad," she said.

Great. I was reasonably sure they could have afforded to come down and see me graduate, but it seemed I was still the family pariah. This phone call and a card in the mail was all the acknowledgment I was getting.

Michael and his twin brother James started some kind of play fight using wooden mixing spoons as weapons. I shook my head and turned away from them so I could concentrate on the phone.

"Hi, Mom."

"Congratulations, honey," my mom said. "Are you happy?"

"Thrilled." It was true, actually, but probably not for the reasons she thought.

"Have you given any more thought to Loyola? You know we'll pay your way if you stay with your aunt and uncle."

"Yeah, I know. I haven't decided yet."

In fact, I'd been saving up my birthday and Christmas money for a plane ticket home, but I didn't want to tell her that just yet. Maybe I'd tell her when I got off the plane in Anchorage. That way, she couldn't stop me or try to talk me out of it.

Michael and James dashed around me in a big circle, whooping and laughing. Aunt Frances tried to hush them.

"Well, you need to make up your mind," my mom said. "And soon. Otherwise—"

"I know, Mom. It'll be another year before I can start. That's fine with me." Especially since I had no intention of attending Loyola, or any other Chicago school. I was going home. Period.

I wanted to see Dex again. Yeah, it had been two years since we'd spoken. Two years since that awful day when she'd found us together. But I couldn't seem to forget him and I needed to know if he still felt the same way about me.

Besides, I wanted to explain what had happened to me. I wasn't sure he even knew where I'd gone. No-one had spoken his name to me, even when I'd directly asked for information.

James barreled into me and I let out my breath in a grunt. "Sorry!" he yelled as he dashed off.

He didn't look sorry, the little monster. I just grinned at him.

"What is going on over there?" my mom said.

"Just Mike and Jimmy playing."

"Those two. I'm so glad I never had twins."

Yeah, I'd bet. Especially two of me. Then she would have had even more girl trouble. Maybe she and my dad could have built a round tower, though, and put all us girls into it and thrown away the ladder. That would have kept us safe.

"So," she said in an oh-so-casual tone. "Guess what I saw in the paper the other day?"

"What?" I said, not particularly interested.

Michael plowed into one of the kitchen chairs with a bang. James screeched with laugher as Mike ended up on his butt on the floor.

"You boys go outside," Aunt Frances said. "Right now! Cass can't hear a word your Aunt Lucille is saying."

"It's okay," I said over the din.

She didn't seem to hear me. She ushered the boys out the back door and into the yard.

"That boyfriend of yours," my mom said. "Dex. There was a wedding announcement."

The noise of my cousins' laugher, the bang of the screen door, my aunt's footsteps on the ancient tan linoleum all faded away. My hand turned sweaty and slick and I almost dropped the phone.

"What?" I said, hoping I'd heard her wrong.

"Dex Morgan got married. Some girl named Marcy. Or was it Marcia?"

"Misty?" I said, sounding choked.

"That must have been it. Give me a minute and I'll find the paper."

"No. That's okay. I don't care."

I had the phone in a death-grip. My eyes closed as my heart dropped through the floorboards. He'd gotten married. It had only been two years and he was the same age as me, so he hadn't wasted any time.

Married. Right out of high school.

I could feel the corners of my mouth turning down as a stupid urge to cry rose up and tried to choke me. He'd forgotten about me. All the time that I'd been sitting around dreaming of him, treasuring the time we'd had, staring at those little photos like they were sacred relics or something...all that time, he'd been messing around with Misty and now they were married. Maybe he'd gotten her pregnant too.

Oh, God. I wanted to sit down but the phone cord wasn't long enough to reach to the chairs so I leaned against the wall. He'd said he loved me, but his love hadn't been as strong as mine. He hadn't waited for me.

"Cass? Are you still there?" my mom said.

"Yeah, I'm here. Just a little distracted."

"Well, I'm sorry to shock you. I thought you should know that he'd moved on."

"I'm not shocked." I tried to make my voice light but it didn't sound very convincing. "We've both moved on. All that happened a long time ago."

"Are you sure?" she said skeptically.

"Yeah. Of course I'm sure. I don't even feel like the same person anymore."

"I thought you might have ideas about contacting him again," she said.

"Nope. Not me." Liar. Pants on fire.

"Well, all right. That's good."

"Yeah."

"Are you sure you won't apply to Loyola? Your dad and I would love to help you out there."

"Mom, I don't want to keep living in Aunt Frances and Uncle Don's house. I already explained that to you."

"Well, why not? They're your family."

They were my jailers. They were kind, upstanding people who meant well, but I didn't want to spend one night under their roof that wasn't absolutely necessary.

"If you'd let me live in the dorms," I said, "then I'd consider it."

"No, I don't think your dad would go for that," she said. "We want you at home."

I was certain of that.

"Then I won't be going to Loyola."

It dawned on me that the money I'd saved for a plane ticket would also work as a security deposit on a small apartment. I could get my own place and a job, take night classes at one of the other colleges—Chicago University or U of I maybe. Because hell would freeze over before I let my parents control me anymore.

No living at home. No accepting hand-outs. I'd rather live in some dive on my own than be under my relatives' thumbs.

I still didn't have any real work experience, but I did know how to type. That had to be worth something, and I didn't care how low on the corporate ladder I had to start in order to get my foot in the door. I just wanted to work so I could support myself.

This was the end of Good-girl Cass, the end of waiting around for someone else to give me permission, the end of waiting for a boy or a man or anyone. From now on, I did everything myself.

Chapter 31

Baggage

Anchorage International Airport, 1982
Cass:

The light outside the airplane windows surprised me even though I'd expected it. There was a lot of light in July in Alaska, even if the weather was cold and dripping rain like it was now. Even at ten o'clock at night.

The canned-air dryness and odor of the plane surrounded me, along with the smell of aviation fuel. Hours in the air hadn't inured me to that smell. It made my stomach churn with anxiety. The only thing I associated with it was my banishment ten years before.

I smoothed my chic, short haircut. It didn't really need it, being so short it kept its shape no matter what I did, but it made me feel better. More in control. I checked my oversized Mabe pearl earrings to make sure they were still in place. Afterward, I pulled out my lipstick and applied it carefully with the tiny attached mirror. In a few minutes, I was going to see my parents for the first time in ten years, and I wanted to look good Chicago-style.

I slipped my arms into my sharp woolen blazer, the pale blue one I'd bought on the discount rack at Marshall Field's. While the plane had felt overheated with all the passengers crammed in the limited space, the air outside would be chilly. Besides, it was easier to carry if I wore it.

I stood up, my trendy black carry-on in my hands, and shuffled off the plane. The flight attendants smiled and wished me a good vacation. Hah. Couldn't they tell I was a native-born Alaskan returning home? The prodigal daughter.

Ten years in Chicago had changed me, so maybe not.

Crowds of people waited in the terminal, craning their necks to catch a glimpse of their loved ones. The passengers around me did the same. I did not.

If we didn't find each other, it was no problem. I'd simply hire a cab and go over to their house. They could catch up with me.

A tall blond guy in a red plaid flannel shirt caught my eye and my heart seized up. My mouth went dry as I scanned the crowd to find him again. And then my shoulders fell as I realized it wasn't Dex.

Of course it wasn't. Why would he be here waiting for me? We hadn't spoken since that awful afternoon when my mom had discovered us together.

He'd gotten married to Misty. He probably had a bunch of kids by now.

No, Dex wouldn't be here. I didn't even know if he still lived in town.

I pushed down the irrational disappointment and continued on my way. Someday there would be a man for me. I kept telling myself so, although I'd stopped believing it years ago.

The Anchorage airport had changed. I knew it had undergone a major update not long after I'd moved away, but it still surprised me. It was ugly. They'd spent tons of money to make it look like this?

Everything was a dirty, grayish shade of brown that reminded me of the darkest spots of dirty snow, the bits where all the grit had accumulated over months of winter. Funny. It sure wasn't a color I would have chosen.

"Cass!"

I recognized my mom's voice and turned my head. There she was, jumping up and down with her hand as high in the air as she could get it.

"Cass!" she bellowed again. "Right here! Here we are, Cass!"

For crying out loud. Did she think she could make this a more pleasant homecoming by making a fool out of herself? Maybe she thought I'd forgotten what she looked like. I sighed and headed her way.

My dad stood next to her, smiling stiffly. They both wore jeans and sweatshirts, bright white athletic shoes on their feet. Typical Alaska wear.

To either side of them were my brother and sister. Beth's hair was still long, brown like Annie's. In fact, I was struck by how much she looked like our cousin. And she was so much older, a woman and not a barely-teenager anymore. Good grief, my sister had grown up while I was away.

Adam, too. His black hair and blue eyes looked the same, but he was so much taller and more filled out. His face, while easily recognizable, was much more angular and adult-looking. The pictures they'd sent me hadn't done either of them justice.

My mom's eyes widened as she took in my short hair. "Oh, my God. What did you do to yourself?"

"I entered the twentieth century," I said dryly.

"Come here and give me a hug." She held out her arms.

I embraced her gingerly. She seemed smaller than I remembered. My dad, too. Had they shrunk, or had I grown taller?

I hugged my dad, and then Adam.

"Welcome back, sis," he whispered in my ear.

"Thanks." I smiled up at him. God, he was big.

"It's my turn," Beth said.

I let her take me in her arms. She wore jeans and a Members Only jacket in dark blue, tasteful make-up on her face. Annie never wore pants or make-up.

"I can't believe you're really here," Beth said, laughing a little.

"Neither can I." I smiled at her too. "Where's Leo?"

"He had some work to do," she said, her smile turning all gooey and lovestruck. "But you'll meet him tomorrow."

"I can hardly wait."

My mom came closer, openly scrutinizing me. "I love your clothes," she said, still looking me over. "Those heels are so high. Aren't they uncomfortable? And your jacket is so tight. And the pants too. Is that what they're wearing in Chicago nowadays?"

Jesus. I could just imagine what she'd say when she saw my exercise gear. That would really set her off. I reminded myself I was only there for two weeks. By the time the termination dust hit the mountains, I'd be boarding my return flight to Chicago.

Adam winked at me and Beth covered a smile with her hand.

"Everything fits perfectly, Mom," I said. "I've got to go to baggage claim now, if you want to wait with me."

"Of course we'll wait for you. Won't we, Pete?"

"Of course," my dad said, sounding like he had the response on automatic.

Great. Lovely. Would we talk about what a slut I'd become? Because that would be awesome reunion material, honestly. I could hardly wait.

Of course, I'd heard it all before from Uncle Don and Aunt Frances. Men don't respect girls who give it away. Why buy the cow when you can get the milk for free? Right. Because I was a cow, and men were in the market for milk. So much wrong with that statement. Where to even begin?

And that wasn't even getting into the religious arguments. According to my relatives, I was going straight to hell, where I'd roast right next to Mary Magdalene and all the other whores. When I'd reminded them that the Magdalene had been a favorite of Christ, it had only slowed them down for an instant. They had an answer for everything, even if none of it made any sense.

Maybe my parents would put a new spin on it, though. I mean, Uncle Don and Aunt Frances had pretty much worn out all their arguments on me and now they were on an endless loop that repeated mindlessly. Even they didn't listen to themselves anymore.

Or maybe they'd hold off, considering Adam and Beth were here.

"The wedding is going to be so beautiful," my mom gushed as we made our way down to baggage claim. "It's out at Big Lake, did I tell you?"

"Yes, you did." About a thousand times.

"We have a pavilion set up for the ceremony."

"I'll be sure to wear all the insect repellent I brought."

Any Alaskan lake in July would be a haven for mosquitoes, although June would probably have been even worse. But July would be bad enough. I would smell like a fisherman casting in hip boots on the Kenai, but who cared? It wasn't my wedding anyway.

"Oh, it won't be that bad. Don't be so negative. I don't want you to make Beth any more nervous than she already is."

Beth and I exchanged a humorous glance.

"Don't worry," I said. "I won't ruin it for her."

"I'm not nervous," Beth said. "I'm fine."

My mom grabbed my hand and gave a big, dramatic sigh. "I just can hardly believe I have my girl back again after all this time."

Yeah. She was the one who'd sent me away. I didn't say it, though. What would be the point? I didn't say anything at all.

"You should have come up a long time ago," she said.

"I didn't have enough money."

"We would have paid for you to visit."

I shook my head. "I'm not taking any money from you guys."

"Oh," she said in a small voice calculated to make me feel guilty.

It wasn't going to work. I was done with the guilt. I was twenty-six years old and I made my own decisions now. I hadn't lived with family members since the day I'd graduated, and I hadn't taken any money from them either, except as birthday and Christmas gifts. Everything I had, I'd earned myself and that was the way I liked it.

The only reason I was staying at my parents' house instead of a hotel was that my budget was still vanishingly small. If I'd had the funds, I'd be staying somewhere else.

Both my parents had a lot of gray hair. I didn't remember that from before. They'd sent pictures over the years, but a photo isn't the same as seeing a person in the flesh. A picture can't really tell you how small they've grown, or how fragile they look. It can't tell you how small they can still make you feel.

I sensed my teenage years reaching out for me, trying to drag me back into that old, familiar family dynamic I'd worked so hard to escape. It happened every time I went to Aunt Frances's house for Sunday dinner or a holiday, only it was weaker there because she and Don were only my aunt and uncle, not my parents. Here the pattern retained its primal power to make me act like a hormone-addled kid.

"So how is your work going?" my mom said as we took up positions next to the baggage claim belt.

I glanced sidelong at her. "It's fine. Pretty much the same as ever."

"How is your boss? What's his name? Ed?"

"Ed is fine, Mom," I said, heroically resisting an eye-roll.

"Has he taken you to lunch again?"

"He's just my boss, not my boyfriend."

She gave an exasperated sigh. "I feel like I can't talk to you."

"Lucille, give Cass a break," my dad said. "She just got here. I'm sure she's tired from traveling."

My mom's lips thinned. She didn't say anything. Adam and Beth shared a glance, but they kept quiet and I had no idea what they were thinking.

Mom liked to hint that Ed and I could get together someday, and by get together she meant get married. I had no interest in the man and he didn't seem to have any in me. We worked together. That was all.

Even if I had feelings for him, I wouldn't act on them. Workplace romance seemed like a bad idea to me. I didn't have feelings for him anyway, so it was a non-issue in my mind. It was just my mother constantly worrying that I'd never find a man.

Dex crossed my mind again. I wondered whether he was happy with Misty, what she looked like now, if they had any kids. If they were still together.

So much for love. I guess two years had been too long to wait, at least for him.

Adam had been right after all. Dex had only wanted to get in my pants. He'd forgotten me almost as soon as my parents had packed my butt on that airplane to Chicago.

I, on the other hand, would never forget him. No matter how many men I slept with, none of them measured up to Dex. Even when they had more technique than he'd had, more bedroom expertise, they still couldn't equal the fire I'd experienced with him. He'd ruined me.

Chapter 32

All The Time

Dex:

The kitchen in our house was almost always clean. This morning was no exception. The counters gleamed because Joe had wiped them down before he went to bed. The garbage can had only a small amount of garbage in it, and the can itself was clean so it didn't stink. All our stray pantry supplies, like canned food and packages of bread, went inside the cabinets, so it looked freakishly neat.

That was how we liked it.

The walls were white now, not the ugly brownish-pink color left over from the late fifties when the house had been built. The bare window over the stainless steel sink let in a lot of light, especially at this time of year.

The weather was typical Anchorage summer—chilly and wet. All the colors in the world seemed limited to the gray of sky and rain and the brilliant greens of the summer foliage. The open window let in the scent of grass and fireweed and birch trees all growing as frantically as they could while the warm season lasted.

I stood at the new beige laminate kitchen counter to pour myself a cup of black coffee and make a peanut-butter sandwich, my standard breakfast. The smell of the coffee almost completely drowned out the green outdoor scents as I poured it into a stoneware mug. Had to have my coffee in the morning or I didn't function.

Our kitchen looked out on the street, not that Susitna Drive was much to look at. This morning, though, I couldn't seem to stop taking glances outside at our average front yard on our average street.

At least, I told myself, it was average now and not the pit of hell it had been when Sin and I were kids.

Sin, Joe, and I had fixed up the kitchen a little bit when we'd finally saved enough money. All we'd really done was sand the cabinets and paint them white, then put down a new beige vinyl floor and the new counter. It was nothing fancy, but it looked a hell of a lot better than it had when I was growing up.

Now we had more than enough money for a new kitchen, but we were so busy at our garage that we hadn't gotten around to it. Three single guys didn't exactly need a fancy kitchen, anyway, so it didn't much matter.

Behind me, Sin rattled the paper as he ate his breakfast at the table. Joe had already left for his first class of the day. He was going to University of Alaska Anchorage, studying computer science and helping at the garage in the late afternoons when his classes were over.

I was fucking proud of that kid. He was doing so much better than Sin or I had ever done. Neither of us had taken any college classes. Hell, we'd barely graduated from high school, but Joe was moving on to a level we hadn't even hoped to reach.

The best Sin and I had done was hold the three of us together and start our business. We got lucky, what with the Alaska Pipeline going through, bringing all kinds of new people and their vehicles into Anchorage. Our business picked up fast and we'd found plenty of customers, so we were doing all right.

I gazed idly out at the neatly mowed front lawn. No weeds. I didn't tolerate them. There was no way I'd let the house go to shit the way our parents had. We were damned lucky we'd even been able to hold onto it, and I knew it.

From where I stood, I could just see the corner of Susitna and Knik, so I noticed when a woman turned onto our street and I got a funny little jolt of recognition and excitement. She looked so much like Cass that for a second I'd thought it was her, coming back to me. Then I shook my head at myself. Cass wasn't ever coming back.

You'd think that after almost ten years I would have forgotten her, that I would have moved on. I'd tried, over and over again. But no matter what I did, no matter how many women I dated or took to bed, nothing drove my first girlfriend from my memory. It was like she was engraved on my bones or something.

As the woman came closer, I could see she had short dark hair. Would Cass cut her hair? Probably not. She wouldn't wear skin-tight spandex, either, like this chick was.

Her body, though. I could see the whole shape of her, fully displayed in the bright red Lycra bodysuit she wore, and the high breasts, the narrow waist, the graceful curve of her hips was all so much like Cass that my breath caught.

What if it was her?

My heart started pounding like crazy. I gulped down a burning mouthful of coffee. It couldn't be her. Not after such a long time. It just wasn't possible.

She'd never written to me. Never called. She hadn't even contacted Jenny. Neither of us had heard a single word, and we'd both pestered the hell out of Adam and Beth Maslanka for information. They wouldn't give up a single tidbit.

Their dad must have put the fear of hell into them or something.

Anyway, after all this time, for Cass to walk casually past my house was just too much to believe. It was just some chick who looked like her, stirring up old memories and feelings I should have let go of a long time ago.

I turned my back on the window and brought my coffee and food to the table. Sin looked up from his paper and nodded, then went back to reading. We both wore coveralls, ready for a day of work, and we both still had long hair. No mullets, either. Real long hair. Sure, we owned a business and a house, but there was no sense getting carried away with all that respectability crap.

I gulped down the rest of my coffee, took one bite of the sandwich and was done. I pushed the plate away and stood up.

"That all you're gonna eat?" Sin said.

"Yes, Dad, it is." I had no appetite.

"Okay. Suit yourself." He turned a page and kept reading.

"I'm gonna put my shit in the truck," I said.

He just kept reading, didn't even acknowledge me. I grabbed my work bag and opened the front door. And there she was, standing right at the end of our driveway, staring at the house.

I came out onto the front stoop and shut the door behind me. Our eyes met. Those beautiful, pale blue eyes behind thick, black lashes, eyes I'd never forget as long as I lived.

"Holy shit," I said. "It is you."

Her mouth opened. Then shut. Then opened again. She turned a peculiar shade of red.

What was wrong with her? She looked like she wanted to take my head off.

"Cass." I started toward her, cutting across the lawn.

"No," she said. She shook her head, over and over again.

"Cass, wait. What are you doing here?"

She took a step backward, into the street. "No way. Nuh-uh."

"Talk to me." I was almost there; I'd almost reached her.

My heart was racing and my mouth was dry. I had the weirdest feeling I was moving through a dream landscape, like nothing around me was real. I'd imagined this day for so long that now it was happening I had a hard time believing in it.

She spun on her heel and stalked off in the direction of Jenny's house. I dashed after her. I wasn't letting her get away this time.

"Cass!"

She just kept walking, her footsteps speeding up. She wore blindingly white running shoes. Her round little ass flexed and her hips rolled from side to side as she strove to get away from me. Damn, she looked incredible in that outfit.

It wasn't the kind of thing I would ever have pictured her wearing. How much had she changed over the years?

"Cass, come back here. I want to talk to you."

"I don't want to talk to you," she flung over her shoulder.

"Damn it. Wait up." I broke into a jog.

She threw a glance over her shoulder and started running.

"Jesus, will you be reasonable?" I yelled.

"Leave me alone, Dex."

"No. What are you doing here?" I called out, still jogging after her. "Why haven't I seen you in ten years? What the hell is going on?"

"I don't want to talk to you."

I caught up with her, running at her left side so she could run on the grass if a car came along. Good thing I'd taken up running the summer before. "I'm not going away. Talk to me."

She threw me a look of such resentment it almost stopped me in my tracks. "Won't your wife have something to say about that?"

"Huh?" I said, bewildered. "I don't have a wife."

"Oh, great. That's real nice." She glared at me again. "Go away, Dex. I would never have come this way if I'd known you still lived in the same place."

Her behavior made no sense to me. Why did she think I was married? Was that why she was so angry?

"I'm not going away," I said.. "You owe me an explanation."

She stopped. I kept moving for a couple of paces before I realized she was standing still. When I turned around, she had her hands on those sexy hips of hers and was giving me a death glare.

"I don't owe you anything," she said.

"Bullshit. What we had—you left and I never heard from you—" I shook my head, at a loss for words. "What happened to you?"

"What happened was ten years ago. It's over. End of story. Now leave me alone."

"I can't." I took a step toward her.

"Dex, do us both a favor and fuck off. I grew up and so should you."

Her words were like a slap in the face. Or maybe a steel-toed boot in the gut. She ran past me, careful to avoid looking me in the face.

This time I stood there, numb and silent, as she ran off down the street without me.

* * *

Cass:

The neighborhood looked a lot less friendly now that I knew Dex still lived here. Jesus Christ. How come Beth or Adam hadn't told me about this? Why hadn't they warned me?

I'd left the house in high spirits, considering the circumstances, determined to get in my morning run. The cool, misty weather was perfect for running and the air smelled sweet and so clean I hardly recognized it as the same stuff we breathed in Chicago. Birds sang in every tree. It was idyllic.

And then he'd shown up.

To be fair, I had stopped and gaped at his house, drawing his attention. I shouldn't have done that. I should have kept moving so he didn't notice me. But I hadn't known it would be a problem, hadn't even imagined he could still be there in that tiny house.

It looked different than I remembered. Neater, cleaner. The grass was green and weed-free, the paint looked fresh. I'd assumed his parents had sold to some other family.

Did he live there with his wife?

He claimed he wasn't married. I didn't know if I could believe that. Although why he'd lie was beyond me. He'd seemed genuinely baffled when I mentioned a wife.

Had my mother been wrong? I didn't know how she could have made a mistake of that magnitude. It's not as if she would have confused him with someone else. Not when he'd been the whole reason I was banished to Chicago.

I passed Jenny's house. There was another person with whom I'd lost contact when I left. My parents and my aunt and uncle had intercepted all my mail. I wasn't allowed to receive anything except what my parents sent. It was practically medieval and I'd never forgiven them for it. Even now, I harbored a lot of rage, which was another good reason for exercise. It worked some of the anger out of me.

Today I had a surplus of anger.

I ran until I was covered in sweat and trembling with exhaustion. Yet when I stumbled back into my parents' house, I still hadn't managed to exorcise Dex's image from my mind.

He'd looked so beautiful. Better than I remembered. He'd lost the few soft edges he'd still possessed as a teen. Now he was all hard angles and masculine power, his blond hair long, a short beard shadowing his jaw. He'd worn dark blue coveralls, the kind mechanics use, so I guessed he must have a job at a garage. The hard, muscular lines of his body had strained at the thick fabric of his clothing, making me long foolishly to touch him.

God, I was such an idiot. He wasn't for me. He'd never been for me. Too much had happened, too much had changed for us to pick up where we'd left off, but even if we could have started over, it wouldn't work.

We were from different worlds.

In my bedroom—the very same one I'd used as a teen—I kicked off my shoes, stripped out of my bodysuit, and slipped into the flannel robe I'd bought especially for this trip. At home in my own place, I went bare-assed naked as much as possible, but here I deferred to my parents' conservative sensibilities. Just one more reason I wanted to get the wedding over with so I could go back where I belonged.

I ran a hot shower in the downstairs bathroom. It looked exactly the same as it had when I'd left, the same avocado and rust colored flowered wallpaper, the same green vinyl floor, same matching green bathtub and toilet and sink. It was like I'd fallen into a time warp or something.

I felt faintly guilty that I couldn't be happier for Beth. I wished her and Leo well, I really did. I hoped things worked out for them and I certainly wouldn't think of missing my sister's wedding. I just wished I didn't have to stay with my parents in order to attend.

As I stepped under the blissful heat of the water, someone knocked on the bathroom door. "Cass, are you okay?" Beth called over the sound of the shower.

"I'm fine," I yelled. "Why?"

"Can I come in?"

"Sure."

It surprised me that she'd feel comfortable standing in the bathroom while I showered; we'd been so big on privacy and modesty in this family when I was growing up. But maybe I wasn't the only one who'd changed.

"I saw you come in," she said, shutting the door behind herself. "You almost looked sick."

"I overdid it a little, that's all."

"Are you sure?"

I squirted some apple-scented shampoo into my hand. "Yep. I'm sure."

"Hm. You looked upset."

"I'm fine, Beth. Don't worry about me. You have enough to think about."

"You've been gone so long. I thought coming back here might be hard for you."

And it was, but I wasn't going to discuss that with her or anyone else.

"Hey," I said. "Did Mom ever say anything to you about Dex getting married?"

She paused, as if thinking it over. "Not that I remember."

I rinsed out the shampoo. "She told me he had."

"When was that?"

"High school graduation."

"Huh." There was a soft bump, like she'd thumped her rear end against the vanity. "She never said anything about it to me. Why?"

"No reason. Just wondered."

"Do you still think about him?"

All the time. "Not much. I guess it's just part of being back in Anchorage."

"I was never able to tell you," she said, "Because of how close they were watching us, but I thought what they did to you was terrible. Way out of line. I'm really sorry that happened to you."

I peeked around the edge of the green and rust striped shower curtain. My sister gazed back at me, so serious and sorrowful, almost as if she felt guilty. "You didn't have anything to do with it. It wasn't your fault, so there's nothing for you to feel sorry for."

"I know," she said. "But I do anyway. I missed you something awful."

I smiled at her. "I missed you too."

Chapter 33

Friends

Cass:

My parents hadn't changed anything about the house in the time I'd been gone. Even the furniture was exactly the same.

My room had the pink walls and rose-patterned curtains and bed coverings I remembered so well. My stuffed animals still occupied the pony wall, staring at me reproachfully for abandoning them. They weren't even dusty. The place looked as if I'd simply picked up and left one day and never come back.

Oh, wait. That's precisely what had happened.

I laid out my second bodysuit, this one in royal blue with white stripes running down the sides from my armpits to my ankles. I had to admit to buying these things because I knew they'd upset my relatives. Immature? Yes, absolutely.

My short hair required nothing special in preparation for running. I slipped into my bodysuit and running shoes and I was ready to go. Breakfast could wait until my exercise was out of the way.

I opened the bedroom door to find my mother standing on the other side. She looked me up and down with that disapproving-mom expression of hers.

"Is that what you're wearing?"

"Yes, it is."

She frowned. "It shows everything."

"Not everything. Just most things." I smiled and made for the stairs.

"Cass, you can't wear that out of the house. It's indecent."

"It's the height of style, Mom. I'm wearing it. Didn't you see my red one? I ran in it yesterday."

She shook her head, her lips disappearing. "What will the neighbors think?"

"They'll think I have a really fashionable running outfit." I opened the front door. "See you later."

"Aren't you going to eat first?"

"Nope."

I shut the door and strode off down the driveway. The weather this morning was clear and sunny, although still somewhat cool. Anchorage didn't get the humid, oppressively hot summers I'd gotten used to in

Illinois. I could have run comfortably at any hour of the day or night here in Alaska, but early morning was what I was used to, so I stuck to it.

Susitna Drive was out today, at least Dex's section. The last thing I wanted was to see Dex again. He confused me too much and made me want things I couldn't have.

I'd built a life for myself in Chicago. I had a job, a boss who relied on me, an apartment. Neighbors who knew me. Friends, even. Anchorage wasn't home anymore.

Hold on. What was I thinking?

It's not like he'd want to get back together with me. This whole situation, as Jenny would have called it, wasn't a situation at all. In two weeks I'd go back to Chicago and I'd never see Dex again.

I ran down Knik and all around the neighborhood. The houses looked so much the same it felt bizarre, like I'd fallen through a portal in time or something. A few of them looked vaguely different, as if their owners had changed the paint color or maybe planted a few extra flowers, but otherwise everything was pretty much the same.

The trees were bigger than I remembered. Birches and spruce that had been mere saplings when I left were mature trees now. The air smelled sweet and clean and I took deep breaths just to appreciate the scent of it. Birds sang, and traffic noise was absent.

Weird. I hadn't realized how much I'd missed that part of life in Anchorage until now.

When I was ready to turn back, I swung around to the other end of Susitna, where Jenny's house was. It, too, looked exactly the same. Even the trees and other plantings hadn't changed, and the paint was the same pale yellow. I ran up the driveway, wondering if the June family still lived here.

The driveway was empty, so I couldn't tell whether people were home. Licking my lips nervously, I rang the bell. Probably whoever lived here was away at work, but it was worth a try.

The inner door opened. Mrs. June stared at me from the other side of the screen door. She was grayer, too, but otherwise looked much the same, minus the polyester blouses she'd worn back in the day.

"Yes?" she said with a polite smile. "Can I help you?"

I smiled hopefully. "Mrs. June, don't you recognize me?"

Her eyes narrowed as she studied me. Then they opened wide, along with her mouth.

"Oh, my goodness. Cass, is that you?"

"It's me."

She turned her head. "Jenny, you'll never guess who's here!"

"Jenny's here?"

"Yes. She's living with us for a while." She opened the screen door. "Come in."

As I entered their little foyer, Jenny came into view. She seemed slightly taller, her blond hair darker than I remembered it and heavily layered. She wore pegged jeans and a cropped rib-knit sweater in pink, and no glasses.

Her face looked kind of naked without the familiar frames around her eyes. She must have gotten contacts.

On her face I read curiosity and wariness but not much welcome. We looked at each other for a moment.

"Hi, Jen," I said.

She crossed her arms over her chest. "You never called me or wrote."

"They wouldn't let me."

Her brows rose. "They wouldn't? What happened?"

"Come on in," Mrs. June said, putting her arm around my shoulders. "We were just going to have breakfast. Would you like to join us?"

"I'd love that."

They'd painted their kitchen cabinets white and put in a new counter of square white tiles. The floor looked different, too. It was gray vinyl in a tile-look. The curtains on the window were blue and white gingham, instead of the brown and yellow ones I remembered.

"You and Jenny sit down and start catching up," Mrs. June said. "I'll finish the cooking."

"We were making pancakes," Jenny said.

"Yum." I glanced at her as we went into the small dining area. "So you're still living at home?"

"Yeah. I'm saving up for my own place."

"And you're at home on a weekday?"

She gave me a look. "Are you checking up on me?"

"No. I'm just surprised I got lucky. I didn't think you'd be here."

"Oh." Looking slightly mollified, she sat down in one of the Queen Anne style dining chairs I remembered so well. "I'm a teacher. Third grade. I have summers off."

"Ah." I took a seat for myself. "Lucky you. I'm here for Beth's wedding."

"Wow," she said, looking surprised. "I had no idea that was happening. She's a little young, isn't she? Not that I'm criticizing."

"You know my parents. They're thrilled she's doing the traditional domestic thing. And her man seems nice enough."

Jenny nodded. "Yeah. I remember how old-fashioned your parents were."

"I wanted to write, Jen. But they checked my mail. The only people in Anchorage I was allowed to communicate with were my family, and even those messages were checked so Beth and Adam couldn't sneak anything in from you or Dex. And after a while, I kind of figured no-one here would want to hear from me. I guess I gave up."

Jenny sat back in her chair with a huff of released breath. "Good grief. What happened, anyway? Why did you leave?"

I looked down at the glossy brown table top. "They caught me and Dex together."

"Oh, my God."

"Yeah. Pretty much." I glanced at her. She looked supportive, a small frown between her brows. "We were—you know—"

"Making love?" she whispered, with a backward glance over her shoulder at the kitchen.

"Yeah."

"That must have been horrible."

"Oh, yeah," I said. "Possibly the worst day of my life. They lost no time packing me off to Chicago."

"Chicago?" she echoed, her voice rising. "That's where you went? No-one would tell me or Dex anything."

"My Aunt Frances and Uncle Don took me in. My parents wanted to get me away from Dex's evil influence, you know."

She gave me a perceptive look. "You're still mad at them."

"Yeah. I guess I am."

"I don't blame you." She shook her head. "What an over-reaction. I mean, couldn't they have just grounded you?"

I shrugged. "They didn't think it would be enough, and they were right. I would have done anything to be with Dex."

Anything except running away.

"You know he still lives in the same house," she said.

"Yeah. I bumped into him yesterday morning on my run."

Her mom came in with a pot of coffee and a platter of hot pancakes. "Jenny, can you get the syrup for me?"

"Sure, Mom." She got up and went to the refrigerator.

Mrs. June set the food on the table. "We missed you, Cass. It wasn't the same after you left. I almost felt like I'd lost a daughter."

My mouth turned down. "I'm sorry." I hadn't given any thought to how my disappearance would have affected the other adults in my life.

"Well, it was hardly your fault. We asked your parents what was going on, but they wouldn't say. All they would tell us was that you'd decided to leave, to live with some relatives."

"I don't understand why they felt they had to keep it such a big secret," Jenny said, returning with a little glass jug of maple syrup.

"Because they were afraid if Dex found out he'd come after me."

She paused as she sat down, her eyes widened again. "Do you think he would have?"

"No."

"Why not? He was really broken up over it, Cass. For a while I was worried about him."

Mrs. June nodded. "All three of the boys were, but especially Dex, of course."

"Sin?" I said. "Sin was upset I was gone?"

Jenny colored and stared at her coffee. What was that all about?"

"He was mainly upset on Dex's behalf," Mrs. June said. "But, yes. He was unhappy about that, among many other things. Those boys had a rough time of it for a few years."

"I didn't even know you knew them," I said.

"I didn't until Jenny started bringing Dex here." She glanced at her daughter. "She convinced me and her dad that we needed to give them some help."

"Uh...that's good. But why?"

Jenny played with her coffee mug. "Their parents died about a week after you left."

"What?" I stared in open shock. "Really?"

Mrs. June sat down next to me, nodding. "It was a car wreck. For a while, we weren't sure if the boys would be able to keep their house or even stay together. The state wanted to split up him and Dex and put them in separate foster homes. And Sin...he was a very troubled young man at the time."

"Yeah," Jenny said quietly.

"I did get that impression," I said. Good grief, his parents were dead. They'd been dead all this time and I'd had no idea.

The thought of him having to struggle through all that alone—or at least with only Sin for support—hurt me. I should have been the one to comfort him, to help him out, not Jenny, but I'd been trapped in Chicago. Of course, my going through a miscarriage would have only made him feel worse at a time when he couldn't have taken any extra misery.

What a mess we'd been in. I hadn't appreciated at the time just how dire it had been or how much farther we could have plummeted. If I'd kept the baby, if Dex and I had gotten back together and attempted to be parents, would we have done any better than his folks had? He'd told me all about how young they'd been when they'd married. What if we'd turned out just like them?

I turned to Jenny: "So, uh, did you date him?"

"No," she said quickly, her face turning red.

"You brought him home but you weren't dating?"

She gave me a sideways glance I couldn't interpret." We were just friends," she said, taking a big swallow of coffee and looking put out by the fact that her relationship with my ex had never progressed beyond friendship.

"I think Dex and Jenny bonded over your absence," Mrs. June said. "But they never dated. Dex couldn't forget you, Cass."

"I wasn't into him that way," Jenny said firmly. "And he wasn't into me."

Then what had that blush been about? I wanted to ask, but her mom was sitting right there and I didn't want to embarrass Jenny.

"Um..." I cast about for something to say that wasn't about her. "My mom said Dex got married."

"Huh?" Jenny gave me another of those disbelieving looks. "That's not true."

"That's what he said, but I didn't believe him."

"He never even came close as far as I know," she said. "Why would she tell you that?"

"She said she read it in the newspaper."

"Maybe she thought you'd try to get back together with him," Jenny said, pouring a mug of coffee and handing it to me.

"She probably did." And she'd been right. That was exactly what I'd been hoping for.

"Wow." She shook her head. "I would never have thought your mom would be so sneaky."

"She must have been worried to death about you, Cass," Mrs. June said.

"I'm sure she was. But she broke my heart." I buttoned my lip after that too-revealing remark.

"So you actually talked to Dex yesterday?" Jenny said.

"Yeah, for a few minutes. I told him to get lost."

She sent me a reproachful glance. "You should give him a chance. At least talk to him. It doesn't have to go any further than talk."

"It can't. I have a job and an apartment back in Chicago."

"That's too bad," Mrs. June said. "Here I was hoping you were back for good."

"I'm sure my mom is hoping the same thing, but I don't think so. I'm too used to Chicago now." But the memory of the sweet, fresh smell of the Anchorage air and the birdsong suggested otherwise.

Living in Alaska was living in the sticks, even in the state's largest city. Fashion and culture were almost ten years behind the rest of the country, judging by the way people dressed. I was accustomed to the fast pace and sophistication of life in a big city, a world-class city, even if I didn't have enough money to take advantage of much of it. Could I return to the slower pace of Alaska life and be happy with it? I didn't know.

On the other hand, I had no sweetheart to hold me in Illinois, just a handful of friends.

"Still," Jenny said. "You two left so much up in the air. You need to talk to him, for both your sakes."

Chapter 34

Invitations

Cass:

I could only take so much family togetherness. My mom seemed desperate to make things right between us, yet she never said she was sorry. She never really brought up the past directly at all; she merely fussed over me and drove me crazy. So I retreated to my room early, pleading jet lag.

No more royal-blue bodysuit. Tonight I wore a light cotton nightgown in a romantic style, with pale blue ribbon trim along the neckline. It was kind of see-through, and not really warm enough for an Anchorage summer night. In Chicago, I wore these to survive the blazing heat that filled my cheap, non-air-conditioned apartment.

Someone tapped on my window. I jumped about three feet in the air, my heart thumping like mad.

The sun hadn't gone down yet. In early July, it's up almost all night, with just about four hours of semi-darkness, so nine o'clock in the evening looks more like four or five in the afternoon. I could clearly see Dex crouched on the concrete path outside my window.

I cranked the window open. "You scared the crap out of me."

"Sorry." He grinned, not looking sorry at all. "You're not looking to behead me anymore?"

I sighed. He was so damned good-looking that I couldn't resist him even though I knew I should. His hair was long and all one length—no trendy bi-level for him. His short, scruffy beard and mustache were equally unfashionable and I didn't care. It made him look slightly dangerous and quite manly, and went with his calloused hands and the muscles straining at his snug, black T-shirt.

"You done?" he said, his dimples showing.

"Huh?"

"You're staring."

Shit. I blushed fiercely. "I was not."

"Okay. Well, I'm staring at you. That's a very nice outfit you've got on."

I crossed my arms protectively over my chest. "It's a nightgown, not an outfit. I didn't think I'd be seeing anyone tonight."

"Does that mean you'll let me in?"

I tilted my head, considering. It would probably give my parents fits. I was an adult and could do what I liked, but I was staying in their house.

"I'll talk to you if you come to the front door like an official visitor," I said.

He nodded. "Okay. Just don't let your dad use that shotgun on me."

"He wouldn't do that."

He met my gaze, suddenly serious. "He threatened to, and I believed he meant it. I still do."

I stared at him, dumbstruck. "He what?"

"I came here the day after your mom found us. I was worried about you. Your dad threatened to shoot me. He wouldn't tell me anything, wouldn't say where you were."

I saw old grief in his eyes as he spoke.

"Holy crap," I said. "That's terrible."

He shrugged. "It was a long time ago."

"Come around to the front and I'll meet you at the door."

We parted. I slipped on the thin cotton robe I'd brought—it coordinated with the nightgown—and dashed up the stairs. It was my bad luck that my dad was coming down just as I reached the door and Dex knocked.

"Who's that?" my dad said.

"A friend." I opened the door. "Hi, Dex."

My dad came up behind me, looming over my shoulder. I could feel the hostility bristling off him as he realized who was standing on his front step.

"You," he said venomously.

"Hello, Mr. Maslanka," Dex said, his voice and gaze cool and reserved, but not cowed.

"Get off my property," my dad said.

"No," I said. "He's my guest. I invited him in."

"You're not dressed." My dad glowered at me. "Is this how you behave in Chicago?"

"Dad, I'm twenty-six. I can behave however I like."

"Not in my house."

"Look, either Dex comes in or I stand out on the driveway dressed like this. Because one way or another, I'm going to talk to him. It's up to you. Outside or in?"

My dad's jaw worked back and forth as Dex waited for us to come to terms. We exchanged a wary glance. Was that respect I saw in his eyes? He almost looked impressed with me.

"Fine." My dad bit out the word as if it tasted bad. "He can come in, but he can't go in your bedroom. You can visit with him in the living room."

"No," I said. "We need some privacy. How about the family room?" That was downstairs, and slightly less available to my parents. Eavesdropping would be possible, but they'd have to make some effort, which wasn't true of the living room.

My dad's nostrils flared. "All right. The family room. But don't think you can sneak off to your bedroom when I'm not paying attention."

Now I did roll my eyes. "Did you miss the part where I turned eighteen?"

"This house belongs to me and your mom."

"Yes, it does," I said, holding onto my patience with all my strength. "And I'm perfectly capable of getting a hotel room if I have to. Now if you'll excuse us, Dex and I need to talk."

He ground his teeth. Actually ground them. I could hear the squeaking sound they made.

"Fine. Talk." He turned on his heel and stomped up the stairs to the living room.

Dex came in with a wry glance at me. "You're fierce."

"That's me. Cass Maslanka, warrior woman."

God, he was so close. So very close. I could almost feel his body heat and smell the scent of his skin. I began to tremble and ache with unrequited desire.

"I've never seen your family room," he said.

"Follow me." My voice sounded remarkably even for someone who was turning into a lust-crazed spaz.

I led him down the half-flight of stairs into our lower level. The family room was directly below the living, dining, and kitchen areas upstairs, but down here it was one huge, L-shaped room. We still had the couch from our first house down here, an antique-gold and green relic from the sixties. In fact, everything down here was the same as it had been when we'd moved in, just a bit more time-worn.

I sat on the couch and patted the cushion next to me. "Sit."

He did, but he didn't look relaxed. He leaned forward, his elbows on his jeans-clad knees, hands clasped. "Thank you for talking to me."

Even his voice sounded deeper, more adult.

"I'm sorry I was so rude yesterday," I said. "My mom told me you'd gotten married to Misty. I guess I was holding a grudge."

"Misty?" His brows climbed almost to his hairline. "I can't stand that chick. Why would she say something like that?"

"To keep us apart," I said. "When I graduated, I was going to come back here and find you."

His face softened a little, his eyes warming. "Were you? Where did you go, anyway?"

"Chicago. They sent me to live with my aunt and uncle."

"Jesus." He shook his head, still looking at me. "I had no idea. I tried to find out where you'd gone, but no-one would talk to me."

I bit my lip. Should I tell him about the miscarriage? He didn't know I'd been pregnant. To my knowledge, the only people privy to that information were my family members. I hadn't even told Jenny yet.

I didn't know how to tell him. How do you inform a guy that he'd almost been a father? I had no idea how he would take that news, and I wasn't sure I even wanted to tell him.

"Jenny said your parents died," I said instead.

He nodded soberly. "Yeah. Drunk driving. About a week after you left."

"I'm so sorry, Dex."

He stared at his hands. "Thanks."

"The state didn't take Joe away, did they?"

"No. We got lucky." He slanted a glance at me. "Jenny and her family helped us. I don't think we would have survived without them."

"Yeah, Mrs. June said something about that today." I bit my lip. "I wanted to write to you. They wouldn't let me. They read all my mail, coming and going, and monitored my phone calls."

He leaned back against the couch. "That's crazy."

"I know. It was basically house arrest."

"And all because your mom caught us together?"

I nodded. "Pretty much."

He gave me a look of deep regret. "I'm sorry for that, sorry I got you in so much trouble. I never meant for that to happen."

"I know." I smiled tightly. "Neither did I."

"I should have protected you better."

"Dex, it wasn't your fault. Or if it was, I was just as much to blame. We were kids. We hadn't thought it through."

"I'm not sure I was capable of rational thought where you were concerned." He laughed a little and ran his fingers through his hair. That gesture sure brought back memories.

"I know what you mean," I said.

He glanced at me again. His lashes were even longer and thicker than I remembered, a deep gold color. Almost brown, but not quite. And those eyes, so green. I could forget who I was looking into those eyes.

"Were you really going to come back to me?" he said.

"Yeah." I shifted on the couch until I was sitting at a diagonal, partly facing him. "I couldn't forget you."

He looked down and nodded. "Me either."

Suddenly my throat was so tight I wasn't sure I could speak. If only I hadn't listened to my mother, hadn't believed her about his marriage. If only I'd come up here and found him again.

"God," I said in a low, rough voice. "I wish—"

"I know," he said.

"I should never have listened to her. I was so worried about you and your family situation. I had no idea your parents were gone."

"We were just kids," he said. "It might not have worked in the long run. My life was— it wasn't good, Cass. It was so hard for such a long time. I don't know how much good I would have been to you."

"But I could have helped you."

"Jenny tried that." His eyes were sad. "She couldn't take the pressure after a while."

"Did you and she—"

"No. God, no. I love Jenny, but like a sister, not a girlfriend." His mouth flattened. "I don't know if I should talk about it. She and Sin—" His voice trailed off.

Jenny and Sin together? I couldn't even picture it. They were so different, even more so than me and Dex. "No way."

"Yeah. But it didn't work out. It was just too much for them. Bad timing, I guess." He ran his fingers through his hair again and stared at the back wall, his gaze far away and abstracted.

"How is he, anyway? Is he still using?"

"No. He's been clean for years. Doesn't even drink or smoke cigarettes anymore."

I wrinkled my nose. "Do you smoke?"

"Nope. I don't want to make it harder for him."

"Wow," I said, smiling. "You sound so square."

"Nah. We're clean and sober, not square."

"I'm glad you don't smoke. It's healthier."

We looked at each other, smiling and not talking. For some reason, it reminded me of that first real conversation we'd had, the one in the darkened library during the Halloween dance. So long ago. We hadn't known each other at all then, yet we'd fallen so naturally into that long conversation and now it seemed we were doing the same thing despite almost ten years apart.

He leaned toward me a little. "Do you think your parents are listening?" he said in a low voice.

"Probably," I replied in the same tone.

"I'd like to hold your hand. Is that okay?"

I reached for him. "Yes."

Our fingers met. I scooted toward him and we laced our hands together. His felt dry and warm, strong, calloused. I could almost see the connection between us re-forming, re-building itself through the touch of our hands. It was dangerous, because I wasn't staying.

I didn't want to hurt myself or him, and if I allowed myself to get re-attached, one or both of us was going to be broken-hearted in two weeks. Yet I couldn't bring myself to relinquish his hand.

"You're not staying, are you?" he said softly.

"No. Only came up to see Beth get married. I have a job in Chicago. An apartment." It was the same thing I'd said to Jenny and Mrs. June.

Dex nodded. His fingers curled around mine, holding on tight. "I figured as much."

"Maybe we can see each other while I'm here." The words left my mouth before I had time to think about what a bad idea it was.

He nodded, still somber. "I'd like that."

"You don't have a girlfriend?"

"No. Not for a while. What about you?"

"I don't have a girlfriend either."

He laughed. "Too bad."

"Whoa, Mr. Kinky," I said, grinning. "I didn't need to hear that." Neither did my parents, but it would serve them right if they did. Eavesdroppers shouldn't expect their delicate nerves to be respected.

"Seriously, I'm glad you're not attached," he said. "So I don't have to feel guilty."

"Same here," I said.

He squeezed my hand. "Come to dinner tomorrow night?"

"Okay." I didn't have any wedding stuff to do, so my mom would have to deal with my absence. "At your house?"

"Yeah. Joe will be psyched."

I gave him a dubious look. "He still remembers me?"

"Oh, yeah. He thinks of you very fondly as the one that got away."

I snorted with laughter. "He does not."

Dex grinned. "No, but he does remember you pretty clearly. You were a big deal around our place for a long time."

My smile faded as I gazed at him. "You were a big deal to me, too."

God, this hurt. It felt good, too good, but it was painful as well because I was going to leave.

Dex raised our clasped hands and brushed his lips over my knuckles. "I'll see you tomorrow, okay? At six-thirty."

"Okay. I'll be there." I could hardly wait.

Chapter 35

Intensity

Dex:

The kitchen looked like an entire grocery store had exploded all over the counters. Innards from the chicken I was cooking sat grotesquely in a plastic bag and bits of lettuce leaves decorated the beige laminate along with a smear of oil from God only knew what. There was a sprinkling of bread crumbs from when we'd made breakfast, and dirty dishes in the sink.

We were a bunch of fucking slobs.

Normally I didn't pay much attention to these details, but Cass was going to see this. The mess reminded me of the way things had been years ago, when my parents were still alive. The stench of spilled whiskey and rotting garbage teased my nose for an instant, like some kind of flashback to my childhood.

The chicken was roasting in the oven, but it wouldn't be done for another hour and it was already almost six-thirty. Cass would be here any minute. Dinner was going to be late.

Sin lounged at the dining room table, still wearing his coveralls and doing nothing helpful, just watching me and Joe get everything ready. He seemed to think my interest in Cass was funny. I didn't agree.

The whole house smelled like roasting bird. I had a chocolate cake from Carrs grocery sitting on the counter, Joe was standing next to the cake and making a salad, and potatoes were baking alongside the chicken. No time to make gravy, though. Did Cass like gravy?

"Joe, did you make sure that lettuce is really clean?" I said.

"Yeah, I did," he said without looking at me.

"And you tore the pieces up nice and small?"

"Yep."

"What about the dressing? Did you make the dressing?" I opened the fridge door and scanned for the Italian dressing Joe had promised me he would make. I couldn't see it in the mess of soda cans, ketchup bottles, and leftover pizza we had lurking in there. I should have picked up some bottled dressing at the store when I bought the cake.

"Jesus, calm down." Sin shot me a dirty look. "Everything is fine and she's going to love it."

"I'm calm," I said. I should have taken a shower when I got home, but there hadn't been time.

Sin and Joe laughed.

"What?" I said. "I am. Calm."

"You're banging around like a crazy pinball," Joe told me. "And you've got this wild look in your eyes." He made a weird face, sticking out his tongue, rolling his eyes, and flaring his nostrils.

"Fuck off."

They laughed again.

"It's okay," Sin said. "We understand, don't we, Joe? Childhood sweetheart and all that. It's bound to make you nervous as a little girl."

"Little girl? I said. "Childhood sweetheart? I was seventeen."

"That's what I mean."

I shook my head. "Like I said, fuck off."

The doorbell rang. I shot toward the front door. Behind me, Joe and Sin laughed. I was going to hurt them severely if they screwed up this dinner.

Maybe I should have taken Cass out for steak or something.

"Clean this shit up," I called over my shoulder as I left the kitchen.

She stood on our doorstep in a pair of narrow jeans and a simple, V-neck red sweater. The low neck and flashy color was something I never would have seen on her in high school. I liked it, though. It definitely hinted at the sexy valley between her breasts.

The short hair, too. It was a little longer on top, glossy and very dark, and cut sharply over her ears. Not the kind of haircut I usually liked on a woman, but on Cass it showed off her slender neck and high cheekbones and made her eyes look huge. She was even more beautiful than when we were kids.

"You done?" she said with a broad smile.

I flushed. "Not by a long shot. But come in. I'll stare at you inside."

She laughed. "Okay."

I let her in the house.

She looked around the tiny front hall and peeked into the living room. "It looks really different from the way I remember it."

"We fixed it up a little."

"It's nice. Really nice." She smiled at me again, with a slightly nervous edge. Did I make her nervous or was it the house?

"Come in the kitchen and say hello to my brothers," I said, wishing I'd made them go somewhere else for their dinner.

"I'd like that."

I wanted to take her hand. We'd touched the night before, yet now I was all bashful and stupid. Seeing her, especially here in my own house, was bizarre. I felt like I'd been shot back in time ten years to the point in our relationship where we'd only just met...except with ten years of baggage in the way.

We stopped in the doorway between the entry hall and the kitchen. Thank God the guys had cleared up some of the mess. At least the chicken innards and lettuce bits were gone.

Joe looked up from whatever he was doing to the salad. He turned to Cass with a huge grin.

"I remember you," he said, extending a hand for her to shake.

"You do?" She accepted his hand. "You must be Joe, but you look so different."

"Yeah, I grew a little." He looked her over with open appreciation. "I've gotta say Dex has great taste."

"Joe, shut it," I said.

My little brother just laughed.

"That's very sweet of you," Cass said, smiling up at him.

He gave her a goofy grin. "I'm gonna have to take you away from him, I think."

"Get your own girl." I put my arm around her shoulders.

I realized an instant later that I was probably moving too fast. She seemed happy to let me hold her, though, and I let my arm stay where it was.

"I'm only in Anchorage for another ten days," Cass said.

"Well, that sucks." Joe looked at me.

"She's got a job," I said. "In Chicago."

I knew she wasn't staying. I knew it would be a bad idea for me to let myself hope, yet my arm stayed around her shoulders. Where Cass was concerned, I seemed doomed to make the wrong choice every time.

Sin ambled over to our group. He stuck out a hand. "Hi, Cass. I don't know if you remember me. I'm Sin, Dex's older brother."

She accepted the hand with raised eyebrows. "Of course I remember you. You look really different, too. I never would have recognized either of you."

"Yeah. I shaved off the beard and quit using drugs," he said matter-of-factly.

"I'm glad to hear you're doing so well," she said, her voice warm.

She really didn't seem to judge him. I liked that about her. She was willing to give Sin a chance because of me, rather than rejecting him at first glance the way her family would have done.

"It smells incredible in here," she said. "What's for dinner?"

"Dex slaved over a roasted chicken," Joe said. "But it's got a while to cook yet."

"Joe—" I gave him a warning look.

He opened his green eyes wide. "What? She asked what we're having."

"I didn't know you could cook," she said, looking at me with a teasing glint in her eyes.

"I couldn't back then."

"I don't know," Joe said. "You made a mean can of chili."

"And then there was his toast," Sin added.

They both laughed, as if they were actually funny. Cass laughed a little, too. I stood there scowling at them and wishing once more that I'd chosen somewhere other than home to feed Cass dinner.

"You three are cute together," she said.

Joe looked dismayed. "I'm not cute. I'm a guy."

"Oops." She winked at me. "Sorry."

Her gaze returned to Sin. "You look like you work in a garage." She glanced at me. "And Dex was wearing the same thing yesterday morning."

"Yeah, we own a place," Sin told her, pride in his voice.

"Really? That's great." She grinned at me, looking impressed. "I thought maybe you just had jobs as mechanics."

"Yeah," I said. "We started the business after our parents died. We had to make money."

"And they didn't want to end up in prison for dealing," Joe said. "Cause they had me putting a major cramp in their style."

"You did not," she said. "They love you."

"I was only joking." He nudged me. "I know I was a good influence."

"Hey, Joe, why don't we go watch the game," Sin said, inclining his head in the direction of the living room. "We can eat at the coffee table when dinner is ready."

"What game?" Joe looked baffled.

"You know...the game."

"There's no game tonight. The only thing going on is tennis and I hate tennis."

Sin grabbed his arm. "Come on. They don't want us hanging around all night."

"Oh, it's all right," Cass said.

No, it wasn't. I couldn't exactly say that out loud, though.

"You only have two weeks together," Sin said. "Make the most of it."

"We're just friends," I told him.

He gave me a knowing look. "Yeah, I can see that."

Sin steered Joe into the living room, leaving me alone with Cass. Finally. Not that we were truly alone, with those two jokers lurking in the next room, but at least we didn't have their eyes on us.

I stood there in the kitchen, staring at Cass tongue-tied. There was so much I wanted to say to her that I didn't know where to start. She just looked back at me, the same awkwardness on her face.

"I—uh—I like your haircut," I finally said.

"You do? My mom hates it."

"It makes your eyes more obvious or something. And you have beautiful eyes."

She blushed a little. "Thanks."

"It's just the truth." I gestured toward the dining room table. "Would you like to sit down and have some coffee?"

"Sure."

I wished I could offer her a beer or a glass of wine, but we didn't keep any kind of alcohol in the house. It was too hard for Sin to resist if we did, and there was no way Joe or I would endanger his sobriety.

I got mugs of coffee for both of us and we sat in the little dining niche off the kitchen. Unfortunately, that gave us a partial view of the living room and my brothers. But at least they weren't breathing down our necks.

There wasn't much to our dining room. Just a small dinette set Sin had picked up at a thrift store, the same old brass modern-style chandelier I remembered from my childhood still hanging over the center. The tan carpet was only five years old, though, not that moth-eaten worn out piece of crap we'd had when I was a kid.

"So you thought I was married?" I said, handing one of the heavy, blue-glazed mugs to her.

"Yeah." She shot me a sidelong glance. "My mom told me on the day I graduated from high school. I'd just gotten back to my aunt and uncle's house."

I shook my head, imagining how much that must have hurt her. "I had no interest in anyone but you."

She drew in her chin, looking dubious. "Even after two years?"

"I'm not gonna lie and say I was celibate," I said. "But I didn't have any steady girlfriends until about five years after you left. And really there was only one. It didn't work out."

"I'm going to ask my mom why she told me that," Cass said. "But I think I know."

I reached out and grabbed onto her hand. Her fingers curled around mine without hesitation. I'd pictured us together again so many times over the years, at first as a real wish and later as a fantasy. I'd given up on ever seeing her again by that time.

"She wanted to keep us apart," I said.

"When we were together, everyone kept telling me you were just using me," Cass said, "so when she said you'd gotten married, I thought it was true. I figured you'd moved on. Abandoned me." Her voice sounded so flat and unemotional that it killed me.

"God, Cass," I said. "No. I would never have abandoned you."

"Even if—" She broke off, sneaking another sideways glance at me. "Even if you knew I was pregnant?"

My whole world seemed to stop. "What?"

She swallowed so hard I could hear it. "I was pregnant," she whispered. "They made me get tested and it was positive."

I blinked. Jesus. That was not what I'd expected to hear today. I was a father? Where was this child of ours now?

"Where? Who? Why didn't you tell me until now?"

She swallowed again. Her hand tightened convulsively around mine. "I lost it. I had a miscarriage."

I took a deep breath and tried to understand what had just happened—I'd acquired a child and lost it in the space of a minute. I'd gotten Cass pregnant and she'd lost the baby. As far as I knew, I'd never gotten any of the other girls and women I'd been with pregnant. I was careful, always used a condom.

"We used protection," I said.

"I know. It must have failed somehow." Another of those sideways glances. "Are you mad at me?"

"Mad?" I said, bewildered. "No. Why would I be?"

"I don't know." She tried to pull her hand away as she stared at the table top. "Everyone else was."

"Who is everyone?" I said, refusing to let go of her hand.

"My parents. My aunt and uncle. Even my cousins seemed disgusted when they found out. Like I was dirty somehow. A whore."

I pictured her alone with her family, pregnant and seventeen, afraid, made to feel like a whore. She'd gone through it far away from me. I could see on her face how bad she'd suffered and I wished I could make it go away.

"So they all made you feel guilty as hell," I said.

"Yeah." She still wouldn't look at me.

"Ah, babe. Come here." I tugged her off her chair and onto my lap. She went willingly. Her ass still fit perfectly on my thighs.

I put my arms around her as she snuggled against me with a sigh. Her face just fit in the crook between my neck and shoulder, and her warm breath teased the skin on my throat.

She smelled different, like she was using a different soap or shampoo than she had back then. Yet she also smelled exactly the same. She was all Cass, and my body responded to her nearness with a roar of desire, my cock stiffening inside the prison of my jeans.

This wasn't the time for a hard-on. She needed comfort. Besides, my brothers were right in the living room, probably hanging on every word we spoke, so we couldn't get too hot and heavy.

"I can't tell you how sorry I am that you had to go through that," I said. "And I wasn't even there for you. I wish there was something I could have done."

"Would you have wanted the baby if you'd known?"

"I don't know," I said honestly. "Yes, because it was yours. I would always want a child that we made together. But we were so young and my life was so fucked up. Adding a baby to the mix would not have been easy."

"I know." She rested her hand on my shoulder. "They were going to try to force me to give it up for adoption, but I was making plans to go off on my own and raise it. And then I started bleeding."

"Jesus." My throat tightened painfully. "If I'd known—"

"There wasn't anything you could do. Nobody could. It was hard, though. My aunt knew it was happening and she basically left me alone to go through it by myself. She said it was a blessing to lose the baby."

I stroked her hair. There wasn't much of it to pet. The short, dark strands felt like silk under my palm. "That was bullshit. It wasn't a blessing."

"You don't think so?" she said, tilting her head back to gaze up at me with watery eyes. "Even though we were just kids ourselves?"

"It was still our baby."

"Yeah. Yes, it was." She rubbed her eyes. "I loved you so much."

I tightened my hold on her. "I loved you too." And I still did, but I didn't think she wanted to hear that. "I just about went crazy when you were gone and they wouldn't tell me where."

We sat there in silence for a while, just feeling each other's warmth and solidity. I didn't want to let her go. In a little while, I'd have to get up and check the food. Until then, I planned to stay right where I was, with Cass in my arms.

In the living room, Joe and Sin talked in low voices. The TV mumbled along in the background. Under my left hand, her back rose and fell with her breaths.

"You know," she said softly. "It's kind of strange how much just a few months can affect your life. We weren't together that long."

"It wasn't the length of time. It was the intensity."

I could feel that intensity swirling around us now, building up inside me. Could she feel it too? Was she as drawn to me as I was to her? We weren't kids anymore. Even if her parents disapproved, that didn't have to stop us. But there was her job, her life in Illinois.

"Tell me about your job," I said. "What do you do?"

"Oh, I'm just a secretary," she said dismissively. "But I've worked for the same company for eight years now. My boss and I are used to each other."

"Do you like it? What kind of company is it?" I wanted to know everything about her life now.

"Yeah, it's all right," she said. "It's a construction company. Ed is a good boss. He's very understanding."

"Ed?" I disliked the bastard already and I didn't know anything about him except his name.

"My mom keeps hoping I'll marry him," she said, a smile creeping back into her voice.

"Then you shouldn't be sitting on my lap."

"Ed and I have no interest in each other." She smiled teasingly at me. "We're a business-only relationship."

"Good."

Shit. I shouldn't have let that slip out.

She laughed softly. "I haven't been interested in anyone but you either. No matter how many men I go out with, none of them are you."

"You go out with a lot of guys?"

Damn. This jealousy crap felt terrible.

"I did." She lifted her hand and placed it over the side of my face. "I was so angry over the way I'd been treated. I wanted to do everything my parents hated. It wasn't very mature, but it was my way of figuring out who I was. I moved out of my aunt and uncle's house as soon as I could, got a job, and did whatever I wanted."

"So you turned into a party girl?"

Cass shrugged. "A little maybe. I was taking night classes and working full time, so I didn't have that much opportunity. But I did what I could to kill off naive, good-girl Cass."

"Hey. I love that girl."

I couldn't seem to control myself around her. I was letting all kinds of things slip, things I shouldn't say.

* * *

Cass:

Sitting on Dex's lap with his arms around me and cuddling into his embrace felt both completely familiar and utterly strange. We'd been here before, but it had been so very long. I hadn't dated in a while, and it struck me how much I'd missed physical contact.

With my face turned toward his neck, the scent of his skin teased my nose. Desire instantly curled inside me as the smell of him conjured memories of heated touching and moans of pleasure. I lifted my face and found him watching me, his eyes heavy-lidded and dark and full of longing.

He cupped the side of my face. "Cass."

I leaned in. He had the most kissable lips of anyone I'd ever been with. Kissing him was a bad idea. It would only make it harder for me to leave when my vacation time was over, yet I continued to lean in, my gaze fixed on his mouth the same way he was looking at mine.

His head lowered, slowly. Our lips clung for an instant. We parted, but only an inch or so hung between us.

My heart thumped hard and fast in my chest. His hand felt warm against my face. We were too close to look into each other's eyes and I stared at his mouth instead.

Then he urged me forward and our lips met again and this time neither of us pulled away. His lips were so soft as they caressed mine, so wickedly seductive. He tugged and sucked at me, gently nipping and stroking with such skill it made me tremble with arousal.

Dex sighed against my mouth. My hand slipped from his shoulder to the back of his neck, under his hair. His skin was soft there, too, and hot. I stroked him right below his hairline and opened my mouth to him.

He lost no time accepting that invitation. His tongue slid into me and I met it with my own and we tasted each other. I moaned a little. I hadn't tasted him in ten years and it was so exactly the way I'd remembered it...only better.

For so long, I'd told myself that I didn't feel for Dex what I thought I felt. That it had been the silly fantasy of a girl with her first boyfriend. That I was an adult now and love, sex, just wasn't like that in real life. It wasn't as hot, as explosive, as tender, as *everything* as I remembered it being with him.

I'd been wrong.

This, now, this simple kiss was better than any of my other encounters with men. I was already more turned on than I could remember being with anyone else even in the middle of full-on sex. And all we'd done was put our mouths together.

His hand came around to the back of my head, his fingers plunging into my hair as he held me steady for his invading tongue. His cock swelled inside his jeans, pushing up against my rear end. His excitement fed mine.

I turned to straddle him, kissing him ferociously. His arms wrapped around me, holding on tight. I lost track of time, of the room, of all thought as we made love with our mouths, our breath speeding into gasps and sighs and low-voiced moans.

Then Dex interrupted the kiss, pulling his mouth away from mine to glare at someone a few feet to his right. "What the hell, man?"

I turned my head. Sin stood in the kitchen grinning at us.

"Sorry to interrupt you two, but the buzzer on the oven was going off. Didn't you hear it?"

Dex's gaze slid to mine, then back to his brother. "No."

"The chicken looks done to me, but you might want to have a look." Sin's broad grin stayed right where it was.

Dex let out a heavy sigh and pressed his forehead against mine. "Sorry about this."

"It's okay." I gave him a tight smile. "We don't want anyone to go hungry, do we?"

"Right now I couldn't care less," he said.

I laughed a little and climbed off his lap. My legs felt rubbery. Holy hell, if nothing more than a little tongue action could do that to me then what would happen if we went further than kissing?

Dex, facing away from his brother, adjusted himself with a wry expression on his face. He went to the oven, opened it and peered inside. Then he put on a pair of mitts and pulled the bird out and set it on the range.

His male gloriousness struck me all over again—the ripple of muscle in his biceps and forearms, the fall of gold hair over his forehead as he looked down at the food, the way his lashes fanned out over his skin. How had someone so good-looking become interested in me? I couldn't understand it.

We shouldn't have kissed. Now I knew what it felt like to be held by him and how he tasted, and I knew I wouldn't be able to leave it alone. I would have to have more and more of him until my time in Alaska was up and I was forced to leave.

I didn't want to leave.

Sin watched me, his expression turned inscrutable as I joined Dex in the kitchen. I ignored Sin as I had a look at what Dex had cooked. The chicken looked perfectly browned and plump, and it smelled divine.

"It looks awesome," I said. "I'm impressed."

"It's just a chicken," Dex said gruffly. He bent and pulled four potatoes from the oven, setting them on the range next to the pan with the bird.

"Don't do that," I said.

"What?" He gave me an impatient glance that took me aback. Was he angry with me now? What for?

"You deflected my compliment. You should just say thank you." I nudged him. "It really does look good."

He looked down, a faint flush on his cheekbones. "Thanks."

"That's much better." I leaned in, smiling, and kissed his jaw.

This wasn't going to end well. It couldn't, because I couldn't leave him alone now that I'd had a taste of him. I couldn't back off or put on a cool facade as if he didn't matter to me. But why had he turned grouchy all of a sudden?

Maybe that kiss had shaken him up as badly as it had me.

Joe thundered into the kitchen in stocking feet. He was even taller than the other two, his hair as black as Sin's and his eyes green but with a hazel tint. With his heavy black lashes, his eyes were stunning. He'd probably broken plenty of hearts already with looks like those.

He grinned at me. "Is it ready? I'm starved."

Dex shook his head. "You're always starved."

"Can't help it." Joe opened the fridge and took out a covered bowl and a small Mason jar of what looked like salad dressing.

"Wow. You guys are really domestic," I said.

"Don't talk that way." Sin gave me a mock stern look. "You'll damage our masculinity."

"Not you," Joe said. "You haven't done anything today except take up space."

"I'm providing needed moral support," Sin told him.

Dex shook his head again, smiling at me. "See what I have to put up with? They're like this every day."

"You know," I said. "In some ways, you three are really lucky. You support each other. It seems like you get along really well."

"You don't get along with your brother and sister?" Joe said, looking surprised.

"I didn't see them for almost ten years."

His mouth fell open. "What? Why not?"

"She was banished to Chicago," Dex said. "Because of me."

"Because of both of us," I said.

He slanted a dry look at me. "You really think your parents would have been as upset if I were a hockey or football jock? A good boy with no record?"

My mouth flattened unhappily. "I see your point."

"Man," Sin said. "That's fucked up. I didn't know they'd sent you Outside."

"Nobody did except my family. They kept it a deep, dark secret."

"No wonder we didn't know where you'd gone." He gave me an odd look. "Your friend Jenny came around for a while, hanging around with Dex. She was really torn up about your leaving."

"Yeah, I heard that."

"I'll be right back," Dex said. "Joe, get the plates out, will you?"

He headed off down the narrow hallway that I remembered led to the bedrooms and bath. The instant he was out of sight, Sin leaned toward me, his green eyes somber.

"Don't break him, Cass."

I drew my chin back. "Break him?"

"Look, I like you. You seem like a nice girl, but Dex—he seems tough, but he isn't where you're concerned. You don't know what he was like after you left. Don't lead him on. I don't know if he could take another let down like that."

"I'm not leading him on." Was I?

"Good." He nodded, his back straightening.

"You need to lighten up," Joe said. "Dex can handle himself."

"You were only ten," Sin said. "You don't remember, but I do. Dex was so down for so long I was worried about him."

"I don't want to hurt him," I said. "I still care about him. Deeply."

I was beginning to think I was still in love with him. But how could I know? We'd only spent a couple of hours in each other's company, and we only had a few more days before I left. Ten days wouldn't give me enough time with him to know if a real relationship was worth pursuing. What if I moved back up here and it didn't work out?

Chapter 36

Stay

Cass:

Dex and I held hands throughout dinner. Sin kept glancing at us, our clasped hands, my face. I ignored him. Did he really think I could sit next to Dex for a whole meal and not touch him?

The food was as good as it looked and afterward he showed me his record collection, which was located oddly enough in his bedroom. Joe laughed at him and Sin just watched silently as we left the dining room together.

All the walls in the house looked freshly painted. I could almost believe that I'd imagined the sad little dump from ten years before, except the carpet was the same in the hallway. It had holes in it.

"We're gonna replace the carpet one of these days," he said, as if he'd read my mind.

"I'm sure you have more important things to do," I said. "And your house looks great. I'm really impressed. No, really, Dex. You guys have come a long way."

"Yeah." He paused with his hand on the door of the same bedroom he'd used as a teenager. "We have."

Inside, the bedroom couldn't have looked more different. First of all, there was only one bed and it took up most of the room. The walls here were also freshly painted, with no dings or smears of dirt, and nothing in the room smelled of smoke. There were real curtains on the window instead of that tacked-up beach towel they'd had before. They were plain and navy-blue, with a black-out lining against the long Alaskan summer days.

"Where are the records?" I said, glancing around.

"In the living room."

I laughed. "You're a sneaky guy, you know that?"

A mural covered one wall, hand-painted directly over the plaster. It was an Alaskan landscape in tones of green, gray, and blue, probably based on a view of the Cook Inlet, with high sharp mountains descending severely to a silvery bay.

I stood in front of it and stared. "This is amazing. Whose work is this?"

Dex cleared his throat, looking a bit uncomfortable. "Mine."

I raised my brows. "You did this? It's great work, Dex."

He shrugged. "I do custom paint work. Thought I'd liven up the walls in here just for fun."

"Wow. You should do some canvases. I'll bet you could sell your work downtown."

"I dunno." He put his hands on my waist. "I didn't come in here to talk about art."

"Oh, yeah?" I looped my arms around his neck. "Why did you come in here?"

It was a simple room, the plain room of a man who didn't care much about decorating or style...except for that stunning mural.

"Cass," he said, drawing me against the hard length of his body. "I really want to make love to you."

I snugged my pelvis in against him as my heart started racing again in excitement and nervousness. "Me too."

It had been a long time since I'd last been with a man. Doubts gathered at the back of my mind that I even remembered how to make love.

He bent his head to mine and I shoved those doubts even further into the background. We couldn't be together forever, but we could be together tonight. Maybe for several nights before I had to leave Alaska again.

As we kissed, my doubts disappeared. All I could think of was how good he tasted, how good he felt, the way his big hand pressed gently at the small of my back.

His erection prodded at my belly. The insistent feel of it excited me and I arched my back against him as a soft moan escaped my throat. He moaned back, his grip on me tightening as he plunged his tongue into my mouth.

His big body trembled in my arms. I was quivering, too, my hands shaking as I reached up to touch his hair. It felt as if I were starving and had only now recognized the fact. I was starving and Dex was the only food I needed.

We stumbled backward toward the bed. He sat down on the edge of the mattress, still kissing me, his hands going to my front. When he cupped my breasts, I whimpered into his mouth.

He shoved his hands under my sweater and up, to my bra. Luckily, I was wearing a front-clasp style, making it easy for him to open it. The two halves sprang back beneath my top, leaving my breasts bare to his hands.

He played with them, molding the sensitive flesh, teasing my nipples with his thumbs. The ecstasy he caused me with just that simple move—incredible. I'd convinced myself that I imagined this passion, but here it was again, just as bright and hot as ever.

Dex pulled the hem of my sweater up. "Take it off."

I pulled it over my head. He stared at my exposed breasts, his lips parted slightly, before he groaned.

"Jesus, you're even more beautiful than I remembered."

"So are you," I said.

He glanced up at me, his eyes dark and glazed with lust. Then he drew me forward again, into his embrace, and his head bent to one of my nipples. His mouth closed on me, hot and wet.

I grabbed his head as my eyes rolled back with delight. My back arched again, pushing my breasts upward, begging for attention. I could never get enough of him.

I glanced down to see his head against me, his lips on me, his dark gold lashes down, hiding his eyes from me. The sight was so erotic I cried out as pleasure speared through me.

None of the naughty dreams I'd had about him over the years compared to this.

His hands slid down to my butt. He clutched me, his fingers digging in, massaging the round globes of muscle. Did he think my ass was too big? As a runner, I'd built up some impressive glutes, especially since I did lunges and squats to increase my strength.

He groaned again, deep in his throat, as he squeezed my rear. Then his hands came around to the front, fumbling with the button on my fly as his mouth continued pleasuring me.

"Damn it," he muttered. "I can't do the button. Get them off for me."

"You need to take something off, then," I said as I reached down to undo my jeans.

He looked up at me blankly. "What?"

"Take off your clothes."

A grin transformed his face. "Yes, ma'am."

I shucked my jeans as he stripped his shirt over his head. I almost groaned too at the sight of him half naked. That body. He'd obviously taken up some weight lifting, to have muscles like that.

I reached for him, smoothing my hands over his shoulders and then his pecs. His skin felt so warm and silky beneath my fingers. I bent down and kissed him at the juncture of his neck and shoulder, then again at his collarbone.

"Come here." He grabbed me around the waist and slung me onto the bed.

He was strong, too. I wasn't very tall and I was relatively trim but my weight was deceptively high because of all the muscle I'd built, and yet he easily hoisted me.

Dex wasted no time in pinning me beneath him. I wrapped my arms around him, pulling him in even closer as he devoured my mouth with a growl. I lifted one leg and flung it around his waist for good measure.

The sensation of all that hot, hard male pressed against my bare body...heavenly.

He shoved his hips against mine. We still had our underwear on, but his cock pressed through both layers of clothing to rub delightfully against my sex and I moaned, clutching at him.

"Dex," I gasped. "I need you. Inside me."

He growled again. "Not yet. There's something I have to do first."

"What? Why?" There wasn't anything else on my agenda, and waiting might just kill me.

He slid down my body, glancing up at me with a devilish glint in his eyes. "I've wanted to do this ever since I met you."

"Do what?"

He smiled a wicked smile. "Open your legs all the way and find out."

"Oh." *Oh.* That.

"Open up, Cass." He pushed my thighs apart and settled his broad shoulders between them.

Oral sex was always nice. No, it was naughty. But the naughtiness was what made it so nice, not to mention it felt pretty good too.

He licked me delicately, almost more of a suggestion than an actual caress of the tongue. I started and gasped at the unexpected pleasure of it. He chuckled, although I didn't see anything funny at all.

His mouth continued to tease me, finding extra sensitive spots I hadn't even known I possessed and making me twitch and whimper. I'd never had a partner who did oral sex this way. Usually they just licked at me like they were licking at the glue on an envelope—a necessary evil they had to endure before getting to the important part.

Dex went about it as if he were worshipping me with his mouth.

Then he swiped me right up the center with his tongue and I almost came off the bed.

"You taste so good," he said roughly, bending his head down for more.

His tongue entered my sheath and I came apart, hollering like a wild animal, my fingers digging into the bedding as the orgasm rocked through me.

I stared up at him, dazed, as he positioned himself over me and rolled a condom over himself. No-one had ever made me come with oral sex before. It usually required hands.

"Not a criticism," I said. "But why didn't you ever do that to me when we were teenagers?"

"Do what?" he said with a mischievous grin.

"You know…"

"Lick you until you screamed?"

I was too turned on, yet paradoxically sated, to blush or feel embarrassment. "Yeah."

"I was afraid it would scare you." He sank into my body with a single thrust.

I cried out as he dropped his head with a hoarse groan, his long hair sliding forward and tickling me. He was so big it almost hurt as he slid all the way in to the hilt. I'd forgotten how much bigger he was than my other lovers.

His hips pulled back, then slid forward for another long thrust. Oh, God, that was even better than the first time. I grabbed onto his waist with both hands, my thighs spread as far as they could go.

He did it again and I came. Three pumps of his hips and I came, moaning and gasping against his shoulder, the bursts of pleasure robbing me of speech.

Dex lifted himself on his elbows and looked down the long line of his body to where we were joined. He groaned, watching his cock slide in and out of me. I looked too. The sight of him pushing into me, pulling out, pushing back in, almost made me come a third time.

I looked up into his face at the same time as he looked into mine. Our gazes tangled up together. I couldn't look away as he continued to move over me, as my hips met his thrust for thrust, as I cried out his name.

The pleasure was building again, tightening, pulling in to that hard knot of bliss that I knew would soon explode through my whole body. Dex's eyes were glazed over and gone with his own ecstasy. The tendons in his neck stood out and his mouth stretched wide, his breath coming in harsh pants and groans. A third orgasm broke over me like a wave of sensation so intense I dug into his skin with my fingernails. He closed his eyes and grimaced, shuddering. Another smaller wave coursed through me and I cried out again, with tears in my eyes. And suddenly I was sobbing and I didn't know why.

He paused over me, our bodies still joined. "Baby, don't. Don't cry."

"I'm sorry," I sobbed.

"What? Why be sorry?" He pushed the hair from my eyes.

I couldn't look at him. Instead, I turned my face into the heavy muscle of his biceps, my tears wetting his skin. "I don't know w-why."

"Hey." He caressed my face. "Did I hurt you?"

"No." I sniffed, fighting to get myself under control. "That was the best sex of my life."

"Really? The best?"

I could hear the smile in his voice.

I opened my watery eyes and looked at him. "Yeah. The best ever. I don't know why I started crying. I've never done that before."

"You don't regret it, do you?"

"No. Hell, no."

Dex laughed a little. "Good. It was pretty damn amazing for me too."

I wiped my eyes. "It was?"

"Yeah." He stroked my face again. "The best, Cass."

The tenderness in his eyes almost stole my breath away. I lifted my head and kissed his lips.

"All these years," he said, "I tried to tell myself that what I had with you wasn't what I'd thought it was. That I'd exaggerated or something, because we were so young. But now ..." His voice trailed off.

"I did the same thing." I bit my upper lip. "Isn't that strange? We were both trying to talk ourselves out of it."

"We were trying to stop the pain." He gazed down at me, supporting himself on his forearms, our bodies still joined, still pressed together from breast to hip.

"Yeah." I clasped my ankles around his waist. "I thought I'd never see you again."

His big hands framed my face. He kissed me again, a slow, wet, profoundly arousing kiss. "I wish you weren't going back to Chicago."

"Me too."

Wait. What had I just said? I didn't want to move to Alaska. My parents lived here. If I moved back, I'd be obliged to spend time with them on a regular basis, and I suspected none of us would survive that.

But Dex...Dex lived here too.

He detached himself from me and rolled to his side, pulling me into his arms. "Stay."

My heart thumped painfully. "Dex—"

"Why not? You don't really have anything holding you in Chicago, from the sound of it."

"Well, no. I don't. But I can't just pull my life apart when— when I don't know if things would work out between us. We've only been together a few hours since I got back."

He looked so serious now, so earnest as he lifted a hand to toy with my short hair. "We might not get this chance again. What if you go back and we never re-connect? Can you live with that? I don't think I can."

I couldn't give him a flippant response. For one thing, it wouldn't be fair to either of us. For another, those words just wouldn't come. And he was right—if I went back to Chicago, we might never reconnect and we'd never know what might have been.

I'd spent the past eight or ten years, depending on how you did your calculations, rebelling against almost everything my parents had taught me. I'd smoked, drank, had casual sex. I hadn't used illegal drugs, but I'd done an awful lot of other stuff, and not always things I'd wanted to do for their own sake. I'd done them because my parents would have flipped out if they'd known.

It dawned on me with sudden shock that they'd been controlling me all this time, just as effectively as if I'd followed all their dictates. Instead of obeying the family rules and upholding the family values, I'd done the opposite, and almost as unthinkingly as I'd conformed when I was still Cass the Good Girl.

That was a humiliating insight.

"I've been letting them control me," I said musingly.

"Who? Your parents?" Dex said, propping himself up a little so he could watch my face.

"Yeah. I thought I was being independent, but really I was just doing the opposite of whatever they would have wanted me to do. That's not real independence, is it?"

He looked thoughtful. "I guess not. I never really had anyone to rebel against, so it's hard for me to say."

I pictured all the hardships he'd had to endure, the neglectful parents, their deaths—the ultimate parental abandonment—the struggle to keep the house and to keep his brothers together against the social services people wanting to split Joe and Dex into foster homes. And I cringed. Here I was, whining about my awful parents when Dex had been through ten times as much strife as I'd ever seen.

"I've been such a child," I said.

He raised his eyebrows. The action made his forehead wrinkle. "You look pretty grown up to me."

"I've been making such a big deal out of what happened to me and how over-controlling my parents are when my childhood was really pretty good. At least I never went without food or clothing."

He tilted his head with a skeptical flattening of his luscious lips. "I think your upbringing was pretty harsh, Cass. They expected too much of you. Nobody could have lived up to those standards, at least not without going a little crazy. And we're not in a contest to see who had the worst childhood. That's not the point here."

"So I shouldn't feel guilty?"

He smiled, his green eyes crinkling at the corners in a way that made me want to trace out the tiny wrinkles with my fingertip. "Not about that. Maybe there's something else you're hiding from me, but not about that."

"I'm not hiding anything," I said. "Look at me. I'm naked. There's no place to put anything."

"Mmmm," he growled, giving my naked self a leisurely once-over. "I am looking. It's the best view I've ever had."

"Isn't it too soon for more?" I said, giggling as he bent over my belly.

"Yeah, but a man can dream, can't he?"

I giggled again as he stuck his tongue in my navel. "That tickles. Knock it off."

"Say you'll stay with me." He licked my belly-button again.

"I'm not sure I can make that promise."

He licked me a third time, using just the tip of his tongue to make it extra-tickly.

"Stop that!" I said, trying to push him away.

"Not until you promise." He kept tickling me.

I wriggled underneath him, but I couldn't get away. He was too heavy and too strong. And he'd progressed from merely tickling my navel to brushing the ends of his hair over my skin, which tickled a whole lot more.

"Okay," I said, giggling wildly. "I'll stay."

He pounced on me and I instantly forgot what I'd promised in the rush of renewed desire.

Later, when we'd worn ourselves out for the time being, I remembered.

"I'm scared," I said as I lay my head on his chest.

"Of what?" He kept stroking my hair, as if fascinated with it.

"I don't really know how to do this," I said.

"Do what? Lay in bed with me?"

I nudged him. "No, you goofball. I don't know how to pursue a relationship with you. Where will I live? Where will I work? There's no way I can live with my parents. No-one would survive."

He gave a soft snort of laughter. "Probably not."

"I'm serious, though. I don't know how to go about this."

"You can move in with me," he said, still playing with my hair. "Just until you find a place, if you don't want to make it permanent. Or if it seems to be working, you can just stay here."

I lifted my head to study his face. He seemed serious. "You really mean that? You want me to live with you? What if we can't get along?"

"Babe, you worry too much. If you think we shouldn't live together, you can just sleep on the couch until you get a job and an apartment. I won't push you for more if you don't want to give it to me."

"The problem," I said, "is that I want to give you everything."

The tenderness rushed into his eyes again. "I feel the same way about you. I love you, Cass. I think I always will."

It was so exactly what I'd hoped he would say that it scared me a little.

I leaned down and pressed my lips to his. "I love you too. But what if love isn't enough?"

"Then it isn't. Do you want to live the rest of your life afraid?" He palmed the side of my face. "Take a chance on us. We won't be like my parents. We'll talk, discuss things, treat each other with respect. Right?"

I nodded. "Right."

He folded his arms around me. "We're in this together?"

"Yes. We're in it together."

"And you'll stay up here with me?"

Was that insecurity I heard in his voice? I raised my head again to look him in the eyes. "I'll stay with you. I love you. I want to be with you."

He gave me the warmest, brightest smile I'd ever seen, and I knew I'd made the right decision.

I was going to have a blast explaining this development to my parents, though.

Then I gave myself a mental shake. It was time I grew up for real. This was my life and Dex's life we were talking about, not my parents', and I would simply explain our plans to them. They could take it or leave it.

Chapter 37

Reckoning

Cass:

The morning dawned gray and cool. Birds sang busily in the neighborhood birches and spruce, but human activity seemed to be absent. It was still only six o'clock and most people were probably just now getting up.

The air held a potent tang of moist earth and damp green leaves. Mist accumulated on my hair and the shoulders of my jacket. I flipped up my collar against the chill. My running shoes made a barely audible padding sound on the blacktop as I walked back to the house where I'd grown up.

The taste of coffee still lingered in my mouth. Dex and I had spent the whole night alternating between long, rambling conversations and making love. I was so short on sleep that the world had taken on a slightly unreal feeling, like everything was a little farther away than it should be. I foresaw a lot more coffee in my immediate future.

At the same time, though, I felt buoyed up by a euphoria I hadn't experienced with a man in what seemed like forever. My whole body glowed in the aftermath of all the sex, even if the place between my legs was a bit sore. He loved me. I loved him. We were finally going to have a chance to make something of the enormous feelings between us.

He'd offered to take the morning off work in order to back me up in my confrontation with my parents, but I'd turned him down. He shouldn't have to compromise his business to babysit me, and besides the whole thing would probably go over better if I did it by myself.

As I turned onto Knik Avenue, I glanced over my shoulder to the east. The Chugach Range rose there like a wall around the eastern boundary of the city. And there was a liberal dusting of snow on the peaks. Termination dust had already arrived, announcing the approaching end of summer, but it didn't mark my departure. It marked my commitment to staying.

The curtains of my parents' house were open, allowing the window glass to take on the dark appearance of eyes. As I walked up the driveway, the house seemed more still than usual, as if it were watching me to see what I would do next. Or maybe that was only my nerves talking.

They hadn't given me a key, so I had to ring the doorbell like a stranger and then cool my heels on the front stoop until someone came to let me in. I used the time to glance around at my parents' perfectly tidy but unimaginative yard. Flat, uniformly green grass and a couple of cottonwood trees near the curb, plus the birch tree in the middle, which had grown enormous.

Two perfectly matched wooden flower boxes full of nasturtiums was all the garden they had. Of course, most of the real gardening went on in the back, where they grew peas, raspberries, carrots, and cabbage. I wondered if Dex would like to keep a garden. We hadn't covered that subject yet.

The door opened to reveal Adam in a gray T-shirt and blue flannel pajama pants, dark stubble covering his jaw. He blinked sleepily at me and flipped the hair out of his eyes.

"You look like you're just getting in," he said.

"I am. Are Mom and Dad up yet?"

He rubbed one eyebrow. "Yeah. Do they know you stayed out all night?"

"They do. Also, I'm twenty-six and I don't have a curfew anymore."

"Were you with him?" he said with narrowed eyes.

I put a hand on my hip. "Is that any of your business? I didn't think so. Can I come in now or are you going to keep me on the doorstep all day?"

He stood back and opened the door wider so I could enter, his posture wary. We'd hardly spoken since I'd come, and I could only assume he held some kind of grudge against me. Whatever his problem was, it would have to wait to be resolved because right now our parents were my first priority.

"Where are they?" I said.

"In the kitchen."

Okay. I had my marching orders.

Kicking off my shoes, I marched right up the stairs, through the empty living room—which looked precisely the same as it had the day I'd left— and into the kitchen, where my mom and dad sat in their bathrobes at our tiny white drop-leaf table drinking coffee. The smell of the dark brew filled the room. They both looked up at me with faint expressions of surprise on their faces as I came into view.

"Cass," my mom said. "We didn't expect to see you so early."

"Dex has to work today." Might as well get the fact that I'd spent the night in an illicit tryst with a man they despised out in the open immediately.

My mom kept a determinedly neutral face, but my dad looked like he'd just bitten into the world's sourest lemon.

"What's he doing now?" he said heavily. "Still selling drugs?"

"No, Dad. He and his brother own a garage."

His brows shot up. "They own a business?"

"Yes, they do. And that brings me to something I need to tell you. I'm staying in Alaska to be with him. We're moving in together."

His jaw pulsed. He stared at me without replying. I guess I'd shocked him speechless. Jeez, you'd think Dex and I invented shacking up.

My mother set down her coffee mug with exaggerated care. "Cass, I don't think that's wise."

"Thank you for your input, but we've already made the decision." My voice sounded so even and unemotional it was almost like I truly didn't care what they thought.

"You don't even know him anymore, honey," she said, sounding concerned.

"Mom, don't try to talk me out of it. We're doing this. If it doesn't work out, then it doesn't, but you're not going to stop me from doing this." I almost added that we loved each other, but at the last instant I paused. They would most likely not believe me and I truly didn't need to justify my actions, to them or anyone.

"He'll never marry you," she said.

My dad nodded in agreement.

"If he can get the milk for free—"

"Oh, God, not the cow thing again," I said, interrupting her. "I'm not a cow. I'm not for sale. And marriage isn't the point here."

"Then what is?" she said. "If he loves you, he should marry you."

"We're giving our relationship a serious shot, but we're not ready to get married," I said.

"Then why move in with him?" my dad said. "You can live here."

"Oh, no," I said with a short laugh. "That will never happen."

"You're still holding Chicago against us after all this time?" he said.

"I'm used to living on my own. Moving back in with you guys would be a huge mistake." I turned back to my mother. "And by the way, Dex never married and I know you made that whole thing up."

She lifted her brows innocently. "What thing?"

"The thing where you said he married Misty. I know that was a lie."

"I never said that," she said, continuing in the innocent tone and sounding as if she actually believed herself.

I took a deep breath in through my nose. "You told me on graduation day that he'd gotten married. You ruined my day, so thanks for that."

She flushed, her lashes fluttering ever so slightly. "I did?"

"I'm pretty sure you remember just as well as I do," I said. "I know you meant to discourage me from looking him up and it worked. For a while, anyway. But we've found each other again and this time I'm not letting you split us up."

She lifted her chin. "I never tried to split you up."

"You sent me to Chicago to keep me away from him." My voice was rising. I took another deep, cleansing breath to get myself back under control. "How is that not splitting us up?"

Mom shifted in her chair, looking uncomfortable. Uneasy. As if maybe, somewhere in her over-controlling brain, she felt the stirrings of guilt. "You were only seventeen years old, Cass. And you were pregnant. That was a different situation."

"Mom, you told me his wedding was in the paper. And he's never been married. So I know you lied."

"Cass, don't talk to your mother that way," my dad said with a troubled frown.

"Why not? She lied to me, about something incredibly important to me. I think I have the right to be angry and I'd like an apology."

"We don't have to apologize for trying to protect our daughter," he said, some heat creeping into his voice.

"You do if it involves lies. And if the daughter in question was eighteen at the time and old enough to make her own decisions."

He glowered at me. I glowered back.

"Cass is right." Adam spoke from behind me.

My parents stared at him in apparent shock. I turned, probably with the same expression on my face. My brother leaned against the dining room table, his hands in his pajama pants pockets, slouching a little and seeming completely unaffected by the tension in the air.

"What?" my dad said.

"She's right. You shouldn't have lied to her. And I don't think you should have sent her away. It hurt the family."

My dad's jaw opened and closed, but no words came out. My mother drew herself up in that disapproving-mom pose I remembered so well from childhood. She was probably getting ready to deliver a lecture on the rights of parents and the duty of children to obey.

"I don't think you have any idea how difficult that was for me," I said. "How rejected and ashamed I felt. How scared. I was terrified I was going to have to leave the family behind completely, that you'd disown me."

"Disown you?" my dad said, his voice rising in shock. "Why would you ever think that?"

"Because I wanted to keep the baby. I never told you, but I was thinking about keeping it. And then I miscarried." I hugged myself, forcing my voice to remain even so I didn't break down in front of them.

"You and Dex weren't ready to be parents," my mother said.

"I agree. But that's not the point."

"Then what is?" Dad frowned at me as if I were being naughty.

"That I got no real support, only blame. Dex and I loved each other, but you didn't believe we were capable of that. I felt like you were trying to erase me."

They both stared at me. I could see in their faces that they didn't understand. Maybe they never would. I couldn't pretend that was okay, but it might be the best I'd ever get from them and I would have to go forward with my life without their approval.

That was nothing new. I would survive.

"Dex and I are moving in together," I said. "I came here to inform you, not to ask for permission."

They continued to stare at me, apparently at a complete loss for words. Since I'd been separated from these people for ten years, I really had no idea whether Adam or Beth had ever rebelled or asserted themselves. I mean, both of them still lived at home, so probably not.

"I'm going to take a shower now." I turned my back on them and left the kitchen.

Adam followed me through the living room and down the stairs.

"Hey," he said as we reached the bottom.

"Thank you for standing up for me," I said. "I appreciate it."

Surprisingly, I saw comprehension in my brother's blue eyes. And something else—sympathy. Maybe he wasn't holding a grudge against me after all.

"No problem," he said.

"Have you and Beth ever said no to them about anything?" I said, only half joking.

He lifted his broad shoulders. "Not about anything this important. Besides, you're Cass, the golden girl."

"The who?" I said in utter bafflement.

He leaned against the wall next to his bedroom door. "I always got the impression they favored you. That they loved you the best."

"I never did."

He gave his head half a shake. "Maybe it wasn't true. Maybe it was just sibling rivalry bullshit; I don't know. But before you left, they were always holding you up to me and Beth as the example of how we should be. Like you were some kind of perfect angel come to earth."

My brows rose. "They did?"

"You don't remember that?"

"No." I glanced around the downstairs hallway, but all I saw was twelve-year-old carpet and white painted walls. "To me, it seemed like they were always harder on me. Like I had to be perfect to set a good example for you two."

"I guess it looks different from other people's perspectives," he said thoughtfully. "I was kind of jealous of you, to tell the truth. I don't think Beth ever felt that way, but I always felt like I couldn't ever measure up. And then you fell off your pedestal big-time. It shocked the hell out of me. I couldn't get over how you'd messed up, how you were human after all."

I had a lump in my throat. "I always loved you guys, you know. I tried to be good because I felt like Mom and Dad relied on me to set an example. But it was so damn hard. And Dex—we couldn't stay away from each other. I don't know if you've ever had that, but..."

"Yeah," he said quietly. "I know what you're talking about now. Back then, I had no idea."

I held out my arms for a hug. "I'm so glad I came."

He put his arms around me. God, he was huge. He'd grown up and I hadn't been around to see it.

"Me too," he said, bending his head down to my crown. "And I'm glad you're moving in with Dex and that you'll be back in Anchorage. We missed you like crazy."

Epilogue

Cass:

The blue-green water of Big Lake shimmered in the brilliant summer sun that was so rare in our part of the world. Our summers tend to be cool and misty, but when the sun shines you know you live in the most beautiful place on the planet and that you can never leave because of days like this.

The usual chorus of early-morning birds chirped and trilled in the richly green birch, aspen, and spruce trees that surrounded the water and our cabin. I lifted my fragrant mug of coffee to my lips as I listened to their cheerful songs. A cool breeze ruffled the hair near my face.

Dex and I had built this place ourselves on ten acres we'd bought years ago near the property where Beth and Leo had been married. Our cabin was a traditional Alaskan log cabin, with dark stained peeled logs for walls, relatively small windows, a wood stove for heat and cooking. Moose ranged the property and we occasionally caught sight of a black bear or even a grizzly. The bears were the reason for the rifle hanging over the fireplace.

So far we hadn't had to shoot anything, though.

The cabin had a front overhang for the porch where I stood gazing out over the lake. I could see another cabin peeking through the trees on the opposite bank. More houses had been built since we'd finished our place, yet there was still plenty of space in the area.

Someone glided across the water in a canoe, too far away for me to tell who it was. One of our neighbors doing some trout fishing, I guessed. Like a lot of other people, we came to Big Lake to fish and canoe the lake in the summers and to enjoy the cold solitude in the winter. Not that we got much solitude with two kids underfoot.

The kids in question burst through the front door behind me and tore down to the shore line, screeching and laughing. Aurora, our daughter, grabbed her older brother Jace by the waistband of his jeans, apparently trying to stop him from throwing something in the water. They were two years apart—Jace was eight and Aurora six—and they were mostly inseparable despite being different genders.

They were also blonds, being the spitting image of their dad.

My mom joined me at the porch railing with her own mug of coffee. The mugs were old ones from Dex's first house, the one he'd shared with his brothers. I loved the seventies vibe of their thick earthenware and earthy blue glaze.

She was grayer than ever, but still strong and healthy like my dad, which pleased me. I loved them, and besides, the kids needed grandparents, and Dex's folks were gone. Not that they'd have been appropriate grandparents in the first place.

"They sure love it out here," Mom said as she watched her grandchildren playing.

"Yeah, they do."

She glanced at me sidelong. "How are you and Dex doing these days?"

"We're great. I love working with him in the garage." I'd taken over the office management for him and Sin not long after returning to Anchorage.

"That's good. I'm glad to hear it," she said softly.

I took a sip of my coffee. My parents and my husband were on speaking terms, but things had never been especially warm between them. The fact that they'd accepted our invitation to spend the Fourth of July weekend with us at the cabin had frankly surprised me.

"I was wrong," she said.

I turned to face her, not even trying to cover my astonishment. "Huh?"

"Your dad and I were wrong about Dex. He's a good man. A good husband and father. I'm glad you two found each other."

I set my mug on the porch railing. "Thanks, Mom."

"You've built a good life together and you have two wonderful kids."

She doted on her grandchildren.

I smiled at her. "Yes, we do."

She reached out and patted my hand. "I just wanted you to know that. I didn't want you to think we were still holding his past against him or anything. And I want you to know that we always loved you and never wanted you to feel rejected or afraid."

Now I had one of those annoying lumps in my throat. I reached out and gave her a quick hug.

"Thanks for telling me that," I said as I released her. "It helps."

The screen door opened behind us and Dex emerged onto the porch in frayed jeans and a black T-shirt. He was just as beautifully male as ever. In fact, in my eyes he'd grown even more attractive as he entered middle age. He was still lean and muscular, and he'd acquired a dignity and self-confidence that none of us had possessed when we were young.

He leaned over me and pressed a kiss to my lips. "Morning, babe."

"Good morning." I looped my arms around his neck. "How are you today?"

"Awesome now that I've found you." He gazed down at me as if entranced.

I was in imminent danger of getting lost in those gorgeous green eyes of his. He smelled faintly of male sweat and sex—not surprising considering the way we'd spent the evening before.

"Well, I'll let you lovebirds have some privacy," my mom said. "Thank you for inviting us, Dex. We're having a lovely time."

He gave her a slightly bemused yet polite smile. "I'm glad, and I'm pleased you could join us."

She winked at me as she went back into the cabin, closing the screen door softly behind herself.

Dex continued to look bemused as he studied my face. "What was that all about?"

"I think we've finally reconciled. And I think she likes you. She told me I was lucky to have you."

He grinned playfully, his dimples showing. "Well, that's obvious. I've known that all along."

About The Author

Tori Minard has published seventeen romance and erotic romance novels and four novellas, in addition to a handful of short stories, both under her own name and as Tessa Tremaine. Her series include The Amaki, Legends Of A Dark Empire, Avery's Crossing, Fortunata: The Jhidris Conspiracy, and Tales Of The Demon Kin.

Tori wrote her first story in elementary school, with a lamentable lack of punctuation. In high school, she spent more time writing fiction than doing homework. Her early stories featured demonic dogs, dolls possessed by evil spirits—no, she'd never heard of Chucky—and politically incorrect post-apocalyptic romance.

She discovered science fiction in the sixth grade, with her dad's recommendation of Edgar Rice Burroughs' **At the Earth's Core,** the first book in his Pellucidar series. Prior to that, her reading had included ghost stories, animal stories and adventure tales. Around the same time, she was discovering the joys of erotica by sneaking her mom's books and reading all the naughty bits. Her mom claims to have skipped those parts.

After a long detour for such grown-up pursuits as working boring full-time jobs (State of Alaska, U.S. Postal Service), getting married and having a child, she returned to her first love—storytelling. She was born and raised in Alaska, and now lives in the Pacific Northwest with her husband, son, and micro-dog

Discover other titles by Tori Minard

Tales Of The Demon Kin:

Novellas:
Malefica
Fury Enchained
The Devil You Know
Taken By Storm

Novels:
Lucifer's Castle
Mastered By Love
Taken By Desire

Short Stories:
Stainless Steel Vampire, story number one in the Skye Donovan series
Love Potion Number Ninety, Skye Donovan story number two
If I Should Die; a Legends Of The Dark Empire story
Price of a Rose, a sexy fairy tale (novelette)
Lemon Drop, a sweet erotic toy possessed by a sex spirit

Amaki Novels:
The Heart Moon
Dragon Moon
Blood Moon

Avery's Crossing Novels:
Rush
Bad Company
Bedeviled: Gage and Nova Book 2
Breaking Free: Gage and Nova Book 3

Fortunata Novels:
Dirty Magic

Legends Of A Dark Empire Novels:
Temple Of The Heart
Darkness Awakened
Darkness Forbidden
Darkness Beloved
Darkness Embraced

Connect with Tori online

To learn more about Tori, visit her blog at http://www.toriminard.com

Twitter: http://twitter.com/#!/ToriMinard

Facebook: http://www.facebook.com/toriminard.paranormalromance

Pinterest: http://www.pinterest.com/toriminard/